WINGED VICTORY

The flak burst in waves and the plane groaned as it was wrenched around. A roar like a blast furnace crashed in a flash of red fire and the nose came off the machine, and the crew of Halifax bomber W. William parachuted into Occupied Europe. It was the start of a hazardous journey, hiding from the Germans, being passed down the network by the men and women of the Resistance. Some will return to England to thunder once again across the Channel on yet another mission. But not all ...

WINGED VICTORY

WINGED VICTORY

by
Dan Brennan

Magna Large Print Books
Long Preston, North Yorkshire,
England.

British Library Cataloguing in Publication Data.

Brennan, Dan
  Winged victory.

A catalogue record for this book is
available from the British Library

ISBN 0-7505-1350-0

First published in Great Britain by NEL paperback edition,
November 1978

Published in Large Print 1999 by arrangement with
Dan Brennan

All the characters and situations in this book are fictitious.

Magna Large Print is an imprint of
Library Magna Books Ltd.
Printed and bound in Great Britain by
T.J. International Ltd., Cornwall, PL28 8RW.

FOR
FLIGHT SERGEANTS
Harry MacDaniels, LeRoy 'Bus' Hill,
Johnny Johnson, Reginald Folkes, Bill
Maisenbacher, Flying Officer 'Crasher'
Dawes, Squadron Leaders Gerald Barrett
and Harry Ratcliffe
NO. 10 SQUADRON
ROYAL AIR FORCE
and
Estelle and Bill
'Who cooked a big kitchen'

Book One
THE MEN GOING AWAY

1 FLIGHT SERGEANT
JACK MCWHINNEY

I knew I was going to have the trouble
again that morning before the mission
when the big rabbit came out of the
bushes and put his fingers to his nose
and yelled, 'Hey, sucker! Hey, boob!' I
was stealing wood off the roof of the 'B'
flight latrine for the stove in my room.

I stopped stripping the roof, put the
crow-bar in my belt, and went back to
my room in the barracks. Better see the
medical officer right away.

Without putting on my battle jacket, I
put on a necktie and started for the sick
bay on the other side of the aerodrome.

But a couple other things shook me on
the way ...

Flying Officer Campbell's big white Pit-
Bull with the black ring around his left eye
ran straight out from behind the officer's
mess and sat up in front of me and held
out a tin can with a slot in the top. He

raised both eyebrows.

'Penny for the Guy!' the dog shouted. 'Help a worthy cause! A penny for the Guy! PENNY for the Guy!'

Then he shot away on all four feet and disappeared around the back of the officer's mess. I took a deep breath, felt better, and began to walk faster toward the sick bay.

'Hoy!' shouted a voice from the doorway of 'B' flight barracks. It was Bobby Paul. 'Got some ale left over.'

I looked at him to make sure it was Bobby. He usually stashed some pints in his room before a mission so he'd have a drink when he got back after midnight. He'd been out last night. It looked as if he might have copped somebody's ale who didn't get back.

'I gotta see the M.O,' I yelled.

'The whammies?' he asked.

'Double whammies,' I said.

'Come on! Six bottles left!'

What the hell, I thought, why hurry? Doc Berins would be there all morning. Maybe a beer was all I needed. I went in through the window. 'B' flight barracks door always reminded me of baling out of Sugar. Walking down the hall an irresistible urge to stop at the second door came over me. It was the room Harold Van Every lived in before he copped it over Emden.

I cupped my hands to my lips and faced the door.

'How you doing, Harold?'

His voice jumped right back through the door: 'Never had it so good.'

I went on and opened Bobby Paul's door. He was sitting on the bed with a bottle of Pale Ale in each hand.

'Ah,' I said, sipping the cold beer. 'Whose beer could it be?' I hadn't been on last night's raid. Bobby couldn't afford two rations.

'Hoy!' he yelled. 'The double whammies?'

'Triple.'

'Give me the picture.'

I sat on the cot and leaned back against the wall. 'A rabbit came out from behind the latrine and thumbed its nose at me and called me a sucker. Then Campbell's dog came at me with what looked like a charity drive coin box in one paw.'

'Did it say anything?'

'He wanted money for Guy Fawkes day.'

'Any print on the can?'

'Didn't see any.'

'Anything else?'

'I stopped outside Van Every's old room and called to him and he answered.'

'How is he?'

'Never had it so good,' he said.

'Have another beer,' said Bobby.

I drank one bottle straight down.

'One for the road?' he said.

'Got to go,' I said.

'Don't let it bother you,' he said in a reassuring voice. 'Goofy rabbits, gabby dogs and dead guys answering are apt to be upsetting. But if you think that's strange you ought to ask Harmsworth what he saw yesterday.'

I looked at him and then it happened. Bobby Paul turned into a red-cheeked man wearing a flat-top old fashioned derby which he doffed and twirled on a cane. When I saw it was Winston Churchill I gulped.

'See you at lunch,' I said.

Bobby—I mean Winston—took out a cigar and sniffed it just before lighting. His eyes looked bloodshot and red-rimmed.

I gave him the V sign with two fingers and went out. I walked fast. I must get to the medical officer, must get there, I walked faster and faster.

Then a man in a Gestapo uniform stopped me. His eyes were black and shining fiercely, black as his uniform. It was Rudolph Hess.

'So Winnie won't see me, huh?' he hissed. 'Think you can continue this war? Think you're going to win, don't you?'

'Listen, Mr Hess. I'm only a—'

'Take me to him. If I ever get you in Germany I'll—' He drew out a black jack and length of rubber hose. I grabbed the section of rubber hose.

'Help!' I shouted at two pilots passing. 'This man wants me to betray all England. He's going to get Winnie to make a deal and betray England. Kill him! Help me kill him!'

I swung the rubber hose at Hess. He fell on his knees. I kicked him in the stomach. I shouted at the pilots to hold him but they ran. They had turned into ostriches. Rudolph Hess had become a small ape, and blood was running out of his mouth.

I rushed away, terribly depressed, and ran into Dr Berins' office, past the line of waiting airmen and told the nurse I must see the Doctor at once.

She took me straight in.

'How're you McWhinney,' he said, shaking my hand. 'Take it easy, son. Tell me, what is the problem today?'

'First a rabbit called me sucker and thumbed his nose at me. Then a dog solicited me for pennies for Guy Fawkes day. Then Van Every who's been missing three months talked to me. Then I met Rudolph Hess and a friend of mine turned into Winston Churchill.'

'Where was this?' asked Dr Berins.

'It looked like Cowes regatta,' I said.

13

'Winnie was standing on top of a cabin cruiser twirling his derby on a cane at the crowd.'

'That's all?'

'I beat Hess up and left him a block away. He turned into an ape.'

I opened my eyes and looked at Dr Berins.

'Now what?' he said.

'Look at yourself in the mirror,' I told him. 'Pointed ears.'

'Yes?'

'Can you feel horns growing out of your skull?' I smiled.

He stopped smiling and stood up and put his hand under my arm.

'Nice try, McWhinney,' he said. 'You must have heard about tonight's op already. Paris.'

'Piece of cake,' I said.

'I wonder what you'll see when you have to go to Essen again.'

He shouldn't have said that. He didn't know how bad it got before Essen or Berlin. Sometimes it went on all day before Essen or Berlin.

'Nice try, McWhinney,' he grinned and patted my shoulder and opened the door. I felt utterly depressed.

The nurse was there covered with yellow fur and big black spots and she was swinging her tail and walking straight

14

at me with her long tiger teeth dripping saliva.

I shot out of the office. The rest of the day was worse. I was leaving after briefing when Flight Lieutenant Poole told me Wing Commander Russell wanted to see me.

I went up to Russell where he was standing on the platform with the pointer still in his hand and the map of Europe on the board behind him with the long red ribbon on it stretching from England across Europe to Genoa, showing the track of the raid.

'What did you try to pull on the M.O?' he said.

'Sir?'

'The M.O has informed me of your rubbish, Sergeant.' He put both hands on his hips and stared down his long thin straight nose at me.

'As long as I'm C.O here, Sergeant, you won't get away with it.'

'You don't understand, sir.'

'I understand.' He pulled on his yellow gloves. 'Sergeant, who's been stealing the roof off 'B' flight latrine for fire wood?'

'Not me, sir.'

'We have reason to believe—' he paused, buttoning one glove.

'No, sir.'

'That's all, Sergeant. Button your jacket.'

15

2 FLIGHT LIEUTENANT JACK GIFFORD: Pilot

The first time I saw Wing Commander Russell he was standing on the platform in the briefing room. He was taking off his yellow RAF dress gloves. It was morning, just before the usual morning roll call for crews and the weather report. Nobody ever wore yellow gloves on the squadron. It wasn't until that afternoon I heard what Russell was, but I might have known before. He wore one of those red striped medals, Air Force Cross. You can win them only during peace time. I missed his tunic lapels. He didn't wear any volunteer reserve badges like the rest of us. He was a regular, the first one our squadron had. Three weeks ago he had come down from training command to take over the squadron since our old Wing-Co, Bruce Hawkins had gone for Burton over Kiel. Russell did not look around the room nor smile after he removed his gloves and carefully set them on the lectern. He looked out over the room, above everybody's head.

'Where is Sergeant Smiley?' he said.

Rows of heads turned to look for Smiley. He got up. Smiley had the face of an owl bug-eyed with perennial hang-over. His hat squatted on the side of his head, raked at perilous angle, apparently supported only by his ear.

He shuffled up to the platform.

'Get your hands out of your pockets,' Russell said. His voice was ice cold. 'Stand over there. Face the room.' Russell looked out across the room, over the ranked faces, his eyes steady, china-blue.

'Stand at attention!' said Russell. 'Tell them! Say it! Fifty times! I am a pig!' Russell stared straight ahead. There was no sound in the room. It was as if everybody had stopped breathing.

'Say it!'

'I am a pig,' said Sergeant Smiley. 'I am a pig,' he repeated, in a monotone. 'I am a pig,' his little owl-face faintly lowered, the dimpled chin creased against the collar of his battle dress.

Wing Commander Russell stood at ease, hands behind his back, his shoes shining like patent leather pumps, trousers creased knife-sharp. His chin was lifted. His gaze was empty. He stared at the ceiling of the room, his lips moving faintly, counting one, two, three ... At thirty Russell stopped counting. Sergeant Smiley's monotone voice went on in the silence.

Then Smiley ceased.

'Dismissed,' said Russell. He waited

until Smiley was seated. He waited while the silence rose again in the room. He could feel silence like a substance, filling the room.

'Gentlemen,' said Russell. He brushed the table top with his yellow gloves, flicking invisible dust. 'I expect all personnel during off duty hours to begin work today on clearing up the area around the Nissen huts. It's a disgrace. All path stones will be white washed by fifteen hundred hours. That is all.'

He slapped his yellow gloves into the palm of his left hand. He strode down the aisle between the ranked chairs as we rose, followed by his staff.

We stood there at attention until we heard the door clash.

I waited five minutes and went along to his office. He was behind his desk but he did not look up as I saluted. He was busy with his report papers to group headquarters.

'Yes, Gifford,' he said, his hand busy with a pen.

'Sergeant Smiley's on my crew, sir. I'd like to know what this is all about.'

He put down the pen. There were the gloves, beautifully clean, neatly arranged, side by side, on the corner of his desk, one glove upon the other, both upon his hat.

'Was he drunk?' I said.

'Quite.'

'Fighting?'

Russell's chin lifted.

'No, he threw up in my hat.'

3   FLYING OFFICER
RODGER CALDWELL:
Navigator on the Emplacement

You could see the flak guns beyond the barbed wire. I often wondered why they have them this far inland. It's been over a year since they raided York and you would think they would put the guns up at Hull which catches a packet every night.

I lifted the barbed wire and stepped through the fence and started across the meadow. It's not long since noon. I kept thinking about the operation that afternoon because it's a short trip to Paris and now that we have the Gee-box for navigation, will it pack up before we even get south of Paris? They are very undependable and Russell wants me to use it as far out as possible.

Captain Barster stood against the radar wagon, scratching his chin, his nose twitching, as though he wished to pick it and glanced over his shoulder quickly to see if anybody were watching him.

'You on tonight?' he said.

I nodded.

I looked at my watch. 'Jennifer on duty?'

'She'll be off in fifteen minutes.'

'I haven't much time.'

'Go ahead,' he said.

The plotting room shack squatted among the trees and a swallow slanted against the empty sky. If it were just dying, if that was all, I wouldn't mind. If just a black door shut and that's all. Just a long dark tunnel and nothing at the end and you don't go on after that, if would be easy, but I don't know. I don't believe in God and I'm scared. I said Mother I don't believe any longer. And when she started to cry that did it, I had to get out. Nothing can help you at this hour because you don't need any help. Maybe pride and fear because that's all that's left.

I opened the door of the plotting room shack and there Jennifer was leaning over the plotting board and the girls sitting on the floor smoking cigarettes and all the plots dead on the board because Jerry wasn't moving anywhere this far inland. I stepped out of the sunlight into the room and the air was hot.

Jennifer turned her head. She looked pretty in the uniform but it's hard to tell unless you see how the men look at her because you've been with her so long. Her shadow turned and crossed my shadow under the lights.

'Rodger,' she said. Her voice was a bell and her smile came into me and I touched her hand.

'See you a minute?' I said.

We went outside and she shut the door and lit a cigarette and leaned against the shack. She was wearing battle dress and slacks and her boots were shining in the sunlight.

'Gifford,' I said. 'Are you going out with him?'

She looked at me but she didn't say anything.

'The American,' I said.

'Oh, Rodger,' she smiled, laughing.

'You're engaged.'

'Why are you angry then?' she said, laughing at me.

'You're wearing his ring,' I said.

She lifted her hand and her diamond finger winked at me.

'Why don't you like Russell?' she asked.

'I didn't say that.'

'Oh?' she laughed.

She kissed my cheek.

'Poor Rodger.'

'Don't fool yourself,' I told her.

She touched my hand. Only she could out run me every time. Sometimes I could catch her. That fast, across the lawn and into the trees like a deer, through the woods to the tennis court. Mother wore a big flowered dress and carried the shears in a wicker basket as we went past whooping.

'Why do you really care?' she asked.

'You know.'

'Poor Rodger. You worry so much. You mustn't.'

'Is it the American?'

'Are you on tonight?'

'Yes.'

'Where?'

'Paris.'

'A piece of cake.' She smiled. She put her hand on the door knob, opened it. 'Gifford'll get you back,' she said. The door shut and she was gone. I looked at the sun, then at my watch. It was almost time for briefing and then I remembered the first time I saw Russell. It was at the strike meeting, in father's office, the day after Boxing Day. If you looked at him then you'd know him for what he was because there were dozens like him in the plant, only maybe not bright enough to be shop steward. And if it hadn't been for father none of them would be working. It was the first time I ever saw Russell and that was seven years ago and even now when I looked at him the back of my neck twitched because nobody had ever talked like that to father. He was standing behind his desk and the strike committee was seated. Father was getting bald. The big clock on the wall was ticking.

'Right,' Russell was saying. 'We've taken the vote.'

'If you want to ruin yourself and everybody,' Father said. 'You could be an engineer, Russell.'

'I'm a better engineer than the one with the degree you hired.'

'What do you want?' Father said.

'It's on your desk,' Russell said.

'That?' said Father and picked up the union newspaper and tossed it in the trash basket.

'I feel sorry for you, sir,' said Russell. 'Come on.' He got up. 'That's all,' he said to his strike committee.

'Right,' said Father. 'That's all.'

The shadow had cleared the corner of the hangar. I stopped outside the door of the briefing room, looking up at the sky.

Russell said suddenly, 'Well ... Are you going in?'

'You ought to see her,' I said.

'I have.'

'She's your girl.'

'That's right and I'll do the worrying about her. Are you going in?'

4 FLIGHT SERGEANT
HARRY SMILEY: Tail Gunner

What I always say is once a bloody bugger always a bloody bugger. Russell thinks he's a nob Bloody yellow gloves. Pulling them on tight, one finger at a time. A used car salesman in civvy street. Hint his posh accent, old boy, old boy. Old boy, my bloody arse. And giving me the bloody thumbs up sign when he got out of the car with his bloody adjutant wearing one of those Guard's mustaches like he's a duke's son. Another used car salesman. They made him think he's an officer when they put the Queen's uniform on him. The adjutant touched the ends of his mustache while the Wing-Co struts around the aircraft. And how are the guns, sergeant? Oh, how awfully nice, I said the guns are synchronized and as good as the night I shot down a ME two weeks ago, sir. He smiles. What a bugger. It's like the first night I saw him in Betty's Bar in York and the girl, a WAAF, at the table next to him she says if she wanted a beer she would call the waitress and he smiled ever so nice and nodded and smiled and asked her for a dance and got turned down and smiled ever so nice at her again, playing the bloody gentleman.

And when it got dark I was swacked and

the floor was moving so I knew I should have gone to the dance. I saw the people going down the cobble stones and it was raining and I fell down twice. Running and panting and feeling sick then and I couldn't see my watch only just thinking if I missed the bus again I'd be up on a charge and rain falling cold as hell. I could hardly breathe. One more block. One more block. One more block until they start pushing you through the door and the bloody driver's telling you it's full up. If it had just been somebody else sat down in front of me when that bus started taking those curves and everybody breathing steam on the windows smelling of stale fish and chips and my stomach starting to go whump, whump, gurgling up and down in the smell of all those bloody wet service coats till I could taste the chips in the wool in my mouth. And if it had just been somebody else when I laid back sick and the bus stopped so quick I got thrown forward, it wouldn't have happened with every bugger in the squadron staring at me because I had to stand up there and be his bloody schoolboy. It was just his hat and because I had to go somewhere and him all the time acting like he's high on a hill and just wanting to knock him off that perch on his bloody clock face that made me do it, picking his hat off letting it go, beer and chips and all by God until his face was quiet and he didn't look so bloody high and mighty with his hat full of vomit. I gunned at him. One more block and I would have missed the bus by God.

So now I watched him walk around the aircraft and look at the bloody machine like he owns it himself. He rubbed his hands together and looked up at the engine bashers on the scaffold and we were all looking up at the sky at the whole bloody squadron setting course for Cromer light and us still on our arse.

'Corporal,' he said. 'How long?'

'Can't tell, sir.'

'Corporal, how long?' He's got a voice like a bloody cop.

'Twenty minutes. Half hour, sir. Can't tell.'

'Hurry it up.'

I went around behind the machine and leaned against the turret and the bloody sun was going down the hour I hate. It's like everything in the world you ever knew is going down in the twilight, everything getting buried in that green light coming up through the trees. I hated that hour. It's like knowing you're going to die, smelling that cool evening air.

He could tell us we don't have to go if he wanted to. He could do that for us. No, he's just a big bag of crap. We're cooked. Cooked. He's going to make us go, and already we're twenty minutes late for rendezvous. It's getting darker. Hell, I can hear the sun setting and smelling cooling leaves and grass and water.

'Look,' said McWhinney. He was leaning against the tail turret with me and we could hear them arguing on the other side of the machine and then they got in Russell's car.

'It's a sign,' said McWhinney.

'Knock it,' I told him. 'It's too late to get out of this op. How long do you think they're going to believe your stories?'

'I can see it.'

'What?'

'Mattson.'

'Knock it.'

Mattson's been dead three months. The fish are eating him in the North Sea. When McWhinney talks like that I don't know whether to worry or not. The sky was different now, almost flat against the earth in the west and the trees were dark clumps. The air felt dead like it was shaping dead all around us and maybe he did see Mattson and now there were no more shadows and they got out of the car and I could hear their voices.

'He's a rabbit,' said McWhinney.

'You're a bloody owl. Shut up,' I told him and listened because it sounded like

Gifford was getting ready to sock Russell since I'd heard Gifford before in bars and it sounded like that again his voice rushing and hot.

'You're crazy,' Gifford said. 'You can't order us.'

'I'm ordering you.'

They were on the other side of the machine and McWhinney kept on pointing at something he thought he saw in the woods behind the machine and all I could hear for a long minute was the fading sound of the machines overhead leaving us and the silence on the other side of the machine.

'Shut up,' I said to McWhinney. 'Listen.'

'You murdering bastard!' said Gifford.

'I could put you on a charge for that.'

'You won't,' said Gifford.

'Are you going?'

'We're half an hour late now,' said Gifford.

'Corporal,' Russell shouted. 'How much longer?'

'Ten minutes, sir.'

'My God,' said Gifford. 'Three weeks here and already you're bucking with group for egg on your hat.'

'Hurry it up, Corporal.'

'It's an order, huh?'

'It's an order,' said Russell.

I could see their legs below the bottom of the fuselage, one pair in blue trousers with black shoes and the other pair of black leather flying boots.

'You murdering sonofabitch,' said Gifford.

'Don't you call me that,' said Russell.

'You know it!'

'Are you afraid?' said Russell scornfully.

'Do you want to kill seven men? Let them stand down. I'll go alone.'

McWhinney was wiping his face with the back of his hand. The sun was dying through the trees. It was fiery red through the trees. The light in the trees was green as lake water. The moon was shining round and the sky was still light above.

'Then you refuse?' said Russell.

'Refuse?' said Gifford. He was shouting now.

'Are you going?'

'To die for you? So you can look big up at group? You told them this morning you had twelve aircraft ready for tonight?'

'That's all, Gifford.'

'Like hell! And twelve it's going to be even if it's our ass, eh? You promised them twelve and you're going to deliver twelve. Bucking for promotion with our lives!'

'Aldington, you're a witness.'

'Yes, sir.'

'Just the two of us,' said Gifford. 'How's

29

that? Just you and me and let the crew stand down. I'll fly it. You drop the bombs. Then it'll be twelve machines on target on your record at group. How's that?'

'Five minutes, sir,' said the corporal. He called down from the scaffold. 'Putting the cowling on.'

'There were magneto drops in both engines when we ran it up!' said Gifford. 'You know that! We're half hour late now. We're sitting ducks! You know it! Who says it at briefing? "Be on time with your wave at all turning points." Who says it at briefing? "It's the stragglers who get killed." We're now half an hour late reaching the French coast so radar has the entire country of France to track us across alone if we're out of that main stream. Oh, I know what's really in the back of your mind. Not the promotion. Her. Only you want both. Russell, you're a phony. I don't mind you trying to get me killed, but do you have to murder other people to get her and the promotion, too?'

'If there are no mag drops,' said Russell, 'you're going.'

'Like hell!'

'I'll run it up,' said Russell. 'Get your hands off me.'

'You're not going to kill my crew.'

'Take your hands off me!'

'You can't! They've only got six missions to go to finish their tour!'

'You're on charge, Gifford!'

'Take it yourself!' Gifford shouted.

I heard the scaffold being wheeled away. The trees were going off into the fading sky. The sun was gone. You could see them now high up, black against the sky where the last rays of the sun still shone up from the rim of the earth. The machines were black dots. Twelve thousand feet up, I figured. Where we belonged. We didn't have a chance now. This was suicide.

'That's what I intend to do,' said Russell. His voice was ice cold. I figured he was probably drawing on those bloody yellow gloves. He came walking around the rudder. His eyes were stiff and pale. He was walking with a wooden-back and a wooden face.

'Ready, Sergeant,' he said. 'Let's go.'

He didn't stop. If he would just walk into a propeller. That would be perfect, the bloody twot. But what was there to do? I knew a bloke once wouldn't go one on a raid night. He had the DFM and bar, and just packed in one night, said to hell with it, so they sent him to the glass house, where you do everything on the double, including going to the can or the special police beat your head off with clubs and when he came back they had

31

stripped him of everything. They couldn't take away the DFM, but they had him on the honey bucket brigade. He might as well have been dead. Nobody talked to him.

'Don't!' Gifford yelled. 'You've only done two missions.'

'Get out of my way,' said Russell, and I saw his legs disappear upward into the fuselage.

5 WING COMMANDER RUSSELL: Pilot

The target came closer and the darkness burst and shattered against the starlight. The darkness was rent by spears of light, rising in monstrous waves. Suddenly below the spears of lights fires crested into the sky, shuddering and sparkling like ice against the ink black earth. The sky hollowed into a huge bowl of fireflies. I felt cold. More light criss-crossed in a vast lattice-work; fenced the fireflies. The black earth sparkling with fire seemed to draw us down. Pennants of smoke from shrapnel explosions swirled past and then the sky suddenly became an immense white bowl of light, into which a fresh phalanx of spears thrust up, row on row, waiting patiently for us to cross out of the darkness. One should not die like this, I thought. My stomach grew colder. I searched for a break in the wall of lights.

Then flak like the thunder of a thousand kettle drums burst around us. Fireflies on all sides fluttered and fell into the lights through drifting waves of smoke. The machine bucked under my hands like a frightened animal. I kicked top rudder and the machine, groaning, seemed to fall away into the lights. Four round balls of smoke burst in front of the port engine. Through the sound of the explosion I heard the navigator's voice, quite calm and steady: 'Four minutes ... four minutes,' and the engines calling to me 'come on, come on, come on.' I was a fool to die this way. I did not have to be here. Why had I taken over the machine at the last moment?

A sea of light filled with black and white flowers rushed up, flowed over us and the machine rose and fell upon explosions like a ship cresting enormous waves. The voices of the gunners came to me, calling, the voices remote: 'Weave! Weave! For crissake, Weave?' Voices far away. I looked down into a bowl of light. Other machines swam past like huge dark fish breathing fire. Enormous chandeliers of colored fire hung suspended all around us. Dripping green and red fiery stalactites, chandeliers drifted through veils of smoke.

I heard the bomb-aimer calling and the crew crying to weave through the barrage. Box barrage. Evasion meant nothing. Any moment unpredicted flak would blow us to pieces; in an instant we would simply run into one of the flowers and disintegrate. Jesus, how could we ever penetrate this flak? It filled the sky, so thick the round white balls had merged in cloud formation like cumulus. I held the wheel steady listening to the bomb-aimer. We started down in a long diving turn.

'Here he comes again,' the tail gunner yelled. 'For crissake, weave!'

'Left, left,' called the bomb-aimer.

Threads of fire streamed past. I lifted the machine and the bomb-aimer yelled.

'Turn port!' screamed the tail gunner. 'Hard! Hard!'

A searchlight beam slid across us. I shut my eyes. The light was gone. Flashes of light glared at me beyond the windscreen.

I don't have to be here, I thought, I didn't have to do this. Now it was too late. We would die. From nobody to nobody, I panted.

I banked to starboard, felt the wheel kick. The machine bounced, terrible sounds of explosions. Then an interval of silence filled with the sound of shrapnel pattering along the fuselage like the sound of hail on a tin roof. It's bursting above us.

Will there be pain? Just one fraction of a second of obliterating pain?

From nobody to nobody, I thought.

'Hey, skipper! Port side high,' called the mid-upper gunner. 'Hun flashing a green light.'

'Watch the tail!' I yelled.

'He's signalling attack,' said the mid-upper turret gunner.

'Seven o'clock low,' said the tail gunner. 'He's closing. Steady. Let him come in.'

'Turn!' shouted the mid-upper gunner. 'Turn port!'

I kicked rudder hard, skidding, and down we went. Dark now. Christ, we'd have to go round again. Never make it. Never make it.

Blue balls of fire winked, suspended in darkness. Fiery threads of tracer streaked over. For a moment I could not see the Hun machine against the dark side of the sky. There went his blue ball eyes again, firing tracer.

I pushed the throttle forward. The air speed indicator pointed at two-fifty. I pulled back the wheel, felt a tremendous shocking explosion. The sky spun crazily. My harness jerked into my shoulders and belly. Then I had the wheel again in both hands and we were stalling, hanging almost straight up and I could hear the tail gunner cursing monotonously.

We flopped like a wounded bird. Searchlight beams rushed past. I shoved the nose down, grabbed the trim tab wheel.

'Bomb doors shot away!' said the bomb-aimer.

'Dump the load!' I said. 'Dump it!'

I was pressed down in the seat. I could not move. The altimeter showed fifteen thousand feet. The machine would not respond to the trim tab. I fought the control wheel. I could not pull it back. I got my feet against the instrument panel. Air speed three hundred. I fought the wheel. It was like wrestling a mad man. It held me fast, my legs pushing against the instrument panel without an inch of gain from the wheel.

'Bail out!' I yelled. 'Bail out!'

I was glued to the seat.

Then the searchlights found their firefly. We were conned. Another explosion rocked the machine, whipping the machine from side to side. I waited for the wings to come off, to fly whipping past overhead.

'All out?' I shouted. 'All out?'

No answer. I tried to get up. My body weighed a ton. I was a thousand pound animal held in irons.

'Goddamn it!' a voice said. 'Give me that!'

It was Gifford. I stared at him. What was he doing here? He reached across my shoulders. He got his hands beside mine.

I felt him pulling. The weight of his whole body leaned on me.

And then it began to work. Slowly, so bloody slowly. The wheel came back in our hands. The cake-like frosting of fires far down in the darkness fell away.

'Easy,' I said. 'Let's not pull the wings off.'

The horizon emerged, darker sky meeting lighter sky, the needle leveling.

I held the kite straight and level. Gifford's face a few inches away.

'Did you think I was going to let you stick me with a court martial?' he yelled. His eyes were wild, rushing whitely.

6 SERGEANT
ROBERT CRAIG: Bomb Aimer

It was a piece of cake until we got south of Paris and my bladder started kicking up so I went back to the Elsan can and something moved in the dark and I took out my light and shined it and, Christ, Gifford was sitting there on the floor with his oxygen mask hooked up to the wall outlet. He held up one thumb.

'I thought—' I heard myself say.

'I thought I'd better come along,' he said, smiling.

'Russell know you're aboard?'

Gifford shook his head, smiling.

Just then I heard the first explosion and bounced and fell against Gifford. I tried to get up only we were diving when I heard the next explosion and then we were climbing and I could feel my feet being pulled straight up in the air until I was standing on my head without touching anything. I hung there upside down and Gifford somewhere in the dark hanging there, too. The plane zoomed and we came down to the floor and the machine went diving and zooming and our bodies kept going up and down, suspended in mid-air. You could hear the flak bursting in waves all around us and the plane groaning as it was wrenched around with the gunners shrieking at the pilot. The engines were screaming and moaning. The hollow boom-boom-boom-boom of the flak pounded the machine and then crack, the sharping piercing explosion of a shell that was almost upon us.

'Bail out! Bail out!' Russell yelled.

I started crawling along the floor in the dark and the wind blew in through a big hole and outside heavy flak was everywhere smashing the sky into pieces. I crawled and prayed that I would get to my parachute before the machine blew up. My head felt as if it would burst. The engineer was leaning against the wall in the astral dome, fighting to get his parachute pack hooked to his harness.

Smiley's neck was dangling out his flying

jacket like a dead goose and he was flopping his hands against the side of the fuselage; it looked like something only he could do, not even the engineer who invented the tail turret, would ever be able to understand how Smiley did it. It took Smiley to figure out how to get himself in such a balls up situation. The turret was half turned with the doors half-open and Smiley was stuck there, half in and half out. We came toward him with the light on him and his eyes blinking over his oxygen mask. He had one hand free and he tore the mask off his face.

'Get out!' Gifford yelled at me and pushed me back toward the side hatch door. 'Get out!' he hollered and pushed me again when I didn't move and I fell against the machine gun cartridge racks and started to feel my way toward the door but looking back.

Smiley's mouth was making some kind of a sound.

The circle of the plane tightened and then the big hole in the fuselage became a sky full of stars.

The front hatch in the floor was jammed. Part of the fuselage was blasted apart but the hole wasn't big enough to get through. I kicked at it and I could hear them on the intercom.

'Are you crazy?' said Gifford. 'Smiley's finished.'

'I'll get him,' Russell shouted.

'We're going to blow up!'

'Get out!' Russell shouted.

'What?'

'It's an order!' Russell yelled. 'Get out!'

A roar like a blast furnace crashed in a flash of red fire and the nose came off the machine. Then the dark sucked me out.

Book Two
THE MEN GOING DOWN

7   SERGEANT PETER MELONY

At the time Gifford and Russell were arguing, a major in the British Parachute Corps was talking with a captain in the dining hall of a stone mansion fifteen miles north of the city of Norwich. The table at which they sat was covered with air reconnaissance photographs. On the wall behind them was an aerial map of France with flags stuck at various locations. The major was big-shouldered and his head was round and close shaven. His face was blackened with burnt cork. On the captain's face under the burnt cork every tiny muscle was visible against the taut skin. The captain was asking questions and listening.

'Are you certain this is it?'

'Look at the photo.'

'Yes.'

'How do you explain the concrete emplacement?'

'I see.'

'Look carefully. All right? Now this photo.'

'The metal frame work?'

'Right. The concrete supports it.'

'Looks like a big electric heater.'

'Absolutely the latest in radar. Five hundred and seventy megacycles. Controls searchlights, flak and night fighters.'

'How will we get it out?'

'No problem.'

'What about air cover?'

'We'll go in the same time bomber command attacks the Renault works at Paris.'

'What's the radar called?'

'Wurzburg frequencies.'

'Range?'

'Fifteen miles.'

'Can't the RAF or our machines simply jam it?'

'Mandrel jamming hasn't worked. If

Jerry gets these up and down the coast we couldn't jam long distance with mandrel. Each bomber would have to carry its own transmitter and as they install more Wurzburg our jamming effectiveness will be progressively reduced. We have to get one and bring it back.'

'We'd never get to the coast with a thing that size.'

'No, old boy. We don't bring it back. Not us, that is.'

'How?'

'Radar wallah going along. Flight Sergeant Melony. Trained. He'll photograph the equipment and remove pieces he wants. All your lads have to do is take him to the river. Boat picks him here will take him to the coast. You know the rest of the show.'

'Oh, yes.'

'You might make it to the coast,' said the major.

The captain laughed.

'Oh, yes,' he said.

Flight Sergeant Peter Melony was twenty-four years old and the night of the drop he was finding it difficult to concentrate on the plan not only during that day but also at the briefing conducted by the major. There would be 115 paratroopers on the drop to surround the installation and attack and hold while he photographed the equipment and removed essential machinery that he could carry. He tried to concentrate on what the major was saying, though he knew the operation by heart, but his mind kept drifting.

He sat in the briefing room and thought of the night to come and the drop, his legs already frozen, sitting among those who had done it before at Narvik, wondering if he would come back, and thinking not of what the Major was saying with his pointer on the map, wishing only that the doubt concerning a woman would stop turning over in his mind.

She would be in her flat now, her eyes bright, sitting at her dressing table, fixing her hair, the blackout curtain drawn, in the cozy slant of that room where so many happy moments away from fear and terror of things to come had been found.

But would she be alone? Would she be going out? Remembering now that night a month ago getting leave unexpectedly, sitting in the cab late the next afternoon going along Cheyney Walk and just as the taxi turned her face—or was it her face?—and the face of a short stocky man with her in RAF uniform, holding her arm.

'Go around the block,' he told the taxi driver, sitting badly frightened, as frightened as he had been the day of his first parachute drop, his guts hollow and cold, his lips tight, only to find the corner empty, and muse beyond with the arch holding only the thin sunlight.

So he asked her when he saw her: 'Were you out walking a while ago?'

Her voice was blithe. 'Why, no. I've been right here.' She was drawing up her stockings, the ones he bought her for two pounds off a Maltese black marketeer in a Soho bottle club. Her legs were beautifully long and slim and her hair was a soft chestnut, cut like a small helmet to her head, her eyes greenish blue and when he kissed her he was frightened of dying and longed to remain here forever, feeling already the loneliness and terror of tomorrow, of walking out of this room perhaps forever.

'I bought you something,' she said.

It was a talisman. He didn't believe in such things. Superstition. Rot. But it was pretty. It lay in the palm of his hand, soft hair, foot of a rabbit, mounted into a butt of gold with a chain from which it could hang suspended round his neck.

He began to put it on. She caught his fingers.

'Look,' she said, pointing at the almost invisible inscription in the gold butt: *'LOVE AND LUCK ALWAYS, ANN.'*

She put it around his neck and he held her in his arm.

'When do you go?' she said.

'Tomorrow night.'

'Where?'

'France.'

She didn't speak. She drew him down beside her, their faces hushed and smooth.

A man's elbow bumped his leg now. 'Opit, mate. Let's go.'

He walked dazed into the dark. It was cold, the night was moonless. He did not remember the ride out in the truck, nor climbing into the aircraft. He did everything automatically. He did not realize time had passed until they were airborne, and he thought only of her as the machine climbed and set course for the French coast.

Remembering was in the sound of the engines, and in his mind it was summer again, and the time seemed long ago, and it seemed he was years younger, but it was only a year ago.

It was spring in London and he was meeting a girl from Weymouth, a Wren, at Paddington Station, and she never came and he walked up and down and while he waited he saw this other girl waiting or at least he decided later that's what she was doing and when he went out to get a taxi she was there trying to get one and that was the way it started:

'Where are you going?'

She was blonde, quite small, very feminine, and careful with her make-up and hair-do, the pride of the female officers.

'Marble Arch,' she said.

'Jump in.'

The taxi went out under the glass roof and turned up the street.

'Leave?'

'Yes.'

'London?'

'I, uh—' she began. She sounded embarrassed.

'I've got three days,' he said. He spoke quickly to cover her embarrassment.

She listened to his accent. North England. The midlands.

'Cigarette?'

She caught his hand and noticed the lighter. She'd never seen one like it before. He saw her studying it.

'Never blow out in a gale,' he said. 'Chap in the regiment makes them.'

'How long have you been in?' she asked.

'Month,' he said. 'I mean, actually, I'm not really a paratrooper. I'm a radar specialist. Government. Sent up to paratroopers for a course.'

'Oh,' she said, not knowing where to take the conversation from there, and he stopped too and looked out the taxi window at the barrage balloons hanging motionless against the sky like monsters left over from a Cannes festival.

That was how it started with them that spring. He talked her into staying in London for leave.

Now in the machine flying to France he thought of her and his belly muscles were beginning to shake. He thought of her eyes, the pale eyelids ...

And the first time he had slept with her; his body and mind absorbed in the wonder of her for the first time, that first great wonder of love, pressing her against himself for the first time, hearing her whimper, her lips tasting of orange blossom, the last drink he had bought her, the band from Hatchett's still beating in his head, hearing her breath escaping from her body into the sound of the drumbeat, feeling the fear of dying grow weaker in him as he pressed himself closer into her without entering, just holding her clasped to his body though they were both naked in a bed in a London hotel, savouring the soft warmth of her flesh for that first time, feeling himself growing strong against her, her soft flesh pliant, her breasts blooming yet soft against his chest. In this instant time stopped, no hellos, and no goodbyes, ever and ever again, ever and ever again,

and he went on with these words going
faster and faster in his mind as his eyeballs
seemed to turn inside out and flicker and
jump inside his skull, ever and ever again
and again and again, tasting her lips,
tasting her breasts, tasting her smooth ripe
stomach, tasting the curves of her stomach
and thighs and arms, over and over again
and again, hearing himself calling out to
her upon her writhing soft, warm body,
thrusting and moving slowly, then ever
and ever again, faster and faster, crying
out as he reached inside her as if for
some memory someone else might some
day have with her if he were to die and
never see her again, wanting her more and
more and more, her breasts invisible in the
darkness but coming over his body bigger
than a moon, then hearing her laughing
softly, holding him, almost lifting him up,
then taking his hands, touching her breasts
with his hands, busying his fingers upon
her nipples, crying out in delight as his
fingers came to life again of their own
volition; as his body returned to him and
he opened his eyes and stared up in the
darkness at her white breasts above him
big as stars until he felt her envelop him
again and the easing loving relaxing sweet
pain of her body turning round and round
slowly above him with her tongue running
over his chest and face until it all became

unbearable, and then her insides moving warm and flooding down into him and through him and both their bodies seeming to pass out through their fingertips as they clasped each other ...

The plane was rising and falling, hitting air pockets and climbing. He felt his heartbeat flicker. For an instant, far back in his mind, a picture wavered ... In the bar, Hatchett's American Bar, looking past Ann's profile at the sunlight in the street beyond, listening to the hum of traffic in Piccadilly. The door of the bar was open and it was a beautiful sunny day in London.

The cigarette was motionless in Ann's hand and her face was smooth, but her eyes were impenetrable. He had loved her now for a year and he was afraid to marry her because of the mission. But he was even more afraid that he might lose her if he didn't marry her, but what if he were killed and the odds were good that he might be killed on the mission and what would that leave, the memory of a few hours of love? But if he didn't marry her she might marry somebody else and he was afraid now for the first time there was somebody else.

He wanted to reach and touch her hand now, but he knew he could not give the gesture the tenderness it needed to reach her with.

'But why can't we get married now?' she asked. He could hear the waiters moving around behind them.

'After the mission.'

'You said that last month. The month before. We could be—'

'And you a widow next week.'

'I'm not afraid if you're not.'

'I am afraid.'

'All right,' she said. Her voice was cold. She ditched her cigarette in the tray.

'Ann. Wait.'

'For what?'

'It's only another week and then—'

She turned and faced him, her eyes blazing, her voice filled with restrained fury, low, almost a hiss.

'I love you. Do you understand?'

'Without a father? How selfish can you get?'

'Is the time so generous?'

He didn't answer. He looked at his watch, then at Ann, her face profiled again.

'Time for one more drink,' he said.

'No thanks.'

'Then you're not coming to the station?'

'Go on,' she said. 'Go to your bloody stupid mission.'

He could see she was almost in tears but

there wasn't time to help her. There was a train to catch, a time to report, and ahead was only the mission, but first there was something else before leaving. Something he had wondered about for more than a month.

'Well, marry him then,' Melony said.

She didn't move for a fraction of a second, and then only her eyes moved, flicked over him and away.

'Do you think I should?' she said.

'Who is he?'

She laughed softly, caught his hand.

'You're mad, Peter,' she said, kissing his hand. 'There's nobody else,' but she was lying.

'I've got to go.'

'I'll go with you,' she said and picked up her handbag and slung the long strap upon her left shoulder.

His mind felt fogged and he knew it should be unbelievably quick and clear ... he looked at the paratrooper's knee beside his and in the darkness he wanted to puke. He told himself he must start thinking about all the complex threads of action he must retain if the mission were to be a success. Everything had been planned, just like a perfect bank robbery, but you never knew what was going to happen. Lots of bits and pieces of trouble and potential trouble could pop up and he knew he lacked the ability the men around him had; to be cool in moments of unexpected stress, and he feared facing such a moment in a long minute, too long, of stunned amazement, that gap that might mean his life or death. He had gone over the mission a hundred times in his mind, and he had been told and shown over and over again every possible minor or major mishap and what the plans were to overcome those mishaps, but now the mission seemed like a blank wall to him, and fear cried out in him, and he could not think what to do. He could think only that he should have married her because now he was sure there was another man. He had waited too long. 'I should have married her and then I would not have worried about that now.' And for an instant he was not sure whether the anxiety he felt was because of her or because of the fear of the unknown potential mishaps ahead. He wished he had talked about all these things with Ann, and then as he felt the machine climbing more sharply he knew what he lacked for the mission that the men all around him had, which he would never have, because there had not been time to give it to him. He wasn't tough enough. He was ignorant enough in the beginning and that stopped all the thinking of fear but now they had trained him, but he lacked experience to make him tough, so now he knew too much about what might happen, the dangers, and he knew he didn't know how he would react, and there would be factors of danger here that not even the most experienced could foresee. He must hurry, hurry, make everything happen fast or new factors of danger would pop up. With each delay in the operation there would be new dangers, but he knew that by both temperament and preparation he was not prepared. Yet as he sat there and thought of his own home wrecked and the thousands of homes wrecked in England an anger enveloped him as it always did after a German air raid because his hate for the Germans was real, the war was real, something he could truly feel, the Germans threatened the lives of everybody. It was everywhere in the wreckage of England, and seeing it, beyond the headlines and the voices of the news broadcasters, you could feel the hate become real in you, so as he sat there in the machine, ten minutes away from the dropping point, he let the anger take over, feeling it rising stronger and stronger inside his body, pouring into every muscle, until he sat clenched like a boxer on a stool, waiting for the bell, waiting and wanting to kill his opponent, as if his insides were filled with a nightmare shriek, and he knew that when he bailed out the shriek would tear from his lips. He gripped his knees waiting for the jump light, holding the crazy desire to scream out the fury building up inside himself, his heart and mind stopped, his whole being filled with a defiance of death ...

The light flashed ...

8 SERGEANT
EDDIE REKER: Gunner

At the same moment Sergeant Reker, falling out of W. William felt the jerk and pull of shroud lines and then the sensation of floating and then his mind cleared and he heard himself out of shocked astonishment mutter, 'I'm alive.' He felt like a cloud falling. He looked up at the parachute billowing overhead and his heart began to race and pound. Through the white canopy he could see the dark sky. God! The chute had been holed! But he felt the gentle sway and relaxed when he realized he wasn't about to roman candle into the ground, with the canopy sucking air and the shroud lines twisting and twirling tighter and tighter.

Then suddenly like a monstrous dragon of fire he saw and heard the machine circling and turning his head knew it was the machine coming at him. It looked like a box-car full of fire. It shot suddenly overhead and he expected the parachute to burst into flames and he buried his head in his hands. A long trail of fire and spark went on across the darkness and he watched it curving away and then circling back and he found himself cursing and praying.

The machine climbed abruptly and turned away and blew up in a ball of fire. It sounded like a bomb explosion.

He felt something cold in his hand and saw it was the rip cord. He pulled on the shroud lines to side slip away from the burning wreckage lighting the darkness below and suddenly he was plunging down. 'God! The shroud lines had twisted and I'm going straight in!' He prayed hard and was certain he would die in a second. Suddenly the chute filled with air again. He stared down into the bottomless dark, wondering how he could judge the ground, wishing for moonlight.

Then in the darkness he saw flashes of light and heard rifle and machine gun fire and the terrible sound of mortars. He thought the Germans were shooting at him. His feet crashed into branches and he grabbed the shroud lines and jerked upward.

A great shocking blow struck his body and in a flash of red light pain shot through his body. I'll be crippled, he thought before he passed out, certain he had broken both legs.

He woke in the dark upon the sound of rifle and machine gun fire. He lay, panting, feeling his arms and legs, numbed, but not broken. The rifle and machine gun fire was over to the right. Crouched, he drew in the chute. Somewhere to his right a mortar shell burst and a man screamed. It was neither far nor close. He felt dizzy and fell down. He lay quietly, breathing hard, his head ringing, listening to the gun fire.

In the darkness he began to see where he had landed. He was in a hollow between two wooded hills and the trees crested in the dark sky, dark against the lighter sky. He knew he must get out of here, contact the underground or have a Frenchman make the contact. He rose, bundled up the chute, pitched it under a tree and started running, away from the sound of gun fire. He ran full speed, panting, climbing, descending, falling, with the gun fire receding.

He fell down exhausted, listening. The gun fire fell away, rose again, far away. He was safe. He gulped air. His chest shuddered. He wished he had brought his side arms, the Webley, but the crew had long ago discarded the idea of side arms. You were liable to be shot if they saw you at a distance wearing side arms.

He felt panic, lost, in an unknown dark land. He tried to estimate how far from the target had they ... and then he heard the sound, and his heart kicked over. A shoe crunched among leaves. It stopped, came on, ceased.

As he lay listening to the sound of somebody approaching, his stomach started to tell him how long it had been since he had eaten and lying there panicky, a corner of his mind was thinking only about how long since he had eaten. He knew it was only three hours at the most since operational tea, two eggs and milky white tea and toast, and now it sat in his hungry stomach in a cold hard ball while hunger or fear (he could not tell which was talking to him) was gnawing into his cold guts. He felt his mouth moving but saying nothing because the words were inside his head, 'I better lay still and let him make the next move.' His body was still inert with shock and fear, and then in the chill dark he heard the slow movement of something soft among the leaves. Then as the sound came again the hunger inside him ceased. He felt fearful but also suddenly cool. He knew he must not move. Somebody was stalking him. Yet his whole being was obsessed with the desire to flee. He crouched on his knees, his face taut with fear and a kind of blind ratlike desperation. With his hands clenched, he waited, longing for the sound to be only a hallucination borne out of fear, and then the sound came again, close, and a dark rigid figure leaped toward him out of the bush. He yelled, cursing, striking out at the figure, and felt himself exploded upward out of the earth at the phantomlike figure he could smell but not see. He felt the bone of his hand go into flesh. Then hands were holding his throat, and then one hand came away, and his mind said, 'knife,' and he kicked and rolled himself free and whirled, crouching, hearing hard breathing above the sound of his own.

The thick dark blot of a man came toward him again and they plunged at each other, grasping and writhing, threshing among the dead leaves. He tried to bite the hand that sought his throat. He saw the lifted arm and smashed his hand into flesh and heard the figure scream and fall away and for a fraction of an instant almost turned to flee only to find the outrage and anger within him which he had never felt before impelling him to kill. He felt his hand go back and smash twice into the flesh as he straddled the man's stomach, searching for his throat, then finding the face and throat with short, slashing blows, he struck again and again. As he gripped the throat an object round and soft pressed into the palm of his hands. From beneath his hands came the gurgling sound of a man swallowing bubbles of blood. Then abruptly the gurgling sound was gone; the far away sound of gun fire came again, then suddenly there was no sound, only the silence of the woods, and then came his hard breathing, but this came before he knew he was running, and the object that had pressed into his hand was still there, clasped tightly, but he was not aware of it. He saw only the dark sky, the darker trees. He ran for half a mile before he slowed. He looked back through the woods. No sound. He looked up at the stars, searching for the north star, stumbling and mumbling to himself, his right hand still clutching the soft, round object. He ran on and on, hearing the squawking of the siren on the road behind him, seeing the searchlight from the weapon carrier sweeping the meadow about half a mile away. His guts ached and his side felt as if it were going to burst with pain. He stumbled down a hill, the rocks jolting the pain in his side. And then suddenly like a monstrous dark hill the woods loomed ahead, a jagged crest of darkness against the lighter darkness of the sky and he heard himself cry out in relief. He stumbled into the high grass, lay there a long moment, sobbing, trying to catch his breath. The siren came again, rising to a scream that seemed to pass out of the realm of sound. He could not tell whether it was on a car or an air raid siren. He lay, listening. There was no sound of aircraft engines. The sky was silent again. He rose and trotted into the darkness of the trees. He longed to lie down. He felt mud clotting his boots. He stopped, realizing suddenly he had stepped out of the grass. He leaned against a tree and advanced cautiously, one step at a time, thinking, 'There's a path here.' He began to dogtrot, then run as he felt the earth harden beneath his booted feet. His brain whirled, rushing with broken thoughts of the shrapnel torn sky, the smell of the trees, the fall in the parachute down the long endless darkness into a ploughed field, the road along which he had walked until the half-track picked him up in the light and fired, and then worst of all, the imaginary sound of dogs following. Or was it imaginary? He stopped to listen, hearing only the sound of the wind drawing through the trees. But perhaps I can't hear because I'm so tired and scared, he thought, slanting his head, hoping he wasn't fooling himself. Then he heard his voice aloud, speaking to himself and for a fraction of a second he thought it was somebody other than himself and he sprang off the back among the trees, plunging against a bush snarled with vines. He struggled against the vines that imprisoned his arms the more he struggled; he lay there kicking and hitting, panic-stricken. Then a part of his mind told him to stop and he lay upon the bush caught up in a hammock-like net of vines, and as he lay there he smelled the berries in the vines. His mouth watered. He felt around the darkness and plucked the berries. He sucked sweetness, listening. No sound of the siren, and turning where he lay he found his arm and leg came easily free. He looked back down through thick shadow to where the German lights had made chalk paths across the meadows. The meadows were dark. Maybe they gave up, he thought, sucking the berry without tasting it now. Then he fell asleep without knowing he slept. He dreamed he was back in London, back in her arms ... he woke in a few minutes, thinking of her face, but he rose immediately frightened and began to walk, bumping against the trees.

He tried to recall where he had been shot down. Intelligence officers at briefings had said to find a whore in a city and she would direct you to the underground who would help you escape. Where was he? The last bearing showed south of Paris, just before they were going to run in. No, they had run in and had drifted back after being hit.

He was so bloody tired and the inside of his right leg hurt; something sharp had struck him just as he hit the ground. If the Germans came now he would surrender. He felt exhausted. Then for a second he saw a light shining through the woods and he hurried. Germans! He paused. The light was gone. I imagined it, he thought, like a star being a night fighter or thinking a night fighter light were a star. Fatigues always played tricks on him. No wonder he had washed out as a pilot.

God, he was tired, tired, tired. His face felt slashed by thorns. If a German appeared now he would gladly surrender. Then he saw the light glimmering again and found himself running, his thighs aching. I must get there. I must get to the light. The light seemed to recede and he stumbled on. Then suddenly the light was there in front of him, and he saw the house. No, it was a small cottage. It was made of stone. He drew back into the trees and watched the light in the window. He looked back into the woods and found himself panting hopefully, telling himself that inside was a kind old man who had fought in the first world war who hated the Germans and would feed and clothe him. A stab of pain ran up his leg. He stumbled toward the light, felt the wood of the door. He must find something to eat and a place to sleep. He couldn't go on running. They'd catch him in the daylight. He would have to come out then for food. He tried the latch carefully, and just as he was about to lift it, the door swung open and he fell into the room on his knees.

He looked up and a woman's voice came out of the dim light: 'Don't move. Stay on your knees.' The voice was quiet but in the dim light he could not see her and then he heard her move and saw her face come into the light. She was young and pretty. There was no sign of fear in her face, and then with a gasp of horror he saw the light catch her head. She was bald. No, shaven. He started to rise then saw the gun pointed at his chest.

'Look,' he said. 'Look here.' His voice sounded dead.

'Stand up,' she said. 'Get against the wall by the light.'

9   SISTERS
LOUIS AND GEORGETTE

About two weeks before the crew of W. William took off to bomb the Renault Works at Paris, Pere Lavier, a priest living at Breche, about fifty miles south of Paris, died. It was reputed by the villagers that Pere Lavier had hidden a cask of brandy from the Germans, but nobody had found it though many had searched the woods behind the village church. In the orchard behind the convent of the Sisters of Visitation, the good Sisters Louis and Georgette had discovered the cask, covered with leaves and dead grape vines, perfectly camouflaged. It was their pleasure in the evening or late at night, depending on the timing that was needed at the moment, to go into the orchard and return with a bottle of brandy which they shared, and which in turn provided them a passive recalcitrance against the time of defeat and ruin so that the tragic events of that year in France seemed but loud noises of the moments to them. For the sisters the brandy took away sadness of the conflict which appeared to them to be a well nigh hopeless ordeal, the two of them joining forces in the bottle against the great common enemy, time, shielding themselves from reality, as if the bottle itself were the shield between them and the fact of the prolonged and interminable defeat. Sister Georgette dreamed at night of the allied invasion, dreaming so often that the dream became real, until she felt certain they were coming, and it would be soon. She confided this to another Sister Aurea, who reported her to the Mother Superior who spoke harshly to Sister Georgette.

'Sister!' she said. 'Do you think there are

enough men left in this country or outside to whip the Boche?'

'They will come,' said Sister Georgette. 'They will come and set us free.'

'How?' said the Mother Superior.

'By air. Many of them will come by air.'

'Stop your dreaming. Pray,' said the Mother Superior. Sister Georgette watched the bomber streams go over at night, once blinking V with her flashlight, wondering if she were seen from the air far down in the blacked-out land. It was cool and dark there in the orchard, and Sister Louis was asleep on Sister Georgette's shoulders and Sister Georgette though not asleep was dreaming. It was as though she were looking at the convent and her home and suddenly the convent and the houses of the town were gone and she was looking at an empty place and it was dark all around her, and then all of a sudden that was gone, too; she was there, and she could see little figures moving far away across the landscape; they were her brother and her father and Sister Louis and herself—and then she heard Sister Louis make a choked sound and she was looking at the high grass beyond the orchard, and there in the middle of the field, leaning forward and firing at a running figure, was an SS officer.

For a long instant they crouched staring at the two figures. Sister Georgette didn't know what to expect at first, but they knew what the SS man was doing. Sister Georgette thought, 'They've come at last, and this is one,' then Sister Louis and she were staring at each other, and then they were crawling back toward the convent without remembering when they had started moving. Then they were running, holding their skirts high in both hands, their heads back, before they reached the convent and fell against the door and plunged into the building.

'It's in there!' Sister Georgette said. 'Hurry! Behind the stove!'

But Sister Louis couldn't seem to move. Her eyes protruded from her head and she stood there pale as if a sleep walker while Sister Georgette knelt down and felt behind the stove and began to draw out the revolver. It was a big Webley and had been left in the yard by a British officer back in 1940. It was lodged between the bottom of the stove and the wall and when it came free Sister Georgette fell back against the wall. They heard footsteps along the hall upstairs, and then they heard the voice of the Mother Superior: 'Who's down there?'

'Hurry!' said Sister Georgette.

'We can't,' said Sister Louis.

'You, Sister!' the Mother Superior said. 'Georgette!'

Georgette clutched the revolver like a loaf of bread.

'Do you want to help them?' she said. 'Don't you want to be free?'

They ran out the door, Sister Georgette still clutching the revolver cross-wise in one hand. They ran through the orchard toward the big meadow and ducked down behind a fallen log just as the SS man, carrying an automatic weapon, came across the corner of the field. They didn't hear the firing, nor the sound of running, perhaps because they were panting so hard themselves or perhaps because they knew it was there without even listening now. Sister Georgette didn't look up. She was busy trying to cock the revolver. She had done it before, practiced, but that was almost a year ago when the priest who was dead told her there would be an invasion. She held it in both hands, and heard the hammer click under the pressure of both her thumbs. Sister Louis was watching her and the SS man, and she cried: 'Shoot! Hurry! Shoot!' And then the sight levelled and Sister Georgette shut her eyes as she saw the man vanish in the sound of the gun exploding. It made a tremendous noise that seemed to build up all around her, and she heard the man scream, but she couldn't see him, hearing only Sister Louis crying, 'Oh, God, there are more! All of them!'

10 FLIGHT SERGEANT BERT NORTON

To Norton the building, the trees, the sky beyond the building, seemed to be receding as he ran. Nothing seemed to come toward him though he knew he was running toward the building. He felt as if he were running in a dream, without an inch of progress. Behind he could hear the shouting and crash of gun fire through the woods. At last he reached the wall of the building. A nun was standing in the open doorway with her mouth open, but he didn't seem to see her. He plunged straight past her and ran on into a room where three nuns stood, two of them red-faced and panting in front of an older nun.

'She shot him!' one nun cried. 'She killed the boche!'

'Where?' The older nun asked, but already she was looking at Norton. 'Sister Louis! Where?'

'In the orchard! By the meadow! There are more!'

The older nun sat down suddenly, her hand at her breast. But her voice did not change: 'Who are you? Sister Georgette! What is he doing here?'

'English!' said Sister Georgette. 'They are here to free us!'

'What?' The older nun stared at Norton, and then another nun was in the room, the one from the doorway and her mouth was still gaped and her face was pale, the color of chalk. Norton heard the sound of motorcycles sliding on the cobblestones and the voice of a sergeant or officer hollering at the troops to cover the front and side of the house and then they came past the window, the coal-skuttle helmets. Then they all heard the rifle butt knock on the door.

'Sister!' Norton said. 'Sister!' But nobody moved. They were all staring at the old nun who couldn't seem to move either, and her face was chalky white, too, and her voice almost failed.

'Georgette! What have you done?' Still nobody moved. Though the room was silent Norton could still hear the crash of gun fire in his ears, and his ears were still ringing, and the voice of the old nun seemed to be coming from far away.

Then she spoke, catching his shoulder with one hand: 'Here! Quick!' And Norton suddenly found himself squatting with his knees against his chin and nothing against his back except the Sister Georgette's skirts spread over him like a tent. Squatting, he heard the sound of hob-nailed boots coming into the room.

And though he could not see him he knew what was happening, the SS officer or sergeant holding the automatic pistol in one hand. It wasn't until later that he knew what they were saying but even then he could guess at it.

'All right, sister! Where is he? We saw him come down in his parachute.'

Norton couldn't see. It was pitch black. He squatted in a smell he did not recognize at first because he would not have believed it even if he had recognized the odor and it was sometime before he realized it was neither her clothes nor her body.

'You are mistaken, sir,' said the old nun. 'Nobody has entered the convent other than ourselves this evening.'

'Where did this gun come from?'

'Where did you find it, sir?'

'Outside the rear door.'

'Then it must have been dropped by the man you are pursuing, but he did not come in here.'

Norton could hear the dead quiet in the room now. He hoped the sister would not move and she did not though he could feel her legs beginning to tremble and his nostrils twitched upon the secret smell he could not recognize. And then he felt a round cold object move faintly against his hand.

'Search the building!' said the sergeant.

'We have nothing to hide,' said the old nun. 'But first—'

'We'll search first.'

'Did you—' she began and her voice died, and she began again, 'did he—?'

'Wounded!' said the sergeant. Norton held his breath.

'It must be his pistol then,' said the old nun.

Norton wondered how much longer he could hold his breath. His lungs were burning, and then he had to let it go, letting it out in faint, tiny surges, making no sound, holding the bottle of brandy suspended on a string in one hand, while he felt in the dark for the cork. He was hardly listening to the Germans now. He had the cork out and the bottle to his lips, and he could feel Sister Georgette's legs trembling heavily as he drank the brandy. And then there was a new voice in the room, a voice of superior authority. The voice was speaking to the sergeant. It was the voice of a German officer, cold without sounding angry.

'How do you know, Schmidt?' he said.

'The men saw him run toward the convent,' the sergeant said.

'You do not have the authority to search a convent,' the German officer said.

'Well, this pistol was found in the rear.

Why should we wait?'

'And one corporal hit in the backside,' said the officer. 'Why was he running away?'

'Haselmeyer is a good soldier, sir.'

'Yes,' the officer said. 'Well, where is the Englishman?'

'He is in here, sir. She said the gun must be his.'

The German officer said nothing. He stared at the Mother Superior, and then at Sister Georgette and his eyes roved down the long cassock-like skirt of Sister Georgette, and then he looked back at the Mother Superior. The Mother Superior's eyes did not blink. 'Is it not true, Mother, that a British officer was buried in your orchard during the Battle of France?'

'Yes, sir,' said the Mother Superior.

'Is it true that he was trying to hide in the convent when he was shot?'

'No, sir,' said the Mother Superior.

The officer turned his head.

'They have not harbored the enemy, sergeant. He is not here. Send your men outside.'

'But, sir, I saw him run in here.'

'Did you hear me, sergeant?'

'Yes, sir.'

'Deploy your men in the yard.'

Not breathing again, but feeling no pain now in his knees, Norton squatted, listening to hob-nailed boots crossing the stone floor. He had not moved, save for his hand which still held the bottle of brandy. It was suspended on a cord tied to Sister Georgette's waist. He felt the stiffness of her legs but her trembling had ceased so he drank again, holding the cork in one hand. He sensed the German officer still there. Then he heard the voice again, harsh and mocking: 'So you have never harbored British airmen? I understand, however, that British airmen were once equipped with weapons such as this but now they no longer carry side-arms. Just as well. Perhaps it prevents them from being shot.' The officer coughed briskly, moved his feet.

'A little wine I can offer you, sir. At this hour if—'

The officer did not answer. He merely stared at the nuns, his eyes bright and hard.

'No, no thank you,' he said. 'This is not the time nor the place. Perhaps after mass some Sunday.'

Then he was gone. Norton heard his boots cross the floor and along the hall, then the door slamming, and then both he and Sister Georgette let go. Georgette went back into a chair with her hand at her breast and her eyes closed and her face wet with sweat; all of a sudden the

Mother Superior hollered. Sister Georgette opened her eyes and thought for a moment the Mother Superior was hollering at the British flier.

Sergeant Norton was holding himself erect by leaning against the wall, limp-kneed, his eyes glassy, with something of laughing showing through the almost idiotic glassiness that was also part shock and amazement. Then he began to grin and almost at once he hiccuped and sat down heavily upon the floor.

The Mother Superior hollered and upon Sister Georgette's face came an expression of concern, consternation; she sat up sharply and tried to swing her legs away from the empty brandy bottle leaning against her ankle below her upraised skirt. Norton looked at her with a happy grin.

11   THE ASYLUM

Ten miles south of the convent, set among rolling hills and august trees, loomed the saddest building in the land, the Boulette Insane Asylum. Among the inmates were three sane men, waiting patiently that night for a signal from a guard they had bribed to secure poison before the Renault air raid.

The signal was to be given to Rene

Gaspard who was not insane, though he acted insane. He had the eyes of a dead fish.

He waited in his cell for the guard to bring the message. It was dark when the guard came, and as the cell door opened Gaspard did not look up. This was the role he had played for six months; extreme melancholia.

'It is done,' said the guard.

'Where?'

'In the yard.'

Gaspard raised his head.

'The yard?'

'They will find him in the morning.'

'Where's the poison?'

'You would have been seen,' said the guard.

'What?'

'You could not have done it in the dining hall,' said the guard.

Gaspard sprang and grabbed him by the throat.

'What did you do with the money?'

'I bought poison!' the guard gasped. 'He is dead. They won't find him.' He shoved Gaspard away. 'Fifty thousand francs—where is it?'

'Jules will take care of you,' said Gaspard, 'provided the pig is dead.'

'He's dead.'

'Where is he?'

'In the yard. They won't find him until morning.'

'Are you sure?'

High overhead came the sound of the passing bomber stream, a steady far faint thunder, then growing louder and louder; they were no longer whispering, standing face to face.

'I want the money this week or—?'

Gaspard laughed harshly.

'Do you think you would live a week if you turned informer?'

'Have Jules bring it to my house.'

'You will be told where and when to pick it up. Contact will be made.' Gaspard's face and voice were cold and quizzical.

The thunder faded into the sound of gun fire. The door clashed. The guard was gone. Gaspard went to the window. To the north searchlight beams sabred the darkness. Moths flickered and fell among the light beams. Gaspard turned away from the window, feeling drawn down into the darkness of the cell. He sat thinking. He had now been here seven months with Bistadeaux and Rampon. If we were outside, he thought, we would be dead. Bleak and chill the night air drew into the cell. Gaspard had been a big man once but now his skeleton rose, draped loosely in unpadded skin that tightened upon a faint paunch. He rubbed his paunch, lifting his face into the wall of darkness with an expression at once fatalistic and of a woman's bland patience, until he rose and lay on the pallet and drew the single blanket about his shoulders. Almost immediately he was asleep and dreaming and in the dream he squatted panting, hearing the whistle of the locomotive crying again across the river bridge from where he lay in the meadow counting, holding his breath, watching the puffs of smoke draw closer and closer, until after the roar of the explosion he realized he still had his hand down on the plunger when he should have been running. It was almost too late, and for three weeks afterwards the running had almost been too late, slipping at night from hiding place to hiding place, farm, field and village, only to learn the Gestapo had been there or would return, until finally the plan came from headquarters in Paris to enter the asylum as inmates. It had been all arranged, false names, false commitment from a doctor, and until a week ago hiding had been secure. Then the informer had emerged, at first only suspicious, an inmate, an old man once wealthy, committed by his wife who had gone off to Grenoble with her lover; a lover of Petain, without any real grounds of suspicion save his own paranoic condition out of which he was looking for something to happen that would confirm to himself he was right, wanting it so long as to see in the first clandestine meetings of the three men in the exercise yard the reality he sought; enemies of his old friends, so crazy as to have imagined what was in fact real: three men were spies hiding from Petain and the Germans. Now the old man, Pierre Villeneuve, was dead, vanishing quietly, almost sedately, while walking in the dusk in the exercise yard, since the asylum lacked the guards necessary to check the inmates by number upon their return from the walled yard at evening. The roaring whine of engines and machine gun fire died away upon the night air high above his body where he lay face down beneath a darkness filled with flickering stars that winked through the drumming thunder of gun fire, locking the sky to the ground in a monstrous veil of a thousand fiery threads.

12 FLYING OFFICER
RODGER CALDWELL: Navigator

Soft. Swinging down through the depthless dark. Pride and fear were gone. He felt as if he were young again because this was the end. He had never known such a sense of release before and down through the darkness, swinging easily in the straps, he knew the war was finished for him. No more fear. No more pride. Pride wasn't worth the burden. Pride was the cross to bear. It was what Jesus had on his shoulder, only he called it salvation. Well, he was finished with salvation, just another word for pride. They pumped you up with words and then put you down as a statistic. God could do so much for people if he just would. God was either lazy or had too much pride. It's because He wants to be alone. If I could just feel He didn't want to be alone, I could believe Him, because when mother died I finally got outside of myself and found there was nothing there. Not even God was waiting. He didn't even know I was there so I went back to grieving because that was better than being alone outside with myself.

From the air he could not see the ground. Then the sound of gun fire came in across the air. It was far away. Father said I worry too much and I said no sorry too much because you've been playing God so long in your head, father. I tried to stop worrying about everything, too, but it made me lonely. So I went back to grieving. That was even better than trying to figure out how to wreck the union which father had instead of mother even before she died.

He felt for his escape kit and slapped

his hand against his chest where the plastic box lay between his flying sweater and flight jacket. One flying boot began to slip. He jack-knifed his leg and tugged the boot top and felt for the hunting knife between the boot and leg.

Just then the chute canopy sagged, and his hand jerked from the boot to the shroud lines. His heart kicked over. And then he was sailing, air blowing on his face, the darkness softening, and it was almost as if the second before had never happened, and the terrible fear that was there was gone. But only for a second, but no longer; his face felt wasted suddenly, like melting wax that congealed coldly. His sight guttered down into nothing. The eternal darkness, he thought, the everlasting salvation, the grace of dying, revealing in an instant our blindness; the eternal fucking about the world at the mercy and ministration of all the half-baked tom-girls and tom-boys; the empty sockets of a billion iron ass-holes.

He felt drunk suddenly in the darkness. It's not like the world cost you anything, he thought, his eyes going black again, feeling the wind on his face as if a girl were slowly lifting a fan across his cheek. If I were dead, he thought, I couldn't feel it. And as he thought this he felt again the wastedness of his face. In despair his hot mouth slacked. No, his mind said quietly, swooning like his mouth, they just never give anybody the price. The thing to do was just save your eggs and bake your cake. Some are going to turn out well.

He slanted for an instant, then swung, followed by the

Vroom   *Vroom*   *Vroom*

of the desychronized engines of German night fighters.

He grasped the shroud lines, turning his head slowly, listening to the sound of the engines, his eyes closed, blank behind the lids.

Once a bastard, he thought. I told Father goodbye, because it was the vanity and the false pride in him. People never deny themselves for their own flesh and blood. Mothers. They have a choice. He stared into blackness and suddenly there was twilight on the sky and the smell of water. In the summer the best smell was water at twilight. For a fraction of a second the flash of flares lay across the horizon in a lake of golden light. Then the world was close and dark again, and he was thinking I am not me anymore who will never be again never never again never.

He could smell the dust in the leaves of the trees and he saw the light explode and lay tranquil shards of silver upon the clouds that trembled a long way off.

He saw shadows flow across his hands and for the first time saw the moon, and then as he floated softly he heard the sirens wailing. Swinging down he smelled dust in the trees as the sirens came up like the crying echoes of bagpipes and passed him and went on into the sky, speaking to him, saying with mocking relevance of a screech owl.

Mother was too proud for me, he thought, and father had too much vanity and pride. The light was gone on the horizon. He could feel the land below. It smelled of rain. The ground smell damped coming up. The dark smelled, too. Who was no who was no who was not; falling, faster, until something hard struck him across the ankles and his brain was isolated from his body and he was kneeling without knowing he was down.

Suddenly there was no sound anywhere. He crouched, then knelt on hands and knees like a dog. He listened, feeling the parachute straps tugging. He struck the release clasp a blow and shrugged off the straps, then crawling and listening he moved along on all fours in the pitch black. The sound of gun fire had died. There was no sound in the sky. He paused a long moment, listening. Then he rose and went on. The night air was cooling. He smelled the dust on his hands. He was about to take another step when something struck him a blow in the head and he sat down. He sat like that, erect, rubbing his head, seeing nothing, hearing nothing. He waited for another blow to fall. Nothing happened. He reached out, groping along the ground. His fingers touched a hard cold object and then he let his finger climb up the surface of the object. Stone, his mind said, and he sprang forward and flung both hands into darkness against the wall. For a long while he just lay prone against the wall that slanted climbing away from the ground, his face cold against the stone. He closed his eyes and stood there panting. Then he lifted his hands and looked up but the wall merged and blended into the darkness. He felt along the wall, came to where it turned and crouched, listening. There was no sound in the dark. He had stopped panting, and he got down on all fours and crawled away from the wall, feeling carefully with each movement of his body; turtle-like, he put out first one hand and then the other, touching the ground apprehensively, keeping his head back between hunched shoulders. He went on. He reconnoitred about fifty feet, not knowing whether he was moving straight ahead or in a circle.

He tried to breathe shallowly, so that the thumping would stop inside his head. He bumped into the wall again and rolled back, rubbing the top of his head. More than anything he must find a way out of here, a door, something, before daylight. Suddenly the darkness was rank; a strange odor. The body beneath his hand was a dark blur, a mound of clothes whose shabbiness could be felt distinctly.

Then his hand sprang back as of its own volition as if it had touched a snake. He listened again, reached out, felt the head for signs of a blow, and then the chest and stomach, but there was nothing. Then he sat beside the body bending forward, and swiftly and quietly, though his fingers were shaky, he stripped the corpse. Now I'll have to hide my uniform, he thought before it gets light.

13   VICHY SOIREE

Candace Compson's party was a success. The band was playing and everybody was dancing and drinking. The Countess Mourdaunt who had sat in the same hall while the Germans danced here in 1917 felt she did not belong here now but she managed a thin smile as the couples swept past. Most of the young men were officials in the Vichy government and were returning from Paris after a conference there with the Germans. They ranged along the wall, eating and drinking from the long table filled with delicacies only the Germans could provide. Some of the intellectual lights of the Vichy regime surrounded Count Griffin and his pretty young daughter. A group of young and old men were chatting and talking among themselves with Colonel Von Helmholtz and Candace Compson.

Colonel Von Helmholtz was not the ranking German officer at the party but he was by far the most handsome. His features were Teutonic, with a touch of Magyar, but his coloring and manners were French. The young men of the Vichy government were pleased with him, since it was rumored that Von Helmholtz would sooon be more than a Colonel. As a group they were discussing the recent Free French bombing of a train in which the Spanish consul had died.

'When will you stop these horrible people from ruining our lives?' said Candace, smiling pleasantly at the Colonel.

Colonel Von Helmholtz adjusted his monocle and smiled indicating he would be happy to explain the inner workings of his benign thoughts.

'He has just returned from Berlin,' she whispered to one of the young Vichy men.

'A personal audience with Hitler,' she went on to the young men on the other side of her. 'How well they get on together.'

'Yes,' said the colonel absently, and then as if he had suddenly remembered something, his lips curved with a subtle smile that at first frightened them, but almost at once his eyes changed, seemed to warm, and his smile changed, too, as though he recalled he must not smile mechanically nor with any subtlety. His gaze held her eyes.

'Who is the lovely lady?' he asked.

She did not realize he was referring to Countess Mourdaunt, and her heart quickened as she saw his gaze leave her face.

'Ah, Countess,' he said quickly as if just recalling the name and he walked toward the old woman. The Countess and the Colonel had those beautifully identical smiles of hosts who are gracious to the world as if their entire life had been lived at a salon ball.

'Colonel,' she said softly.

His lips barely parted. 'Countess.' He bowed, lifting her hand to his lips. Long ago she had been a beautiful woman, breasts and figure and skin, more beautiful than these would ever know. They day-dreamed of diplomatic careers, looking at her, with their courteous faces.

The young men admired Candace because she never played the coquette. They liked and feared the Colonel because of his subtle smile. It changed and moved, but it was as unquestionably false, always and forever; and as cold as the air of age and death the Countess seemed to carry with her. But the Countess' smile was as warm and gracious as the light in Candace's eyes. The smile seemed even to increase the patience of death that was in her face, and her smile shone in the lights as she touched the Colonel's fingers. Almost at once their heads inclined.

'Do tell us, Colonel,' she said, and young men of Vichy moved closer to the colonel.

'They are in every field and nothing is done,' said Candace, raising her eyebrows and smiling subtly at the Colonel and then at the countess.

'Something is always being done,' said the Colonel, faintly astonished that anybody would question the ability of German troops and German intelligence.

'I hate to see your men outsmarted,' said Candace in a tone that sounded at once innocent and sincere although the subtle smile remained on her lips.

But her eyes were almost arrogant, yet the Colonel could not discern whether he was being mocked or teased.

The Colonel quickly explained his plans. It was known that in the French underground collaborators had been placed by the Germans but in this province none of the key members of the French underground had been caught. The Colonel explained that shortly suspects in various towns would be picked up and hostages would be taken from the towns in which sabotage was committed, and that shooting of German soldiers by the underground would be repaid by the death of the hostages.

'That should stop them,' said the Colonel with an inquiring glance at the faces that ringed them.

'Ah,' said the Countess, fanning herself. 'You Germans are so efficient.'

The Colonel smiled, not certain whether he was being complimented or baited, but just then Candace, who had been watching an old man, saw that he was speaking in a fast and heated voice to a German major. She hurried away to stop the old man from talking too much. Candace knew this could be dangerous, especially since the major was listening carefully.

The old man was Pierre Micheleaux. He owned a truck company which no longer made trucks. He still controlled the company personnel but the Nazis controlled production: train wheels.

'The Americans are not fools ... Henry-Haye bore the taint of Laval,' the old Pierre was saying, speaking about the first Vichy ambassador in Washington, D.C. 'It was not the Americans who trapped him ... foolish to have published a decree depriving Frenchmen of their citizenship because they join De Gaulle. It only turns more French against you. If you are to save the world from the peasants, you must first save the world from the British ... And to let that writer go to America ... Maurois ...?'

'What would you have done?' said the Major.

Just then Candace caught Pierre's arm, squeezing it tightly, and smiling at the major, asked if he would like to meet some of the young women. The German major at once became pompously Prussian, clicking his heels, bowing, smiling the set smile he always kept for women.

'I would be enchanted,' he said, 'and from what the Colonel tells me I would be more than enchanted to see madame's collection of Monet.'

As he lifted his head there came the sound of voices from the terrace, and then through an opening in the hedge, two German soldiers emerged. Between them stood a British flier, hatless, smiling. He wore battle dress and black leather flying boots. Below the battle dress tunic hung a long white sweater, reaching almost to his knees. He bowed his head and apologizing in German, and still smiling, he reached down, drew up the sweater and rolled it around his waist.

14 FLIGHT LIEUTENANT JACK GIFFORD: Pilot

The woman was beautiful. But there was something too perfect about her beauty. It was too dazzling, the face of a movie star, and then Gifford saw the two German officers watching her as she walked toward Gifford. The tall German moved, crossing in front of her.

'Colonel,' she said, and her eyes caught Gifford's gaze. But he did not appear to hear her.

The Colonel's eyes were piercing and black. Gifford stopped smiling, clicked his heels, saluted. Even when he answered in German his expression did not change, but he knew he had him fooled, though the Colonel's eyes and face were hard and rigid as stone.

Good old New Ulm, Minnesota, Gifford thought; the nerve ends in his back twitched where he had struck the fence on the last swing on the parachute. Then he thought again in that fraction of a second of New Ulm as he heard this Kraut voice. It was the same: and he felt more disgust and determination, as when you suddenly sense a snake beside a garden path. He stood rigid, sweating, staring up at his dark eyes. He tasted sweat on his lips. He thought he had lost the memory of that other Kraut voice forever.

'Unter Officer Paul Schmidt,' Gifford heard himself say, snapping the voice. 'Abwehr. Section Thirty. Paris.'

Ah, Franz, he thought, if you could hear me now: the perfect little Prussian playing marbles behind the Standard Oil Gas. Franz Poehler. Father Poehler, keeper of the Iron Cross. Immortal Prussian. The whole town immortal Krauts. Dear New Ulm, Minnesota. Kraut talking Kraut in every store in town. Might have fought the Krauts even without Hitler starting the whole business. Learn it before you learn English. And with old man Poehler's Prussian accent. And he's sitting looking at himself in the yellow photograph in the Hussar uniform with the spiked silver helmet.

It was commonplace practice by both British and German intelligence services to have officers dressed in enemy uniform walk around airfields to test security, and Gifford had seen it happen several times, including one air base on which two

English had walked all over the field unmolested in Luftwaffe uniforms. He was gambling the Germans used similar methods to test security.

Gifford explained in German that he was from central security and giving the name of an imaginary German airfield, he explained he was checking security; chuckling he told how he had walked through the field and out the gate and now asked if he could use the telephone to call his headquarters so he might be picked up.

When Gifford ceased talking the Colonel who both hated and feared Intelligence, thinking it might be Gestapo and not Intelligence, said quickly:

'Won't you join us?'

'I should have returned long ago.'

'How far is the field?'

'Two miles. I was to rendezvous with my driver.'

'Candace, show him the telephone. Join us later.'

The Colonel smiling, clicked his heels. Gifford saluted, clicking his heels. His downcast eyes followed the blue veining in the curves of her breasts swelling above her dress. She sees me. Imagine squaffing some of that. Wonder if the Colonel is getting any of it. Immortal lusciousness. June. Shouldn't be allowed to eat. Her breasts all ambrosia. Enjoy her.

He followed her across the garden into the big house. The hall was cool and dim. The sound of his boots echoed along the hall.

'For God's sake,' she said suddenly. Her voice was hushed, restrained, yet cased in violence.

He felt her fingers clasp his wrist.

'What the hell,' his voice cried, his arm jerked itself loose. He struck at her in the dark. He heard her cry out, yet feeling he had not struck her.

Again her fingers caught, her nails dug the flesh of his wrist.

He caught her other arm, the wrist. With astonishing strength, as he held her, she sprang back, dragging him against the wall.

It was dark. He could not see her face. Her breath touched his mouth and he knew her face was only inches away.

'Why?' she hissed. 'Why now?'

Her accent, the falling intonation of her voice was unmistakably American.

He found himself laughing suddenly out of fright and exasperation.

He held both her wrists and he pressed her forearms back against the wall.

He wanted to curse at her for frightening him, but he was so tired he felt suddenly a relapse of memory, and in the relapse he felt all the muscles of his body collapse; for a second all his dead body weight leaned against her.

'Come on,' she hissed, shrugging at his weight. He leaned upon her like a tired boxer, without feeling.

'Shut up,' he said in a tired voice. 'Just shut up.'

She found her arms free and she pushed him away. He went back and came forward, and as he came forward his hands struck her shoulders and held her pinned to the wall again.

'Nestor,' she hissed through his fingers. Her body surrendered helplessly beneath his hands. 'Nestor,' she gasped.

He released her throat and she fell down and knelt holding her throat and choking.

Almost at once he thrust his hands under her arms and lifted her erect. She slumped against him but he still did not trust her. He stepped back. She leaned against the wall, touching her throat, brushing her hair away from her face.

'Get out,' she said. 'Get out while you can.'

He thought: I'll chance it.

He said: 'I've been shot down.'

'Christ,' she said. 'I thought—' and he heard her voice break ... 'I thought you were Nestor.'

'What—?' he began. She waved him away.

'Go on.'

'Get me some clothes,' he said.

'Get out,' she said. 'Get out.' Her voice was cold now with fury.

He seized her throat again.

'I'll kill you,' he said. 'I'll kill you here.'

She struck at his hands.

Her voice was a dying sigh: 'All right. All right.'

He followed her down the dark hall. They mounted through darkness a cold stone staircase. He felt the stone walls along the halls, a dampness seemed to be congealed in the air. They turned and she caught his hand and drew him into a room. Almost at once the light exploded in his eyes. He blinked and felt without seeing anything for an instant: the gun was against his ribs.

'Who sent you?' she said.

'I was shot down.'

'Where?'

He watched the gun. Her hand was steady.

'Half an hour ago,' he said.

'I'll kill you if you're lying,' she said. 'Get in there. Against the wall. Face it.'

He listened to her walk backward, heard the door clash and rasp of the bolt. He touched the wall in the darkness. He began to feel along the surface of the wall. It was pitch dark. His hand struck something cold. A mansard window, he thought, breathing faster now.

15   RUSSELL AND SMILEY

Russell began to see light; the mouth of the cave through which moonlight shone, almost overhead.

'Smiley?' he said. He still had the flashlight he always carried in his boot and he flashed it in the darkness.

'Smiley? Where are you?'

He knelt in darkness, shining the light. No answer. He flashed the light overhead. It rose into darkness, then into the moonlight. He listened to earth shifting behind him. Where in God's name are we?

'I'm dying!' Smiley wailed somewhere in the darkness. 'I'm dying!'

Russell moved the beam of light. It sabred the darkness. He heard again the sound of Smiley somewhere in the darkness. Then the stench of rotting flesh came to him. He thought for a fraction of a second how they had stumbled through the woods; Smiley half-carried, bleeding, then Smiley screaming as the earth moved under their feet plunging them downward.

The flashlight beam found Smiley's face. He lay on his side, his face caked with blood and dirt. Again the stench of decayed flesh struck through the darkness and Russell lifted the light beam, shooting it into the darkness toward the smell of flesh. It splashed light upon a ruined concrete wall curving downward beneath the gaping cave-like mouth in the earth above. Stacked like cord-wood, were rotting corpses in field grey and leather boots, layered between corpses in French tunics; at once Russell realized he was in the bottom of a French fortress blown up in the 1940 retreat and used as a common grave. He snapped off the flashlight.

'We'll get out,' he said. He flashed the light up to the cave-like mouth.

Smiley screamed again and Russell flashed the light upon his face and laid his hand over Smiley's mouth. Smiley made a choking sound and then was silent.

Russell began to climb the pile of earth. Smiley called to him from the darkness.

'I'll be back,' Russell answered and Smiley began to scream again.

'We'll get out,' Russell called to him.

He felt the earth slide beneath his flying boots. It slid downward and he almost lost his balance, trying to hold the light aloft.

Then he saw the night clearly, stars a

different darkness, a lesser darkness and smell of fresher air.

The earth slid beneath him and he tumbled backward. He halted, digging his feet into the earth and shone the torch upward. Through a faint veil of dust he saw the stars, and he started down toward Smiley.

'I'm dying!' Smiley wailed. 'I'm dying!'

'Shut up,' Russell said as he helped Smiley to his feet. He thrust him ahead, half pushing and half holding him erect. He made whimpering sounds like a dog crying. Russell cursed him and shoved him. Then Smiley was out in the fresh air, and he began to laugh crazily, and the fresher darkness enveloped them.

Where are we, Russell thought, taking a deep breath, leaning against a tree, feeling the dust and burning in his lungs. Where are we, and which way shall we go?

Russell looked up at the stars and Smiley began to moan and wail again.

16 SERGEANT
ROBERT CRAIG: Bomb Aimer

All that next morning Sergeant Craig, hiding in the basement of the bombed stone ruins of a house, watched the house across the street into which the police had carried the German officer whom Craig had stabbed the night before. Craig was twenty-three, a Scotsman. He had a short, snubby nose, small round head; his blond sideburns showed reddish hair, and his cheekbones were high, roundish, almost Germanic above his full lips and small straight teeth. He had worked in a draper's shop in Glasgow before enlisting in the Royal Air Force.

The night before, in the darkness in which the German officer was returning from a tryst in the fields with a French farm girl, Craig was walking across a barley field near the town. In that chill early morning darkness, that was neither night darkness nor the beginning of dawn, the smell of the fields and trees blew slowly across the cool air, one blending into the other. Part of the barley field had been freshly ploughed. It was there on the road that the officer captured Craig as he stepped out of the field on to the dirt road. To Craig it had all happened so fast he could not recall having seen the officer until given the order to halt and put up his hands. On the edge of the town Craig stumbled and fell. They were in front of the bombed ruins. The German officer stood directly over him, cursing him. The knife which Craig carried on each mission was in the side of his flying boot. He came up swiftly with the knife and the blade went straight into the German's belly, almost disemboweling him in the single upward heave of the blade.

The sirens began after Craig was in the basement of the ruined house. Now he had the officer's pistol. From the basement where he lay hidden, Craig could hear the police sirens rise and fall twenty minutes after the policeman on the bicycle passed the body in the road. 'They'll never look for me here,' Craig thought. 'Not this close. They'll think I ran from here.' The sirens were two miles away across town, but he could hear them as though they were inside the ruined basement itself, rising and falling, rising and falling. It was as though he could see them upstairs in the house across the street where they had carried the German officer, with the ambulance standing in front of the house now. Only they had not brought him out. Then he heard the rats run across the floor upstairs, the whispering scratch of the small feet.

Though it was now morning, a light shone in the window of the bedroom in which the German officer lay dying. Craig had watched the doctor go in, and now he watched him come out, open the ambulance door, remove a small box, and re-enter the house. 'They're still trying to keep him alive,' Craig thought, hearing a

100

part of his head talking to himself: 'You haven't a chance. You can't leave here until he dies.' He wished to be back in London and he lay quietly for a long moment with his eyes closed.

He imagined himself coming into London on leave, walking out of Charing Cross station, wanting to jump up and down in the sunny street, so happy with life to have leave. But maybe he would never do that again. Bad luck had overrun him. He wanted to leap out of here, run up the street, shouting for a miracle to take him back to London. The thin whispers of rat's feet came to him again. He was hungry. He wished he were in London having a horsemeat steak in Cambridge Circus and Eda were with him.

He was thirsty now, too, and he opened the collar of his tunic, and the talisman slung on a cord fell on to his hand. He looked down at it. The talisman consisted of a fox's eye mounted in a silver butt. Alice had bought the talisman in the Flea Market. He lifted his head, watching the house, the street, listening to faraway sirens, thinking of himself running among the sirens.

He lay there all morning. That afternoon he saw the doctor come out, in his Wermacht uniform, and get in the ambulance with his driver and drive away. He lay very still and watched the ambulance vanish up the street, and then he discovered he had been holding his breath until he felt faint and he let the air back into his lungs, until his breathing was regular.

Then he saw another officer come out of the house and look up and down the street. It was quite light out now. By this time the Gestapo cars were stopping people in the streets and on the corners and making checks of their identity cards, and Sergeant Craig watched the police cars pass slowly along in front of the ruins. The sirens were still howling intermittently at sundown throughout the town. They were howling in the darkness, when Sergeant Craig climbed out through the rear basement window and entered the orchard where the moon was shining. He began to run. From faraway and near he could hear the police klaxon wailing as the cars searched the town block by block. He heard a cat rush past him, and near the end of the orchard, also running, he passed another man. For an instant, without breaking stride, they stared at each other across the darkness, their eyes shining. Craig plunged out of the orchard, and running full speed, he doubled his fists, gasping.

He ran on across the mooned land. He did not know where he was, but at home he had hunted, and, running, he sought the north star, and as he thought of the men who would hound him as he had so often hounded game at home he spotted the north star. He dog-trotted two miles and turned south. He travelled twenty miles that night, occasionally doubling back, crossing two shallow streams. The next day about noon he knew he was being sought even this far from the town when he saw two men, both in leather coats, too well dressed to be peasants, wearing brown wide brimmed hats. He watched them from a thicket, dismount from a small open car and search in the dust of the track that ran parallel to the stream in the woods. They were young, tall, and he did not doubt they could catch him running if they saw him. They would probably go on, he decided, because he had not walked in the dusty track. So he decided to sleep here the rest of the day. He had not eaten in almost forty-eight hours and he wondered why he did not feel hungry. 'But I must sleep,' he thought. He could hear the loud beat of his heart as he told himself this. He lay down but he could not sleep, and though he knew he needed rest with sleep he could not understand why he could not sleep. 'Maybe I forgot how to,' he thought.

As soon as the dark came he began to move south again. He thought he would walk slowly to wait for hunger to come, thinking he would tire before he felt hungry, but as the dark thickened he found himself running. He was in a wood, and he could hear himself running as though he were somebody else apart from himself, and he ran listening to his breathing, his feet crashing in the leaves and brush. When he felt his chest feeling burning and choked he stopped and rested, but soon he was walking again, but still he did not feel hunger. For a while he was lost, and then he checked the stars and estimated how far he had been walking east and he turned south again. Suddenly he stopped, not believing what he heard, police sirens, telling himself they were only echoes in his mind from the time he had spent in the ruins. Listening now, all he could hear was the thudding of his heart. Then the police sirens came again, and he wondered for the first time how far he had walked, thinking perhaps he was near the outskirts of a new village or town. Then the siren ceased abruptly, cut-off, and he halted smelling a wood fire. When he looked again, they surrounded him, though he could see only four or five, pointing guns at him; the leader came toward him, a short man in a leather coat, wearing a leather cap, carrying a machine pistol, and then with a light in his face he heard the voice. It spoke English, carefully and slowly.

'We heard it might be one of you,' the short man said. 'Keep moving. You can't stay here.'

'Why? Who are you?'

'Maqui. We will feed you. That is all. We cannot keep you.'

'I don't want to stay.' From faraway came the sound of the police siren.

'Take this with you.'

He accepted the parcel that smelled of food, and turned and went down into the woods again, heading south. It was almost dawn when he stopped. 'I have passed them,' he thought. 'They've lost me now.'

He sat down and ate the bread and cheese wrapped in the newspaper. Then he dug a hole with his hands and buried the paper. Then he rose and moved slowly as the light increased. He lay down in a patch of cattails and covered himself with leaves and went to sleep. He dreamed he was running down a long hill. He was lucky to have covered himself, for, waking suddenly in the waning light of afternoon, he saw two German soldiers. They were big, tall; they stood about twenty-five feet from where he lay hidden; they looked school-boyish in their uniforms.

'This is bad duty,' one said.

'Damn those fliers, I have a date tonight,' the other said. 'We better come in with some information.'

'Yes.' They looked about, up into the trees, and one of them drew off his boot and rubbed his heel. 'Damn those fliers,' he said.

'What the hell difference does it make if one man gets away?' said the other.

Just before dark, from the broken window in a house ruined by shell-fire three years before, Sergeant Craig looked down into a town two miles away. He could see trucks and motorcycles between the houses where German soldiers moved in the street, and the sidestreets were filled with field weapons, heavy artillery and anti-tank guns and weapon carriers. He waited until darkness and circled the town.

In the middle of the next morning he came face to face with a German soldier. They looked at each other down a narrow path in the woods—the German small, youthful, almost child-like, apparently weaponless; Craig, bearded, gaunt and desperate looking. The German froze for an instant, his mouth gaped. Craig took a single step and the German ran, plunging through the underbush.

That night, lying in the undergrowth, Craig felt something soft and furry brush his cheek. He struck at it out of a sudden

106

fright, hungry and weary. He lay back, quite exhausted, thinking, 'I don't want to die.' Then he thought it again, 'I don't want to die,' the thinking going in long slow waves in his brain, while feeling the deep desire to live slipping faintly away in exhaustion.

He woke hearing his own breathing, as if already he had been running. His lips felt dry and thin and he could feel them going in and out as he rose and squatted beside a stream to wash his face. This was the day on which hunger caught up with him. He could smell himself, not so much the sweat, but the fatigue and fear inside himself as though his tired flesh were turning into stale water. But he did not eat that day, nor the next.

17 INTELLIGENCE REPORT

Documentary Records

EXCERPTS FROM CONVERSATIONS DEALING WITH THE EXPERIENCES OF THE CREW OF W. WILLIAM. THESE CONVERSATIONS TOOK PLACE SEVERAL MONTHS LATER AND CONVERSATIONS WITH MEMBERS OF THE FRENCH UNDERGROUND TOOK PLACE ONE WEEK AFTER CRAIG'S RETURN TO ENGLAND.

Speaker: Flight Sergeant Craig. This is an abstract of an interview between Flying Officer Harry Benson, an intelligence officer and Sergeant Craig upon Craig's return to England.

'Did I know Wing Commander Russell and Flight Lieutenant Jack Gifford were at odds with each other? Sure, you mean old yellow gloves. Yes, that's what we called him. He was a good pilot, we thought, but we thought he would go out of his way for glory, and if necessary, get us killed. He was gong happy.

'I can't remember how I got down that night. It was a nightmare. Guess I was blown out of the kite. Do I think Gifford was responsible for Russell's death? Gifford wasn't that kind of a guy. Why would he do that? and how would I know.'

Speaker: Jacques Benzoin, a farmer living near Neuville de Bois, former member of the Resistance. The following are extracts from Benzion's statement, with interviewing questions omitted. Recorded three years after the war.

'It was just after midnight when I heard the RAF going over. We were out in the woods laying wire. I was wheeling the barrow, working the pigs truffling ahead of the wire party because there were Germans all through the area. The machine exploded in the sky about five miles away. We always used the pigs out truffling when laying wire so we could scout ahead of the wire laying party. The Germans cut our wire three times to the resistance camp.

'The sky lit up like daylight. I didn't hear anything until about half an hour later when I saw this man hanging in a tree and he was shouting. I told him to shut up and I would get him down. But when I went back to the wire party, they would not come up and help since it was more important to get the wire laid than risk getting picked up. When I got back to the tree he was down and shouting at me. I mean, he was hanging down, upside. How did he act? He was crazy.

'I mean, he kept calling me Hitler and raising one hand and then the next minute he would be laughing. I was afraid to go near him, but I knew I had to get away then or help him because the German patrols were around. So I cut him down.

'He started truffle hunting with the pig, sniffing and snorting, and we were headed right into the patrols. I managed to lead him back to the wiring party where they held him down and took off his uniform and got him dressed in trousers and jacket. He actually seemed pleased to see my pig as if it were a dog. He kept saying I was an owl.

'Needless to say, we ran into German patrols. There were seven of them. How did we get by? Like I said, he acted crazy enough, sniffing, but he wasn't that crazy. All he could say was Heil Hitler. Thank God, he didn't talk, just flapping his arm up and I tapped my finger to my head, and the Germans let us pass. It was impossible for them not to let me go. All those staff officers and aides-de-camps; in short, no me, no truffles for them.

'What ever happened to him—what was his name—McWhinney?'

Book Three
THE GIRLS THEY LEFT BEHIND

18   EDA BRAUER

As Eda braided her hair she enjoyed stroking it, the long, soft warmth of the braid felt cool in her hands, and she paused to sense the fresh softness of the hair now. She admired herself in the mirror. She was quite happy about what she saw; a good looking, yes, striking woman of twenty-three, with the two long braids of hair, one finished, the other in her busy hands, the hair chestnut colored, and soon she would wind the braids about her head. But now was the time of day she liked best and this was also her favorite day in the week. It was her day off, her free day. She heard the baby crying in the front yard, and without stopping her hands or turning her head she called down from the bedroom.

'Oh, Harry! Turn Michael over, please.'

There was no answer from downstairs save the sound of footsteps crossing the kitchen and the back door opening. It was a small house, a cottage, with two bedrooms upstairs, a kitchen, bath and sitting room downstairs.

She studied herself again and smiled with pleasure. Her teeth were beautifully white and straight. Her skin was dark without being olive colored, yet underlaid with a rich soft plum colour that gave her skin a glowing warmth. Her eyes were hazel and her cheekbones were high and round and soft.

'Harry, put on the tea, please.'

When she finished her hair she put on a black linen dress which she had bought before the war, the summer she had come to England, the summer she had married Harry. The hem was bordered with flowers, and the neckline revealed just the faintest swelling of the tops of her breasts. The dress amused her. At the pub she enjoyed bending over at the bar, not too far, but just far enough. Eda was a tease and she loved being one.

It wasn't that Eda was a bad girl. But she was bored with being a wife and a mother, but when you marry a man for the convenience of leaving Germany alive with citizenship in a new country, you were apt to get caught by new responsibilities, and though she loved her children who were not the products of love, she still felt that the years she had been married had deprived her of what every girl deserves, those years when you could flirt for its own sake and have a drove of boys chasing you.

Because she had worked out an agreement with Harry, her husband, who was assistant manager in the fuse section of the munitions factory, her free day, that delightful day away from the babies and the house, fell on Friday. This was Harry's day to stay home with the babies; Michael, a year, and Tommy, almost three.

On Fridays, Eda frequently was the first client at the King's Arms. Over a period of two years she had known by sight, or to say hello to, scores of fliers, but Sergeant Robert Craig was the only one whom she had ever allowed to buy her a drink.

She first saw Craig sitting alone at a table in back of the bar, a small round table, big enough only for two. She saw him again five or six weeks in a row. Their eyes happened to meet and because they had seen each other so often she nodded when he nodded, for it was early, but past noon, and only three people were in the bar, a farmer sitting alone sucking a mild and bitter over his gum boots, and Craig and herself.

She had always thought Craig looked like an unhappy version of Tommy Trinder, the comedian, but this day he smiled cheerfully as she nodded, and then suddenly he winked, which seemed so out of character to her that she wondered what he had been drinking. As she walked to her table she heard him whistling softly a lewd tune that kept time to the motion of her hips. Eda pretended not to notice it. But even after she had ordered her drink and sat sipping it she could hear him whistling softly a few tables away, the same lewd tune. It went on too long.

'Would you mind!' said Eda, looking at him.

He smiled and said, 'Mind what?' He

bowed his head as if he were doffing an invisible cap.

But his voice was so friendly and innocent, that Eda couldn't be sure that he had understood her intentions. But the next Friday Craig whistled the same tune as she crossed the room alone and as Eda passed his table she said, 'Some people become officers and other remain sergeants forever. Little wonder.'

'It costs too much money to be an officer.'

'Some people couldn't buy manners with a fortune.'

'Who wants to be that rich?'

The next Friday she sat on the other side of the pub, but there he was alone at his table, reading a magazine. This time as he passed her table on the way out to the toilet he went into an elaborate act of stumbling, falling against the walling, rolling backward on the floor like an acrobat to end up face down, moaning, beside her table. At the moment in concern she reached down and touched his shoulder and called to the bartender, Craig rolled over on his back and burst out laughing.

'Funny,' said Eda. 'Very funny.' She stood up and left the King's Arms.

The next Friday she decided to get even with him for embarrassing her in front of the people at the bar, but she could think of no way save to ignore his glance and, more and more, she found herself wanting to go to the King's Arms simply to see him.

So the next Friday when she arrived at the King's Arms, instead of going directly in she hesitated at the door, feeling foolish and embarrassed. She was standing in a complete state of indecision when Craig came up behind her, tip-toeing. When only three or four feet away, he made the sound of an air raid siren, perfectly imitating the sudden rising and falling wail.

'You!' she shouted, terrified. She wished she had an umbrella. She would have struck him, but now suddenly she didn't know which way to go, and the next thing she found she had entered the pub and taken her seat in the back of the room.

A few minutes later, Craig came in, but Eda did not look at him, staring, in fact completely in the opposite direction. Craig looked worried. It was apparent he had carried things too far and she was angry. He walked over to her table.

'I'm sorry,' he said.

'I don't care. Just go away. Please. Just leave.'

'I was only having a little fun.'

'I don't think it's funny.'

'You looked like a girl with a sense of humor.'

115

'I fail to see the humor in anything you've done. Frightening people isn't funny.'

'Really. I'm sorry. Please let me buy you a drink.'

For a long moment she hesitated, then said, 'All right, but act your age. I'm a married woman.'

He sat down. She fished in her purse nervously for a cigarette.

'I said I'll buy.'

'I'm looking for a cigarette.'

Craig laughed. 'Oh,' he said. 'In that case, have one of mine.'

'I don't even know you.'

'You've seen me often enough.'

'What is your name?'

'Robert Craig?'

'Yours? I mean, your first name. Not your married name.'

'Don't you try anything funny again,' she said. Then added: 'Eda.'

He ordered two India Pale ales and though she tried to discourage intimate conversation she found herself talking freely and easily. She also noticed that every now and then while he was either talking or listening, he got a kind of beyond-look in his eyes, as if he weren't even there in the room. It lasted only a second or two, but each time the corners of his eyes turned down and his eyes seemed to go out of focus in a blank sad way.

At closing time that afternoon he still had not asked her married name; she knew only his name and the fact he was a bomber aimer on a squadron stationed at Pocklington. At the bus, where he asked her to stay for a film, she merely shook her head, and hopped on the bus before he could say goodbye. She was afraid to look back because she felt sure he was still standing there waiting for her to smile or wave to him, and she knew the look he had in his eyes now. She had seen that just before she got on the bus.

The next Friday he was not there and she felt cold and lonely and went home early. Usually she went by herself to a film in the afternoon, and then came back to the pub in the evening where she bought her own drinks and exchanged smiles and small talk with the fliers. She never told them her name, not her real name, and though she flirted with all of them, she never accepted any invitations to attend the nightly dances at the De Grey Ballroom. Now she discovered she missed encountering Craig. But the following Friday he was there again, and he bought her a drink, and after two drinks she found out all about him him; that he was Canadian, she had known from the first by his accent; that he was married she had not known before, and that he

117

had a child, lived in Winnipeg. He also told her he had worked as the head electrician in a lumber camp, had been an amateur boxer, had never smoked in his life, had a sister in the Canadian Wrens, thought the English didn't complain enough, and wished he could get more leave, because every three months was not often enough. Eda told him about herself in terms of the facts that she had been born in Stuttgart, Germany, that she was partly Jewish on her mother's side who was half Jewish, had studied music in Berlin, had married her husband an English traveling salesman after her father had been killed in a street pogrom, loved bicycling, missed German cooking, had two children. In a month they knew all about each other, enough to fall in love, but both became cautious, waiting for the other one to make the first move.

One afternoon Eda said, 'I'm going to stay overnight at my aunt's house in Bury St. Edmunds tomorrow if you want to meet me there.'

'I thought all your relatives lived in Germany.'

'No, mother was part English.'

'You mean overnight?'

'Yes. I can go up on the bus and you can—'

'What about your husband?'

'I hate him.'

'Well, I wondered, you know.'

'I don't think you understand. When you marry, you're supposed to be in love with the person. Maybe I was fond of him in the beginning or maybe just grateful getting out of Germany. But we just don't fit together. It was his idea. He asked me to get married. We were going to separate and then there was the first baby. I think every time we have a child I hate him more than before. I can't help it, because we don't mean anything to him. You've been nice to me, and meeting you, Bob, you might as well know because I'm in love with you.'

'That's why I asked to be transferred to another squadron. It'll wreck both of us.'

'You'd leave here?'

'They've cut the papers on my transfer. Next Tuesday. God, I think of you all day, even when I'm flying.'

'Well, now you know!'

'I'll get the orders changed, Eda.'

And remembering all those times with Craig, as if each memory were a part of his body, or a part of her body, each time: her breasts swollen with love in the orchard beyond the field at Marston-Warden and his hands, and his hands on fire, filled with sunlight, tracing her body, sunlight heating flesh against flesh; his thigh raveling the cool sheet in the hotel room at Coningsby, her hands seeking the hard muscle of the thigh to stroke softer and softer into the long shuddering spasm of their bodies quivering against the reverberations of the guns firing and bombs falling in the fields beyond the town and his shoulders reaching above her in the dawn, the sweet-honeyed dawn, the light moving as slowly through the worm-like cracks in the black out curtains as her thighs feeling the clench of his leg muscles parted with the sun rising until there were no limbs or bodies or minds, only a vacuum in which she lay, until as if waking from a long blissful lassitude her body seemed to grow again, assume size and form and touch, evolving out of an immeasurable inner depthless pool of warmth. And each place was a limb of love, a time never to forget, his lips those nights in the warm fields, the summer fields, filled with stars and sky, the long, long twilights at Middleton Moor, lying beside the pool, his lips upon her breasts, her hand trailing in the water, feeling the water growing warmer and warmer beneath her fingers, holding and holding tighter the lily stalk beneath the water, until her hand crushed the stalk, that sweet ever-lasting sweet night that only he had ever given her, nerves ravishing nerves until it seemed even a voice cried out from the end of her spine, seeking some enormous anguished release in an ecstasy so unbearable she no longer knew where she was until she saw his face and the stars beyond and he was stroking her cheek softly, gently kissing the lids of her eyes, calling to her, darling, darling, darling, darling ...

That was three months ago, and now it was four days since she had heard that Craig's aircraft had not returned. She started down the stairs. Harry was standing at the bottom.

'Well, Missus, where are you going?'

'It's Friday.'

'You're in a hurry,' he said slowly, quietly.

She paused.

He said nothing.

She came down to the bottom of the stairs. The hall was narrow and she could not pass Harry who stood in the kitchen doorway.

'You're not fooling anybody, Eda.'

'Oh?'

'You're not going there anymore,' said Harry.

'What?'

'He won't be there.'

She looked at him.

'You're not leaving this house,' he lifted his arm.

'Lay a hand on me and I'll call the police.'

'You're not going down to that pub.'

'You miserable, dirty spying ...' she said.

'Listen, you bitch, you're not going out of here!'

She ducked under his arm and ran across the kitchen and out the back door.

It was after midnight when she returned. The kitchen door was unlocked. The man who brought her to the door wondered why she laughed when she kissed him and why she opened her mouth and held him hard and tight when she kissed him again and said she would see him next Friday. Going upstairs she thought that she hated and that seemed to ruin her life forever. And God awful part was she blamed Harry and not herself and knew this wasn't true, but the worst part was she knew there was nothing she could do, nothing about Craig or Harry, or any of them, but what was even worse was when she got into bed her husband touched her, and for a moment the terrible thing was she felt herself giving in. 'Let me alone!' she heard herself scream, just as she was about to give in, and knowing, too, she would be back at King's Arms next Friday, and all the Fridays to come.

Mary Alice Evans looked at the silver framed photograph of Flying Officer Rodger Caldwell. Upon the ledge above the white fireplace beside the photograph sat a full bottle of gin. Mary Alice looked at that, too. Through the open window above Curzon Street everything was violent and still, the sky green paling into gold beyond the gable of Chesterfield Gardens. A plume of smoke rose from the chimney across the way. She listened to the all clear of the sirens dying away. A fire watcher looked up into the sky from the roof across the street. She could hear a lorry starting up somewhere. Mary was thirty-seven. She looked thirty, at the most. 'Oh, hell!' she said, and fingered her lower lip. She was wearing black velvet slacks and a white sweater. 'Joan!' No answer. That stupid Mick, she thought.

She looked at the bottle of gin, shook her head, turned away, then seemed to change her mind, and looked back at the bottle of gin again. She walked over to the fireplace and unscrewed the bottle cap and put the bottle to her lips. It wasn't a big drink, nor was it short. She put the cap on just as Joan appeared.

'Some ice and soda, please.'

'Yes, Miss Evans,' said Joan. 'I'll fix

a fresh bottle.' She left the room and Mary Alice watched her maid's figure as it crossed the room and wondered what Joan did on her day off. She went to the window as if to get away from the bottle until Joan returned with the tray of ice and bottle of soda. Mary Alice was fixing herself a drink, splashing the soda when the doorbell rang. Joan went to the door, and Mary Alice tossed off the half-made drink and put the glass behind a chair and sat down suddenly.

Joan reappeared. 'It's that American. Sergeant, uh—'

'All right. All right. Show him in.'

What are you drinking? Rodger said. You've got to eat something or what's the point in coming to a place like this? Here. Get this down! He handed me a piece of mutton on the end of the fork. We sat there on the davenport with the windows blacked out and the sound of the squadron going out against the moon. Can't you eat anything? Rodger said. How can you keep doing five and six shows a week and drink like this? We went through Piccadilly Circus in the black out and up to Bobby's club. It was full of red tab staff officers, all puffs, with their bum boy corporals and privates. It always made me laugh, how sore they got when I came to pick up Bobby for the show. He had a yen, too, for Rodger Caldwell but I'd warned Rodger, though competition never scared me, not after what I could do for Rodger.

When the American sergeant came in she didn't get up. He stood in the doorway and smiled at her.

'Was that a nice thing to do?' she said.

'Well, frankly, I don't enjoy people putting live cigarettes into my navel when I'm asleep,' he said.

'Were you able to get any Chesterfields?'

'Camels.'

'There's some gin in the kitchen. Call Joan.'

'I'll get it. Any scotch?'

'Right on the mantel.'

She looked toward the liquor cabinet.

'Ectchually, you're a princess,' he said.

'As a matter of fact, yes.'

'How'd you make out with George?'

'Oh, he's nice. Very nice. Thanks a lot,' she said.

'You mean that wavey hair?'

'Beautiful. Thanks a lot,' she said.

'I think he's real nice.'

'Funny boy, aren't you?'

'Did you burn his belly button, too?'

'Don't drink so much scotch,' she said. 'I won't have to wake you up then.'

'You out of gin or something? You're not drinking.'

'Pacing,' she said. 'Just pacing myself, sonny boy.'

'I'll fix you one myself,' said the sergeant and went out of the room. He was gone only a few minutes and returned with a tall gin drink. 'I want to know if you're going to pull that again,' he said, handing her the glass.

'I'm the one who deserves an explanation,' she said.

He told her for fifteen minutes and fifteen different ways he didn't like to be awakened in the middle of the night by somebody using his navel for an ashtray, if she didn't mind. They went through three highballs in the next half hour during which time the sergeant explained that he had not gone to see another woman after leaping out of bed in the middle of the night and dressing and leaving the apartment in something more than a huff.

'See if there's some more scotch. Where is that Irish biddy?'

'I'll get it.'

'Never mind. I'll be back in a second. I need the walk,' she said.

She stuck out her right hand to be pulled up and he caught her hand, pulled her erect and she went out of the room.

Rodger's mouth was almost unbearable. What did he do that nobody else had ever done? What was it? His kiss kiss. Oh, God, how could it be that good and before never

126

with anybody never like that. What do you think of that? The night he came over to the piano after the show in the squadron hangar with the oh-you beautiful girl look on his face. So damn young looking yet older than the other boy faces. God, I'm thirty-three. That's a lie. You're thirty-four. The touch of his hand still on my back after two weeks like I can turn the touch on and off.

I'm glad your mother isn't alive, Rodger, said his father, bringing a west end actress into her house and Rodger across the table not looking at me. It's not for this harlot I raised you and you will stop it and I ask both of you to leave my house. And his hand coming back red from his father's face. You'll never come into this house again, Rodger, said his father wiping the blood from his mouth where he sat on the floor. Take your harlot out of here. Get out. Here father let me help you. Get your bloody hands off me, Rodger. Get out. Get out. Get out.

She came back into the room, walking barefoot now across the deep white pile carpet. The whole room was white, including the furniture.

'Well, what was I saying,' said Mary Alice Evans. 'I think you're a fraud, coming backstage telling me Lady Beaumont sent you. I'm gonna call her at the—uh—what's the name of that service club? George Washington, and tell her, look here, what's the big idea of sending some smart pants Yankee sergeant around to my dressing room, saying I ought to meet him. Listen, who the hell do you think Lady Beaumont is? Esther Cartwright, and her father owns a chain of hardware stores in Kentucky. Big deal. Did you know that?'

'News to me. She has kind of an American accent.'

'Well, she's okay, but kind of a phoney. I've a good mind to call her. I suppose you jumped into the sack with her, too. You're quite a lad, Sergeant MacDaniels, aren't you?' She paused and leaned forward and smiled to herself: 'Aren't you, sergeant?'

'Yes, mam.'

'How long furlough do you have?'

'Couple days.'

'Have some more scotch,' said Mary Alice Evans.

'How about some gin?'

'I'll take care of myself, sonny boy.'

She handed him the bottle of whiskey and the seltzer bottle, and he handed her the gin bottle and waited for her to pour, then he shot the seltzer water into her drink and fixed himself a big drink. They looked at each other over their glasses, smiling.

He began to grin.

'Oh-he,' she said. 'Let me tell you. You don't know the half of it. I wrote your squadron commander about you breaking my door down that night I wouldn't let you in.'

'That's only two nights ago and I—'

'And he called me on the phone and you're in a sling, sonny boy, when you get back. And I guess you've broken down a few doors before. At least he said same and you've had a court martial coming for a long time.'

'Now, listen, Mary, I don't blame you.'

'So it's true. You've got a lot of nerve coming back here.'

'You got more nerve sticking a lighted cigarette in my belly button. I ought to tell the cops. How'd you like that?'

'You wouldn't dare. Not with a court martial staring you in the face for breaking and entering.'

'And I suppose you'd like News of the World to hear about that ... "Mary Alice Evans Spears Sergeant's Navel." How's that for a headline?'

'Go on. Go on. You wouldn't dare, not after they put you in the glass house for six months. Assaulting a lady, too.'

'Ha. That's rich. You kill me,' said the sergeant.

'Oh? So I kill you. How do you like it? Sure, I've been around, and you're a nice kid, but how do you think I felt having you bust the door down and those nice people next door knowing about it. What if I'd called the police instead of finally letting you in?'

'What people next door? That bomb knocked the windows out next door. There's nobody—'

'I don't mean next door. Down the hall. They heard you. What if they had called the police and it got in the papers?'

'People mind their own business.'

'I've got a public name to think of.' Miss Evans' lips trembled. Her eyes blinked. 'I've been in this country fourteen years and I've got a public image to maintain. I've been a star and no punk kid like you is going to get me in a jam the papers'll pick up.'

Miss Evans began to cry.

You'll be off the stage in six months if you don't stop drinking the doctors say if you don't stop drinking and I won't stop I can't stop not since I couldn't cry the whole year after he died and now they say Rodger's gone the same way. I can cry and I couldn't cry after Howard like his death froze me and Rodger unfroze me until now he's gone and all there is his father bellowing and bellowing and his voice hammering back into being frozen again but I can't stop drinking I can't.

The sergeant smiled suddenly and raised his eyebrows. 'I've got a great idea,' he said.

The tears were still there only less numerous for a moment. She raised her head and applied a handkerchief to her nose and eyes.

'What?' she said.

'You said you've got a couple free days. You ought to get out of town. I know a pub. It's one of those places Cromwell slept in.' He saw her smiling. 'Yeah, I know. He slept all over England. Every pub. This is a good spot. I'll get us two rooms. It's just what the doctor ordered.'

'What doctor?'

'It's only a saying. We'll go up there and just take it easy. Maybe a couple mud baths. There's a mud joint near it. No booze.'

'Where is it? Yorkshire?'

'How'd you know?'

'I think I've been there,' she said.

'Doesn't matter. I need a little drying out myself.'

'Sounds like a great idea. Sounds great. We'll go tomorrow. Here. You bring the scotch. I'll carry the gin. You know where it is?'

'End of the hall.'

'Right, honey,' said Mary Alice. 'Wait a minute. I want to make sure Joan's left.'

It was crazy, but it did not kill the loneliness. It did not kill the picture of Caldwell in her mind. Nothing would kill that, all she wanted was to feel him with her again and she closed her eyes, forcing her mind to turn the sergeant's body into the body of her lover, forcing her body to fill with desire, while an old poem kept roaming through her mind:

The passions will come, and bring
Every unhappy thing,
Troubles that turn the wits
And tear the heart to bits,
Troubles and grief and care!
Where shall we hide, ah, where?

The odor of Caldwell's flesh lay in her mind like the remembered odor of autumn nights, and holding this tight in her head she began to feel her body tremble. Caldwell's face evolving behind her eyeballs, in the darkness of her swirling brain, as she felt his image move her body in a long swoon of ecstasy, and a tingling throe quivered along her spine. She felt the blood charging in her loins and her mouth softening. Ah, Rodger, Rodger, Rodger, sweetheart; she felt the fingers upon her nipples, her breasts reaching upward, and then her body becoming only a long, deep sensation of liquid rhythm. She felt Rodger melting inside her, the melting feeling mounting steadily as if striving toward some unbelievable crescendo of an agonizing ecstasy that would pass her body out of and beyond bliss into some kind of luminous explosion of her entire being that would transcend and make real the sergeant's mind and body into Rodger Caldwell. For a flashing second fear struck into her. 'I'm not going to! I'm not going to!' she cried out. Then the fear vanished and she felt herself, her brain, falling into a bottomless darkness. She had lost herself, her body and mind were gone. She was blind. There was nothing of herself left. She heard a voice.

'Hey, baby.' It was the sergeant. 'How was that?'

She felt her body coming back, her mind. She touched herself, rolled away from the sergeant.

'Hey, baby!'

'Shut up,' she said and began to cry.

20   JOYCE MOWBRY

The barracks door was shut but the windows were open and she could hear the engines revving up for the night's mission. Oh, God! He was dead. He must be dead. Not a word. Six days, and no report. Oh, darling, darling, darling, she wanted to writhe and toss and turn, but she'd already done that and nothing happened except grief knifed deeper and deeper until she wanted to scream; scream, until she drove out all the grief. The door opened, and Joyce Mowbry heard the voice of Nora Leak whom she hated. Nora's voice was tinged with the quality of the slow fixed smile on her face: 'Joyce. Nancy wants to see you.'

'Why?'

'I think you're up on a charge,' said Nora.

'My foot!'

'Right,' said Nora and went down the hall into her own room.

Joyce got up from the cot on which she had been reading Lilliput magazine. She put on her tunic and buttoned it and looked at the polish on her boots and on her tunic buttons. She picked up her battle-dress jacket, hung it on the hook above her bed. She snapped out the light.

She was half-way out the door before she remembered the note from Eddie Reker. Flight Sergeant Eddie Reker. The note lay on the desk. She reached back inside the door and snapped on the light and went over to the desk and picked up the note and put it in her tunic pocket.

Junior Commander Nancy Cumming's (ATS, 560 Mixed Ack-Ack Battery, Royal Artillery) office was on the other side of the battery site, and walking across site Joyce wondered what she had done. There was a difference between 'Nancy wants to see you' and the 'Junior Commander wants you.' It couldn't be too bad because Nora had said 'Nancy wants to see you.' So it couldn't be too bad. But what? What could it be? Heavens, all she could think of was the time she had the girls paint the tables in the Mess Hall instead of painting the stones which divided the paths to the Nissen Huts, but Nancy didn't bother about such small things as that. The trouble might be something else: the Major in a bind and picking up the tables as a starting point to raise hell with the battery.

The Major was a bloody young bastard, only twenty-three, a piece of mathematical cornstarch; with his head buried in his hands he could compute the firing on a ME 109 in the pitch dark, taking evasive action, at twenty thousand feet, with changes in elevation and course.

For such a minor offense as not recognizing a JU-88 in the aircraft re-cognition test Major Showers made all the gunners polish every piece of brass on the ack-ack guns.

He also insisted that every officer play poker, and if they didn't know how, they were taught how, and their losses were added to their Mess Bills.

Joyce knocked on Nancy's office door and a man's voice said, 'Come in.'

Major Showers was sitting at Nancy's desk, his hands folded on the desk like a judge or a priest.

He was smoking with his gold cigarette holder upthrust saucily from the corner of his mouth. Light caught his major crown momentarily and it glinted like a brooch.

'Nora said the Junior Commander wanted to see me,' said Joyce.

'No, I do,' said Major Showers. He took the cigarette out of his mouth and slowly tapped ash into the tray and added. 'I wanted to see you.' Then he took a long time inserting a fresh cigarette into the holder lighting the cigarette with his gold lighter bearing the Royal Artillery Crest. He wants to sweat me a little, thought Joyce. But for what unearthly reason? He wants to make me play the dangling woman and torture myself a little trying to figure out what I've done wrong. To hell with you, Major Showers, but she was still anxious.

'Sit down,' said Major Showers. He lifted his head, leaned back in his chair, jetted smoke from his nostrils.

'Mowbry, you've been an officer now for—almost two years?'

'Yes, sir,' said Joyce Mowbry. She sat down and waited while the major inhaled and exhaled smoke.

'Hmm. Two years,' said Major Showers. 'Odd, and a year with five-six-he battery, I believe. Odd, and I thought I knew all my officers. Apparently, I don't. Tell me something about yourself. I have your file but I never look at my officer's files.'

'I try to know individually first, but tell me something about yourself.'

'Really, nothing much to tell,' said Joyce.

'Now, now, everybody has their personal background. Come along now.'

'Well, uh,' Joyce said, uncrossing her legs. 'I was born in British East Africa. Actually, Portuguese East Africa. My father was a colonial officer. He's retired now. I was raised in Kenya and attended school in Nairobi. Is that what you want to know?'

'Go on,' the Major smiled from behind his cigarette, a plume of smoke drifting across his damn self-satisfied face.

'Well, I didn't live there all the time. I got black water fever and my parents sent me to live with my aunt in Rhodesia. I stayed there three years and then Daddy came home to England just before the war and we lived in London and then in Bournemouth.'

'Thank you. Go on.'

'Well, Mother and Daddy stayed in London and I went to school in the

Channel Islands. Jersey. Two years before the war. It's all in my officer candidate record, sir.'

'Right. You've certainly seen more of the Empire than most of us. I have always wanted to see Africa. Did you like Kenya?'

'I was quite young out there. Yes, I enjoyed it at home in Kempala where Daddy and Mummy lived.'

'And do you like England?'

'Of course.'

'You wouldn't want to go back to Africa?'

'Oh, I don't know, it's a lovely country. Perhaps after the war.'

'Oh, perhaps?' said Major Showers. 'With all your travel, you've seen many social systems, naturally, I suppose you have many opinions concerning practices within these systems.'

'I don't know. I never, uh, thought about it. I like most people and I think I get along well with most people, if that's what you mean.'

'Yes. Hm. Of course.' Major Showers squinted at her through the cloud of smoke. She was sitting upright now, both elbows on the desk. Then suddenly he dropped both forearms with palms down flat on top of the desk.

'Subaltern Mowbry! Whose picture is

this? Answer me!' Major Shower's voice was cold and flat. He turned over the snapshot that lay face down on the desk, and in it Joyce saw the face of Flight Sergeant Edward Reker.

'Do you have a brother in the service? A cousin? No,' said the major answering for her in a hard voice. 'I've checked your records.'

'It's Flight Sergeant Edward Reker,' said Joyce, looking down at the snapshot. She felt happy as she spoke his name.

Major Showers continued holding out the snapshot to her view. She could hear the clock ticking on the wall, for how long she could not tell but it seemed like a long time, several minutes, though it was probably only a few seconds. Then he tossed the snapshot down on the desk in front of her and swiveled sideways in his chair and studied a blank point on the wall for a long moment. Then after some thought he turned and stared at her, joggling the cigarette holder in the corner of his mouth. 'I have spent five years of my life in the army. My father spent his entire service life of thirty years in the Royal Artillery. This is my battery, my regiment. I'm proud of it and I'm proud of the men and officers. I have been with the regiment four years. I intend to stay with the regiment after the war. I have demanded certain standards of conduct for officers of the regiment because I believe in them. I believe we cannot function efficiently without those standards of conduct and I have done everything in my powers of communication to make clear to my men and officers what those standards of conduct are. I intend to maintain those standards.' He paused and removed the cigarette holder and plucked out the cigarette. 'Mowbry, there's no room in my battery or in this regiment for officers who go out with other ranks.'

Joyce Mowbry did not say anything.

'There's no place here for that type of officer! Did you hear me?'

'Yes, sir.'

The Major turned over the snapshot again and glanced at it and set it down on the desk. 'This flight sergeant is attached to the bomber squadron next door. I found it on your desk during inspection and further details concerning your relationship with Flight Sergeant Edward Reker have been brought to my attention. I instituted the search for such details. You have been seen in Hutton-Rugby with him more than a dozen times, in fact, dancing with him publicly three times. The hotel clerk states you have been registered in the hotel on three week-ends under your name, of course, while Reker was registered in a room on the same floor. I want you to know how I won't countenance this in my battery, nor will I condone such conduct in the regiment. By God, if I could I would have you transferred to Africa, but perhaps a spell on the Thames Estuary commanding some of those lice laden ATS dockies, will bring you to your senses. You've failed the battery, Mowbry. Get out!' The Major appeared to be panting.

Mowbry stood up. 'Edward Reker was shot down last week.'

'Get out!'

Joyce Mowbry saluted and left, closing the door, but not softly.

She returned to her room and lay face down on the bed, without removing her tunic. At first slowly, then faster, she began to cry, at the same time cursing the Major, cursing Nora, then the Major, then Nora, while thinking over and over again, 'I hope he isn't dead. I hope he's alive somewhere,' knowing now, since yesterday, she was pregnant.

Knowing and fearing she would never have those moments again with him, all those hotel rooms, the lovely rooms that were their home, the only home they had ever known together, his hands smelling of sunburn against her cheek, feeling the soft sheen of her flesh endowed with a God-like power over him and over herself, her arms entwined around his neck and his mouth fiery and wild coming down upon her, searching and searching every soft crevice of her flesh, feeling her eyes dilating, pressing against the sockets, her mouth breaking in exultation beneath his caresses as her flesh began to dissolve, flowing out into a warm glowing light, her thighs and arms and body flowing far away, melting and flowing, utterly drugged only to come back suddenly in a wild rushing of fresh tenderness and passion, making him press harder and harder with all his fullness and strength until she could feel all his nerve ends trembling, their naked muscles reclining laxly, her body filling with a soft humming as of the sound of summer afternoon fields, and she lay entranced, floating effortlessly, floating endlessly, forever and forever, lying there speechless, no sound, hearing only the far-faint murmur of her nerve ends still quivering, lying there until the sound was gone, until again she felt herself crying out for him, her flesh glowing freshly, pink and white.

'And now,' she thought. 'All that. All that gone. And he's dead and all I have is maybe a baby.'

She felt herself falling off the earth, the globe spinning on its axis, the depthless sky swallowing her.

21   THE HONORABLE
MARY HUNT

Cresting the hill against the soft afternoon sky, the huge grove of trees looked almost tropical. They rounded against the sky like a great green sleeping monster, shielding the rolling gorse from the castle. Then the monstrous dark green leafy shadow seemed to drift backward in the wind like a huge rolling sheet of sea wave.

Then they entered the gorse, and Mary thought, with quiet astonishment: 'Two more birds. Then there won't be time.' She thought of Flight Sergeant Harry Smiley, holding now in her mind for a fraction of a second his knobby face, the cheeky smile, ruddy cheeks below the shock of red hair, while her gaze rested on the man ahead in the gorse. Almost at once the other part of her mind spoke to her, and she heard the voice inside her head saying as it had said a week ago: 'But why can't we just run away, Harry?' remembering how two weeks ago the game keeper had seen them—cum butler (There's a war on, you know) going into the woods together, remembering this now, as a feeling of hopelessness struck her.

She called to the man, watching the two pointers quartering slowly now, faintly stalking in the gorse: 'Won't you try to understand, just this once?' The man's name was Rodger.

Rodger did not turn, but his voice came back over his shoulder: 'You fool!'

His rigid attention to the dogs did not abate despite the cold fury in his voice.

Then Mary began to think again of a future in time which filled her with dread and despair; the future filled with her father's face, the white hair, the waxed mustaches, the milord-ramrod posture, even now like Rodger in the field, with the double barrel shot gun crooked in his arm: 'How can I do it? How can I? But if not, what then?' For a second she looked upon herself with surprise.

Mary was nineteen. She lived near Goale, two miles from the airfield, with her father, third lord of Goale, in a massive stone castle. She was homely, almost ugly. Her mother, a baroness in her own right, was dead, her brother was fighting in Africa. The castle resembled one of the big red two-block square county court houses found in American metropolitan cities, replete with six towers, one at each corner and two in the middle, with a huge clock set in one tower. It was surrounded by three thousand acres of forest, gorse, farms and deer parks. The land abounded in game, both pheasant and partridge. Upon his land she rode horseback almost daily, often meeting the young men from the aerodrome, speaking to those who spoke to her, and pretending not to notice they were poaching her father's game with skeet guns designed for squadron air gunnery practice. In the rear wing of the castle, wounded soldiers recuperated, but she did not see them, nor did she give up hope that one day one of the young fliers would ask her to a squadron dance. The girls from the village attended. For a few moments she would rein her horse and speak to the young fliers:

'You mustn't come too near the house.'

'Why?'

'My father. He'll see your guns.'

'Thank you, miss. The Mess is a bit thin of rations.'

'Be careful.'

'Thank you, miss.'

Upon the big chestnut Irish hunter she would be smiling, yet waiting apprehensively for the invitations that never came. And they would pass on, and she would return to the castle, and enter the huge stone hall and look at the silver-plaque, fox tails on the walls which her brother had left behind. Weary from riding, she would enter the long stone hall, passing the religious figures recessed in the stone walls, to the long table at the end of which sat her father. She would look down the long empty table at his immaculate cold face, feeling hopelessness. They would be served dinner in silence by the one remaining servant, Rodger, in his full funeral-dark suit. Then it would be dark and she would take the torch and go up the long labyrinth of passages to the fire-lit stone bedroom, thinking, 'If only he would let me out of here ... into the army ... anything.' Then she would lie exhausted from hating her life, sometimes falling asleep in her clothes, dreaming of running away, only to wake and think: 'Why don't I run away?' Knowing it would not help, no matter how far, for her father would have her returned.

Then one morning she met Harry Smiley at the edge of the willow swamp. He was squatting, holding a shotgun in one hand. He looked up at her with veiled eyes. She did not move astride the horse.

'You don't even shoot them now, so it doesn't matter,' he said.

'Don't let my father see you.'

'With the mustaches?' Harry laughed. 'Come here and talk.'

'What?' Mary said, pretending she did not hear.

Smiley laughed.

'You look like you need to talk to somebody.'

146

Her face reddened.

He laughed at her and stood up and caught the bridle and put up his hand. With a feeling of fright and excitement she found herself being helped down from the saddle.

Then she was on the grass, talking, but still not surprised until Harry left, then wishing she would see him again, which surprised her.

'What do you do all day in that place?' he asked.

'Aren't you supposed to be flying?'

'Not if I can help it,' he said.

The next day she met him again among the willows. He asked her to a party that night at the aerodrome; she said she would meet him here in the woods if she could get away. She waited until dark, then slipped out through the kitchen.

It was ten o'clock. He was waiting. When he told her there was no dance and caught her hand, she sprang back.

'Why? What are you going to do?'

'Come on. You're out with the troops.'

'What?'

'Sit down.'

'No.'

He kissed her hard then, flattening her mouth, and holding her with both hands pressed into the small of her back. She did not move even after he released her.

She stood there speechless, then her voice came urgent and tense: 'You mustn't! You mustn't do it!'

'Come on.'

'No. You're horrible!'

'You'll like it.'

'I have never done it.'

'So what? Come on.'

'I can't.'

'It won't hurt.'

'No! Please!'

He laughed.

'Teaser?' He laughed again.

'I've never even kissed a boy,' she said, sighing.

'Sit down.'

'No. I have to go back. He'd kill me if he knew I—'

'Tomorrow?'

'No.'

'I'll be here,' said Smiley.

She went in through the kitchen. Her father had gone to bed. She could hear herself panting as she sneaked up the stairs, thinking with a crazy amused excitement: 'A cockney! A cockney! Father would kill me if he knew I were out with a cockney air gunner.'

Two days later Harry Smiley knocked at the big wooden castle door and asked for Mary. Rodger, the butler-cook-secretary, gamekeeper with the face and suit of an undertaker, brought him into the circular study on the wall of which were more silver-plaqued fox tails. Mary was standing at the window, her father reading, the white hair shining above the neat waxed mustaches. He sat on a lounge. Mary turned and walked toward Harry. Her father did not look up, nor appear to see or hear Harry's entrance. Harry stood in the door.

'Are you daft?' Mary said in a low tense voice. 'Are you completely crackers?'

Then she turned and walked, smiling, back to her father. The old man lifted his head, a tall man, stiff, the mustaches spike-ended, his eyes gaunt and assured.

'Father, this is Flight Sergeant Harry Smiley,' she said. 'He's here about a contribution to the squadron music fund.'

Her father did not appear to hear her. 'What?' he said.

'Flight Sergeant Smiley! From the air-field!' she raised her voice. 'The music fund.'

Her father's head jerked, the mustaches thrusting upward as he rose and left the room, his finger inserted to mark the book page.

'All right,' she thought. 'All right.' That night she was back in the willows. She lay with him in the darkness, kissing, keeping her dress down though his hands already

149

sought her loins. Her blood and heart pounded in her mouth as his mouth flattened her lips and her body writhed as if repressing some exquisite pain she could no longer endure beyond the measure of one more open surrender of her mouth. Then she felt the full thrust of his passion, and lust struck and stunned her like a blow of sunlight. Her body felt at once cold and feverish and she felt her hips arch, seeking, her loins writhing fiercely. She caught his shoulders and drew him down, her body now arching slowly downward. Then her whole body pressed upward toward an exquisite torture. She felt headless until she heard herself moaning. When he touched her she clawed at him with both hands.

'Don't hurt me,' she cried, whimpering, pressing his head down upon her breasts. 'Don't hurt, please.' She began to grind against him, dragging her lips over his face. 'You won't hurt, will you? Come on. Now. Please. Please.'

She didn't seem to be aware that he had already entered her.

Her voice expired for an instant, then her mouth opened as if she were going to scream, but he held her tighter and she seemed to take one last despairing look up at the cold remote stars and then her eyeballs drew back into her skull and she cried out: 'Oh, God. Oh, God,' in a long shuddering swoon. He held her gently, whispering to her softly.

She dragged his face down against her lips. Her mouth gaped. 'Oh, darling, darling, darling. All night ... touch me again. Please ... I didn't know this. Oh, darling, darling, darling.'

She writhed against him. She felt small and lonely and strangely grateful and tender toward him and then the anger came again, the vision of her father.

'A cockney air gunner!' her head said, loving his mouth, his lips, his anguished loins. 'Cockney air gunner,' wishing she could see her father's face, and Rodger's, almost laughing to herself, until she heard the sound, thinking at first it was the last of a pheasant convoy fluttering into sleep in the willow softness; and then she heard the footfall and the fatuous, unctuous voice, not loud, amusing, contemptuous: 'If he could see you! Bitch! If he could see you!' And in the darkness she recognized Rodger's voice upon the sound of his feet rushing away in the darkness as she sprang up.

'Who the hell is that?' Smiley said slowly. He had not moved. He still lay on the ground, on his back, propped up on his elbows, looking up at the stars, no moon, grateful he was not on call that night for a raid.

'No matter,' she said. 'I must go.'

She did not wait for him to answer, if he would. Already she was running toward the house while he rose without haste and folded his air force ground sheet, neat as his mother had folded his bed sheets at home.

She went in through the kitchen, not having to open the window, for somebody had left the window open for her. The halls were dark, and she knew the way without her torch, no longer walking softly, not caring now, not because she did not have to pass her father's door, but now because she had to pass Rodger's door. She lay on her bed panting, undressed, thinking. 'He never even put his fingers in me. Never even touched me. But in the dark who could tell the difference? He was on me.'

She woke feeling exhausted and dull, surprised she was undressed and in bed because she could not remember taking her clothes off.

Frightened she went down to breakfast, but certain Rodger had said nothing because her father greeted her warmly, and Rodger did not even glance at her while serving the meal. Soon her father walked down to the village to see what he might do for an old tenant who was sick. The door of Rodger's office was open, his back to the door where he bent over the desk. He did not turn when he heard her enter, nor did he move when she shut the door.

She stood behind the chair.

'All right,' she said. 'Did you tell him?'

Still Rodger did not move. She could not understand why he was not in service. He was at least thirty, black-haired, like a village boy, but not from the village, from where she did not know.

'Did you?' she asked and when he did not answer nor turn she shouted: 'What am I supposed to be? Why won't he let me go in the army? Anything?'

Still Rodger did not move, his shoulders hunched, the inscrutable black head and black cloth shoulders motionless.

'Oh, you think!' she said. 'Think what you want! Oh, you'd like to think he did it, wouldn't you? Wouldn't you?'

Then Rodger turned, his smile cold and fixed.

'Ha!' Mary cried. 'Why, you ruddy cockney! You're jealous of the other cockney.' She began to laugh with thin exhilaration, until there was no longer exhilaration in her voice, but only mirth.

Two days later in the post office in York she bumped into Smiley and they went to a corner.

'Did you get in any trouble?' he asked. 'Anything? I mean—'

'I'll go to London with you,' she said. Her face was pale but her eyes were bright. 'When do you get leave? I'll meet you.'

'Two months,' Smiley said. 'What's the matter?'

'Two months?' Her face waned more palely, her voice dying sadly. 'Two months. Oh, God. I would do it tonight with you in London.'

'What about here?'

'No.'

'Forget it,' he said.

'If I do it once with you here, will you take me away when you get leave. Will you meet me in London?'

'Hell, that's a long way off. Maybe I'll be dead by then.'

'No, you'll just do it once and get leave and go home to some other girl.'

'For crissake,' he said in a low angry voice. 'You don't even know me. What're you pulling? You work in that house or is that your father?'

'You saw him?'

'How about your brother?'

'They're both in Africa.'

'Him in the black suit?'

'Rodger? He's after me.'

Smiley laughed softly, covertly, with almost amusement, as if out of some half-stilted memory.

'A cousin?'

'Shut up,' she said. 'I didn't say I'd marry you.'

'That's what I mean,' said Smiley. 'You knobs want it like everybody else only you go around looking pretty pretending it's only to pass water through. Who you crapping?'

'Will you?' she said, her voice tensed again and hushed, as if she had not heard his question.

'Yes,' he said. 'I'll meet you again tomorrow night. I'll show you and then if you still want to go to London when I get leave I'll take you. But don't ever think I'd marry you either. Not with an old man like yours and that bloody house. I'd be a laughing stock.'

But he was not there the next night, nor the night after that, nor for the next week, and then two weeks later when she'd given up seeing him her fourth cousin returned from the desert, a young man two years older than Mary. It was to be a planned marriage, planned even before the war, but now it did not have to be planned, though she never knew it had been planned, even before her mother's death. He was a captain in Fourteenth-Sixteenth Hussars who would some day be a colonel if he lived long enough after he went back to the desert. He was a wiry little man, with a mustache like her father's, whom she had met many times as a child before the war had snatched him up into becoming an impeccable officer with a swagger stick and MC and his hair sun-burned waxy white as some of the Saxon Germans he had fought at Tobruk. He had six weeks leave and he spent five weeks at the castle, riding and shooting daily, kissing her only a few times, and then in the castle, never in the willows. His lips were flaccid and cold as a child's, and she hated his mustache. It reminded her of being kissed before going to bed by her father, only the captain's mouth was thinner. She thought several times she was going to cry and she even tried but there were no tears, only a dead deep dullness in her soul. 'He won't even be killed,' she thought. 'He'll go back and never be killed, but it won't be necessary because we're all dead now.' Thinking this now she had the feeling she had been dead a long time, that even her father had been dead a long time, and she tried to think when this feeling had started but it had been going on so long she could not even remember when it began. The wedding was to take place when he came home on leave again. He was not going back to the desert, and he would be home again from a training camp in six months.

Then the day came that came but once a year, that day when milord went to sit in the House of Lords, that single day in the year when milord accepted his hereditary obligations which were no longer meaningful; he departed for London. A week passed and he did not return, and she no longer went riding but hung about the great monstrous empty castle, avoiding Rodger save when he served the meals. She moved as if in a dream, listless, thinking slowly of being married, not caring, but as if waiting for some inexorable fate over which she had no control. Then one day her father returned and shortly afterwards told her that her fiance had phoned from camp asking her to come down to Surrey for twenty-four hours leave. An hour later she reached Smiley in the sergeants mess at the airfield by telephone, thinking, 'How can I ever marry? Not him. Never. I cannot.'

'I don't know,' Smiley said.

'Only twenty-four hours. I'll meet you at the station.'

'I don't know. I'll—'

'It's only twenty-four hours.'

'You'll change your mind in London.'

'I'm not scared. I want to.'

'After that what?'

'Who cares?' she said. 'Hurry. I'll meet you at the ticket window. At noon. Tomorrow.'

'If I can get leave.'

The next noon when Smiley went to the ticket window at the station in York, she was not there. He bought a ticket, deciding to go to London, anyway. He was opening the door of his compartment when he heard her voice behind him, and he whirled as she sprang past him into the compartment, her voice filled with fright and haste. 'Shut the door!' she said. 'Shut the door! He'll see me!'

He stood there staring into the compartment and then he turned his head and looked over one shoulder.

'Get in! Get in!' she cried, catching his wrist, dragging him in and shutting the door before he was seated. Then she began to laugh as she drew down the curtain.

'Who?' said Smiley.

'Rodger.' She went on laughing. 'We fooled him. He didn't see me. He can't tell father anything now.'

'Why now? Why haven't you phoned before?'

'Where would we go? I will not go in a field,' she said. 'I will not.'

'No!' he said suddenly, watching her hands. 'Mary! No, not in here.'

'Bolt the door,' she said.

A week later, pausing outside the study she could hear her father and Rodger talking. She stood to one side of the door, their voices remote and indistinguishable.

Then she heard Rodger's voice cease. She stood still as he came out of the study. She let him pass and then followed him into the kitchen. He was opening the huge ice box that filled one of the kitchen walls. Rodger turned and they looked at each other for a long moment.

'You're a clever girl, Miss Mary. Your father still does not know you did not get on that London train alone.'

'Shut up!' Mary said.

'Oh, I have been quiet.'

'You better be.'

'I'm sure it would kill your father. Sleeping with a cockney sergeant.' He glared at her, smiling.

'He is not a cockney and he has the D.F.M,' she said.

'I can understand his being brave, but listen to his voice. I'm sure your father would be proud to have you bear his cockney children. You must not see him again.' Then he stopped and smiled and walked toward her, put his hands on her shoulder. 'Unless ...' he smiled.

For a moment she did not appear to understand and then she jerked away as if his hands were diseased.

'He is more than you will ever be,' she said.

Rodger smiled slow and indulgent.

'Unless ...' he said in a soft voice,

ceasing, watching her for a moment after his voice ceased. When he spoke again his voice was patient: 'I'll come to your room.'

'I'll kill you!' she said furiously.

Rodger looked at her wild eyes.

'If not, I shall tell your father,' he said. She did not move and he took a step forward, reaching out as if to embrace her.

'Get back!' Mary cried, striking at his face.

He drew back carefully, smiling.

'Come here,' he said softly.

Her eyes glared.

'Tell him! It won't get you what you want! Tell him! I slept with a cockney sergeant in London. Tell him he was better than the men I've seen here.'

'The bell,' Rodger said. 'Your father wants me.'

When he was gone Mary went up to her room and locked the door. She lay awake a long time, listening, hearing the clock strike nine on the tower, feeling the pistol beneath her pillow. At the stroke of eleven she called the sergeants' mess and got Smiley on the phone and told him she would meet him in the willows in half an hour. Despair filled her as she dressed. She ran down the hall, barefooted, carrying her shoes, and climbed out the kitchen window and sped across the lawn and fields. At the edge of the willows she called, 'Harry!' There was no sound. She moved along the edge of the willows calling his name. She heard the far away *vroom vroom* of a German bomber going home across the sky. She waited, shivering. She heard him coming as the bomber sound died away. She heard him through the willows.

She heard him crash against the thicket and emerge on to the moor of gorse. She went straight to him and caught his shoulders in both hands.

'What the hell,' Harry said. He wore battle dress. 'Calling me at this hour!'

'Sit down,' she said in her tense, low voice as if she felt somebody might be within earshot.

She looked over her shoulder, first left, then right, and then sat down.

'What do you want?' he asked, standing above her.

'Just sit down,' she whispered. When he did not move she reached and caught his trousered leg and clutched at him through the cloth.

'Harry!'

'Let go!'

She rose and flung herself against him, holding his arms, pressing her face against his face, shuddering.

'He knows! Listen to me! He knows!'
From faraway came the distant thunder of
engines going out against the dark sky.

'Who knows what? What the hell are
you talking about?'

'Oh, darling, tell me you love me, please.
Please tell me.'

'Who the hell are you talking about?'

'Rodger. Unless I sleep with him.'

'For crissake!'

'He'll tell father. He knows we were in
London. He saw us here once.'

'So what? Bugger Rodger.'

'Oh, darling, please. I'll marry you.'

'Are you kidding? Listen, it was fun.
Now forget it.'

'But he'll tell father.'

'So what. Listen, I could be dead right
now. They scrubbed a mission to Essen.
You take care of yourself. I'll take care of
Harry Smiley. Let go!'

'Please, just this one thing. It would kill
Father. Just this favor. Please.'

'What?'

'You know how I come out riding
some days and now I'll be going out
shooting, with Rodger because Father's
too old. And as we come past this thicket
I could ... if you would back me up ... if
I miss ...'

'What?'

'Listen. They'll never know. It will be

an accident. I'll swear. Listen! Harry!'

He stared at her in shocked astonishment but not for long. She reached for his hand, her whole body shaking, her voice filled with despair. 'Harry, you must help me!'

'And if you miss on purpose I'm to shoot him?'

She did not move, her face chalk-white in the moonlight.

'And you'll testify it was an accident?' Harry said. 'Nice, eh?'

'Please!' She gasped. 'Please! Harry!'

He pushed her, though wanting to strike her, and she fell back into the gorse. She lay there listening to the sound of running and then on into the dark silence until there was no sound in night. After a long time she rose slowly and walked dazedly toward the castle.

Even the castle seemed more empty and silent in the morning than ever before, and she heard her father's voice from far-off when he spoke. She nodded answering words she did not hear at breakfast.

That was on Friday. On Saturday her father asked her to shoot some grouse for dinner with Rodger. Even now in the morning the fields seemed silent and peaceful as they had been that night. He hasn't spoken, she thought, as she walked behind Rodger. I remember right here I shot my first bird. God's teeth, how long ago. Was I ten? Was I twelve?

'Mary,' she heard his voice call to her. She pretended not to hear. 'Do you want me to tell him? Last night? Do you want me to tell you were out again?'

'Tell him!' She watched him, casting the dogs, his lips busy with the whistle. Ahead the pointers, quartering, bobbed whitely through the gorse.

He paused and turned.

'I'm going to tell you something you must not tell your father. Your brothers are dead. It came in the mail. Yes, I kept it from him. That would have killed him even quicker. Well?'

'Do you think I sleep with household servants?'

'You can't run this place after your father dies. You don't love the captain.'

'I'll marry him.'

'You'll sleep with a ruddy cockney and not me? Why? Why, Mary?'

'He's a man.'

'Why him?'

She did not answer. The dogs went on across the field. Now she saw the edge of the willow swamp. She thought: 'I wonder if he came. I wonder if he's waiting.' Rodger's voice came to her faintly, though now he was walking beside her: 'How can you do it alone, Mary? A bloody cockney. Are you mad?'

'Here,' she thought, watching the curve of the willow thicket. 'He should be just there in the corner.' The field dropped down past the willow thicket. She paused, as if watching the dogs working though they still were not making game, their tails high but neither wagging with interest nor showing any sign of a point. She laughed suddenly: 'Father to a cockney child? Would you like that?'

'It would not matter. No one would ever know. Remember, I'm asking you now,' he said. 'For the last time.'

She laughed.

'All right. If I tell your father and the captain, they'll have the cockney sent out of the country.'

'Go on,' she said. 'Tell them.'

'I shall,' he said. She waited for him to go on; at that moment the dogs began to quarter furiously, their muzzles raised high, body scenting, their tails lashing from side to side. Rodger began to run to catch up with the dogs, cocking his gun. As Mary flung a last look over her shoulder toward the willows, knowing, sensing now in this last instant of despair that she was helpless, that Harry was not there, would never be there, the gun came to her shoulder, the finger cocking. 'Tell him!' she screamed swinging the stock of the gun against her cheek; 'Tell him!' sighting along the barrel as the dogs came to point. She fired just after the grouse burst, not hearing the explosion of Rodger's gun, knowing only the sudden shock of the gun butt against her cheek as Rodger fell down against the sky. 'Oh, God,' he cried, staring up at the sky, 'you shot me! You shot me!' When she stood over him, his eyes round and empty with death the words 'You shot me!' still seemed shaped on his lips. Then abruptly his mouth opened and as he lay there his mouth gaped and a rill of blood crawled down his neck like a monstrous wound.

Into the silence from faraway a sound began to rise, high and far-faint at first, then closer, a wasp-like snarl rushing down across the sky to die away in the whining crescendo of a diving Spitfire. She stared down at Rodger's body. 'And now there's nothing,' she thought. 'Only Harry. And he'll tell if they find him. He'll tell them I did it.' She began to cry a little, slowly sinking down on one knee, staring dully at Rodger, touching his shoulder as if out of some desperate urgency she thought he might be alive, as if by shaking his shoulder she might rouse him as one rouses a sleeping person. 'I just wanted to scare you,' she said to the corpse. 'Rodger, I didn't mean to. I really didn't,' she said, watching the rill of blood widen across his jaw. From faraway came the sound again, the high wasp-like whine. She listened to it, thinking, 'I must tell Harry. I must explain.' The wind blew the sound away.

But even then it was too late. Harry was on the revetment at that hour, waiting to take off, and when she called the next day she heard what had happened; Harry was missing. She looked at the telephone, rubbing the tip of her finger around the head piece. 'Oh, God,' she thought, 'I'll have to tell the captain or go to bed with him right away so he won't know it isn't his baby.' At the coroner's inquiry two days later there was no question; the coroner's report judged it a 'hunting accident.' Riding home she thought: 'It's me now. I have no one. No one.' Then she thought of the child and for a moment was happy. 'I wonder how much it will look like Harry.' She sat quietly in the car, looking out at the bleak Yorkshire fields, the wind sighing in the telephone wires.

22 KATHERINE ALCOTT

Yes, it was better she came to the club today, or so she'd thought for the past six mornings, but that was a big fat lie. It didn't do any good at all. You looked at people and didn't see their faces and listened to their voices and didn't hear what they were saying, all the time telling yourself this was better than sitting alone in a room thinking about things you didn't want to think about. She was glad Diana had gone north to visit her relatives; she couldn't have borne with Diana commiserating with her, and that's all Diana would have done, but it was wrong to condemn Diana even though she would be annoying. Yet she couldn't get Diana out of her mind. Why? Why did she think of her? Diana wouldn't have any way now of knowing about Jack because the Times didn't carry any 'missing in action' notices until the end of the month, and probably wouldn't carry anything about Jack because Jack was American and his family wherever they lived wouldn't be putting notices in London Times from America. So there wasn't even the slight chance Diana would hear anything about it. Which was all for the good. Because only Diana knew what had happened between her and Jack Gifford.

Then she felt another part of her mind, the part that seemed to be worked by her eyes, by what was in her line of vision, saying: 'Go on. Write the young man's name on the registration card and give him a room.'

She wrote the sergeant's name, Harry

Appleby, his serial number, and his room number on the card headed WASHING-TON CLUB, relieved to finish the card, as he smiled across the counter, and gave the young man his room key.

She turned away from the desk and walked to the window and looked out at Curzon Street. It was a sunny day. She remembered suddenly for some reason that George had tickets to Shaw's *Doctor's Dilemma*. The last time she'd seen Olivier was a navy benefit party. She wondered what made her think about the tickets. Olivier's eyes? Not that Gifford had eyes like Olivier, but there was something similar, something a little merry, kind, and yet sinister, deadly in earnest, yes, that was it, that same quality in Gifford's eyes. But the strange thing was George's reaction five days ago when he'd come to the club to pick her up, and that Flight Lieutenant, at the desk, mentioning right in front of George that Gifford had been missing three days. George hadn't said anything except sorry to hear it as if he couldn't recall who Gifford was. But it wasn't so strange, after all, even though Gifford always stayed at the Washington Club when he was in London on leave. George had only met Gifford once, that time in the Landsdowne Club when George who was standing at the bar with a couple of fliers nodded to her as he might have nodded at any one of the many English volunteer ladies who manned the desk at the Washington Hotel which had been turned into a service club for airmen. And being near the bar while waiting for a table they had talked casually and just as casually she had introduced George. No, no reason at all why George should remember Gifford. Gifford was just another American face in an RAF uniform.

'I say, you remember Gifford,' said the Flight Lieutenant, a Canadian, that afternoon at the club desk. 'Went for Burton last week.'

Those were the words, the same words in which so many people were described as missing or killed in action. In the first world war they called it 'going west.' And it was all so casual. Just a few words and somebody was dead, bad show, rum do, bad luck, was the way they made it sound. How old was Gifford? She'd never asked, and he'd never offered. Perhaps twenty-five, at least 'ten years younger than I am.' They would have her age in her obit. Thirty-five. Could he be dead? Or a prisoner? Or in the bottom of the North Sea? Where was he right now? Had he been blown to bits?

All that big body, and brown wavy hair, and those dark eyes. Could all of that be gone? Wiped off the earth? And his people back home. She wondered who they were or what they were like? Rich or poor? And girl friends? How many in America? How many here?

I would have gone away and slept with him, she thought. I should have asked him when he didn't ask me. He might have, if I would have asked him. It was odd the way they had met, and odder still that nothing had ever come out of that day, that crazy afternoon. Was it two or three years ago? She wasn't sure. She was sure only that it was the day she and Diana were walking away from the Washington Club and right at the Curzon Street entrance to Sheperd's Market, somebody said hello and they turned and here was Gifford whom she'd waited on half a dozen times at the club desk and with him was another man, a Canadian flier whose name didn't matter now because she could not remember it. They were both high and should not recall now what they said except they had made both women laugh as they walked along with them. Neither she nor Diana had any notion of having a drink with the two fliers. George was still out in the desert then. But as they walked along laughing, they found they had not resisted either the funny things said nor the fact that the two men literally steered them into

Sheperd's Market and then into Sheperd's bar where she and Diana often stopped for a drink together. They stayed there until it closed and Gifford mentioned something about having a house in Chelsea, and both woman thought he was joking, even after they got in the taxi for Cadogan Square where both she and Diana were living. How could a flier have a house in Chelsea? Well they would prove it. No, we must get home. No, one more drink at my Chelsea town house. So they'd gone as a lark. Neither woman ever had been mixed up with any men while their husbands were away in the desert, and Diana's had stayed there, buried outside Tobruk. Yes, it was going to be only a lark that afternoon, so they had gone to Chelsea. Well, it was funny because Gifford did have a house, right at the foot of Battersea Bridge, Cheyney Mews, a lovely place, a sculptor's house, with a studio downstairs, and a winding stairway upstairs to the three bedrooms with kitchen and small dining room downstairs, but how he got it nobody seemed to know, and after the wine and the dinner nobody really cared, and she had wandered into the studio with him. God only knew where Diana had gone. Diana's Canadian was really quite a nice type, though not quite Diana's type, but nice nontheless. By nice, the women meant he had manners which was more than you could say for a lot of Americans. And Gifford was nice too. But more than nice. By this Katherine meant he was attractive. And also had manners.

'Well, well,' Katherine said. 'You Americans live well. Don't you know there's a war on?'

'It's reverse lend lease. House, wine and food. We have to get our money back some way, otherwise you British will spend it all on boot polish and blanco.'

'Are we really that bad?'

'Not nearly as stuffy as the American Naval Air Force,' said Gifford.

'How do you mean?'

'Well, before Uncle Sam's washed me out, I spent more than a year learning to be a navy officer. Fine training for a hotel maitre d'.'

'Where did you get that wine tonight?'

'Black market. Here?'

'All right,' she said. They drank the whole bottle and he opened another. She didn't move all the time, leaning back against a table while he sat on a davenport about five feet away.

'That ring,' Gifford said. 'Where's your husband?'

'Middle East.'

'Why did you come out with me?'

'You guess.'

'Spur of the moment?'

'That's it,' she said.

'I haven't run into many girls like you over here,' he said. 'Where do they keep them all? Do they lock them up at night?'

'With people like you around they should,' she said.

'Oh, I don't know. I don't feel dangerous until I meet somebody like you. Too bad you're married, or I'd ask you to—ever been to St Ives? No, forget it. Know what?'

'No.'

'You're damn good looking. What're you? Thirty?'

'Sweet boy.'

'Thirty-five?'

'Thirty-five.'

'I bet you've been married almost fifteen years.'

'Twelve.'

'I always thought they married older in England. The men, I mean, before the war. God, you are a good looking woman. You're the nicest dish I've seen over here. Woo! That wine is something!' He rubbed his forehead, smiling. 'Sit down, beautiful United Kingdom? Lovely British Isles! Down the bloody Hun! Sit down, beautiful England! Britannia darling!'

She sat down, not close, but close enough for him to reach along the back

174

of the davenport and draw her over with one arm, and in a moment (it was almost two years since a man had kissed her) she was being kissed and her lips were open and she lay against him, letting herself go, becoming all body against him for one long delicious minute, clinging to him as if he were the first and last man on earth. She was kissing him when she realized he had stopped kissing her, and as she drew back her head, seeing in that second the almost empty bottle, and remembering, too, he had been high when they met in Curzon Street, she realized he had passed out, not cold, just sleeping softly, exhausted.

Katherine never forgot him. She didn't see him face to face for almost a year, just catching a glimpse of him, getting out of a taxi in front of the Washington Club; avoiding him when he came to the desk by quickly going into another room, but she thought about him a lot. And then George was sent home from the middle east, and her life with George before the war, her married life, the life she loved with the man she loved, began all over again with a freshness engendered by George's absence. She was relieved when she didn't see Gifford anymore. Apparently he didn't stay at the Washington Club anymore when on leave. But after a while she longed to see him again even asked about him; he was alive, still flying, according to his squadron mates and flying friends, most of whom stopped at the Washington Club. Finally, she went down to the house in Chelsea one day and rang the doorbell and found herself face to face with an M.P.'s wife who was also the sculptor who owned the house to whom she made some lame excuse about the American Red Cross at the Washington Club having a request from a squadron to pick up a uniform left there by an American. The woman almost laughed in her face, and said, smiling, she was no longer subletting the house now that her husband was back from a trade mission to America. Oh, God, why do I want him so badly, she thought, walking up the street.

Then she knew she would have to stop thinking about him because she thought about him now all the time in bed at night, and she found herself asking other women on the desk about him and checking the register to see if he had stayed there on her days off. This was the time Diana twigged, as the saying goes, as to what was going on in her mind, and Diana asked her directly what it was all about, the questions, the checking of the room files.

'I never slept with him or anything,' Katherine said.

'I believe it.'

'It's terrible, but I never wanted a man like this before.'

'I wouldn't mind knowing him better myself.'

'You know, this sounds crazy, but he reminds me of my brother Bert,' said Katherine. Bert had been killed at Crete.

'You were always crazy about Bert, weren't you?'

'He was wonderful to me when I was a little girl.'

'Well, forget it. What can you do about it?'

'How'd you guess it? I've thought about him for months. Sure, I could write him. He'd think me mad.'

'Right. Forget him. You know those Yankees. Here today. Gone tomorrow. Watch your bicycle, girl.'

'I know,' said Katherine. 'But somehow, oh, I don't know, but somehow, this is different.'

'You'll get over it. The war will end and he will go home.'

'What if he dies and I never see him again?'

'Don't try to,' said Diana.

'I even thought of taking a train up to the town his squadron's stationed near and telephoning his base and asking him to meet me in York.'

'Listen, you owe a debt to George. Three years in the desert. You have a husband. You don't know what it's like being alone.'

'Haven't you met anybody yet?'

Diana shook her head, faintly sad, averted her eyes. They never mentioned Gifford again and Katherine stopped asking about him in the club but she never stopped thinking about him, no longer wondering what she would do if she came face to face with him in the street, but knowing what she would do if he ever asked her out again for another drink, not even a whole bottle of wine.

Now, standing at the desk in the Washington Club, a year and a half after that first meeting with Gifford she thought of the moment in which they had kissed, wondering if he ever thought of it as she did, wishing she could talk to somebody about it, somehow explain to somebody, yes, even to herself the way the man had made her feel. She stood there, feeling a pointlessness and emptiness of life more profound than ever in any moment of her life. Somewhere, someplace, she was certain he was dead, certain because she knew so many other dead people, so few ever returned after being reported missing in action. In fact, she tried to recall friends and relatives who had friends and relatives reported missing and dead; no, she could not think of any who had ever returned. Oh, yes, Virginia Montgomery, her husband was a prisoner of war in Italy. Maybe, oh, maybe, he was somewhere safe in German hands, and someday—but how?—someday, after the war she would see him again, but she knew this for a foolish thought. She would never see him again if he were a prisoner of war. She closed her eyes and clasped herself, holding again in her mind those long minutes in his arms in a time that seemed a century ago. Somebody called her name. It was her husband. He was standing directly in front of the desk. She dropped her hands.

'You scared me,' she said.

'Come in the lounge where we can talk.'

The lounge was empty. George was carrying his coat. He took off his Colonel's hat.

'Did you ever know a chap named Gifford?'

Her heart hammered and she felt the skin on her body turn icy cold.

She could not speak. She was panic-stricken.

'An American,' said her husband. 'Flier chap?'

'He used to stay here. Why?'

She felt she couldn't move her eyes from her husband's face.

'Did you know much about him?' he asked.

'No.' She could hear her heart pounding and she kept watching her husband's eyes but his eyes said nothing.

'Well, I have to go up to his base. Near Selby,' he said. 'I'll stay in Selby. Diana was up there and she took an overdose of sleeping pills when she heard he was shot down. She's dead.'

'Diana!'

'She left a note addressed to us. You know Diana's American. No people here of her own since Steve died.'

'Dead? I don't believe it.'

'What?'

He looked at her curiously.

He kissed her awkwardly.

She said nothing.

'Don't worry, darling. I'll be back in a day or two.'

After he left she went into the woman's room and cried, not for herself, not for Gifford, but for all the women like Diana who would never have a man or child after the war but as her crying diminished, a vague gladness touched her which she did not understand until she was back behind the desk again and thought suddenly of that moment when Gifford held her in his arms. 'I'm glad he passed out that night,' she told herself.

But she could not stop herself from thinking what it might have been like to make love to him, to sleep with him, to have him beside her, and though she knew she was only torturing herself with the thought she could not put it out of her mind, and the next night when she lay in her husband's arms she closed her eyes and called up the face of the man who was not her lover and never had been but had become now for just this one time, and she gave herself up to him as she had never given herself to anyone in her life, to kill all the years past, all the dead, dull years of marriage. She felt cat-like, feline in her husband's arms, feeling her body sending out wave after wave of excitement as she had never done before in her life to her husband, feeling a voluptuous hysteria rising in her flesh. She thrust and twisted her loins into her husband with a passion he had never known before, and in the darkness stars bloomed inside her brain like gigantic, soft flowers.

She felt her husband's body flinching and jerking, and then growing larger and larger, bigger then he had ever been before, and she heard his breath making a sound as if he were dying, and then she felt him hurl himself into her deeper and deeper, her hands dragging his head down, enveloping him with her arms. After a long time, he freed himself.

'Oh, my darling, my darling,' he said, touching her shoulder, wanting her again, but she had turned her back. You bitch, she thought, you bitch, worrying now, knowing she would never be able to do it again like this for her husband.

23 JENNIFER CALDWELL

Jennifer walked down the lane and up the hill into the woods. There. Now she could be alone. Not that they wouldn't leave her alone in the house, but out here it was different, though open, more alone here than in the house. She always came here as long as she could remember when she wanted to be alone, even when her mother and father thought she'd only gone up the hill into the woods to play. Her father had sympathized all he could; there was a point beyond which it was meaningless and ghastly, and she wished he would just say nothing. Which was why she had come out here. She would not have to listen to him, telling her not to worry, not to worry. That's all he ever told her as a child. No, that wasn't fair. He had told her that as a girl because he loved her and didn't want her disturbed or worried.

She fumbled in her purse for a cigarette. All she had was an old package of Gold Flakes. She felt ashamed because she had promised herself she was going to give up smoking, and she had carried these for over a month without touching them. She had smoked so many cigarettes in her life. Without knowing it for an instant she began to cry. Then she felt the tears on her face and knew why she was crying because beside the package of cigarettes in her purse lay Jack's lighter with the RAF crest on each side. She did not want to cry, but she could not help herself. She had cried enough, she told herself, trying to stop the tears but they would not stop so she let herself go and sat down beneath a tree and sobbed, as she had sobbed so often during the past week.

She looked down at the empty shotgun shell in the grass. It was red and faded now by the sun and rain. It did not make her feel happy because it reminded her of Jack and also the fact that she did not enjoy hunting but she had enjoyed hunting with Jack. She tried to recall the day they had been out here for pheasants but that day ran together with other days and she could not separate them from other pictures in her mind. Her thoughts were confused. Her memory was fuzzy today, but she remembered one thing, sitting out on the terrace with him on a sunny afternoon, playing the phonograph. He had brought a record down from London, *I Can't Get Started With You*. It was by Bunny Berigan. Or rather it was his trumpet playing the song. She had danced to the song with Russell at the Mirabelle. If she had married Russell now she would be perhaps a widow rather than a woman with a lover missing in action ... But even the best of fliers go for Burton, but she could not understand how Russell and Gifford had been together on the same machine because the RAF did not carry two pilots. But there was no blaming either Russell or Gifford for being shot down, or one having taken the other down with him. God, she wondered which one was alive.

She was sorry that her father thought so little of either man, hating Russell for standing up to him in the labor negotiations so long ago, and it was funny, though, how her father's attitude had changed, and she resented it, his half-admiration of Russell when Russell had become an officer in the RAF, as if that made Russell a gentleman at last. But she knew her father didn't really care whether both men were dead, but cared only because it affected her. She wondered what her father would say if she had told him she were going to break her engagement to Russell and marry Gifford. Well, she wasn't sure now she would ever marry either one of them, if either were alive. Oh, damn you Jack Gifford, why did you have another woman? She would never be happy until she had that cleared up. How could a man make love to two women? What similar moments of tenderness had he had with that other girl? What did she look like? I must find her, she thought. Blast!

I'm going to have a cigarette ...

It had been a mistake coming home like this. She decided she should have stayed at the gun battery instead of taking leave. The trouble was there was nobody in the world she could talk to about Jack Gifford. No other woman that she knew personally knew Jack. She didn't want to talk to any of his men friends, and besides she did not know with whom he was close because so often nobody lived long enough to develop a close friendship with another flier. She thought about Flying Officer Steve Palmer, a Canadian friend of Gifford's who'd once tried to get her outside in the dark during an intermission at the squadron dance. Gifford had told him to run along, or he'd sock him. No, she had nothing to say to Palmer, yet Palmer would know what kind of man Gifford was; she'd seen them together a lot. She wondered how Palmer felt about Gifford gone missing, as the saying goes. No, he wouldn't have any grief. It was difficult for any of the men to have grief, least of all to show it; they'd been through grief so many times it didn't touch many of them anymore because death was an every day event, like eating or sleeping. Suddenly she thought she wanted to see Palmer, just to talk to him, anybody who had known Gifford intimately. She would go back to the squadron and look up Palmer. No, Palmer wouldn't really care and he might even make a pass at her, if they were alone. She suddenly hated Palmer. He probably didn't give a damn about Gifford, not a single thought, now that Gifford was gone, might even, like some people she knew, have gotten Gifford's shoes.

What was there to do then? Four more days. Not here, she hoped. But where could she go? Dear Rodger, she thought suddenly, wondering if any of her tears had been for Rodger. No, the shock had stopped all that. It was only Gifford who gave her grief, and Rodger's absence only caused shock which was probably why everybody said how well she was bearing up. She would throw up if anybody mentioned that word again. Bearing up. Bah! If only she had another brother or another sister, somebody older, and she could stay at their house and feel they wouldn't bother her, and would understand.

Because she did not want to be alone. She wanted to be with people, yet she knew they would disturb her. Anything, anybody would disturb her.

If only Jack hadn't specified that his possessions go to her in case he was shot down ... if only he hadn't done that, she would never have known, but you'd think the adjutant would know better than to leave his personal letters intact in the foot locker ... Oh, God!

Go to London and find the woman, meet her. That was the only thing to do. And be kind to father until she left. Suddenly she felt better, not so mentally confused, as if the decision to do something had cleared her mind. Father was an old man now. He was of the Victorian age, there was no denying it, and he wanted to own everybody in the family, all their feelings were his possessions, and you must surrender them to him, as if this were a debt each member of the family owed simply because he was the father. No, that wasn't it either. He was just born meddlesome. Look at the way he had defeated mother's wishes at every turn and how he had confused Rodger all his life, making him dependent until Rodger got into service, and now trying to ruin Rodger's life because Rodger wanted to marry an actress. She wished she knew where Gifford lived, his home address. Was it Chicago or North Dakota? He had told her, but never the street address. If she knew she would write his parents.

She lit a cigarette and there was a taste of copper in her throat. She knew she would cry again soon. She could feel it coming. Diana, she thought, who are you and what are you? She would find her and find out. Diana Bisbee. The cigarette tasted terrible. It was time to go back to the house. Her father was sitting in the sun on the terrace. He looked older and no longer imperious. 'I'm going to London for a few days,' Jennifer said. Why did he have to sit there and look at her as if she had done something so ghastly wrong. He did not speak. Does he expect me to stay here with him in this big empty house? How are we ever going to get over it if I stay here and we just keep thinking of both of them every time we see each other. How she hated grief suddenly.

'Don't leave me, Jennifer.'

His face looked a hundred years old. His eyes were taut with despair.

'It's only for a few days,' she said, and then he began to cry and she took him into her arms, and she knew then she had never really known her father before. She had never seen him cry, not even when her mother died. She didn't care now how hard he had been all his life just so some of his tears now were for her and Gifford as well as for Rodger. She held him close.

24 FRANCES MCWHINNEY

She wondered why he had picked a place like this. It was apt to be filled with airmen, and, surely, one of them might recognize her from the last time she was here with Jack. It looked like a tea room from the outside, but it was a bar, she knew, because she had been in here before with Jack. You could have tea upstairs and downstairs was where all the life was, especially at night. She passed the tea room and went downstairs and sat at one of the small round tables. A waitress came to the table and she ordered a mild and bitter, half-pint. The waitress went to get the drink and came back with what looked like ale. Frances tasted it and called to the waitress as she turned to leave.

'This isn't mild and bitter,' she said. The waitress came back to the table and looked down at Frances.

'There's a war on, you know,' she said. 'No mild and bitter until tonight.'

'Thank you,' said Frances, smiling. 'As

long as you only charged me for mild and bitter.'

The waitress left. A couple of airmen came in and walked past her, and then a sergeant of the Royal Artillery came in, and she looked up and smiled.

'Hello, Bert,' she said.

'Waiting long?' he asked.

'Just this minute. I came straight from home,' she said. She looked at the M.M. ribbon on his battle dress tunic. He had won it at Dunkerque. 'I thought you might be in civvies.'

'I couldn't get a week,' he said. 'Only forty-eight hours.' He ordered a mild and bitter and changed it to Pale Ale when the waitress told them there wouldn't be any mild and bitter until tonight.

'Did you get my letter?' she asked.

'Sorry, but there wasn't time to answer,' he said. 'I had to go on a gunnery course at Oswestry. They ran us ragged day and night.'

'When did you get in?'

'This morning.'

'Oh?' she said. 'Are you sure?'

'I ought to know. I came in on the eight forty-five.'

'Yesterday morning. You mean.'

'Are you daft or something?'

'Don't worry. I can't force you to explain anything to me,' she said.

'Listen, you wrote me. I didn't write you.'

'Forget it,' she said. 'Why did you pick this place?'

'What difference does it make at this hour?'

'It could always happen. Somebody who knows Jack.'

'No flies on you, is there?' he said. 'Well, let's not worry about it.'

'Easy enough for you.'

'All right. All right,' he said. 'Any news about Jack?'

'Not a word. Nobody saw him go down. He was with the Wing Commander, you know.'

'Why did they let him keep flying?'

'They don't believe him. They keep telling him he's gold bricking.'

'But those headaches and can't sleep. He didn't make that up.'

'How's he going to prove it?'

'That must have been a hell of a night he spent.'

'You wouldn't sleep either after getting bashed on the head with a gun turret and then spending three days and nights in a cave with water dripping on you while you were going crackers trying to keep a dead man alive.'

'Jack was the only one survived that crash?'

'Yes. He crawled two miles from the crash with that cut in his head, dragging a corpse with him he thought was dead.'

'You think a lot about him, don't you?'

'What about your wife?'

He frowned. 'How'd you know?'

'I called your battery and left word for you to call your wife and the switchboard didn't seem surprised.'

'So you're the one?'

'Why not? You could have told me. It wouldn't have surprised or killed me.' Her eyes were filled with anger now. 'Would it? Do you think I wouldn't have come here if I had known you were married? Really.'

He laughed. 'Look, Frances. I wasn't trying to fool anybody.'

'Not much.' She drew her hand away as he sought to cover it with his hand. 'This is my lucky week,' she said.

'Did you come here just to tell me all this?'

'No. How long have you been married?'

'Just after Dunkerque.'

'I'll have another ale, please.'

'What about a Gin and Lime?'

'All right,' she said. He called the waitress and ordered two Gin and Limes.

'Now I suppose I'm Number One rat in your book,' he said.

'Oh, everybody's got a wife or husband nowadays. I'm going back home next

Monday and you don't know where that is, so what does it matter?'

'Where is it?'

'Cheddington. Near London.'

'I could meet you in London.'

'How would I explain that to my folks with Jack gone?'

'Up to you,' he said.

'Why doesn't your wife live in town here?'

'She did until a couple of weeks ago when the battery got posted for overseas.'

'How many women have you picked up since she moved back home?'

'Come off it. I didn't come here for this kind of talk. And I don't think you did either.'

'So I'm the first and only?'

No, no, she thought, that was not the point, the point was loneliness, and they had done it to kill loneliness. It was the great killer of loneliness, even when there was no love, but when there was love you could drive loneliness away for awhile, but not forever because you could not kill it forever, but what they had done, she told herself, had not been wrong, they had needed each other, and she would need him again and again. There was nothing else and she liked him most above all, but she felt terrible every time it was over, and every time they were in bed, it was lovely. Oh, God, what could be better, she thought, remembering: the sound of his hands moving her clothing in the darkness, the secret darkness filled with such delight, the soft, secret dark, her soft nude warm body beside him, tasting the sweetness of her own lips, the sweetness of his lips upon her breasts, feeling their bodies becoming one central point in time with no morning or night or day, until they slowly went down together blissfully into a dark whirlpool, a pool gradually lighting as they seemed to rise out of it.

'Think what you like. I'm glad you came. I'm glad I met you at the dance that night and I'm glad I saw you again and glad you wrote me. I'm not going to get you in any trouble or make you do anything you don't want to, and you're not just another pick-up.'

'What am I then?'

'What do you want to be? I made love to you and you didn't dislike it and I didn't either and your husband has trouble doing it because something's wrong with his head.'

She looked away. 'Don't talk about it, please.'

'I didn't bring it up.'

'I know what you think of me. I'm just a cheap tart you picked up at a dance a couple months ago when her husband was away flying ...' The waitress set the drinks down. 'When are you going overseas?'

'Should have been a week ago,' he said. The waitress left.

'Do you know where you're going? A lot of the lads are out in Burma. Do you think you'll go there? I really shouldn't be here,' she said. She pushed back her chair.

'Wait,' he said. 'Listen, I've got a room and everything. You can't back out now. I had a hard time getting a pass.'

He reached and caught her hands and she drew her chair back to the table.

'Please don't go,' he said. 'I'm sorry. I was in town last night.'

'I thought I saw you. Going into the De Grey rooms.'

'You're right.'

'All right,' she said. 'I don't know what I'll tell the folks. I told them I'd be back home today. I don't know how I'll explain it.'

'Tell them there was a bomb on the tracks.'

'That's so old.'

'Always the best. Wait a minute. I'll phone and see if I can get some theater tickets for tonight.'

She squeezed his hand, and for one who felt ashamed and guilty her face was curiously lit with happiness. 'I shouldn't stay, Bert. We mustn't do anything crazy.'

He went upstairs and outside on the street to the phone booth on the corner. 'Sergeant Morris, please ... This is Sergeant Bert Haugen, Corporal will you get him, please ... Hello ... listen, will you do me a big favor, George ... Send a wire right away to the George Hotel ... I'm to report back to the battery immediately. Posting overseas. Right away. I've got a real problem on my hands.'

25 JENNIFER CALDWELL

Yes, this must be the place. Jennifer opened her purse and drew out the letter and looked at the address again. Yes, this was it. Apt. 2. She opened the door and looked up the long stairway into the apartment building and she was filled with a mysterious fear. Going up the stairs the fear increased and at the top she found herself panting. She rang the bell and a tall dark woman, about thirty-five, with beautiful black hair which she wore straight back above a long oval face, opened the door.

For some reason—oh, why? oh, why?—Jennifer couldn't speak. She stared at the woman.

'Diana?' Jennifer heard her mouth say.

'No.'

'I'm looking for Diana Struthers.'

'Won't you come in.'

'Thank you,' Jennifer said.

The woman shut the door.

'Why do you want to see Diana?'

'Well, you might say. I'm a friend of a friend of hers.'

'Care for tea?'

'Thank you. When will she be in?'

'She won't. Diana is dead.'

'What? When?'

'She committed suicide. I'm Katherine Alcott.'

'Good Lord!'

The women smiled and nodded at each other and introduced themselves.

'Did you know Diana?'

'No.'

'Won't you sit down. I'll fix some tea.'

Jennifer sat down and Katherine Alcott went to the kitchen.

She wasn't gone long, but long enough for Jennifer to see the framed photograph on the piano. It was Gifford but he looked younger, as if the picture might have been taken during his training days. She went to the piano and felt better after inspecting the photo: there wasn't any inscription on it. She had it in her hand when Katherine came back from the kitchen. Without stopping or even looking at Jennifer, Katherine set the tea tray down on the coffee table and spoke

197

without lifting her head where she stooped for a fraction of a second over the table.

'Did you know him, too?'

'No,' Jennifer lied.

'How did you know Diana?'

'My brother knew her,' Jennifer said, feeling safe. It was all in the letter in her purse. She knew Diana's husband was dead, and she knew Diana had been up to Yorkshire to see Gifford because she had said she was coming in the letter.

'It came as a shock to all of us,' said Katherine, stirring her tea. 'Milk? I think there's some condensed milk.'

'Just a touch, thank you.'

Standing above Jennifer, pouring the milk into the cup, Katherine Alcott's breathing deepened suddenly, as if some strong thought had suddenly seized her. She finished pouring and stood up and stared at Jennifer.

'What's the matter?' said Jennifer who felt Katherine suddenly looked angry.

'You—knew—him, didn't you?'

'Oh, really. What is this?'

'You did, didn't you?'

'Didn't I—what?'

'Who is Flight Lieutenant Jack Gifford?'

'I don't know.'

'Oh, you don't know.'

'Oh, really. You are interesting.'

'Yes, I knew Jack Gifford,' said Katherine Alcott.

'Yes, you must have. I'm afraid I've know him longer than either of you.' Then: 'God, God, no. You don't mean, you, and Diana.'

Jennifer put her cup down and stood up.

'I want you to tell me some things. Important things.'

'I suppose you think he belongs to you. Yes, I know he's missing. She killed herself when she heard.'

'I still want to know.'

'I suppose you think I would tell you.'

'I have to know, if he's still alive some place. Did you ever—?'

'I won't tell you anything.'

Jennifer opened her purse and held up the envelope.

'Now you know why I came up here,' she said. 'They turned over his kit to me. A letter from Diana.'

'You're his true love, I suppose?'

'I thought so. How do you happen to know him?' Jennifer asked.

'I met him when he came to the club. He took me out once. And that's all.'

'Where did he meet Diana?'

'She was with me. But what can you do? He may be dead.'

'Maybe.'

'What difference does Diana make? She's dead. And if he's alive, there's only two things that matter. You and Jack. And you're both alive.'

The bell rang.

'That's probably my husband.'

For a fraction of a second, just as the door was opening, Jennifer tried to decide what to do, perhaps slip out, but then Colonel George Alcott was there, hair smoothed back, bat stick under his arm and hat in hand, replete in red-tab uniform, his boots gleaming. He was smiling.

'I saw Freddy Waters,' he said. 'Going to the palace next week. Another gong. Lucky he's alive. Oh, I say, sorry,' he turned, seeing Jennifer for the first time, and bowed, apologizing, and Katherine introduced Jennifer as a friend of Diana's. He stopped smiling.

'Rotten,' he said. 'Diana was a grand girl.' He shook his head, put both hands behind his back, clasped his hands together, shook his head again. 'Be a good girl, Katherine, fix us a drink, will you, please. I feel like a double whiskey.'

Katherine turned her face away suddenly.

'I say, I didn't—' George began. 'I mean, you mustn't let her place here and her things upset you like this. I'll fix the drinks.' The two women said nothing and

George went out to the kitchen.

Jennifer walked across the room and put her hand on Katherine's shoulder.

'Katherine.' Katherine's face was turned away.

'What?' said Katherine.

'I know. I know.'

Katherine turned her face and embraced Jennifer and began to cry. 'Oh, God, you don't. Nobody knows how I feel.'

Book Four
BY LOVE AND ARMS

26 SERGEANT EDDIE REKER

From the glassless castle window the five French peasants watched two figures moving across the plains to enter the woods below the castle and come up the hill and halt at the empty ditch that had been a moat three hundred years ago. One figure was tall, a man. He stared up at the shot-torn castle walls. Shrapnel scars upon the walls looked like some miraculous and gigantic form of small-pox. The man wore a weathered green hat and a long leather great coat. Beside him stood a figure in a weathered brown dress, hatless, with the long blonde hair of a woman.

One of the men at the window lifted a Mauser rifle and laid it on the stone casement. An elder man struck down the man's arm and seized the rifle.

'No,' said the elder man.

'The coat,' said the younger man. 'It is German.'

'No,' said the elder man. 'That we will find out.'

They watched the couple staring down into the empty ditch. The rim of the ditch crested with sandbags, sagged where the bags had been blown away by gunfire; it turned at the corner of the castle, but a narrow trench had been dug running straight out from the castle, and it sloped down into a field that had once been a pasture. The sky was cloudy and the clouds blew over the plains.

They watched the man put his hand under the woman's arm and lift her up on to the wall of sandbags. They stood poised for an instant and then as the woman appeared to lose her balance, the man caught her about the waist and leaped with her down into the ditch. From the corner of the window they watched the man and woman scale the other side of the ditch. Then they heard them scaling the pile of rubble that almost filled the doorless castle entrance. They listened to them climb.

The old man spoke to the young man. 'Go down!'

The young man did not move. His hands touched the Mauser. An old woman, perhaps fifty-five, who looked older, stepped past the young man and descended the stone stairs in the rear of the room and walked along the stone hallway, making a loud shuffling sound, since she wore French army boots that were too large for her feet. She descended another stone staircase, this one circular. She stopped at the foot of the stairs and looked up at the rubble-filled doorway. Light, faint and grey like muddy water, filtered through the tunnel-like opening at the top of the rubble. Her high, almost oriental shaped cheekbones were plum colored, but her eyes were blank and cold and hard. She looked up at the blonde-haired woman scrabbling her way on hands and knees down the pile of rubble. The blonde woman was young. The dress reached below her knees. She paused, lifted her head, looked at the older woman, the shot-pocked stone walls.

'Sergeant Reker and I—' the young woman began. Her voice ceased as she saw the expressionless eyes of the older woman.

Then her voice came on again: 'He was shot down three weeks ago.' She paused for a long moment, the two women staring at each other, their faces motionless. Then: 'He wants to reach Spain. May we rest here?'

The old woman did not appear to hear, yet her thin lips moved faintly and her voice issued as if solely out of her throat between her lips that were almost closed as she spoke: 'Wait.'

'We will pay for food,' said the young woman.

'Money?' the old woman said; she had started to move away; she stopped now and looked over her shoulder. 'Pay? Where would we spend it?'

The young woman raised her hands. 'Please. His hip. He must rest ... Please?' Then the young woman heard the noise. She saw the older woman look up. Powdered back and shards tumbled down the pile of rubble. Stepping carefully, grimacing with pain, the man in the leather coat who was named Sergeant Eddie Reker made his way down the rubble pile into the hall. His face was pale, with blue eyes and flaxen hair, his cheeks almost cavernous beneath hollow red-rimmed eyes. But he stood erect. He was nearly six feet tall. The torn leather coat revealed mud-stained blue trousers and battle dress.

'Hello,' he said, smiling, speaking in broken French which the girl had taught him since the night she had held him against the wall with a pistol at her house. 'Could we get something to eat and rest for a few days?'

The old woman stared at him, squinting, searching his face and eyes.

Then she said: 'No.'

'I have money,' Reker said. 'French and English. Later the English will be good.'

The woman shook her head. She turned and began to mount the stairs. She paused. The older man was now descending the stairs. He came toward Reker.

'I am Sergeant Reker,' said Reker. 'I wish to return to England.'

The old man studied him, roving his gaze over Reker and the woman as one might study the purchase of live stock. 'The Baron is dead. Now this is ours.'

Reker looked first at the old man, and then with an air of arrogance he stared at the old woman. 'Jean,' he said to the young woman, 'go with the old lady.'

The old man said nothing. He did not move as the young woman crossed the room and mounted the stairs toward the old woman. Then the young woman saw the soldier boots on the old woman and she smiled. She did not look back as she mounted the stairs, smiling.

The old man and Reker stared at each other, both erect, with the air of two strange animals studying each other.

Upstairs in a room next to the room from which the men had watched Reker approach the castle, a young girl sat upon a broken box that had once contained German rifle ammunition. She was nineteen, tall and slim, with black hair coiled in braids about her head. She wore the blue coat of a dead French officer above a skirt fashioned from field grey wool. She was leaning forward now, musing, her head slanted. She listened to the feet mount the stairs and then the sound of the men's voices in the next room.

The room in which she sat had once been a wood paneled library. The wood had been stripped away for fire, and the brick wall stood cracked and charred. Through the crack in the wall she listened and watched the men in the other room.

She looked at the bare floor on which lay empty bottles and neat piles of French and German rifle cartridges. Her two brothers, squatting among the bottles, were sorting the cartridges, and the English sergeant leaned against the wall beside the door. The girl wondered why they had not killed him as they killed the others and took their clothes.

'Here,' said her younger brother, and

without looking up where he squatted, lofted a bottle with one hand. 'Drink.'

She watched the English sergeant drink and then saw her brother turn, lift a hand full of cartridges and a German automatic pistol from the floor.

'You know these?' said her younger brother.

'Only in pictures,' said the sergeant.

'They are better than your Sten.'

'Shut up.' It was her father's voice. The younger brother who was sixteen turned his head and spat on the floor.

The old man looked at his son briefly, then back at the English sergeant. The English sergeant's eyes were strained.

'Drink,' said the younger brother, while the other brother watched him and the sergeant, but the sergeant did not move.

'Nobody's going to poison you,' said the older brother. 'Take a drink.'

'Thank you,' said the sergeant and reached for the bottle of wine. He lifted the bottle to his lips.

'A sergeant,' thought the girl, watching first the sergeant and then her brothers' hands busy among the cartridges.

'The Germans thought they drank it all,' the older brother laughed.

'Shut up,' said the father.

The sergeant smiled. 'Eventually the English will drink it. Save it for our army. They will be coming.'

'A sergeant,' the girl thought, watching. She watched Reker drink again and then walk past her brothers, the bottle still in his hand.

'Where are you going?' asked the older brother. The sergeant looked at him over his shoulder. 'Where is she? She needs a drink, too.'

The girl studied Reker's face as Reker stared at her brother. He is not afraid, she thought.

'Stay here,' said the older brother. 'You bloody English.'

'So it's my nationality, not me,' Reker said. 'Soon it will be other men, many nationalities.'

'Take her a drink,' said the father. Reker still did not move. He stared at the older brother and the father spoke again. 'Go on.'

'An English sergeant,' the girl thought again, breathing faster now, the color bright in her cheeks, her eyes shining. 'An English sergeant,' she said softly, taking a deep breath.

Jeanette was sitting upon a legless piano bench in a room down the hall, empty save for a broken bed filled with a straw mattress. In her hand was a potato. She gnawed slowly at the skin.

'Thank God somebody is eating in this

country, even if they're bandits,' she said. 'I'm almost starved.'

'Try this,' Reker said, handing her the bottle.

Jeanette paused, stared at the bottle.

'Well,' she said. 'Where did you get that?'

'Wine,' he said.

'They'll poison us,' she said.

'Drink up. I'm not dead yet.'

She took the bottle, regarding it suspiciously. She sniffed the top, grimaced, shook her head, made a sour face.

'Did they make this?'

Reker did not answer. He began to polish one of the potatoes with one hand.

'Go on,' he said. 'You'll feel better.'

'It smells terrible.'

'Sour, that's all.' He polished the potato.

'No,' he said. 'It would be cheaper to shoot us, if that's what they want.'

Her lips recoiled from the bottle. She slapped her chest and coughed.

'Horrible,' she said. Then she laughed. 'But it's good.'

Reker opened his coat and reaching inside his trouser pocket, he drew out a small black automatic.

'Put it away,' she said. 'They'll kill you for it.'

'They have plenty of guns.'

'Just to kill. That's all they want.'

Reker looked at the gun.

'Let me carry it until we leave here,' she said.

'Don't worry. They're partisans.'

'You fool! They're bandits!'

'They cook here,' Reker said slowly. 'I'll get you some soup.'

'Give me the gun. Let me keep it.'

'Stay here,' Reker said. He thrust the gun into his pocket. He went to the door, listened. He looked back at her briefly, then he turned and vanished down the hall. She crouched listening to the hollow sound of his boots along the barren stones. She touched her hair, felt the wig adjust, and crouching, thought of dying days in between: *He dug and I dug with him. One night I had him against the wall and the next night he was in my bed. But he saved me. I would die back there if I hadn't gone with him. When I saw their eyes with the scissors in their hands I began to cry. I saw their eyes and began to run but it was too late. After we buried father there was nobody. The door was thin and old. You wait at the corner, he said. I waited. He came back with the wig. How many days have we walked now?*

A sound came. The young French woman, Jeanette, stopped thinking and rose quickly and went into the hall and along the empty stone corridor. She passed doorless rooms that had once been bedrooms, rooms with charred walls and floors littered with bricks and empty shell and grenade boxes. A sound and smell came again. She stopped, taking a deep breath, listening, and then the sound came softly at the end of the hall. She went up narrow stone steps that mounted into another stone corridor, and the sound and smell filled the room. Cooking, she thought. Reker? Where was he?

At that moment the young girl who had been watching her brothers, raised her head. She looked at the blonde woman.

The two women stared at each other.

27 FLYING OFFICER
RODGER CALDWELL

Thin sunlight shone in the sky. In the meager yellow light the old faded stone walls of the asylum and the guards' cages on each corner of the wall loomed above the men walking in the exercise yard. From the woods beyond the walls the invisible birds called to each other in the soft summery air.

Six figures stood against the wall, hunched together talking. One man leaned against the wall, one hand covering one eye, the other eye fixed on the guard's tower; blind in one eye, but only recently blind. He said he cannot yet focus the single eye without covering the blind eye with one hand.

'You don't need the hand,' another said. 'You're already blind in that eye.'

'The good eye still doesn't know it,' the one-eyed man said.

'What? Do you think your good eye is connected only to itself?'

'Parisians don't have any brains,' a third said.

'Why don't they take us out and shoot us if they know we're not crazy?'

'Did he lose his brains with his eye?' a fourth said. 'Was he tortured much?'

'He blew the bridge at Rislon. Isn't that right, Jacques?'

The man with one eye lowered his head and looked at the faces around him. Then up at the tower again and around the yard. When he spoke his voice was flat. 'She didn't even know what she was doing. I gave her the basket to carry through the station. I was carrying the gun in a suitcase.'

'What?' the fifth man said. 'What's the matter with him?'

'Shhhh,' said another. 'It's about his girl. He made her a courier two weeks before they were to marry. She didn't even know it.' His voice sounded tired. 'Thought she was going on a picnic when they took the train to Rislon. They picked her up, and

212

he had to go on to Rislon. We met him there. They got her with the explosives. Shot her. He didn't know it till after the bridge when he got back home. Except he knew they would find the explosives. He'll show you her picture. Just look at it.'

'Sure,' the other said.

'Wait,' said another. 'Hold it. Here he comes.'

The men turned and looked across the yard.

'Who?' said the man with one eye. 'Is it the Boche?'

Nobody answered. They watched the man coming across the yard toward them; a stocky man. They watched him silently. Nobody talked. The man stopped in front of them.

'Have you sent a message to England?' Caldwell asked.

'Yes, Flying Officer,' the first man said. His voice was mocking. 'They say you are a Wing Commander.' The others laughed.

'I tell you,' said Caldwell. 'I swear it. Look, that is my uniform.'

The others looked across the yard at a tall man wearing a Flying Officer's uniform. The man was tall; he carried a bat stick, but something was wrong with his eyes, gaunt and strained, with something blank in them above the foolish smile.

'For the fiftieth time,' said Caldwell. 'I parachuted in here. There was a dead man in the yard. I took his clothes. That man has my uniform.'

'We are all Wing Commanders,' the fourth said.

The man in the uniform appeared utterly oblivious of the seven men as he passed. They watched him strutting past, watching him quietly, as if he might be on parade. His eyes were dead.

'You're not insane,' said Caldwell.

'Shut up,' said the first. 'Get away. Keep moving.'

Caldwell walked on. Still watching, they saw him walk up to the man in uniform, a real mad man, tall, with erect back, the stick, and beside him Caldwell, slightly stooped, limping from the night when he fell on his leg against the wall.

'Is he a Boche?' the one-eyed man said. 'Is he trying to find out about the break-out?'

'We'll take him with us,' the first said. 'And we'll send him to Rabbit. The Boche will follow and we shall follow him.'

'Two agents,' the fourth said. 'We'll bag two. The Englishman and whoever betrayed Rabbit's section.'

He felt as if he were in a warm lake, at night, far out in the lake, swimming easily, steadily, the water feeling cool because the air was feather-soft and warm; not even a faint breeze after the long hot humid summer day. The hour is one of utter stillness, unbelievable tranquility, everything velvet soft in the darkness, the islands rising all around like sleeping monstrous fish, and faraway he could see car lights flashing through the branches of trees heavy with leaves. He felt himself swimming slowly, drawing his arms back in a slow breast stroke; the dark hulls of boats ran past, flashing red and green lights. The water chuckled softly against his chin and he thrust his arms forward and drew them back letting the cool water flow over him with a delicious sensation. His back arched and relaxed and arched again as he thrust his legs frog-like, and in the dream he was having, a woman was the lake in his mind and he was swimming into her in long easy strokes and her flesh was the cool water flowing over him in smooth undulant waves. He felt himself going deeper and deeper inside her and it was all one long easy swimming stroke with the water flowing over him smoothly and softly, her flesh enveloping his arms and legs like water, taking him deeper and deeper inside her. The trees seemed faraway in the darkness, the lights receding through the leaves and he felt his body going further and further out into the dark water, swimming with long smooth strokes through the moonlight marbled water. He wakened, shocked to find himself in bed with a woman, the room dark, the woman's voice soft in the dark, her hand seeking him, his memory filled with pleasure while he thought, feeling hollow and empty, 'what kind of a whore am I.' For instantly memory twined the image of Jennifer Caldwell and Diana. 'Is the flesh always just this hungry for flesh? I love Jennifer but here I am sleeping with another female. Again.' Yet he did not feel guilt or revulsion, only a warm tenderness. He turned and embraced the woman in the darkness.

'Listen,' he said. She did not move. He drew her head back and looked at her in the darkness. How can I love Jennifer, tell myself I do, and lie here with this woman and enjoy her and feel tenderness for her. Quit kidding yourself, he said to himself; you did it with Diana, too. Poor Diana. He couldn't tell her he had not been serious. She had been so serious.

'Candace,' he said. She would not listen.

Her mouth came against his throat and she moaned softly, quivering. God, he thought, is there any way to satisfy this one?

'Two weeks,' he said. 'I've been—'

'Shhhhh.'

He thought about up on the Yorkshire moors at the squadron field that fall, after having met Diana at that party in London. Yes, he was only killing loneliness with all of them, loneliness for Jennifer, but none of it helped because all of it came back only to loving Jennifer. He could whore forever and never kill his loneliness for her. Perhaps that was all love was; the person who makes you feel the least lonely. He was afraid he would lose the feeling for her when she wasn't around. No he was weak, that time with Diana, all those times, shouldn't have happened simply because Jennifer had gone home on leave, and you tried to kill the fear of dying in the warmth of another woman's body. But even now as he touched Candace he knew the tenderness he was feeling here was the tenderness he had for Jennifer, and the longer he lay here the more he longed for Jennifer. How long since he had come in that night at the party? Two weeks. Nearly two weeks. This woman was insatiable, but without her he would be in prison. But now he knew even more than that ... that no matter how long and how often he slept with this woman nothing would ever stop his loving Jennifer. But why if she thought he had been sent in to her as an agent from England, why didn't she send him on, if that must be her duty? She'd get in trouble if he stayed here. All the time talking about Nestor and something about sending him to a town to see somebody. He wanted to get back to England. He had never been so happy any place before in his life as in England, even if they were going to kill him for it, and he had his whole life ahead, if he could stay alive. He would stay here after the war. He would never go back to the States, to that cruddy midwestern town where the biggest deal in town was to be the biggest car dealer or grain buyer while your wife ran around playing Lady Bountiful in the Junior League or some hospital auxiliary. God, was that the ultimate in success, the great standards of western civilization, two cars in every garage? Was this all that Democracy was about, the opportunity to make money? Well, it was the same here, but his love for Jennifer would make it easier to swallow the crap that people told each other so they could go on selling each other something. No, he was afraid he didn't love it in England that much. He loved excitement, change of scene, new people. Now if that was the way he wanted it after the war, perhaps he could have it, running a small airline of his own. He felt her lips against his ear.

'Candace,' he tore his mouth away. 'Listen.'

'S-s-sh.'

'You lied. You can get me out of here.'

'Please. Just shut up, darling.'

'What the hell is Nestor?'

'There's plenty of time, darling.'

He sprang up, caught her arms.

'I've been here damn near two weeks. Two weeks you've been saying you're going to put me in touch with the underground.'

'I'm waiting to hear.'

'Who?'

'You can be such a bore.'

He began to twist her wrist.

'You're hurting me.' She smiled, averting her head.

'You are part of the underground. Quit kidding.'

He dropped her arm. Her face changed. The smile was gone. Her eyes were serious, a little hard.

'You'll get out,' she said. 'When I say so. I've done plenty for the French. Now I happen to want you. Yes, use you. Call it what you want. He looked like you. He's dead. They killed him in the retreat.'

'You're mad.'

'Maybe.'

There was the sound of footsteps coming up the stairs. She turned, crossed the room, slid the bolt on the door. A man with a mustache and a machine pistol stood in the door. He was wearing jodhpurs and the machine pistol of German make was held in the crook of his arm. There was no sling on the gun. He was perhaps nineteen years old.

'London's going to hear about this,' he said. His voice was cold and flat. 'Nestor's gone. They nailed him at the drop. Rabbit close down. London's orders.'

She jerked her head toward Gifford.

'What about him?'

'London okayed him a week ago. I thought he'd left.'

Candace did not answer. The man stared at her.

'He'll have clothes in the morning,' the man said. He spoke in English with an American accent. He gave Gifford one more searching look and departed. Candace bolted the door.

'What the hell is this Nestor business,' Gifford asked.

'London sent him over. There have been too many arrests in my section. The Germans know too much. I think there's a German counteragent working in our circuit. Nestor was to locate him. You'll have to get out of here quickly.'

'How?'

'You'll have to chance it. After we get your clothes you'll go to this cafe. I'll give you the name of the place. Roger will meet you. He's a new agent. Watch him. I don't trust him.'

'Does he know you?'

'No, but my last cut-out who went there hasn't come back.'

29 SERGEANT
ROBERT CRAIG

The mist was clearing away. The skies were paling with morning light. Craig looked out from under the low branches of the tree under which he had slept. The world beyond the hill was wide and green, rolling, the horizon blue and far away. Craig came out from under the tree and began to size up his position. Down below the hill a road ascended curving behind him. The road below cut through the hills and vanished in the hills below. Beyond the hills a plain shimmered bluely in the dim morning light. Far to the south mountains marked the horizon. He could see anything that moved within a range of five miles. Somewhere pigeons called softly and through the trees came the chuckling of a stream. A plume of smoke hung drifting against the sky a mile behind his right shoulder. He looked at his watch. Six-thirty.

Then he heard the sound of aircraft. He scrambled back under the low branches of the tree. The machine came from the west, flying low, a Fesler-Storch, with its high-wing parasol structure. It banked and began to circle the hills. It was so low Craig could see the two men in the machine. One man swept the hills with field glasses. Craig tried to flatten beneath the trees, but as the machine came skimming past the top of the hill Craig knew he had been spotted even though he had concealed his face in his hands. The machine immediately turned away and sped eastwards as Craig lifted his face.

They spotted me, he thought; I'll have to keep off the road. He looked at the hills again. They were bare of cover. He climbed the next hill and looked down into two valleys. Still no cover in this treeless land.

He decided that the people in the aircraft would tell the search party to look for a man cutting across country so that perhaps the best bet would be to stick to roads now, but that would mean a change of clothes. He couldn't walk the road in daylight in his flying uniform and he couldn't stay here because they would look for a man in the hills. Well, the only thing to do was to get on the road with the hope of finding a French who might give him clothes. He descended the hill and walked out onto the dusty winding road.

The air was hot, humid, and the sun hammered down heat, and though the area seemed empty of life, desolate, he felt hemmed in, watched. He walked south keeping close to the side of the road. The road climbed and from the top of the next hill he could see far down a long valley, with the road winding between hills, and faraway, a column of dust that could be made only by a car or truck. Then something moved, a dot, another dot, about five miles below in the valley. He squinted against the bright sunlight. A company of soldiers! Combing the field. But perhaps they were not looking for him alone. After all, he'd come almost fifty miles from the place where he was shot down. Maybe it was somebody else they sought. Maybe!

But he could not go down the road. He would have to head west and come around behind the search party. Now across the still air he could hear the sound of the car approaching, far-off, but quite clearly, a faint humming noise. He began to run, up one hill, and down the next, moving farther from the highway.

He had a terrific impression of being hemmed in, and tried to tell himself it was all in his mind. He longed for trees, even some brush in which to hide, but the hills were bare. The sharp spears of grass beat against his legs.

Then suddenly coming up a short path was a man. He looked at Craig with frightened eyes and stepped back.

The man was old. Craig grabbed him by the shoulders. The old man cringed. Craig shouted at him to take off his clothes. The old man began to cry and shake his head. Craig tore off the man's coat. The man fell down. He began to pray. Craig removed the man's shirt. He pointed at the man's trousers. The old man did not move. He knelt shaking and praying. Craig pushed him over into the ditch. Craig stripped off his trousers. The old man huddled naked. Craig tossed the old man his uniform. He watched the old man dress. Then putting one finger to his lips, Craig drew one finger across the old man's throat. The old man smiled feebly. Craig shoved and the old man ran up over the hill.

Craig enjoyed walking across the hills that afternoon. Twice German planes passed low. They were observation machines. Craig looked up at the men in the machines. The planes flew on. Craig passed flocks of sheep. He nodded at the sheep herders. They nodded at him. As the sun faded he came out of the hills into a small wood. He sat down and waited for the dark.

The grass was high in the wood. Before dark he made a bed of the grass. He sucked on some grass. God, he was hungry. He felt how weak he was becoming. Then he slept, dreaming of squadron sausage, fried eggs. Before a mission. How he hated that stinking bread sausage! Oh, but how wonderful it would taste now! Even cold and stale it would be so delicious.

He woke in dawn light. His back and shoulders were cold and stiff. He looked up at the pale blue sky. The leaves made a network through which the early morning sun was beginning to shine. He sat up and looked down into the valley. At once he sprang up. A row of men were combing the hills.

Craig crawled through the high grass. He knelt behind a boulder and looked out. The row of men were coming up the hill. About half a mile away. He crawled back through the high grass and ducked down at the top of the hill and rolled down the other side about fifty feet. He rose and began to run. He ran full speed down the hill into a ravine. He ran along the ravine about a quarter of a mile. The ravine turned to the right and he turned, panting, and halted. He heard a shout, and knew he had been seen.

He ran up the hill to his left. For an instant he paused on top against the sky. Then he descended and circled the hill and came back down in the ravine which he had just left and climbed the hill to the top where he had slept. Just as he thought, he saw a line of soldiers going down into the ravine and climbing up the opposite hill.

He waited, watching them disappear. Then he started down the hill into a low flat valley. Here were trees, a shallow stream. He followed the stream. He heard dogs, then whistles; the sound came down the wind from the hills. He stumbled through the brush beside the stream. A line of soldiers stood for a moment against the sky line. He fell down, rose, stumbled on among the trees. A house, bigger trees, loomed suddenly. A man seated in the bay window rose and looked out. Craig stooped to hide, but the man waved him on. The man was tall, white-haired, with a long thin nose, and beady eyes.

Craig looked back. The baying of the dogs increased. He ran on, and the door opened. It was a big house with two chimneys, a wide garden.

The man slammed the door shut as Craig entered.

'I'm—' Craig began, but the man raised his hand.

'I know,' he smiled curiously. 'An escaped airman.'

'They're only half a mile away.'

'Come with me,' the man said softly. He led Craig into a library. He pointed at the door on the far side of the room. 'Go in there.'

The room was dark, shuttered. Craig heard the dogs cease. He sat down and almost at once began to think of food. God, if only he could get a decent meal here. His guts were cold and empty, gnawing into his chest. He lay down for a moment and fell asleep. A hand, voice, roused him. Light shone in his eyes.

'Come on,' said the voice. 'They're gone.'

'What'd you tell them?'

'You weren't here,' said the old man. He paused, tamped tobacco into his pipe. He smiled slowly. 'But now that you're here, perhaps you can clear up who you really are.' His eyelids blinked. Craig felt cold along his spine.

'I told you. I got shot down and—'

'Oh, yes, we've heard that story before. Now stop lying.'

'Why didn't you turn me in?'

'I thought we'd play their game.'

'Game?' Craig said in a sudden rage. 'Listen, I haven't eaten in God knows how long.'

'You won't either. Until you talk.'

'Look at my escape kit. Here.'

'A very neat fake.'

'Are you crazy?'

'Not quite. Who sent you?'

'What in hell are you talking about?'

'Come now. Give me your name, rank, and serial number. Perhaps I can clear you with London.'

Craig gave him the information.

The man drew a pistol.

'Walk ahead of me,' he said. 'Keep walking. Down the hall. Open the door at the end of the hall.'

Craig opened the door. A cool, fetid cellar odor rose out of the darkness. The door clicked. He heard the bolts shot into place. Awkwardly he felt his feet descending wooden steps.

30   FLIGHT SERGEANT JACK MCWHINNEY

And me at the gate of Buckingham Palace with all the girls from Soho waiting in their beds after my chest was covered with V.C.'s by the Queen's own hand, taking each girl one at a time after the celebration party and giving each a miniature medal for souvenir.

He lay still. His mind thought about the palace and all the lovely girls waiting outside the gate for him after the queen pinned him. After a while, he thought he heard a groan. But there was no more sound. Only the creak of the wheels beneath his shoulders.

He lay on a flat moving floor made of wood. But he had the feeling as always that only part of himself was there, just his body while another part of him (was it another body? another person) marched rigidly into Buckingham Palace courtyard toward a vast glory, passing the rows of Horse Guards drawn in line, toward the throne invisible somewhere in the sky down from which the queen would descend from a cloud. He wasn't sure which part of himself saw this. Was it this part lying here on the wooden floor? or the part already in the courtyard? He heard himself laugh lightly as he turned on the wooden floor against the side of the coffin.

Thus were the mechanics of his travelling, of each day, the same stretching back to a time he could not recall, only hanging by his feet in the dark. Each day the wagon lumbered along the road and the coffin was removed and remained inside until dark. It was like a film, hours long, all of the same action, repeated over and over again; a single day out of many days, a scene to which constant sleep attached him. He did not recall eating but neither did he remember being hungry. So maybe his other body, the one getting the decorations from the queen, was getting the food too. But it is all right, he thought, because I am not like myself now. But things are easier this way. It's quieter than dying.

He closed his eyes, savoring his ease though the floor was hard. Beneath him the wheels of the hearse, like all the other hearses beneath which time had passed him, followed the rough country road where even in daylight it was dark in the hearse for the curtains were drawn. From somewhere close behind, through the steady sound of the horse's hoof beats, a mourner released a cry of pain and grief. It seemed to cease almost as it began, and into the silence came only the sound of the horse's hooves, thudding upon his ear, through his breathing.

He did not move. And his mind went on thinking again, sliding softly, sweetly into dreams.

Across the darkness of his eyelids the queen descends from her throne in the sky, walking down a stairway of soft white clouds. From side to side the hearse swayed against the vision of the queen, the silence of heaven punctuated by the thudding of shod hooves. He can see the queen's sweet smile and sunlight glinting on her crown. The queen wears an ancient white robe, sashed with a golden cord, and she seems to move across the courtyard upon invisible feet, gliding and he thinks of the girl on the stage in London coming down the long gang plank toward his uplifted face, the silken white robe swinging rhythmically about her white thighs, not knowing she was the queen, too.

The walls of the hearse felt cold, of glass. It was night now, or at least twilight, and the vision died in his mind, and his body seemed to grow into one large eye and look down upon a carcass that was his own, decaying steadily beside a coffin. I am the resurrection and the life, he thought, and worms will never touch me here.

It was lighter now in the hearse. He must have slept. Then he remembered why he was here. Then the first bomb fell down the road while he lay in the quiet peaceful hearse with the waiting, soft countryside beyond, and then that swift, rushing reverberant sound came down upon heavy summer air. He felt the hearse slow, then lurch upon the first explosion. Then the soft silence closed down and the hearse which had halted moved again. Then the sound of the

231

second bomb came heavy and monstrous, stirring the curtains on the hearse. As he sat up the coffin beside him moved too. He could hear the silence outside, then the frightened snorts of the horses struggling in harness as if against the dying reverberation of the third bomb. He felt the curtains on the glass wall moved inward against his face as to a gigantic breath. He knelt on his hands and knees, feeling his head and guts were jogging now with the joggle of the hearse moving rapidly. While he knelt there, drooling faintly, the fourth bomb came.

He felt the hearse creak and crack. Perhaps it would hold together, he thought, because it had already been spent in age by creaking. But somebody was always getting killed in a war. He heard a groan again somewhere in the darkness. The Frenchman, nameless, like the others who had performed the same office, who had placed him in three other hearses alongside three other coffins, had told him not to move in case of a bombing attack. They'd make a corpse of you to protect themselves. With them, if you were a flier, it was better you get killed in a jam because if they helped you to escape you might even come back and bomb them later by mistake. Maybe you would. The French are so wise. They have learned how to live with war and the Germans unconfused by reality, perhaps even impervious to war. Too many wars. It was dim.

And the Queen pinned the medal. It was dim, a dim light now filled with the pattering sound of shrapnel falling on the roof of the hearse. The sound was cold, almost stealthy, scurrying like rain across the roof in whispers of minute sound as the reverberation of the flak guns in the woods died away up the still air. Faint light slanted along the bottom of the curtain; he watched lights flickering from shadow to shadow in the silence filled with the gusts of minute shrapnel fragments rattling across the roof.

'I want to get out of here,' he said, shaping his lips soundlessly in the dim light, but the queen ascending filled his mind again. He could see the flowing robes and glittering crown, and he thought of that round, pink Scottish face, bred of Highland faces in the damp green hills of Scotland, the face fused into the green valleys of England.

'McWhinney,' a voice said.

'McWhinney,' he heard his own voice repeat. He mused for a moment while the voice he did not recognize spoke again, and the lid of the coffin lifted and opened and let the body through. 'McWhinney,' it said. Yet the face had an astonishing and exasperating way of suddenly filling his mind with trivial bits of past information that had escaped his memory.

'You're lying,' McWhinney said staring at the face.

'Christ, I've been asleep,' the face said. 'When did you get in?'

'Lie still,' McWhinney said. 'That's all you have to do. They told me. Don't move. They'll get us through.'

'Don't believe those frogs,' said the face. 'This is the fifth hearse and second coffin I've travelled in. Where the hell you been?'

McWhinney groaned.

'I don't believe you,' he said and repeated it.

'All right. All right,' the face said testily. 'I won't argue. I'm just telling you.'

'Yes,' McWhinney agreed sourly. 'At least, it looks like you.' He lay still against the window, in a silence filled alternately by the sound of shrapnel bursts and the pattering of fragments upon the roof. He felt himself, body and soul, slanting downwards through blue tunnels, flickering with dying sunlight and then himself dissolving dimly upwards out of the tunnel mouth, resting at last upon windless cloud. All around the remote stars, and his body lay quietly on the moonlight dappled cloud, peaceful far above wavering echoes of gun fire.

I want to get out of here, he repeated, shaping the soundless words into the sound of shrapnel patterings, just me and the queen coming down out of the high heaven. When he opened his eyes and looked up at Norton sitting on the edge of the coffin, the fifth bomb fell.

Norton leapt down. He landed on top of McWhinney just as the coffin slid backwards and crashed through the plate glass and vanished, leaving the lid on the floor.

Norton got up and pulled at McWhinney's arm as the hearse lurched and sloughed into the ditch. Then suddenly above the two men a voice in German shouted at them to halt.

They looked into the mustached face of a German sergeant. For a time the three men started at each other, perhaps only a fraction of a second. Then the sergeant made a peremptory gesture with his machine pistol and began to unsling it. Jerking McWhinney's shoulder, Norton vaulted through the shattered pane of glass.

The sergeant sprang back, trying to watch them and unsling his machine pistol at the same time. Norton plunged past him and onto the road, falling. As he turned and started to rise, the sergeant kicked him in the stomach. The sergeant kicked him again, striking at the face and throat. McWhinney knocked the sergeant down, where he lay on his back trying to bring his strap-slung pistol to bear. Then the sergeant freed the gun from his side and fired point-blank from his hip at McWhinney.

Norton sprang upon him before he could shoot again, trampling one hand. The sergeant screamed as the boot ground the bone in his wrist. His mustache twitched and his scream came out high like a woman. The sergeant was a big man, and McWhinney began to laugh. Then he stopped the screaming by holding the sergeant with both arms while Norton kicked his face in. McWhinney stood there drooling and spitting. Up the road lay two bodies of Frenchmen. Then McWhinney was in the woods. McWhinney did not remember getting there at all. He was on his hands and knees, vomiting savagely. Norton stood and watched. Light was coming through the trees.

31 WING COMMANDER RUSSELL

When the shadow of the tree lay down across my leg it was between nine and ten o'clock but I was not sure what day it was, Friday or Saturday, listening to the church bells, knowing they were telling the hour. Was it a week? Two weeks? Longer? I was not sure. The time had revealed to me only my own follies and that success is an illusion. Why had I ever wanted to be one of the upper-classes? What had made me believe that was the most important thing in life, to ride in a railroad carriage, speak with the right accent, to be an officer and a gentleman? Officer and gentleman, the graveyards of despair. How silly it seemed out here the past two weeks, grubbing for roots to eat, thinking that running hot water and hot food were the only important things in the world, or even clean sheets. And all my life chasing for a victory which is an illusion of fools, oh, to join the upper classes. I wanted to be one since I joined her father's company and she was part of being one, Jennifer, but she's better than that; she's human, but they're all bank accounts and saying the proper thing at the proper time so that everything is always proper and nobody must ever feel too much or show it because that would be a bad show. Spending all their thinking and breathing hours being ladies and gentlemen to make the wheels of finance and society go round. What a waste. God, if ever I get out of this I shall live in the woods, have a few children and teach them about the woods and how to feel how many beautiful things there are in the world other than being a proper gentleman.

The church bells were a mile away and I lay listening to them. Hearing them toll and echo. Each tolling of the bell struck the long chords back in time for me. The crap I used to breathe—be a success, be a gentleman, be a success, make money, be a success, be a gentleman. How did I ever dream there were things more important than sunlight, stars, water, trees, grass, earth, fresh, hot food, and the flesh of a woman? How did I ever come to believe otherwise? Now that it is all taken away, all the vainglory prestige of success, business success, ah, is there nothing more profoundly sacred and sincere than a successful business man?

Through the trees screening the road I heard the German trucks grinding up the road and Smiley breathing in sleep upon his bed of leaves: I got up and touched the bandage on his throat and his face was the boy-face of my younger brother, Harry, his bones rotting in the desert sun. The shadow of the tree fell across his face, and I knelt there listening. I had learned to tell almost blind which way a truck or car was going. Nobody dies in peace time;

they're just worn away by the clicking of the machinery piling up crap all around.

So as soon as the bells stopped tolling, I knew I had been wrong because the shadow had shifted. It was not ten o'clock. It was Sunday and I was two days behind myself.

If I hadn't had to think about what we should do next I would have looked up through the leafy branches of the trees, thinking whether I had fallen in love with Jennifer because she was rich or because she was Jennifer. But what is love but somebody filling a gap in another's image? Thinking it would be a good night for a raid if the weather stays clear like this. Is it raining in England? I said I love her because she's Jennifer, not because marrying her would make me a gentleman, mother, I said. Money makes gentlemen. Money and cunning, mother. If you make a million dollars and don't get on the Queen's honor's list after dedicating fifteen hospitals and contributing to ten of the Queen's charities, you ought to get your money back. Let my sons live in the woods. Burn down Eton.

Smiley lay on the bed of leaves, blinking his eyes against the sunlight, as though he'd just wakened.

'Are we going to move this morning?'
'Can you make it?'

He stared up at the sun. 'It's going to be hot.'

'I think we ought to move.' He was still looking up at the sun, his lips faintly open. 'I'll have to go slow. I can't stand falling down again. That doctor told me we should have stayed there and—' He slanted his head as if listening to the church bells.

'You'd better find a way round that town first,' he said. He turned on his side and looked off through the trees.

I got up and went to the toilet behind a tree, listening to him humming some tune I couldn't make out. He was sitting up when I came back pulling up my trousers.

'I think we better move out together.'

'Not till we're sure about that town. Go ahead. I'll be okay here.'

He lay back on the leaves. Sunlight flowed in checkered shadows over his face. His eyes closed. Then I heard the church bells again. I went along among the trees and knelt down in the bushes that screened me from the road and watched them going by in their trucks, the same ranks of coal scuttle helmets I had seen in the first world war history books rushing past in rigid seated rows, and the face on the last truck turned in profile like my brother's. Calling Jennifer my fortune's mother. Poor

240

boy, Jennifer said, if he's foolish enough to prefer the army to business for a career. In England you are ashamed of being a shop keeper. The highest level of success is to live off an unearned income. Now that's a real gentleman. Because not working is the only difference between us and not being gentle folk, father said.

He said it was machines that really invented the English gentleman, not the king nor the wars he made gentlemen out of. Father said being a gentleman was a little like death, only you still had a state of mind. And I said but what else is there to believe in in this country and he said, that's why England is such a sad country, the king won't give them anything else to believe in, and I said, she doesn't even have a title, it's her father's milord and he said that's even worse; you won't even be able to change her name because I can't give you any land that would give you a hyphen with her, and my brother said if he marries or doesn't he ought to go into the forces if he wants to look like a gentleman and I saw then what I wanted to be, wearing the king's uniform, only I didn't really see myself then, I saw only myself a gentleman, her officers we, and I said to father didn't you ever want to be something, somebody. Didn't you? Didn't you?

A rook shot through the trees and sat down in the road, dusting his feathers. The bells sounded again, and the rook slanted his head as if he were listening for the time of day. Then he jumped up into the air and vanished. Even after the bells sounded and were gone I thought I heard them. Because if it's only hell or heaven to look forward to we might as well get as much of this here as we can; if that's all they have to offer you after you've finished here. Get all you can of it now because heaven might leave you thirsty. If I had only seen myself then before I became what I was. It's not too late now because I no longer need those things to help me that I thought counted like money and religion and prestige and success. Those are only aids to fill in the illusions of our follies and shrunken souls.

I got up and went across the road. I walked down into the ditch and across a field of woods and entered another wood. The sound of the bells seemed to linger in the bright air. I went on. My bruised leg began to hurt. There was a church steeple beyond the woods. I came out of the trees onto a dirt road. It curved away from the town. I followed it for a mile. The steeple tip grew smaller. When the bells sounded again beyond sight of the steeple I went back. The road was empty all the way.

The shadow of the tree trunk no longer lay across his legs. I stood behind a tree, studying the length of the shadow.

Smiley said, 'Well, did you ... can we get round it?'

'With luck,' I said.

'You sure it's Sunday?'

'I'll find a bandage for you,' I said. 'And something to eat.'

'Let's eat,' he said. The tree shadow lengthened. We stepped out into the sunlight, watching our shadows moving ahead of us.

32   SERGEANT EDDIE REKER

The young French woman was bending over a large fireplace in which logs burned beneath two iron pots suspended from an iron rod thrust into the brick walls. She was stirring one pot with a German bayonet. She looked up at Jeanette, watching her with a cold gaze. Jeanette crossed the room and stood beside the girl.

'God help us,' Jeanette said. 'If this war goes another year, nobody will have a home.'

'Where have you come from?' the girl asked.

'Soisson.'

'Where did you meet the English?'

'He crashed outside our town.' Jeanette's pale skin glowed pinkly against the blaze. 'I'm going out of the country with him.'

'Out?' the girl said, frowning, watching her hands busy with the bayonet in the iron pot. She did not raise her head as she spoke.

'England,' said Jeanette. 'The underground sent me with him.'

The girl lifted her head. Her eyes were steady and cold. Her busy hands did not cease.

The older woman entered the room, carrying German army field tins and poured the boiling food into the tins, and left the room without speaking or looking at the two younger women.

'English,' said the girl. 'My brother thinks you are Communist spy.'

'Your brother wants to kill him for that?'

The girl stared at Jeanette.

'Why should he fear the Communists?' Jeanette asked. Her eyes blazed. 'Maybe you've lived out here alone too long.'

The young woman's wooden gaze was fixed on Jeanette's face. 'Communists,' she said. 'George says he is a Communist.'

Jeanette did not answer.

'Are you his lover, too?' the young woman asked.

'No.'

Jeanette blinked. 'Where did you steal the wine?'

'Ask George.'

'How long have you been here?'

'We were all born here,' said the young woman. She paused, studying Jeanette. Then: 'I suppose the English has a woman at home.' She lifted one of the iron pots off the fire.

Down the hall Sergeant Eddie Reker sat upon a broken machine gun barrel box, between the father and across from the two sons. Upon the floor sat bottles of wine.

'George says you were an officer,' the father said.

'Sergeant,' said Reker. He looked at the father. 'Does George hate the officers more than the Germans?'

'You are all murderers,' the father said.

'Just the officers,' Reker laughed, but the father nor the sons did not laugh, nor smile. 'Tell me about all the Germans you have killed?'

George lowered the bottle, spat on the floor between Reker's legs.

'George!' the father shouted.

Reker stared at George.

'You are stupid,' Reker said.

'English,' George said. 'You will never leave this country alive.'

'Fools,' Reker said to the father. 'I have nothing to hide from you. I'm not an officer. I am not a Communist. I am a Royal Air Force sergeant.'

'You were in bombers?' George said.

'I was.'

'What kind?'

'Halifax.'

The father shook his head, looked at Reker. 'Forget what he says. He was in the war. Now he thinks the Communists run it. He will not fight with them, but he likes war.'

'Wine,' said George.

'No thanks,' said Reker. He did not trust the wine.

'Drink,' said George, lifting the machine pistol that lay on the floor beside his leg.

Reker took the bottle and then his hand stopped moving. He was looking at the doorway. The young woman stood there now. Her mother stood beside her.

'My daughter,' said the father.

'Do you think she is pretty?' asked the brother.

'Come in,' said the father.

'No,' George said. His voice hissed.

'I am old, George,' the father said.

'The Communists will go away,' George said. 'The war will end and the men will return.'

'Who knows?' the father shrugged.

'No,' said the son. 'Not a German or English. No.'

The father rose and went to his daughter and took her hand. He spoke softly to the mother and daughter and they left. He looked down at Reker. 'Stay with us until the war is ended,' said the father.

That night in the room that was cold and dark save for the faint heat from the fading fire, George lay upon a straw pallet and thought of Reker. 'He carries a gun. I shall get it and—' Footsteps came along the hall. 'Father,' he called into the darkness. Then a hard hand caught his shoulder, rolled him on his back, snatched the gun beneath the pallet.

'Do not harm him,' said the father.

'They are not our friends.'

The boot struck George across the back, making no sound through the thick German great coat.

'Shut up,' the father said. 'Sleep.'

Outside in the moat where she had fallen, Jeanette lay against the wall, looking up at the sky. She tried to rise, one hand on the wall.

She listened, then after a long moment she crawled along the bottom of the ditch, looking up at the cold stars. She rose, stumbled, fell. She lay on her stomach. She tried to rise and fainted.

When she woke she heard them moving, voices, first Reker's, then the mother and the father.

'In here,' the father said. 'The back window.'

Reker and the father carried her. She lay in a blanket as on a stretcher between their arms.

Reker touched her forehead, her cheek. She pushed his hand away.

'Bandits,' she said. 'Murderers.'

He stroked her cheek. She turned her face away violently. 'They will kill us,' she said.

'Lift her up,' the father said.

'Easy,' said Reker. 'She must have climbed out the window in her sleep. It's only her ankle.'

'George,' the father called. A head emerged from the window. 'Take her up,' said the father. George drew in the blanketed figure, the two men supporting her shoulders.

'Go on,' the father said to the mother. The woman vanished into the darkness.

'You must stay at least until she is well,' the father said, looking at Reker.

'Of course.'

'There are no men left in the area,' said the father. 'My daughter is beautiful. She would make a good wife. Better than this one.'

'No,' said Reker. 'I must return to England.'

'Remember,' said the father, 'I have asked you.'

They went into the ruined castle. Jeanette lay on the stone floor. George stood in the doorway. Reker picked up Jeanette.

'Move, please,' said Reker to George.

'Let them pass,' said the father.

Reker found their room and put the woman down into the straw pile. Her ankle was swollen but not broken. He lay down beside her in the darkness and put his arms around her and held her close, covering her and himself with two old German great coats. 'If only there was something we could ride out of here. Even a cow,' he thought. He listened to her breathing as she slept. He lay there thinking of England, Joyce Mowbry. She seemed unreal, as if he had never been in England.

Then he heard a sound. He drew in his breath, touching the trigger guard of the gun against his chest. He slowly lifted his hand. His eyes were motionless in the dark, fixed upon the direction of the sound. He could make out the door by the rectangular shape of lesser darkness. Then as a figure moved against that rectangle of lesser darkness he said: 'Don't move!'

'No,' said the voice, the voice of

the mother, filled with urgency and desperation. Then she was crouched over them.

'George will kill you. He thinks England and Communists will ruin France.'

'Maybe he's right.'

'Don't you see,' the mother cried out with despair. 'They want you for her. To stay. Like the Baron was. They got all their ideas from him. Family, family. It's all they think. But more children for what? To die? They believe the castle is theirs now that the Baron is dead and his family is dead. They want you for her man. You must take her away with you.'

'I can't get her through.'

'Where are you going?'

'Marseilles.'

'Take us.'

'They may not let me go. What happened to the Baron?'

'The Germans killed him. They shelled the house.'

'Why?'

'He was of the underground. S-s-sh. George.'

'Where?'

'S-s-sh. There is a truck. I must go.'

She fled soundlessly. Reker held his breath, listening.

33 FLIGHT LIEUTENANT JACK GIFFORD

A small fire burned against cobble stone wall beneath the bridge. The wall was fungus grown and the light was fitful in the early twilight. The river clucked and gurgled over the stones.

The two men crouched against the wall, squatting with their backs against the damp stone.

The man named Rodgers said: 'We'll make Montlucon tonight.' He was dark and tall. He was French but his English was perfect. He wore dark trousers and a white shirt.

Gifford said: 'It's a garrison town, isn't it?'

'Don't worry.'

'I thought we were going to Lepuy. Candace said Lepuy.'

'She doesn't know this section.'

'Those were the instructions she received,' Gifford said.

'Don't worry.'

'If you go into a garrison town like Montlucon.'

'We'll stop at Bourges tonight.'

Rodgers moved, stirred the fire. His eyes were bloodshot.

'How long have you been doing this?' Gifford asked.

'What?' Rodgers asked. He turned with catlike indolence.

'The resistance.'

'Oh?' He turned back to the fire. 'A year.'

At dark, Rodgers put out the fire, and they rose.

Gifford followed Rodgers across a field. They walked slowly, tentatively, stopping now and then to listen. There was no light. The sky was dark, cloudy. Gifford felt a pulse in his head beating, almost as if it were a warning.

Suddenly the darkness burst into light. Rodgers turned to run. Gifford did not move. Bluish-white light blazed down on the two men. A rifle crashed. Rodgers halted.

He walked back to Gifford, squeezed Gifford's shoulder, and walked steadily toward the lights. There was no sound, no voices. They walked on, into the light, until a voice shouted to halt.

Out of the light came figures. Shirts and trousers. Maqui! Each man carried a rifle. They searched both men and as Rodgers spoke concerning identification a single voice laughed at them from the darkness.

A hand ran over Gifford's body, drew out the pistol. Another voice rang out from the darkness. A gun prodded him in the back and as he stepped forward, he felt a shocking blow against the back of his skull and his brain disintegrated in a whirl of sparks.

He woke sitting upright, his back against a tree trunk, his hands tied behind him. It was daylight. Fifty or more figures lay about fires, their heads covered in slumber, others smoking and talking. Gifford's head sagged with pain. He closed his eyes. His mouth tasted dry and copperish, salty with blood from the gash in his skull.

The sun was high when Gifford woke. A scream split his mind. His body heaved and his eyes opened. He stared up into Candace's face. But she did not see him. Her eyes were narrowed, the lids closed as a cat's eye closes, the slit of the eyeball shining, her face rapt with a kind of cold pleasure. Gifford blinked and gasped.

Upon the ground, spread-eagled, lay Rodgers, each leg and arm shackled to a stake.

Four men squatted, cross-legged beside Rodgers.

'Why were you not in Lyons on the twenty-third?' said the short, dark one.

'I told you,' said Rodgers.

'You lied,' said the second.

'Where is Adrienne?' said the first.

'I don't know,' said Rodgers.

'She did not come back from Lyons,' said the second.

'I followed instructions,' said Rodgers.

'He's lying,' said the first.

'Where is Nestor?' asked the second.

'He never contacted me,' said Rodgers.

'Liar!'

'Paul,' said Candace. She turned toward a tall, blond man. In his hand he carried a whip. 'Paul,' she said. She nodded her head.

Paul walked toward Rodgers. Rodgers screamed.

'I don't know! Please! I don't know!'

'Why was the Jedburgh team caught?' Candace said, her voice rising. 'How did the Gestapo trap the wireless operators in Lapalisse?'

Rodgers screamed and writhed against his shackles.

'Nestor?' she screamed, leaning above his writhing body. 'What happened to Nestor?'

She lifted her hand. The lash whistled down upon Rodgers legs. He twisted and writhed. The lash struck again and again into his legs. He cursed and screamed.

Ten minutes later he confessed and they shot him where he lay.

Gifford thought she had left, but an hour later she came to him and had one of the guards untie his wrists.

'You would have been shot long ago,' she said, 'if I did not believe you.'

'Who are you, really?' He was impressed by her power over the men.

'You wouldn't be the pay master?' he winked.

She laughed but did not answer. She must get the money from England, he thought, and handle the pay to the Maqui.

'Rodgers suspected we were using you as a decoy to find out to whom he betrayed Nestor,' she said. 'He wasn't taking you to the Gestapo agent or whoever he uses. He was going to turn you in for a reward. We had you followed and he must have suspected. He was to take you to Lepuy.'

'He wanted to go to Montlucon.'

'That would have been even quicker for you,' she smiled.

'I know.'

'All right,' she said. 'We will send you to Lepuy and when the time is right ... you will hide at Lepuy. We have a place for you. An apartment. Our man will take you. You are not to go out. It's a wireless hide out.'

'I thought—'

'Wait,' she said. 'We need an airman to trap Rodgers' contact in St. Fleur. When the time is right, you will get instructions. Where to go. It will be a cafe. We must reestablish Rodgers' contacts.'

'Are you the local pay master?' he asked.

She grinned.

'Wine?' she said.

34 FLYING OFFICER RODGER CALDWELL

A mile beyond the Insane Asylum they came out of the sewer, five men, stinking of human excrement, panting and running through the dark across the countryside. It had been hours of horror, the waiting in the asylum until all the locks were picked in the doors, and then down through the basement into the sewer only at the end of the sewer to have the sewer lid jam while they stood in the stench and fought the lid free.

But now they were out. Panting, Caldwell felt his chest ready to burst, and wanting to vomit, without being able to stop, he felt he could not run any farther. A voice pushed him forward and he stumbled on, his legs weakening, turning to water. At last somebody called for the party to stop. It was so dark. Caldwell could not see whether they were in meadow or woods, and then a branch scratched along his face, and around him the men fell sobbing down on the pine needles.

A voice said: 'We'll sleep here.' It was the voice of the man with one eye, Jacques.

Half past three. The stars sputtered

through the trees. Caldwell flattened himself against the ground. His body throbbed and already was stiffening. He wanted to curl up but felt he would snap when he wakened if he curled his body now. His hand, as if of its own office, slipped out along the ground and fingered a leaf. He knew the men did not trust him and yet he could not understand why they had taken him in on the plot to break out. They must have had a fix inside to get the keys to the doors. Somebody had been bribed. Suspicious. But he could see nothing behind their eyes in all the time he had been there, save the one time in the yard when he had tried to be friendly and they'd told him to move along, and then two days later they had come to him, telling him they believed his story that he was an English flier and they would take him out. Was it a test? But why? Surely, they could tell by his English he was neither French nor German.

The stars through the trees seemed to hum in his head. He stared at the round moon and the branches like huge eye lashes brushed across the gigantic white eye. His hand twisted the leaf, and in the fresh, bright odor of the leaf he smelled her hair again. Mary Alice, he thought, and for a second he was no longer in the woods. He was alone with the smell that reminded him of her, of days he had forgotten, sunny fading twilights in Curzon Street and beer and sandwiches in Sheperd's Market, smell of petrol in the air at Hyde Park Corner and her soft perfume beneath her hair in the darkness of her room and breakfast with the carpets clean and white, smelling of English sunlight.

The stars were blinking again. The men were sleeping. Mary! Her image ringed his mind. The moonlit sky yawned vast through the trees; the leafy branches hung motionless; loosen your collar, he thought, try to sleep.

Tomorrow ... tomorrow.

Morning came in a rolling cannonade of thunder and lightning and rain hissed rattling through the leaves. Along the edge of the woods the men walked despondently in single file. The sheets of rain like monstrous grey waves flung broken glimpses of trees and fields up ahead, and a sudden pennant of smoke from a factory chimney hovered then swung in the wind and vanished into waves of rain.

The smell of the trees in the rain wakened Caldwell's appetite to the point of pain, but he went on wearily, swaying in the wind like an old scarecrow. He felt utterly alone, as if he were at the end of an empty street.

The morning dragged on through the

fields and woods, dripping with rain, with a smell of undergrowth everywhere. Almost noon before they rested, stinking more than ever in their rain-soaked clothes, though the rain had ceased now. Their faces looked burnt-out, stubbled, and red-eyed. Caldwell's guts ached. He sat on his buttocks, bent over as if the motion might stop the hunger. A gust of rain shot through the trees again and leaves showered down in the wind upon their faces. The men rose silently, grateful for the rain only because it made tracking difficult for the Germans.

Rain hammered down through elms and oaks and beeches and at the end of many broken woods and fields a lonely woman turned from a cottage door and waved. But as they turned to her she shut the door.

Caldwell found his mind repeating meaningless sentences over and over again, almost as if he were in a dream, and looked only at his feet, watching them plod forward as if they were the mechanical feet of another image. And then the rain ceased and the light of the day brought the realization of afternoon to his consciousness. He smelled a hop field and for a fraction of an instant thought he was back in England. He stared ahead at the line of muddy feet that slogged on an endless path between trees. He thought of the field back in England, of the faces sitting now in the briefing room, lifted to the map, staring perhaps at the very area in which he walked. He felt his whole being reaching back across the skies to England, to his sister and Mary Alice, and he was moved by thoughts of standing with them, of touching gently their hands. He spat and laughed. He might never see them again. What kind of masquerade was this? Where were they going?

Evening. Along the wooded path, shrouding in the dying light appeared the faces of his crew, all so clearly through the trees, each with his different face and expression. Every tree he passed rose like the bare radio poles around the air fields in England, and in the pink and gold light dying beyond the darkening tree trunks the hour struck an echo in time as a clock chime beats into silence memory of the past and thoughts of days to come. 'Life is nothing,' he thought. 'Thirty years is no longer than a second.'

Then twilight coming again, the stars sprinkling through the sky, the earth's dark rim eating into the blood red circle of the sun.

The man ahead said: 'Look! The light!'

'Where?' the men cried.

'S-s-sh,' hissed the one-eyed man.

Suddenly the sun was gone and darkness blackened the forest. In a moment a torch threw up light among the leaves, and sleeping birds cried out and fled; the light probed, twisting among the leafy branches until it turned back upon itself and gave up the face behind the torch, gaunt and sun burned, a giant of a man, hard-faced and curly haired and a gun in. his hand ready to fire.

'Gus!' cried the one-eyed man.

'Jacques!'

Blackness and night, the darkness seemed to say, as their voices entangled in a welter of arms gripping hands and shoulders. Caldwell wiped his hand across his mouth and spat. Now he could run. But where? They were not watching him.

A hand curled about his arm. A cold, harsh voice said:

'We've got him, here Gus.'

35 SERGEANT
EDDIE REKER

Morning light, blue and cold, fell upon the plains; as the sun rose the plains seemed to lift into the rising light. But Reker still did not unbutton the great coat in which he had been sleeping.

'Don't go,' said the father.

'I must get back,' said Reker. 'You know that.'

'You will die.'

'But the girl?'

'She is not married to you?'

Reker did not answer.

The father said: 'The Baron is dead. The family is dead. After war we shall have the land.'

'I have to go.'

'I advise you. Do not.'

'Thank you. But I—' Already the father had left the room. Reker got up and went along the hall, peering into each room, searching. When he returned to his room the mother was there, looking down at Jeanette who was still sleeping.

'Take us with you,' the woman said. 'We will help you get through.'

Reker shook his head.

'Too many.'

The woman looked at Jeanette.

She spoke without taking her gaze from Jeanette.

'I can show you their trucks. They stole them from the Maqui.'

'How far do you think we can go in a truck?'

'At night many miles.'

'Where are the trucks?'

'Half a mile. Straight west. Tomorrow at dawn. We will wait for you.'

She turned and went out. Reker sat down beside Jeanette. It's our only chance, he thought.

Another dawn and in the darkness the two figures crouched in the moat again. The ruined castle loomed stark and huge against the waning moonlight.

There was no sound. The castle was dark. Reker put one arm under Jeanette's shoulder.

'You'll have to help me again,' she said.

He half carried her up the side of the moat. He looked back toward the castle. It was chilly in the dark air. Darkness and veils of fog swallowed the castle.

Against the darkness a jagged crest of trees lifted into the paling sky. They went on stumbling, waiting for the sun to show faintly. At last lilac colored the eastern sky. The fog began to burn away, though in the trees moisture still clung to the leaves. A figure shaped vaguely came at them, and Reker reached for his gun. The figure evolved into a woman.

'Hurry,' said the mother. She began to lead them, grasping his arm.

'How can you drive trucks out of here?' asked Jeanette.

'Shut up,' said the woman.

'Hurry. They'll've missed me.'

'Where's your daughter?'

'At the castle.'

'I'm not going,' said Jeanette.

'Shut up,' said the woman. She grasped the girl's wrist.

There was no path through the woods. The woman seemed to follow an invisible trail, winding in and out among the trees, dragging Jeanette.

The sound came across the air in rough jerky shapes, the coughing of engines.

'Oh, God,' said the woman. 'Their car. We can hide in the marshes.'

'I told you,' said Jeanette furiously. She flung the woman's hand away but the woman did not appear to notice it.

Reker drew out his gun.

He said: 'We can't move in this daylight.'

'Come on to the marshes,' said the woman. She sprang up and began to run. Reker plunged after her. He heard the first explosion and thought it was his own gun. When he heard the second explosion he saw the woman fling up her arms. Her body slammed into the bushes.

On a road to the right above the hollow in which he squatted he saw the woman's daughter come out of the woods. He watched her kneel beside the body of her mother. The girl screamed. She thought it was Jeanette, he heard himself say. The

German great coat fooled her. He heard a noise.

As Reker turned two men emerged from the woods, and he watched with quiet horror as Jeanette whirled, running. A branch struck her shoulders, then her hair; a blonde wig hung suspended suddenly from a branch. Reker watched her running toward him, her eyes round with horror. Then she turned and ran toward the men, screaming, her arms upraised. One of the men lifted a machine pistol. The muzzle stopped. Jeanette fell to her knees, her mouth gaped on a soundless wail. Her eyes seemed to widen slowly as the morning light shot down through the trees, and for an instant her eyes held an expression as if she had never seen such light before, and in the crash of gunfire Reker saw the edge of darkness still clinging to the trees behind her and the explosion tore the sky away and Reker could not feel the earth beneath his knees.

Then he was running. He could hear other feet running, and see the daughter, the elongation of the gun barrel in her hands. Her figure grew larger and he wondered if he were running or whether he were motionless and she was running toward him. He could feel nothing, save the hard butt of the gun in his fist.

His hand lifted and he aimed straight at

the girl. Without breaking stride, though it all happened in a fraction of a second, and seemed centuries long, he held the sight on her chest.

Not breathing even as he ran.

'Halt!'

Still not breathing, his arm rigid as steel, straight out in front of his face, he was running full tilt.

I can hit her now. Why hasn't she fired?

He saw the bullets hit her twice in the chest before she fell down. A thin wisp of smoke dissolved over his head as he raced past her body. The sky, the land wheeled as if it were coming at him through a piece of multi-colored glass.

He whirled in a blind-furious rage born of fright.

Kneeling he shot the first man coming out of the woods and heard the feet bunch skittering on the leaves of the second who was invisible but coming fast.

Reker crouched with his eyes half-closed.

The second man fired twice with a parabellum German pistol, and Reker thought, the son of a bitch can't shoot, watching him coming. He was a bigger man than the first.

Then the man fired the gun again and almost at once flung the gun at Reker and leapt. Reker heard the gun go off in his hand and saw the face of the man sailing down on him as if he had sprung from above out of a tree. Somewhere a cow lowed suddenly against the violet sky paling into sunny light.

Then Reker held the man's throat between his hands and was bumping the head against the tree.

'Stop! Stop!' the man screamed in French.

Reker caught the man's wrists.

'Please! Please!' the man screamed.

Reker knew he couldn't stop and he caught the throat again and slammed the head against the tree.

The man tried to break the hold on his throat. Then slowly at first, and then faster, everything emptied out of the man's eyes, and all of a sudden they looked like the eyes in a statue, blank and serene.

Reker caught the man's wrists and dropped him to the ground. He felt the blood surge in his head in terrifying accelerating beats.

'You son of a bitch,' Reker said aloud. The unseeing eyes stared up into the trees where the sun slanted and the birds called.

'You son of a bitch,' Reker said. He could hear his heart beating and beating against his chest. He began to run again. His body felt dead and cold.

French underground fighter found hanging from a light pole. That's what'll happen to me if I don't start scrounging around for food instead of copping looks at popsies' legs, I told myself. It scared me. It's the second time it's happened that Norton sent me into town in the evening to scrounge food. I start following a pair of legs down the street instead of knocking on a likely looking door to ask for food.

Here I was standing on a street corner looking at the girl's legs and I don't even know the name of the town. All of them have red knees and red calves, just like the girls back in England. I should come in when it's darker because then I couldn't see their legs and I wouldn't stop like this on street corners and stare at them. The trouble is, these little towns don't have any underground toilet stairways. That would be a good place to stand as they come back up above on the walk, because you could get a good look then, right up their legs, all the way. What town is this? And where are we going? Norton keeps telling me we're going to Lay—Lay—something, to a cafe, and we're going to ... I can't remember. These small towns aren't any good for ... Oh, oh, maybe I'm wrong, here comes one now, swinging that thing real fine.

I looked right at her breasts and she kept right on coming, holding her chin high, and her eyes straight ahead, but she knew I was looking at her, keeping her shoulders straight, and swinging that arse like it was iced cake frosting. Then she pulled her skirt down so it would be tighter over that little apple hard fanny when she passed me, and she knew what she was doing pulling that skirt down tighter, and pretending all the time nobody was looking at her, Miss Innocence.

I gave her my bold strip glance, like I was taking her clothes off with my eyes, right straight up, from ankle to ear lobe, and she came on pretending the street was empty. Jees. They're not fooling me, I know what they're doing, trying to put the old burn on a chap's crotch, so they can get their kicks, grinning to themselves like they know they're being watched. Look, but don't touch.

I followed this one, chestnut hair, and she went round the corner, and I tailed her about fifteen feet, watching that little arse swinging hard and tight, like she was trying to make me go cross-eyed before it got so dark I couldn't see it. This one wasn't scared. In the last town, I followed one little Frenchy for seven blocks and then she broke and ran.

If one of them yells, I'll have had it. Shot by the Huns for chasing French pussy. What a way to die. Man, man. Wizard. All this poon around stretching skirts, and nobody to take care of it except the Huns.

Her fanny wiggled a little like? Who am I thinking about? Why doesn't Norton come in and help ask for food? Oh, yes, he's got the gash on his face. Police might start asking questions. Yes, that's it. But one of these nights I'm going to walk up to one and ask her if she goes for poon, and if she's a Hun lover, she'll turn me in, and if she isn't, she'll take my hand and we'll go get some of that extra poon that's lying around this country going to waste with all the Frenchies in German prisons. Guessing which one is a virgin and which one isn't. You can always tell the married ones because their fannies have dropped flat from having kids. That's what's fun, trying to figure which one is cherry.

Then suddenly this young girl came along going the other way, and she looked at me, shaking her shoulders a little. I don't like them too young. They're liable to be amateur prick teasers who yell their heads off the first time you touch it. And they expect the world, like necking all night, without getting in. They want to be romanced without putting out. So I turned round and started following this young one. About sixteen or seventeen, I guessed. She was carrying a sack of potatoes. Maybe a peck. Cherry. Strictly. She wore rope soled shoes, some kind of a cotton looking dress. She was Frenchy which means she looked better than she really was because those babes all do something with their hair and clothes that makes them look clean and fresh, and she had a beautiful pair of legs. She stopped and looked in a shop window, and I wondered what she could be looking at because there wasn't much in their shop windows. So why did she stop? I stopped and looked in the window full of old ladies hats and I was standing about three feet from her and I looked straight at her reflection in the glass window. She pretended she didn't see me by turning her face slightly to the side. That's a laugh. She moved a little away, as if she were trying hard to see a hat in the far corner. Then I saw her eyes come back and she started to look at me so I pretended to look away, but just as she started to turn away I gave her a bold look again like my eyes were taking her clothes off right there on the street. She knew what I meant but she pretended she was looking at another hat, and then she turned away and started walking slowly up the street.

She scratched her fanny just as she turned the next corner. I felt funny watching her do that like she didn't know I was following. I thought maybe she was trying to put me off, then she turned another corner, and I started running because it was getting dark, and when I came around the corner she was gone. I could hear her running, but I couldn't see her. There was the sack of potatoes on the corner where she'd dropped it. So I misjudged her, but maybe we needed potatoes more than I need poon and now I wouldn't have to knock at any doors.

But on the way back out of town to the woods where Norton was hiding a girl came out of a house, and when I looked at her, straight in the eyes for a couple of seconds, she smiled, and walked swiftly down street, and I thought here's a sure thing, but at the next corner there was a big Hun all decked out in some Hun uniform, like you see on one of those Hitler Youth Posters, flaxen hair and high cheekbones, waiting for her with what looked like a bundle of goodies under his arm. So I cut out.

I got to the edge of town and felt washed out. Where were all the French prostitutes you hear so much about? Nothing but cherry and old maids on the streets. I used to think French girls were nymphs. But so far there aren't even any whores in France. At least, I haven't been solicited and I'm not a bad looking guy.

I want to find one who looks like—like—who? Who am I trying to remember? She had good legs.

But if I find one that looks like her what will I do about it? If I'm not careful I'll be showing it on the streets after dark. Court martialed by a Hun court for exposure in France. That would look nice on my record. But it might happen yet with all this good looking young poon running around, asking, just asking to be taken care of. I knew what they really wanted.

It's dark. I better get back to Norton with this grub.

37 FLIGHT LIEUTENANT JACK GIFFORD

Candace had briefed him well and he felt amused as he drove the pony cart along the highway toward the town of St. Fleur. Before outfitting him in the disguise he now wore, the clothes of a lady, black taffeta, with a first class blond wig, Candace had told him exactly what the problem was, how the underground organization was set up in different cells so that one cell could not communicate with the other cell without the correct pass word, and that the key men in the organization were mostly English. The cells were divided into radio communication, guides, and finance, which she headed. Intercommunication was sealed off by means of pass words, but somewhere along the line a double agent was revealing the cells, one at a time, and the man from England with the code name of Nestor, had never arrived at his rendezvous point after being parachuted according to schedule. The agent who was to meet Nestor at the cafe in St. Fleur claimed Nestor, the British agent, who was to take over the entire underground organization in the area, had never arrived. This agent who served as the contact in the cafe in St. Fleur was suspect as was the madame who operated the whore house a block away. Since Gifford could speak German they were sending him to the cafe to eavesdrop on anybody who might come in and speak in German or appear German and make contact with the suspected French underground agent whose job it had been to lead escapees to the cell which furnished guides either to Marseilles or Spain.

Riding along in the pony trap, Gifford felt a curious exhilaration, almost as if he were on a holiday. He passed a column of German troops marching in the opposite direction and waved at the men and winked at the officer, giving him a lascivious smile.

It was almost three hours to the town, and Gifford rattled along the highway in the high sunshine, enjoying himself. When he reached the town he parked the pony cart in the market place and walked to the cafe which was called the Fiocca. It was more a bistro than a cafe.

When the bartender saw Gifford come in the door the bartender looked up and then across the room to the far corner.

'Give me a glass of wine,' Gifford said in broken French, emphasizing his German accent. Gifford put the money on the wood and the bartender handed him a glass of wine.

'Where is the troop house?' Gifford asked.

The bartender did not answer. He just looked over Gifford's head and said, 'Wine?' to a man who had come in.

The man nodded. The bartender put out a bottle as if he knew the man well.

'Where's the troop house?' Gifford asked, hoping he looked like a proper whore.

'What?' said the man. He looked surprised, but only for a second. He wore a long dark turtle neck sweater and black cap and dark trousers. He looked Spanish. It was the man Gifford was looking for; he fitted the photograph Candace had shown him.

'The troop house,' Gifford repeated.

'It's full up,' said the man.

'They sent me from Holland,' Gifford said.

'You ought to know where it is then,' said the man.

'I don't want to work in a house.'

'You better go if they sent you.'

'I'll go,' said Gifford. He felt scared. He hoped the powder still covered his closely shaven beard. He shouldn't have talked so soon, but now he was positive this was the man.

It was dark when he came out onto the street. He followed Candace's instructions. He drove slowly out of town, one mile, past a factory, the third house on the right. He parked the pony cart in the yard, and knocked on the door. A tall, fair-haired man opened the door.

'I would like to buy some food for my pony,' said Gifford.

The man smiled. 'Come in.'

An hour later Gifford was informed he would have to make contact with the man he had met in the cafe. He was to wait at least a week and return and ask for guides to take him into Spain. If anything went wrong at the meeting, French underground members would be waiting in the street to help him; in case the contact was a double agent and brought the Gestapo with him to the cafe.

38   WING COMMANDER RUSSELL

The jingling of crickets softened in the darkness to a low murmuring sound. Russell lay in the top of a hay stack deep in sleep dreaming of Jennifer Caldwell. Now in his mind she lay naked in the sunlight and her breasts were fresh melons. He could taste their sweetness against his cottony dry mouth. Then looking down from her breasts he saw her stomach, a huge beautiful egg plant stuffed with chicken and her arms became long rows of dumplings covered with hot peas and as he kissed her mouth he tasted the fresh aroma of coffee, and then her whole body dissolved and he sat looking at an array of food upon a picnic table cloth: a lovely dish of corn beef and meal cakes and syrup and grouse smoking on a silver platter, surrounded by a bed of rice inlaid with freshly fried fish. His hunger mounted in the dream, and then as he reached for the smoking delicious grouse a scream tore his dream apart and he sat bolt upright in the darkness, hearing Smiley coughing and moaning, knowing by the sound that Smiley was bleeding again. It was dark, dark, dark under the hay. The farmer had hollowed them a resting place two days ago. Russell touched Smiley's hands. They were cold. Russell felt his heart drowning. Oh, God, don't let him die. I've brought him this far. From somewhere came the barking of dogs. Russell closed his eyes and a row of coffins slid past inside his head. A long row of dead faces from the squadron stared at him out of the open coffins, faces white as angels, the coffins ascending through the darkness of the dead. If only it were not night he would not bleed. Always at night Smiley started bleeding again. They shouldn't have moved so often. Maybe they should turn themselves in to the Germans. The wind outside was filled with the sound of death, and then the silence came and the silence seemed filled with the sound of death, an immense silence surrounding the hay stack.

Under the hay, deep in the darkness, the silence seemed to have an echo of its own, almost a substance, hushed, and then the darkness began to change, became a soft violent color, and pushing aside shocks of hay Russell stared out into the moist air that was green, the color of leaves, and against the side of the hay pile he heard the lappings of leafy boughs, stroking the hay, as if the tendril-like boughs were long fingers searching the hay, seeking something, seeking somebody, and suddenly the wind began to blow and the great green tree began to swell in the wind with the branches and leaves sailing back and forth.

Russell began to pray, listening to the moaning, gurgling sound of Smiley. Russell had not prayed in years. Not since he was a boy. He could not remember when he had prayed last. He knelt beside Smiley, praying, asking God not to let Smiley die. God, you mustn't let him die. He's just an ignorant boy. Why Smiley? What will it prove to the world if Smiley dies? You can stop it, God. You can save him. Don't let him choke to death on his own blood. Poor kid. He doesn't even know what the world and life are all about. He's never had a chance. Give him a chance, God. Give him a chance.

But Russell knew Smiley was dying, and he knew there was nothing he could do about it. He knew that he had been lying to himself for days, that Smiley had been slowly for days, just putting it off because he was a tough boy, but putting it off nonetheless.

Russell could hear Smiley breathing hard, deeper and faster, and he turned away, filled with terror, wanting to flee from the terror rising inside himself, a terror he had never known before, a terror that was tearing at his insides. He felt if he could get outside and run away from Smiley he could escape the terror that was small inside him now. A terror that was growing bigger each minute he stayed with Smiley. He began to curse Smiley, yet not moving as if he were bound by some invisible umbilical cord to Smiley's body. He wanted to twist and turn and run and he could not move. Why does he have to die with me? Why am I chosen to have him with me when he dies? A frenzy to escape seized Russell but his limbs remained numb, frozen. Then as Smiley's moaning stopped, and there was no longer any sound of his breathing, the frenzy and anger inside Russell slowly ebbed. He lay back shivering and cold. He felt ashamed for being so angry and frightened. God, but poor Smiley's death seemed so unjust. Smiley was nobody. But why have I become so attached to him? It was as if Smiley represented suddenly the whole human race in a single man. Yet it seemed futile to look upon him in this way, but to Russell at this moment the death of Smiley seemed an enormous error in the scheme of life. Better I were dead than Smiley, because he saw now that it was himself he was angry at, not

Smiley, and he saw himself as he had been all the days of his youthful life, arrogant and proud, with pride based on all the trapping of station and prestige which he had so greedily sought.

He felt Smiley's cold face and hands and in the silence there was no sound and he knew Smiley was dead. He opened the entrance in the hay stack and climbed out, and began walking across the fields, not knowing where he was going, nor how long he had been walking.

All his dead friends. He had never felt much about them during the war, had never felt he owed them any debt for being dead, for having died before he died, and all the lower classes on which he had looked down so arrogantly, all of them stupidly trusting to faith and their own irritating sense of endurance. But he had never felt anything about them because he had been too worried all his life thinking about himself.

Just a moment ago. Was Smiley really gone? With all the Smiley's of the world. Did he owe them anything? He saw now the anguish he had felt had been born in the shame he had stifled so long for not feeling deeply about others. He could no longer feel that way. He had been blind to the world before. He was no longer blind to life and the world. It meant caring about others, and not being bitter about one's self. He had rationalized his life too long.

But what can I do? He longed to fight. He felt a new rage. He must get out of this vacuum. Evil. He must do something against it, something for all the heedless years of his life.

He began to run. He looked up, seeking the North Star.

39 SERGEANT ROBERT CRAIG

His body ached from the dampness of the cellar. What day was it? How long had he been in here? They fed him three times a day, and would not answer when he asked if they had checked on him through the underground to London to determine his valid identity. There was only a cot to lie on. If only they would open a window for him, but apparently they were shuttered from the outside, and finally after—was it two days or three?—they had given him a single light bulb. God, he'd have rheumatism the rest of his life if he stayed in here any longer. Fetid and chill the wall emanated an odor of mould that was almost a substance upon the cellar air. He could hear footsteps overhead. Part of the time the house was silent and part of the time he could hear footsteps, sometimes a man came downstairs and removed one of the boxes stacked against the wall. What were they going to do with him?

He thought wistfully for a moment of the Germans. Perhaps he would have been safer in their hands.

He knew it must be nearly noon because he had a stomach ache again. It was the only way he could tell time, by the hours between meals. But was it lunch or dinner or breakfast? You couldn't tell by the food because it was always the same, bread, cheese, wine and some kind of sour gamey meat. If he hadn't been angry most of the time he knew his sense of defeat would have overwhelmed him. He was furious that if these were underground people why shouldn't they trust him? He hated them suddenly more than the Germans.

He paced back and forth in the room. He opened one window and tried as he had tried over and over again, to open one of the shutters, but it would not budge. It was barred from the outside.

He kicked one of the crates, and hurting his toe, he kicked it again furiously. One board cracked and he kicked at the cracked board. Something caught his eye and he knelt and pulled at the cracked board, drawing it away from the case.

Something fell out on the floor. It was a

small cardboard box. He opened it. Inside were detonators. He reached in through the hole and drew out another box. It also contained detonators. He searched again inside and felt a larger box and drew it out. It contained cord for fuses.

The wooden crate stood at the bottom of the pile so he lay on his stomach and stuck his hand up inside again and searched as far as his shoulder would permit. He stopped and listened, thinking he could hear footsteps. No sound. He rose and kicked the crate hard and tore at the boards. Boxes of all sizes tumbled out.

He opened one of the large boxes. Inside lay a square of what looked like clay, molding clay. He kneaded it in his hand. He saw what it was. He hadn't worked in the mines for nothing. Gelignite.

Hell, it would take only a small particle to blow out the wall. Provided he didn't blow himself out with it. But how much was enough? He wasn't sure. He had only seen this stuff a couple of times in his life, but he had never seen a charge laid.

He would have to guess and take a chance. Christ, he could blow himself to bits if the charge were wrong. Or maybe just blow himself half way across the lawn. He was damned if he was going to stay in here any longer. He shivered and his guts coiled in a cold hard ball. No, I mustn't think about killing myself. Just guess and take a chance. Don't think about blowing myself up. Sure. Just don't think about it. Just go ahead and blow yourself up. Sure.

He fixed a detonator to a length of fuse. He squeezed a lump of gelignite. It was a lump as big as his fist. He flattened the clay-like explosive against the base of one window and inserted a detonator into it. God, he wondered if the explosion would set off all the rest of the explosives in the boxes. In that case he'd be blown straight back to England. But the only thing to do was to take a chance.

He lit the fuse with his cigarette lighter and rushed back across the basement and where the wall turned into a coal bin he crouched. No sound. Was the fuse lit? He began to count.

Suddenly he felt himself sucked into a roar filled with yellow light and bluish heat. His body and mind seemed to dissolve in a single powerful blow and he felt himself falling down into darkness.

Just as quickly his eyes opened on light. He felt sick and he vomited. Smoke filled the basement. He felt his way toward the square of light in the wavering smoke. The window was gone. Brick shards jammed the floor. He climbed over the pile of bricks and out through the jagged hole torn in the wall.

He staggered and fell against a tree. Somewhere a voice shouted. He ran, staggering across a vast lawn. He looked back. Smoke poured from windows of the house. He ran, choking and panting. He could never get away in this country.

He passed a barrel. No, it had wheels on it. He turned back, saw what it was. One of those barrels on wheels used to carry wine so that it could be dispensed from the street. He looked at the round cover.

He pulled at the handle which came free like a huge plug. He looked inside. The barrel was empty. He climbed inside. He crouched down, his knees jack-knifed against his chest. Holding the cover reversed with the handle inside, he drew the cover shut, pulling hard.

If nobody noticed the cover lacked a handle he was safe.

Suddenly he passed out. He woke sweating, his head throbbing. From somewhere came the sound of men's voices. The voices came closer, ceased, then suddenly were quite loud and he realized several men were standing a few feet away. He felt the cask move faintly. Somebody was leaning against it. He held his breath. After a long while he heard the voices diminish.

He began to long for water. His tongue thickened. He licked it dry, trying to suck saliva into his mouth. His mouth cottoned and his tongue grew sour and sore. Through a single minute crack in the cover he could see it was light out.

He lay sweating and almost suffocating while the crack darkened and outside there was only silence.

He felt for the handle and pushed. Night air drenched him cool as water. He crawled out into a pitch black night. He must find water. He felt his way through low brush.

Branches struck at his face. Fifteen minutes later he was deep in woods. Neither moon nor stars. He was completely lost. He went on. He walked until the moon rose, dreaming of water.

He was walking in a trance when he stepped off what he thought was a ridge.

The next instant he knew where he was. He'd fallen into a river. He felt as if his skull had cracked open when he hit the cold water.

40   SERGEANT
JACK MCWHINNEY

McWhinney was walking along the road when he saw the first body. It lay in the grass on the side of the ditch. The man lay face down, his head covered with blood. There was blood on his back and holes in his back. There were flies circling his head.

McWhinney wandered off the road and

over to the body. Then he saw the others. There were a couple piles of dead bodies and more lying face down in the high grass about fifty yards off the road. Around them lay rifles and some grenades.

He stared at one dead man who lay on his face. His face was swollen. At first he could not understand who they were. Then it came to him slowly. Free French, and they had all been killed by rifle or machine gun fire. There were no shell holes. There was no one in the woods except the dead.

Jack McWhinney had seen no one since he had become separated from Norton. He had walked along roads, through woods and across fields. Now he walked through the woods, thinking he might meet some people who had survived this fight. He came out of the woods into a huge circular meadow, surrounded by trees on all sides. This was all he could see.

He walked on across the meadow toward the woods. Suddenly somebody challenged him. He stopped and from behind a tree stepped a young Spanish-looking man with grenades on his belt and a bandolier of rifle ammunition slung across his chest. His eyes were yellow as if he were suffering from jaundice. He pointed a sub-machine gun at McWhinney.

'Who are you?' he asked in an American voice.

McWhinney started to explain.

'Prove it.'

McWhinney showed him a silver identification bracelet he wore on his wrist. It
bore the imprint of his name. The man
began to jerk the bracelet off McWhinney's
wrist.

'Hey!'

'Take it off.'

'I won't.'

'Take it off before I shoot you.'

McWhinney took it off.

'If you don't believe me,' he said. Then:
'Who the hell are you?'

'I'll ask the questions.'

'Have you a wireless?' asked McWhinney.

'None of your business.'

'Who's in command?' McWhinney asked.
Everything was a blank. He could recall
bailing out, but he could not remember
how he got here. He knew he had been
shot down but he could not remember
what had happened after that.

'You'll find out soon enough,' said the
man with the American voice.

'I—' McWhinney began and the man
jammed the muzzle of the machine gun
in McWhinney's stomach.

'Turn around. Start walking. One move
and you're dead.'

The sound of the man's voice frightened

McWhinney. It was the voice of a scared, tired and nervous man. He didn't like the way the man waved the sub-machine gun around.

'Listen,' said McWhinney. 'All I want is something to eat and drink. Take that gun out of my back.'

'I ought to shoot you,' said the other. 'The damn country is full of spies.'

'Come on,' said McWhinney. 'Let me talk to your commanding officer.' He was beginning to feel scared around this man.

A major, very British looking, tall and lean, in British battle dress, came out of the wheelless bus lodged in mud alongside the farm house that apparently served as brigade headquarters. McWhinney saluted him and the major returned the salute.

'Well,' said the major, 'we have no way of checking your story now. Jerry is trying to infiltrate us all the time. It's rather bollocked up for you. Where were you shot down?'

'That's the trouble. I can't remember.'

'Name's McWhinney, you say. Hmm.'

'Bloody black out. Can't I get out of here?'

'We'll have to check you.'

'How long?'

'I can't tell.'

'I should have turned up with a pocket

full of Cadbury. Maybe you'd believe me then.'

'Would you like a drink?'

'No. Just something to eat now.'

'You'll have to stay here. What do you mean you can't remember?'

'I'm crazy, I guess.'

'Come inside and lie down. You look done in,' said the major.

McWhinney went inside the bus and lay down on a cot. He wondered if they saw him as he felt they must see him. He felt like crying. Maybe he should take some liquor, whatever they had. No, that would only make him forget even that he was here. He couldn't drink anymore. He knew that. It frightened him to think about it because now it was all clear. He had lost part of his mind back in England and nobody would ever give that part back to him again and nobody believed that part of his head was gone. They all thought he was putting them on. If only he could get back to England maybe he could remember what had happened to him since he had been shot down because now everything was clear in his head about what had happened to him in England. But suddenly he had the feeling he was in England and if he got up and went outside he would be back at the squadron and then suddenly as he thought this everything ran together in his head and he lay back confused again, and he lay there trying to insist to himself where he was. He got up and looked outside. There was a guard on the door and now he knew for sure where he was again. He lay down again.

What frightened him more than anything was not remembering the way he had been in England but the fact that he couldn't remember getting here except for that moment when he had jumped out of the plane. That part he could remember.

The door opened and a man came in carrying a bottle of wine and a plate of food. The man muttered something in French and went out. Suddenly McWhinney did not feel hungry. He drank some wine and lay back and wanted to sleep but felt frightened of sleeping, fearful he would wake having forgotten the past few minutes. He sat up and ate the food.

The major, accompanied by Norton, opened the door and came in.

'Yes,' said Norton. 'That's him. Hello.'

'Norton,' said McWhinney and stood up. He felt himself grinning. 'Where have you been?'

'Looking for you.'

He was going to ask Norton how long he'd been here and then he thought better and said nothing.

'McWhinney,' Norton said. 'We've got

to get out of here. This outfit is getting the squeeze and they're moving out. We can't stay with them. The major's told me where we can contact the underground and maybe get to Marseilles or over the mountains to Spain.'

'I know the major thinks I'm silly,' said McWhinney, 'but I can't remember anything after we bailed out.'

Norton glanced at the major.

'You just wandered off one night,' said Norton. 'After we got out of the hearse. What a squeak.'

McWhinney shook his head. He rubbed his forehead. He felt the blankness coming again.

'Don't you remember?'

'Yes, yes,' said McWhinney. He tried to fight off the blankness taking hold of his mind.

'We'll take off tonight.'

'Sure,' said McWhinney. Oh, God, here he was slipping away from both of them. Here it was again, everything going away from his head.

'I've been here four days,' said Norton.

'How do you like?' McWhinney heard himself asking. There. He could feel his head thickening. There it was again.

Norton said something but McWhinney did not hear him.

'Yes,' he said. 'We better get out of

here. They'll kill us, if we don't. They killed a bunch of people down the road. They'll kill us, too. If you can get us out of here, we better go.'

'Where have you been?'

'All over the damn country, I guess.'

'Do you feel well enough to go?'

'Any time,' McWhinney said. 'I don't want to hang around this bloody place.'

'Take it easy. Have some more wine.'

'Sure.'

He lifted the bottle, dropped his head back and there on the ceiling he saw the back of the man's head with the flies buzzing around it.

'God,' he said. 'Let's get out of here.'

'I'll help you,' said Norton. 'Don't worry.'

'Where do we go?' He sat down on the edge of the bed.

'St. Fleur,' said Norton. 'The Fiocca Cafe. Isn't that right, major?'

'Yes,' said the major. 'You can make contact there.'

41 SERGEANT
EDDIE REKER

When the rain began late in the afternoon Reker found the small cave and crawled inside. He squatted in the mouth of the cave and stared out at the rain. He hadn't eaten in three days. He was getting faintly delirious and he thought that Wing Commander Russell had just called him out for another mission and he was waiting to hear what the target would be. For a long time he stared at the sky and told himself the mission would be scrubbed because the weather was socked in heavy. Can't make us take off in this stuff, Reker thought. Even if it's for Essen. Russell isn't so crazy about dying he'd make us go in this stuff, he thought.

The rain came in thin sheets and sometimes the thunder sounded like cannonading and sometimes the cannonading of German guns shelling resistance groups in the hills sounded like a rolling barrage of thunder. After a while Reker knew he had been delirious. He drank the rain water, holding his mouth open. His head stuck out in the rain. He knew the sounds he had heard were the sounds of heavy artillery.

I'm crazy, Reker thought, if I had any brains I'd find the Germans and give myself up. If the French had any sense they'd stay at home until the invasion and save themselves for the real fighting instead of letting the Germans kill them now. Bloody frogs.

He couldn't remember seeing the rain fall so fast and thick as this in England. He crouched back out of the entrance because the wind was blowing the rain into the cave now. It was green-looking outside the rain was so thick. He was aware now more than a second or two before that he had been a little delirious from hunger and thirst. He felt as if he had wakened from a short dream. He felt the beard on his face. My God, I haven't shaved in how long. He felt the water gurgling in his stomach.

Then the artillery fire increased and he listened intently. It sounded like tank fire but he couldn't be sure. I ought to give myself up, he thought. Twice in the past three days he had approached French families and they had told him to keep moving. They were afraid to help him.

After a moment he closed his eyes and felt his mind drift away again. He forgot where he was and how he had arrived here. He dreamed he was eating a cheese sandwich and drinking a cold glass of beer. What a sweet life, he thought, God, the beer was wonderful, cold and beaded. Nice to be here in London on leave. Just think. Ten great days. Nothing to do but sleep late in the morning and get up and sit in Berkeley Square and read the newspapers and go out to dinner and shows. He felt the need to urinate suddenly, and he squatted because the mouth of the cave was small and wet his boots. He sat back and closed his eyes and dreamed about smoking a cigarette. After a while he was sure he was actually smoking. He inhaled three or four times and blew out the smoke. He saw himself lighting another cigarette, taking deep drags. He lay there against the wall of the cave savoring three dream cigarettes.

Suddenly a noise wakened him. At first it seemed part of the dream, just as part of him was not dreaming, and then the part of his mind that was not dreaming told him to wake. The noise was high and when he looked out he saw the rain was gone and the moon was shining and it was dark outside. Then against the moon light he saw the high wing parasol monoplane coming in low, about two hundred feet. What the hell is that kite doing over here, he thought. He fumbled in his trousers for the German pistol he had stolen at the castle. He felt it in his hand.

He climbed out of the cave. The machine passed over him, banked and came back low as if looking for somebody or a landmark. It waggled its wings twice. He walked down from the cave through the trees to the meadow and watched the machine turn again and make another pass low at the meadow and while he was watching something fell out of the machine, then a parachute opened.

Reker saw the man swinging back and

forth holding to the shroud lines. Reker saw the figure land hard and spill the air out of the parachute and then unbuckle it and stand up. I'll find out who he is anyway, Reker thought. He drew out the pistol. Reker waved and yelled and ran toward the man.

The man saw Reker and put up his hands.

'All right,' said Reker, 'don't move.'

Then he saw it wasn't a man, but a woman, with short hair.

'Bloody hell,' he said. 'What the—'

'Stop waving the gun at me,' she said. 'Where are the rest?'

Reker didn't answer. He stared at her.

'Who are you?' she asked in English.

Reker explained and she laughed. Her hair was blonde. She was short. She wore slacks and a British army battle jacket.

'We better get out of here fast,' she said. 'They were supposed to meet me.'

'I wish I knew where I was,' said Reker.

'If he dropped me in the right place,' she said, 'we're about five miles from St. Fleur. There's a contact there.'

'Let's go. I'm starved.'

'Here's some chocolate,' she said, reaching inside her battle jacket. Then suddenly her voice was different and she was pointing a pistol at him. 'Drop it.' Her voice was harsh, quite cold.

'Really,' he began, but she only said, 'Hurry up. Drop the gun. Throw it over here.'

42 FLIGHT LIEUTENANT JACK GIFFORD

They sky showed blue outside the window. There was no sound in the house. Gifford had been inside for four days, sleeping most of the time and now he'd had enough sleep and he wanted out. But every time he talked to the old guy who owned the house about putting him in contact with the underground to move him out the old guy told him to take it easy and the time would come. But when? Gifford knew one thing though. He knew where they were going to take him. The name of the cafe. When the time was right. Fiocca. He knew that much because he'd been there before. But the waiting was killing him. Just sit on your ass day in and day out and look out the window.

'Hey, Papa, when do I move?'

'A couple days.'

'You already said that. What's the trouble?'

'All the roads are being watched.'

'Hell, if you say the guides are good, what're we waiting for?'

The old man smiled. The light began to fail in the window.

'The guide will come,' he said.

'Sure,' said Gifford. 'And I'll be a thousand years old.'

Then it was dark and time to sleep again. He climbed the stairs to the big bed. What the hell, the room was warm and the meals were good, what was the hurry. Am I out of my mind? Get back to England so I can get my ass shot off again. But he'd never been able to sit around like this. Too much time for thinking. Christ, action was the only thing. Otherwise what was a war about? He climbed the stairs, undressed in the dark.

43   WING COMMANDER RUSSELL

Russell had been watching a house now for two hours. It was a smallish dwelling, standing in what looked like large grounds. An old man walked about the lawn. When it was dark the old man went inside. Well, no children or young people to cope with here and it was far enough from the edge of town.

He felt in his pocket for the wood knife. He sat and watched the stars. It must have been past midnight when he moved. In the moonlight he climbed over the low railing surrounding the yard. He got in close to the wall and leaned against the house and listened. No sound. If there wasn't food here he would go crackers. He tested the windows and doors, keeping close to the house. He found the top of the kitchen window opened outward. He climbed up on a wooden box and reached down inside and slipped the catch on the main section of the window.

He crawled inside into a thicker darkness. He felt around. He touched a chair. No. Not a chair. It was an old style toilet. He felt along the surface of the stone wall.

He felt the floor. Also stone. He crawled along on the stone floor in a narrow hall. A clock ticked somewhere. Moonlight shone on a fireplace. Russell picked up the poker beside the fireplace.

He felt a desk and opened the drawers. Inside he found four cigarettes which he put in his pocket. He went on along the passage and found himself in the pantry, then the kitchen.

He opened a cupboard, smelled cold meat and potatoes. He ate squatting on the floor. He took off his boots.

He decided to find some clothes. He couldn't travel during the day in his uniform. The trouble was to get trousers meant going upstairs. He went back along the hall and listened. The house was silent. He tiptoed up the stairs, feeling along the wall. At the head of the stairs his hand touched a door knob.

Suddenly he felt panicky. He turned to go and then he found himself thinking, if you're ever going to get out of France without starving, you're going to have to travel by day, and you better get trousers if you're going to move in daylight, and where there are trousers there's bound to be a jacket and cap.

He turned the door knob softly. The door creaked. He pushed it open. He stepped in swiftly and flattened himself against the wall. He gripped the poker tightly. From somewhere came the sound of breathing in the darkness. Russell felt sweat running down his back and arms.

He stood and blinked his eyes, squinting into the darkness. Then he saw what was apparently the wardrobe. The door opened easily. Then suddenly the door made a strange sound. It sounded like an animal. The poker fell from his hand.

He knelt, feeling for the poker, and something shaped of darkness and a roaring human voice leaped upon him. He struck at the invisible figure with the poker. The man roared with pain and rage. He flung himself on Russell and they fell.

Russell felt fingers clutching his throat. He

stiffened his neck muscles and reached back and grasped the man's thumbs. He jerked the thumbs upwards and the man screamed and fell backward.

Russell slammed his knee into the man's stomach. Light burst into the room. An old man stood framed in the doorway. He pointed a pistol at Russell and shouted in French. Suddenly light flooded the room.

Russell backed against the wall, raising his arms, watching the gun. Standing there, his gaze caught sight of the figure on the floor. For God's sake! Gifford! He stared, tongue-tied.

Book Five
RENDEZVOUS

44   WING COMMANDER
RUSSELL

'She doesn't love you and never has, Jack,' I said. Gifford sat on the broken chair with his back against the wall, slanting his head a little, wooden-faced. His long uncut hair drooped down in bangs over one eye. He sat squinting out of the other eye, past his bangs, looking out across the roofs of the town to where the hills cut off the other half of the town.

'Are you listening?' I said. High overhead, against the pale blue sky, they passed in fading blasts of sound. We could not even see them and if we could they would only be specks, heading toward Calais.

'She's engaged to me,' I said.

'Screw you, buddy,' he said. 'Screw you.'

I could not make him see that he was wrong, that even if Jennifer had kissed him, she still loved me first. His idea of love is all sex. He will never understand.

Snoring, the German machines sped past, the clouds hanging high and white and motionless.

Wooden-faced, he rose and went to the window and looked down into the street, brushing the hair back out of his eyes. He could see where the street ended and the other street bisected it, turning, and a mile beyond was the cafe. Coming back from the window, shaking his head.

'Screw you, buddy,' he said. 'Maybe you're not going until you get the word from downstairs.'

'You can't go yet,' I said.

'I can go any time I please,' he said. 'And if there's a contact in that cafe to get me out of France, I'll find it.'

McWhinney squatted in the field, sitting on his ass, like he was nailed to the ground. His face was whitish grey. He lifted his lip like a hurt sick child.

'No,' he said. 'I won't. Not matter what the frog says I won't go near a frog's house.'

'Jack,' I said. 'It's our only hope. There are two others there. He told me.'

'He's lying,' McWhinney said.

'It's our only chance. We'd better go.'

He rolled over on his side and stared at the trees, leaning on one elbow. For an instant I resisted kicking him in the ass, and then I thought why not just leave him, and then: no, we've come this far, maybe we can go all the way, and the shape he's in the German wouldn't bother but to kill him.

'It's a place where they keep fliers before they get them out of the country,' I said.

'Don't believe any of those bloody frogs,' McWhinney whined. He curled a blade of grass between his teeth.

I sat down beside him and he wouldn't look at me until I brought my face around in front of his face and then he raised his eyes.

'Go on,' he said. He looked away.

'Come on, Jack,' I said in a pleading

voice as one might use with a child. He didn't move.

I stood up carefully and dusted my clothes. I made slowly as if to move away, just turning my foot one way to see if he was watching me.

'Wait, Bert,' he said. But I wasn't going to wait. He almost moved for a second, then the complete despair seemed to seize him again and he rolled onto one side like a weary man seeking sleep. I turned and walked behind him. He did not move.

'Goddamn you,' I said. 'I brought you this far.'

I kicked him in the ass. His face jumped red with fury.

'Goddamn you,' I said. 'Get on your feet.'

SERGEANT EDDIE REKER

The parachutist said we must go into town, but not to the cafe. There is another place. I didn't like the way she said it. But her face began to shine when she talked about getting into the town.

A man and woman coming down the road, looked as if they wanted to pass us and yet pretended they didn't see us because they kept looking straight ahead as we approached. Then they looked down, faintly hang-dog.

'Hello,' the girl said in English. I wondered if they couldn't see by her slacks that she looked pretty expensive for that part of the country. The man and woman did not stop.

'Hey!' the girl said in English and pulled a pistol on them and pointed it straight at the man. Her eyes looked like glass and they either understood English or the sight of the gun told them about stopping in whatever language they knew.

'Stand there,' she said to the woman. Then to the man, 'Come here.' He didn't move. 'You,' she said.

She was like a man. Cute. But a man.

'We're walking home,' the woman said humbly. She was middle aged with a black scow of a hat and an old-fashioned black dress. Her English was quite broken.

'Ask if there are a lot of troops in town,' I said.

The man was small, with eyes like a fish.

'Shut up,' the girl said.

'Ask them,' I said.

She didn't appear to be listening.

'Do you know the Fontaines?' the girl asked.

The man and woman nodded. The girl asked their names.

They talked rapidly, blurting out their names. The girl waved the gun at them and said something in French about the Fontaines. Both the man and woman nodded. Their faces were pale, down looking.

The girl asked them the same question again about the Fontaines, then said something rapidly in a threatening voice and waved them on with the pistol. The man and woman scurried down the road like scared chickens.

The girl put the pistol inside her tunic. She stuck it in her belt. She brushed the tip of her nose with her finger tip. Her lips curved in a secret smile. 'Piece of cake,' she murmured. She adjusted the pistol in her belt. She pulled down her blouse.

I looked over my shoulder at the man and woman scurrying down the road.

'Let's go. We're set,' the girl said, her face shining a little again.

SERGEANT ROBERT CRAIG

They had him against a tree, tied to the trunk when I told them who he was. A bunch of cut-throats, calling themselves French patriots.

'He's in my crew,' I said. One of the Frenchmen had one eye, and he kept wiggling the blind glazed one at me when I talked. 'His name's Caldwell,' I said.

They didn't say anything and the boy

who had pulled me out of the creek after I got a crack on the head looked at the one-eyed man like he had made a mistake.

I think they were looking for somebody to croak. And they were disappointed we weren't spies or double agents or something they could take out and shoot because they'd been locked up so long in jail, some of them, they needed a shooting to feel free again, but they knew they couldn't do it when I called Caldwell by name.

Caldwell looked all-in, washed-out, and later I found out he hadn't eaten in forty-eight hours because they figured to croak him, and not spoil any food on his guts that they could use.

He got up, when they took off the ropes. He stumbled wooden-back against the tree.

The one-eyed man that was the leader or acted like he was carried the German machine pistol cradled in one arm. His face was calm and sullen. But his eyes were alert and watchful.

I could see us in his eyes, both Caldwell and me.

He kept watching us like he didn't believe me, but almost did, and hated to do what he knew was right, holding that machine pistol like it was a baby he was going to nurse.

Caldwell looked suddenly as if he had waked from sleeping. His face took on an expression of intent and concern. He stared at the one-eyed man.

'I told you,' he said. 'I told you in prison.'

The one-eyed man set the machine pistol down against the tree, his back arching like a big dog when he bent over.

He sat down in the grass in front of Caldwell and told me to sit down. We sat cross-legged like a couple of Indians waiting for somebody to light a campfire between us.

The others stood silent behind him.

'I told you!' Caldwell said. He sounded rocky.

'Go on,' said the one-eyed man. 'Say it again. Then shut up.'

'How do we get out of here?' I said.

'Let him say it again. It's all he's said for three days. I want to hear it again. The English are never happy unless they hear themselves being right.'

'Just tell us how you want to get rid of us,' I said.

'You're going to St. Fleur. There's a house. The people will put you in contact with somebody who will take you south.'

'When?' said Caldwell.

'Tonight. If you're lucky.'

'God, I'm starved,' I said.

'We're all starved,' he said. 'Give them a drink.'

The bottle moved down between us; the soaring heat of alcohol bobbed for a second in our stomachs. The sadness and fatigue inside started to diminish and disappear.

FLIGHT SERGEANT REKER

It was just before sundown. The second day since we'd all been in the house, and all of us in the same room now.

'Who was that coming up the street?' Norton said.

'They live a couple of blocks from here,' said Gifford. 'You see them every day.' He was looking at the floor. 'Well,' he said. 'How do the rest of you feel about it?'

'No,' said Russell. 'We're going to wait.'

'How long you been here?' said Norton.

'That isn't the point,' said Russell. 'I'm in charge. Do you want me to make it an order?'

'Sure,' said Gifford. 'Make it an order.'

'Nobody leaves this house until I give the order,' said Russell. 'Fontaines will tell us when.'

'Hell,' said Gifford. 'How are they going to know when? They're scared to go to the Fiocca themselves.'

'Right,' said Craig. 'How are they going

311

to know if he's there if they don't go down and see.'

'What does he look like?' Caldwell said.

'You're not going to let these fools talk you into it,' said Russell. He looked at Caldwell but Caldwell was looking at the floor, too, with Gifford.

'Well, tell us,' I said. 'What does he look like?'

'I told you,' said Russell. 'All the Fontaines know is he's there some Thursdays.'

'How long since he's been there?' I said.

'Couple weeks,' said Russell, and he looked down like he didn't want to say what he'd said.

'Maybe he's dead,' said Norton.

'What the hell does he look like?' said Craig.

'Black hair. Black mustache. About thirty,' said Russell. 'That's all I know. The Fontaines didn't go last Thursday because he wasn't there the week before.'

'They're scared,' said Norton.

'We could rot here the rest of our lives,' I said. 'If there's no contact any more. If he's dead, we'll never get out of here.'

The light began to fail beyond the window. The vivid blue sky began to turn green, the color of glass.

'Let's vote,' said Gifford. 'If the Fontaines—'

'No,' said Russell. 'It's an order. We sit tight.'

'The hell with that noise,' said Gifford.

McWhinney's eyes looked like marbles.

'Can't I go, too?' he said. 'Can't I?'

'Shut up,' said Norton.

'Vote,' said Gifford.

'There are witnesses, remember,' said Russell. 'Deliberately flouting an order.'

'All those in favor of going down to the Fiocca?' said Gifford. He looked round at the faces. Norton, Caldwell, Craig. They had their hands raised. McWhinney stared at the wall with his marble eyes.

Gifford looked at Russell.

'That makes it,' said Gifford. 'Are we going to sit here?'

Russell did not answer. He put his jaw between his hands and leaned his elbows on his knees and looked at the wall.

Gifford turned to the rest of us.

'Okay,' he said. 'Now listen. We know this much. The location of the cafe. This guy who is the contact who hasn't shown up for three weeks is the guy who can get us out of France. Down to Marseilles. The Fontaines say he has contacts there who can arrange a sub pick-up. I go in first. I sit down. We can trust the guy that runs the place. This much the Fontaines know.

The contact word is Frank if I have the right contact. You guys wait in the street. If anything goes wrong, bust up, and head back for the house.'

Gifford looked at his watch.

'One hour,' he said. 'It'll be dark.'

Russell lifted his head.

'I'll go in with you,' he said. I thought he was going to sigh, but he didn't. He just lifted his shoulders and went back to looking at the wall.

WING COMMANDER RUSSELL

We stood in the street. It was dark. The cobble stones shone in the moonlight. I thought of a pub, a rainy night, the door opening suddenly on the rain-glistened street. Glasgow. The streets here felt bright with emptiness.

We knelt on our knees at the corner of the building and looked up the empty dark moonlit street.

'Count three hundred,' said Gifford. 'If I don't come out, come in.'

He rose. I caught his wrist. He jerked it away but he didn't move.

It hadn't been any problem getting guns from the Fontaines. I think the Fontaines were scared, even happy we were going to get a look at the Fiocca. Which was why I felt we didn't belong there. If they were that frightened there was something wrong with the Fiocca.

'Count three hundred,' Gifford said. 'But slow. One thousand one. One thousand two.'

I watched him go up the street. Quite a lad. But I hated him. I tried not to. But I couldn't help it. It was as though I could hear the others breathing, though they were a block away.

If something went wrong, would I go in? Not just because the others would know I was there and saw it go wrong. No. All in the same trap. Couldn't kill him off like that. I felt one eye film with sweat and I rubbed it, and then I heard the first footstep.

They couldn't wait.

'What in bloody hell are you doing here?' I said to Norton, and without turning my head I could smell and hear others. They were kneeling behind him, single file.

'Has he gone?' one said. It sounded like Reker.

I didn't answer. Somewhere a train whistled. The moon slid between clouds and the cobble stones turned dark. I was counting.

'What?' said Norton.

'Shut up,' I said, thinking I must have counted out loud because I was thinking about things other than counting, so I must have forgotten about counting. 'One thousand ten,' I heard my mouth say, and shut my lips tight and stopped thinking about Gifford knowing it wasn't thinking going on inside me but jealousy and hate and half-thought out hope that something would happen to him inside the cafe.

Maybe he won't come back, I thought, and for a second forgot why I was counting, not even remembering I had promised to go in.

'We ought to go in with you,' Craig said. They were kneeling around me now in a kind of semi-circle.

McWhinney blubbered something and I could feel Norton shake his arm without turning my head to where they squatted in the darkness.

The moon came out and the cobble stones started shining again.

'Bloody hell,' said Craig. 'What's taking so long?'

Just then we heard boots coming along the cobble stones. It was too dark. The boots were coming from the other direction, coming out of the dark. They sounded like about five pairs of feet.

'Sh-h-h,' I said. 'Get back.' I pushed at Craig's chest. 'Back.'

I snapped off the safety catch on the gun.

FLIGHT LIEUTENANT GIFFORD

I opened the door of the Fiocca and stepped inside and reached into my pocket and drew out the franc note. There were ten tables. Only two tables were empty. I chose the one beside the wall. From there I could watch the door and see everybody in the room.

I sat down and by this time I had a good look at the faces. The one I was looking for, the Spanish face, the same face Candace had told me to meet, the same face the Fontaines said was the contact, was not there.

I ordered a glass of wine. I had the glass at my lips when the door opened. The man was wearing what the Fontaines had said he would wear, but it wasn't the Spaniard.

He was the right size, with black hair and black mustache. He caught the whole room, all the faces with a single practiced glance and came cross the room toward me.

I looked past him, and he sat at the next table. It wasn't until I heard him order that I knew he was a wrong number.

His accent was Frenchy, but beneath it was that guttural sound I had heard all my life in New Ulm, Minnesota. This wasn't a French man. His eyes were china-blue and the skin was drawn tight over his cheekbones.

When the light caught his hair as he took his cap off there was something funny about the shine of the black, and a second later I thought, it's dyed.

Somebody came through the door. It was a tall man. Almost all the people in the room, men, save for two women, were short, middle aged. This man was perhaps twenty-five. A finger touched his head as he saw the dark-haired man and he nodded and came over.

I finished my drink and started to leave. I was half-way across the room when I felt a signal had been given. I heard two chairs scrape together along the floor.

'Halt!' a voice shouted in German and I turned.

Both men were standing. The tall one had the pistol. He was pointing it at me. I stared back into the light, the blur of gaped faces.

'Hands up,' said the stocky dark man in English. 'Behind your head.'

I felt my fingers touch the back of my neck. The tall man's face got bigger and bigger. He walked across the room, the gun looking longer in his hand.

Then the shout of a voice and the crash of gunfire punctuated with screams. His face vanished, and I heard my name shouted.

FLYING OFFICER CALDWELL

Sitting there counting to himself out loud, I heard Russell go past two hundred and then he must have been counting to himself because there wasn't any sound. Just our breathing, all six of us, as if there were only one of us because that was what it sounded like, just one sustained breath of waiting, going in and out in all our lungs.

'Rodger,' he said. He must have stopped counting. He put his hand on my arm. I was kneeling beside him. 'You're going in with me. Cover me. I'll go in first.'

When I was a boy I first learned what it was like to be really scared physically at school when they made us box. Sick-scared, waiting to get hit, and then being hit and learning the sick-scared-waiting hurt more and was more frightening than the blow.

'Come on,' he said. So quickly I didn't even have time to be scared because we were running up the street, keeping close to the building. I was ten feet behind him and I could see the gun, swinging back in his hand as he ran, pumping both arms like a sprinter.

The fear came while I was running, after all that had happened, after all the times I had been shot at in the air, the fear came now worse than ever, almost unbearable, so unbearable I was too frightened to stop, thinking that if I stopped it would be beyond what anybody could bear.

Then it seemed that everything happened at once. We stopped running and breathing and being afraid all in a single fraction of a second that happened at the same time we were doing something while we seemed still to be running.

I saw Russell spring at the door, then the crash of gunfire rose, met me as I dived through the open door and ducked behind an overturned table. I was tugging at my pistol as I saw Russell fire three times at two men in the far corner. One of them vanished abruptly as if he had fallen through a trap door in the floor. Through the crash of gunfire a woman passed me shrieking.

I felt as if I were sitting outside time, and then suddenly back in time, surrounded by mask-like shrieking faces of men and women pouring out the door.

'Come on! Come on!' Gifford shouted. I felt his hand under my arm. 'Get up!'

I rose and saw a short man with a mustached face I had seen a fraction of a second before. He came ploughing through the overturned tables; in his hand a Luger.

Russell swung his arm and fired point blank into the mustache.

SERGEANT ROBERT CRAIG

Gifford had Mr Fontaine against the wall in the basement. He was holding him by the throat. Fontaine was a stocky man with iron grey hair, and the sad face of a street sweeper. He wasn't even crying, just staring out of those bluish grey eyes with despair and resignation written all over his face.

And then Gifford began to torture him again. It was the only thing to do. Gifford held him by the throat and twisted his right arm higher until Fontaine's face changed and he began to scream.

I wondered if his wife upstairs could hear him. I wondered what Eda was doing at this moment. I love you Eda I love Eda. Fontaine screamed again. Gifford's French was bad but good enough to keep asking the same question over and over did you set us up did you set us up and Fontaine's face shaking and turning purple no matter how high the arm was twisted.

'Look, Jack,' Caldwell said. 'He's telling the truth.'

Gifford turned, keeping Fontaine's head

pinned to the wall. God knows how we ever got back down that street from the Fiocca. All I can remember is running, and alone, and getting to the house in the dark, and the police sirens blowing.

'How do you know?' Gifford said, his eyes wild and red. 'The cafe,' said Caldwell.

'Don't be a fool,' said Gifford. 'Maybe they'll leave us here to draw more bait until those fools up north get word their unit is busted down here.'

The sad sound of sirens blew out across the darkness. Gifford began to choke Fontaine again. Caldwell sprang forward and caught his hands and dragged them away, and they stood there, face to face, their eyes a couple inches apart, shouting.

'They'll tear the town apart looking for us,' said Caldwell.

'Not the town. The countryside.'

Gifford began to question Fontaine again, but it wasn't any use. Fontaine's face was the color of chalk. His eyes were closed. He looked like something in a meat market gibbet, his neck loose in Gifford's grip, and his head lolling over Gifford's wrist, his body still upright against the wall.

Gifford held him there, looking straight ahead.

'Get him some water,' he said.

The next morning Russell and Gifford told Fontaine to go down town and find out if there was going to be a house to house search. We all sat in the kitchen and listened to Gifford talk to them. He told Fontaine if he betrayed us and brought back the Gestapo his wife would be shot before the Gestapo took us. Fontaine sat there like he was drugged, looking at his hands on his lap while Gifford talked. His wife looked dazed, as if not quite believing any of it had happened, sitting on the kitchen chair, her face blank and bovine. Looking like one of those French paintings of the peasant wife.

'I'll go part way with him,' said Russell. 'Get me a coat and cap,' he said to the wife.

Caldwell said: 'A cap won't make you look French.'

The wife mumbled something to Fontaine and he mumbled his mouth back.

Gifford looked at both of them with that look in his eyes that said he was figuring how right or wrong he had been about Fontaine and waiting as if he were listening for Fontaine to come clean and confess the whole business of betrayal.

'You shouldn't have shot him,' Gifford said.

'What the bloody hell,' Russell said.

Gifford didn't look at him. He went to the window and looked out at the street. We were all watching him. He looked out through the curtains at the empty street.

'Let's hope he wasn't Gestapo,' Gifford said.

'Are you crackers?' said Russell. 'He was going to shoot you.'

'Sure,' said Gifford but he didn't turn. I could see his breath moving the curtain as if an invisible finger was pushing the fabric slowly in and out.

'Don't go,' said Gifford. 'We'll wait in the woods out back. After he leaves. We can spot anybody coming back that way and take off if he tries to double on us.'

'I'm going,' said Russell. I could see the pistol in his belt. The woman handed him a cap and coat. He put them on.

Gifford laughed. But his eyes were hard.

'Good luck,' he said. 'You still look like a bloody Limey.'

WING COMMANDER RUSSELL

Fontaine walked up the street ahead of me, turning the corner, limping a little.

He carried an empty wicker covered jug for wine. As he turned the corner I saw his face, different now, calm and sullen, his body thrust forward like a dog going on alert. From the set of his neck and thrust of his shoulders I saw he was a different man that we had questioned in the house, almost as if he had changed personalities, and all the time he had been acting for us. So I didn't know whether it was intelligence and courage showing now or deception and cunning and perhaps all four things which he had hid from the Germans so long he hid it naturally from us. He turned the next corner and went halfway up the street. It was empty. He opened the door of the Fiocca and vanished inside. I turned round and up the street came Gifford, walking slowly.

'He's playing both ends against the middle,' Gifford said. 'Otherwise why is every resistance person I met so damn nervous about this town. Something's been going wrong for a long time and they haven't been able to run it. There's been a double agent in here a long time, and they don't know who.'

'He could turn us in now,' I said.

'A few fish when if he waits he can get a net full,' Gifford said.

The door of the cafe opened and Fontaine came out. He looked sick, more ill than when we twisted his arm. His face was ashen. He walked steadily toward us, without looking at us. As he passed his eyes were like marbles. His face looked funny around the nostrils.

SERGEANT REKER

'You have to,' Gifford said.

'The hell I do,' said Russell.

'Well, it was you, wasn't it?'

'It could have been any of us,' said Russell.

We were all back in the kitchen and Fontaine had brought in the news and it was bad.

'What'll they do to him?' Norton said.

'Depends,' said Caldwell. 'They could shoot him.'

Fontaine shook his head. He mumbled something in French. He looked bloody scared. His eyeballs were wet with sweat.

'What's the scare?' I asked.

'Fontaine thinks if Russell turns himself in they'll sweat Fontaine's name out of him and that means the chop for our host.'

'He and the old lady must be hot anyway. If they were going to get out they better get out with us,' said Craig.

'I'm not turning myself in,' said Russell. He didn't look angry. He was holding on, playing the senior officer, but he sounded defensive.

He opened his mouth to speak and his face sagged.

'Oh, all right,' he said. 'What difference does it make.'

He looked suddenly like a man at the end of his rope, but then just as suddenly he raised his face, and there was a change in his eyes, the resignation gone out of his face, and his eyes bright and flashing.

'No,' he said. 'I'm not going to die for twenty Frenchmen.'

'Who said anything about dying?'

Gifford had a gun in his hand and he was pointing it at Russell.

WING COMMANDER RUSSELL

The gun didn't frighten me. What frightened me was myself. I thought I had gotten over Jennifer, as the saying goes, but when I saw Gifford and thought of him going back and having her, taking her from me, I was my old self again, wanting all the phony things my old self had wanted, except she didn't seem part of those things, vainglory and money and power and prestige. Too sweet and gentle and genuine to be any part of that even if it were her world which had been a temporary state of my mind until these last weeks and which was now becoming a temporary state of mind again when I looked at the gun and thought about staying here to save the lives of twenty

Frenchmen hostaged to die if the British flier who shot the Gestapo agent isn't turned in or turns himself in in twenty-four hours. Or was it a story Fontaine has made up. No, I believed him, and I know why he is afraid. He does not wish to die. He wants to see the end of the war because he can smell it coming. And if I hadn't heard it from his lips outside the cafe I would believe only that Gifford thought it up. It isn't that I hate him anymore. It's only that I want Jennifer's love, and I could not have that hating him as I've hated him. You can't know love with jealousy eating you. But no one will be arbiter of my life after this war, nor now, not even England nor twenty hostages. I will not die for Freedom nor Brotherhood nor the good of my fellow man. I will live because I love and if some must die because I love they will have to die. No, I do not believe we are just accumulations of dust and the old dust simply fills up a new set of dolls. Nor did Christ die for me. This I cannot believe, either, and He will have to have done it for Himself and then if that's the way He wanted it I will believe Him. Yet what is my life against twenty lives, and how many babies, wives, husbands, how much blood can one bathe in? How much blood is needed? How many bits of ribbon? Suddenly I could feel for the first time in my life a profound calm.

'What about it?' Gifford said.

The gun barrel slanted at me.

'O.K.' I said. I opened the door and walked out up the street.

Book Six
THE RENDEZVOUS

45 SERGEANT ROBERT CRAIG

It is two days now since Russell walked out and gave himself up. Gifford and Caldwell sat on the two chairs set back from the window on the second floor and watched the street, day and night, while we laid awake, and Fontaine tried to figure out some way for all of us to get away because he knew he had to leave too. Gifford turned his head as I crossed the room now and picked up the bottle of wine and pulled the cork and drank.

'Where's Mrs. Fontaine?' Gifford said. I don't think I'll ever get used to wine. Rusty, all of it rusty compared to beer. You have to be born to drinking wine. You can't just take it up after drinking beer all your life. Not even champagne. Give me a cold ale any day.

Even warm it is better still. I used to go down to the pub with dad, waiting for him to take his turn at darts, so I could sip his pint when he wasn't looking. It was plain old mild and bitter, bloody strong then, lovely amber colored, and maybe sometime it would be Burton's dark ale. That's the best. Then I got my first job. I would go to the pub on Saturday night and order Burton's dark ale, listening to my old man telling me on my pay I better stick to mild and bitter wondering if I was going to have to wait as long for a woman as I had for my first beer.

Gifford's face looked different, his cheeks gaunt and his eyes red-rimmed every day, from not sleeping enough or it's the crummy wine the Fontaines gave us. Besides he had a beard, kind of a scrubby Van Dyke.

On the floor behind his chair lay his coat. It looked crude enough to have been woven by hand and cut without a pattern with sheep shears. Reker had gone to town with Mrs. Fontaine. For the funeral driver's suit. And she was to get a nun's habit.

I sat the bottle on the floor and licked the wine off my lips. The wind was blowing. Outside the trees were bending.

'In town with Norton?' I said. 'Don't you remember?'

'Yes. Yes,' said Gifford. 'Aren't they back yet?'

I walked down the hall and looked out the back window. Mrs. Fontaine and Norton were washing the big, black hearse. They were shining it up, black as patent leather. Mrs. Fontaine was washing the wheel spokes. Norton and Reker were fooling with the scrolled carving, all fat little angels and faces of Jesus and God, and clouds. Norton was washing and Reker was polishing the angels. They were joking about something. Reker was laughing.

Mrs. Fontaine shook her head and called to them. They worked faster. Reker moving his arm, jerking his head up and down with each stroke of the polishing cloth. With the angels and God and Jesus sweeping above them in a carved symmetry, Norton and Reker sure looked strange.

When the angels inlaid upon the black wood behind the driver's seat were washed and polished, Mrs. Fontaine got up where she knelt busy among the wheel spokes and stood back and inspected the work. First she shook her head and then she nodded at Norton and pointed at the big rectangle of glass that made one side wall of the hearse. It was spotted and dusty.

They nodded and waited until she had

circled to the other side of the hearse. She knelt behind the spokes and set to work again. I opened the window and Reker cursed the angels for being so dirty.

They began to scrub the window, their arms pumping furiously up and down. Soap and water ran down on some of the freshly polished tableaux of angels. Reker short, jumping up and down to reach the window top, fell on his ass.

'Hey,' Norton said, 'take it easy. If the horse doesn't make it to Marseilles, you're going to pull this baby.'

The horse, an old white nag, snorted where it was tethered to a tree. The window began to shine, the two men scrubbing rapidly with rags upon the glass. Carrying a bucket, Mrs. Fontaine rose and walked away from the hearse. From fifteen feet she remarked her handiwork as a painter might survey his canvas, cocking her head from one side to the other. Norton slung a rag into his bucket and walked over to her. Reker joined him. They squinted at the big black old-fashioned hearse.

'Bloody hell,' Reker said. 'If we can keep McWhinney from blabbing inside that coffin, we might make it all the way.'

They had two of us. I couldn't see the other man. They pushed us into a dirty room with dirty walls. A light struck my eyes. There were five German guards along the rear wall. At the table were two men in civilian clothes scrabbling around papers.

The door opened at the rear of the room and they brought in some more prisoners. About six, I think. They were all middle-aged men, dark-haired. The man in front of me, facing the table, had a scar like a scimitar along the back of his neck. He kept pulling his ear lobe.

They made us stand while they questioned us. I thought we were going to be first because we were brought in first. I felt immensely tired, a great sense of lassitude. I wanted to lie down and go to sleep. How often I have felt this way, sitting up in the cockpit, waiting for the green flare, just before take-off when one should feel so alert.

The guards marched the prisoners up to the table. Each man was asked his name and occupation. They asked a lot of questions, nothing to do with our party at the cafe, mostly about railroad sabotage and where were you on such and such a night at such and such a time.

The civilians were Gestapo. Neither

appeared to listen to the answers. They were writing while the prisoner was answering. They asked the man next to me if he were with the Resistance.

'Whose identification papers are these?' asked the man behind the table.

'Mine.'

'This is not your photograph.'

'It is.'

'You lie.'

The man's lips trembled.

'It's my brother's. We got them mixed up. I had nothing to do with the bridge.'

'Take him away,' said the man behind the table to the guard and the guard took the man out the door.

The man on the right lifted his face, looked at me.

'You are?'

'Wing Commander Gerald Russell.'

'Where did you get those clothes?'

'I found them in a field two weeks ago.'

The two men behind the table looked at each other.

'Did you shoot a man in the Fiocca Cafe?' the man on the left asked.

'When did I give myself up in the street?'

'You claim you are an Englishman?'

'Yes.'

'Liar.'

'Do you still plan to shoot hostages?' I asked.

The two men did not answer. They talked in low voices and began to write. Then one of them summoned the guards and the guards took me out through the door in the rear of the room. The man with the scar on his neck was standing in the hall.

'Who are they?' the scarred neck asked one of the guards.

The guards looked at him and laughed.

'Who?' one guard said.

'I've been picked up before,' said the scarred neck. 'But why are they writing?'

The guard smiled, drew a finger across his throat and smiled again. 'Come on,' he said. He prodded me with the rifle.

FLIGHT SERGEANT MCWHINNEY

Locking me in the room until they're ready to go, thinking I couldn't see what they were up to, shining and polishing the bloody rig. Where they figured they would put me. Where I won't open my mouth about what they have done to Russell and get all the Krauts on their backs. Thinking I don't know what they're going to say. Now Jack you just get inside and don't make any noise. I already told them to go to hell. I've done enough time in coffins crossing this country. I said bloody hell if you want a real corpse kill me but don't ask me to lie in that bloody casket all the way to Marseilles. I got to do some of the walking too. I'm bloody poorly enough not lying in a casket. Like I told Gifford, why can't we take turns being corpses because most of us look like walking death now and all we have to do is close eyes and our guts aren't big to look breathing.

And all of them looking at each other when I said that, like they'd already taken a vote when I was out of the room about who was going to be the corpse. Pasty-faced, more dead looking than me. I said if you expect me to practice looking dead all day and every day and just get me out at night and walk around who is going to take my place in the coffin after dark. I'm not going to be the only corpse in this bunch. I watched them turn the hearse round and polish the other side in the sunlight. Norton and Reker and that woman working like a couple bar swampers. And Gifford and Caldwell talking so fast I couldn't tell who was talking because they sounded like one voice coming and coming about what I had to do, and their bloody lips going faster and faster. All you have to do. All you have to do. All I have to do until the Krauts jump us and they run off and leave me stuck in the coffin. If I had had enough sense to make that stupid doctor believe me back in England and got myself taken off flying, I wouldn't be sitting in a frog house waiting for a two hundred mile lift in a coffin. What the bloody hell I have done to be the corpse and I could be sitting home in a pub and a pint and cheese and a job in a powder factor all cushy and no officers yammering bloody about what to do. What to do. What to do. What to do.

WING COMMANDER RUSSELL

They put us in the basement of a school. It was the town prison. I sat against the wall, holding myself warm against the drafts blowing through the room. It was light outside now and I had shivered for two days. There were two men with me. I couldn't remember their names but one spoke English and claimed to be English. I guess he was. Said he had been dropped into France. I wasn't certain. But it was better than being alone. The second day guards put a bench in the room. We slept on the floor, a blanket on the bottom and blanket on top. The other man was only a boy, about seventeen.

The man who claimed to be English and

who was named Harry said, 'Ruddy balls up. We've had it.'

'Yes,' I said. 'What's the boy in for?'

'Nothing really,' said Harry. 'Something about being a mile from a bridge when it blew up.'

I looked at the boy. He was sitting on the bench, resting his face on his hands with his elbows on his knees. He wasn't paying any attention to us.

Harry said: 'You know what they did with the last batch they picked up north of here two months ago? Took them out in the country in a truck and shot them in a field and then reported it as escaping prisoners.'

'Par for the Gestapo,' I said.

I hoped the boy couldn't understand English. He looked scared enough without being spooked completely.

'They have a lot of tricks to get rid of people,' Harry went on. 'Look at the draft in this room. Or they open the windows when you're asleep and give you pneumonia.'

'Well, they haven't started on us yet,' I said.

Through the window the eastern sky was turning violet and gold. Morning. Not far away.

Harry rubbed himself, first his arms, then his legs and stomach. 'Pound me on the back,' he said. 'I'm freezing.'

I pounded him on the back and then he pounded me and we asked the boy if he were cold, making signs, but the boy only stared at us a long time and then after many signs shook his head.

'Christ,' Harry said. 'Sit with your back against me.'

So we sat on the bench that way and it was better. Full morning light came into the room. About noon a priest came in with two guards. The guards stood in the door and he came into the room and the guards shut the door behind him.

'Russell?' he said and I nodded and then the priest spoke Harry's name and the boy's name. He was a big old man with a broken nose and a shock of black hair. He looked to me Polish. His English was not too bad.

'You've been sentenced,' he said. 'You're going to be shot.'

He spoke in French to the boy and the boy rose and began jabbering excitedly, clutching the priest's arms as if he expected the priest to tell him it wasn't true.

'He was only near the bridge,' said Harry.

The priest nodded but did not look away from the boy.

He asked the boy in French if he wanted

to say confession and then asked us if we were Catholic.

We shook our heads.

'When's the party?' Harry asked.

'Next week,' said the priest.

'It would be nice to know the date,' I said.

The priest did not answer. He raised his hand and made the sign of the cross, blessing each of us and left.

Harry said, 'We've had it.'

'Looks that way,' I said. 'They ought to let the boy go.'

SERGEANT REKER

Gifford came into the room and shut the door and we all turned and looked at him. He didn't appear to be looking at anybody.

'All set?' he said.

'Mrs. Fontaine get the nun's habit to fit?' I said. He didn't answer. 'Well?' I said. He looked at Caldwell. Craig started to relight his pipe. The match went out and the pipe did not smoke. He tapped the bowl on the back of his hand and let the dead black burned tobacco fall to the floor. Gifford stroked the side of his cheek slowly. He looked past me through the open window down into the street to the corner around which at any moment

340

troops could come. Mrs. Fontaine and her husband were watching him.

'We can't stay here another day,' Gifford said.

'Tell that to McWhinney,' I said. The cap Gifford wore had a tear across the back. He wore it raked, jauntily as if it might have been his officer's cap. I half expected to see the sides of the cap pulled down. He had come to the squadron wearing one of those operational boffin hats, faded, and he admitted that he had aged the cap two hours after he bought it in London at Moss Brothers by wearing it in a shower-bath in the Green Park Hotel. I wondered if he thought hats like that brought good luck. I had known enough dead fools with good luck charms around their necks.

'McWhinney will ride in the coffin,' Gifford said. 'Don't worry about it.'

Craig tapped the pipe bowl against the back of his hand. He wouldn't have tobacco for a long time again.

'If I have to make a real corpse out of him,' Gifford said. 'Don't worry. I won't have McWhinney walking the road with us. I haven't rehearsed him in that coffin three days for nothing.'

'Sure, but how we going to keep him in there once you get him in?' I said. Gifford still did not look at me. He went on looking out the window. Since he got the beat-up French looking clothes he looks like some kind of poorly dressed American gangster, a burglar or thug. His face had a mean look.

'You better make him come out of that room if we're going to get in gear today,' I said.

'He's a very sick boy,' Mrs. Fontaine said. She looked huge in the nun's habit. I wondered what order. She looked like St. Joseph but I wasn't sure.

'Better we left him here,' Craig said. 'We get stopped in road block and he stops playing dead we're dead.'

'He must go with us,' said Caldwell. 'There's no place to leave him here. They would pick him up and be on us in no time at all.'

Gifford looked at him. Caldwell's face and voice were calm, almost bland, and his eyes were still, more blue than I had ever noticed before. He stood up and for the first time I noticed how tall he was.

'Be quiet, all of you,' Gifford said. But he didn't even appear to hear his own voice. From the look on his face he appeared to be listening to something inside his head. An idea. A plan. Who could tell? He rubbed his cheek.

'All right,' he said. 'Let's go.'

FLIGHT SERGEANT NORTON

'I won't go. It won't work. If you—'

'Get up. Goddamn you, Jack, get up off that floor.'

'I'm telling you I rode four days in a coffin. You know that. I almost died. I won't if—'

'Get up. You cloth-eared baboon, get up!'

'If you think I can hold my breath that long in the dark again you—'

'Get up, or I'll shoot you!'

'I'll stay here and—'

'Get up, you bloody fool! I got you this far and you're going all the way. Get up!'

FLYING OFFICER CALDWELL

Gifford looked down at him. We were all looking down at him. Gifford's face was red and angry. His eyes were bright and hot. He lifted his lip, his voice cold and furious.

'Drag him downstairs if he won't walk!' he said.

He stopped and grabbed McWhinney's arm and heaved him so suddenly to his feet McWhinney started to fall as Gifford released him. I caught his arm. He began to fall. Craig caught his other arm and

McWhinney lay back, slanting between us, supported on our hands, heavy, bigger than we expected. Then we pushed him erect and again he fell backwards like a dead log, inert in our grasp. His face was chalkish white, his eyes closed. He looked dead, his lips pressed together. Then all of us rushed at him suddenly and heaved him to his feet. I could feel the breaths of everybody blowing hard.

We dragged him like a sack of potatoes across the floor, bumping his feet, and then picked him up at both ends, and down the stairs.

'Easy,' Norton said. 'Wait.' He paused and lifted McWhinney's shoulder higher. Gifford pulled at his boot.

'Hurry up,' he said, his voice harsh and low. 'Let's go.'

We carried him carefully down the steps. We tried to grasp his limbs through the thick rough garments, but our hands slipped, bumping his bottom along the steps. We gained the rear door and laid him on the kitchen floor. He did not move, nor open his eyes. Gifford opened the door.

'Wait a minute,' Norton said. 'He's heavier than he looks.' Norton panted.

'Come on,' Gifford said, grabbing and lifting McWhinney's ankle. 'Come on.'

'The sonofabitch can walk,' said Reker. 'Make him get up.'

'Pick him up,' Norton said. We grabbed his limbs and lifted him, spread eagled, a man on each limb, his bottom bumping along the grass.

Gifford began to dog trot. He moved faster, so that the limber body of Mc-Whinney distorted suddenly as if he were being stretched, one leg longer now than the other. He cried out as I tried to move faster to bring the limbs back in line, feeling his wrist slipping in my grasp.

'Hold up,' I said. But Gifford only moved faster. I began to run and Norton who was holding the other wrist broke into a trot. McWhinney felt lighter. He began to struggle and just as I was about to drop his wrist, Gifford dropped one foot and McWhinney seemed to hit the ground running and then we were all running and McWhinney was running and rubbing his wrists. The back end of the hearse was open and McWhinney seemed to run straight off the ground into the open entrance where the lidless coffin rested and beside it the lid against the glass wall, his face back turned for an instant just after he lifted it from looking down in the coffin.

'Christ,' he said. 'Don't I even get a pillow for my head.'

The second day I began to dislike the boy. He looked too scared. I hated being around anybody who looked that scared. He looked like an old man. He smelled of urine. He had wet his pants and didn't know it. The thought of feeling sorry for him seemed to horrify me. His skin was a dirty white and he seemed unable to speak. He had not spoken for two days. Even his hands were a dirty white color. He sat there staring at the ground with big open eyes. Harry put his arm around the boy's shoulders and the boy jerked away.

The boy began to blubber.

Perhaps we should both have comforted him. It would have helped us forget our fate and not think about ourselves, but the boy would not help us by accepting comfort. The boy was annoying. No, it was dying, having to die, to think about it that was annoying. I had thought about it so many times but never with this reality. Before death was possible yet remote, unreal.

'Were you a fighter pilot?' Harry asked.

'No,' I said. 'Bombers.'

'Then you never killed anybody?'

'You mean an individual? Probably several hundred.'

'Not face to face?'

'No.'

'I killed seven just two weeks ago. Shot every bloody one in the back.'

He stared at the wall. He didn't realize he was going to die. It did not seem real. I thought about being shot and remembered what a friend had told me; how it felt, just a sudden hot sledge hammer blow, not a lot of pain, no pain for some time afterwards if it were only a machine gun bullet. I felt calm. I don't know how long I sat there thinking about what a friend had told me about being hit. Perhaps it was several hours. Perhaps longer. When I looked at Harry he had turned the color of the boy. Beyond the window the sky was paling, turning green. Soon it would be dark.

The door opened and two guards admitted a woman. She wore a white jacket like a doctor and told us she was a doctor.

'What do you want?' I said.

'Would you like a cigarette?'

She held out a box and we took cigarettes.

'Come on,' I said. 'What do you want?'

Suddenly, as I drew on the cigarette which the guard had lit I didn't care why she was here. I simply no longer really cared about anything, not even the cigarette. If it hadn't been in my mouth I wouldn't have cared even to reach for the cigarette, let alone smoke it. The female doctor sat down in a chair which the guard produced. I leaned back against the wall and closed my eyes. For a long time I slept. When I woke I felt as if I had a fever. I could hear heavy breathing. It was the boy. He lay on his back, eyes closed, the doctor bending over him taking his pulse. The boy breathed with a choking sound. The doctor dropped the boy's wrist and seated herself again across the room and made some notes on a scratch pad.

Nazi bastards, I thought, she's probably working on some medical paper. She lifted her head and looked at me.

'How do you feel about it?' she said.

'What?'

'Being shot.'

'None of your bloody business.'

She laughed, a mocking laugh, and only then did I realize that my teeth were chattering and that flesh felt dead and cold all over my body. I was terrified and almost didn't realize it. I clapped my hands against my sides like a man keeping warm in a snowstorm. Yet it did not seem to matter. I wanted to smash the smile on her face but now suddenly that did not seem to matter, either.

But I found my hands rubbing my arms and shoulders again and I felt the cold going directly into my chest and stomach. The boy opened his eyes and sat up suddenly and said: 'Will it be very long?'

'They will let you know.'

'When?'

'Stop worrying,' she said in a comforting voice. 'It won't hurt.'

'How do you know?'

She did not answer. I got up and paced the cell. It was dark outside now and they had turned on a light for her to write by.

SERGEANT MCWHINNEY

It was easier than I thought; much easier. Almost fifty miles of road the first day coming right up through the bottom of the hearse, where my ass counted the miles by the bumps. But it's always the troops in this officer-run world getting the short end of the stick. A bunch of nobs, living off unearned income, starting wars to keep themselves busy after they're tired of screwing the natives out of the copra and hemp. It isn't the working man, nor the troops. I wonder if God ever has a mind to change things or just goes on letting it happen because it amuses him. All the time the nobs telling us to go out and die because there's a reward upstairs for good dead religious people, but it's time we started getting some of the heavenly swag on earth.

It's too long being dead that counts, seems to me. It's wrong if the officers are supposed to be setting an example all the time to the troops to be always giving the troops the rotten jobs and short end of the stick. We moved along the road for two days and then got stopped by the Krauts and the Fontaines never did catch up with us. I heard them say they were going to bury some money in the woods and would join us but there's no sign of them. And you wouldn't believe how stupid those Krauts were if you hadn't seen them yourself.

But now I don't have to lie in the coffin because we got a real corpse. Bless my bun. It feels better walking. It does.

GERMAN SERGEANT

It was just before dawn. They were lying in ambush, listening to Gottfried's platoon that was trapped two miles away when a hearse came along the road with four mourners beside it and the driver on the seat up above the horse. The German sergeant stepped out and raised his hand and called to them in French to halt. At first they did not appear to hear him and then the driver raised his hand.

'Who are they?' the first German said: he was new and the sergeant did not think he would last a week against the Resistance the way he would not lie down when told.

'Frogs, from up north,' said the second German. 'Farmers.'

'Where do they get food for that fat old horse?' asked the first German.

'Maybe they heard how much you like horse meat,' the second said. The hearse went on.

'That horse would taste fine,' said the sergeant.

'Wait until they run into that road block,' said the second one.

'Where are they going anyway?' said the first. 'There isn't a cemetery around here.'

'Probably hauling an old relative back to where he was born,' the first one said.

'They'll wind up in the hearse if they try running that road block,' said the sergeant.

'Schmidt. Pann,' said the sergeant. 'Stop them. We send guns and ammo through the French with the hearse. Schmidt and Pann. Inside.'

The sergeant yelled at the hearse. It stopped and the sergeant went to the hearse and told them what he wanted.

The man's face on the driver's seat

looked funny. The mourners looked down at the road. The sergeant opened the rear door in the hearse. Inside there was room for one machine gun and two men. The sergeant ordered Schmidt and Pann to bring up ammo and the gun. They set it inside on top the coffin and pulled the curtains. The sergeant shut the doors.

The sergeant went up to the driver and warned him what would happen if he opened his mouth when he went through the French lines. A runner who had come from Gottfried Company came up and the sergeant pointed out the aid he was dispatching.

'Tell Gottfried to hold on,' said the sergeant. 'And watch for the hearse.'

He shouted at the driver. The hearse started up.

WING COMMANDER RUSSELL

I looked out the prison window. Harry had a sour look on his face and his lips were blue. Around his nostrils there was a scared taut look. The sky was sprinkled with stars, beautifully cold and remote. I thought of turning on track over the Cromer light, the North Sea foaming like white fire light against the dark edge of Norfolk, and in the morning coming home, the Dover beaches white against the cliffs, the sky amethyst, vivid and bright as glass; and I thought of leave in London and walking down Curzon Street in the noon light and turning into Sheperd's Bar to drink ale and eat upstairs; and then with the sun shining in the afternoon walking through Green Park under the shade of the trees and the high sky shimmering, sun-filled, radiant with motionless whip-cream clouds. But suddenly all that seemed exhausting. I could not feel again. I sat down and stared at the wall.

Harry mumbled something, but his voice was a blur and my mind was a blur. We could not look at each other, both of us beginning to freeze with fear, and then an acrid smell came again through the blurred sound of his voice and I lifted my head, trying to understand what he was saying, but his voice went on in the strong odor:

'Will they shoot us together?'

'How do I know?' I said.

'All of us against a wall?'

'Maybe one at a time,' I said. I wished he would stop talking.

'God, one at a time.'

'Shut up about it.'

'I can feel the bullets going into me now.'

'Come off it.'

'No, really.'

I wanted to tell him to shut up because

I knew what he was feeling. I was feeling the same way but if he went on talking about it, everything became more painful. But what difference would it make? What difference would anything make at that time?

'Sure,' I said. 'And then you'll be dead.'

He went on mumbling. I couldn't tell what he was saying. The German doctor kept watching him, the student, checking reactions to death.

'I wonder,' Harry said, 'if even after we're pronounced dead, we're still alive and can hear them saying we're dead.'

'What difference will it make?'

'You'll be able to hear the officer coming to give you the coup de grace, behind the ear.'

'What a blessing. Then you won't feel those other bullets hurting.'

'Do you believe in God?'

'Yes.'

'Why haven't you prayed?' he asked. 'I haven't heard you pray once.'

'Just shut up,' I said.

I sat there, feeling alone, and his death did not seem to matter to me, nor mine, nor the French hostages for whose ransom I was here. Why had I done it? I could feel nothing toward them now. Well, that was the way I had made myself, and perhaps for the best because it was easier to take these hours when you felt like this and kept yourself feeling like this; nothing matters; there is nothing of any importance except not breaking down before they kill you.

But Harry wouldn't shut up and he went on mumbling and mumbling. I did not say anything. Perhaps he was keeping himself from cracking up, and the mumbling helped him. I was as frightened now as he was but I was forcing myself to fight against the terror, yet I knew I was as pale as Harry and probably looked just as scared.

'Do you believe in heaven?' Harry said suddenly, quite clearly.

But before I could answer he sprang up and ran to the corner of the room and pissed against the wall. The doctor went on writing.

My body felt colder, almost as though it were dying by itself, and I gripped my arm and wrist and leg, as if reassuring myself I was still on earth and that my body was intact, that, in fact, it was still my body that I owned and not some other force that was fighting inside me to take it over.

The boy lay on the floor as if he were dead already, face down, body motionless as one lies sleeping on one's stomach, his head turned on the side, resting on his forearm.

I began to feel at once nervous and a

great lassitude, as if I were divided into two beings, one that wanted to shout and run, and the other that found any movement an impossible effort, and for a moment I was reminded of the first mission I had flown and the immense lethargy fear creates.

I leaned my head against the wall and closed my eyes but as soon as my head touched the wall I saw in my mind the firing squad and my body arching in agony against the crash of rifles. I started forward to meet the bullets with my chest and I woke. Again the great lethargy came over me and I thought that if I kept myself awake longer I could induce such a numbness in a few days that when it came time to die I would be utterly beyond all feeling and thus beyond any sensation of fear or pain.

'You're cracking up,' I thought.

SERGEANT REKER

So I figured when we got near the shooting all we had to do is duck in the ditches and let the frogs take the Krauts in the hearse because the Krauts couldn't see out with the curtains drawn so all we would have to do is run. The trouble was the minute the back end of the hearse opened there would be two Krauts firing machine pistols right in your face.

I could see all of us looking at the ditches on each side of the road, and everybody thinking the same thing, until Gifford figured what we had in mind.

Norton walked close to the hearse and talked to Gifford. I could not hear them. Gifford shook his head. Norton kept on talking, waving his hands. I could not hear them above the creak of wheels.

Then Craig came up beside Norton and they both talked and waved their hands and Norton drew his pistol and waved it at them and they went back and took their places as mourners again and marched.

Caldwell was walking on the other side of the hearse. I went around the hearse.

'Go back,' he whispered. 'One of them just opened the curtain a crack.'

I went back to the other side and nudged Norton and pointed at the hearse window.

'I know,' he said. 'They just took a look at us.'

'What's Gifford up to?' said Craig. 'They'll shoot us over there.'

'Don't worry,' I said. 'Gifford'll get you a medal.'

The road went along dipping and rising and up ahead the woods were crashing and shaking with machine gun and rifle fire and then it stopped and somebody fired a bazooka and it made one hell of a loud noise and then all the rifles and machine guns started cracking again.

We were still about a quarter of a mile away, I figured. I was tired and the wood when I looked at it started to sway back and forth over the road. And then tracers coming over high like long threads of fire of something you see on Guy Fawkes Day going straight up in white fiery streaks up and up and up, fiery threads burning out.

'What the hell is he going to do?' I said. 'When we cross with the Germans and they get that ammo to their friends, they'll give us the chop.'

Norton said: 'You don't think Gifford's so stupid we're going to let these Krauts get past the frogs, if we gotta pass the frogs first, and that's what it looks like.'

'Look,' said Craig. 'It's Gifford's ass, too.'

'We ought to jump in the ditch,' I said.

'Don't get any ideas,' said Norton. 'We leave Gifford and Caldwell alone, those Krauts will see we're gone and come out shooting.'

I still didn't believe we would see the French first. I didn't believe it at all. All the time I thought the Germans were lying to us and they were between us and the Frogs.

It was like when we first hit the Krupps works at Essen, down into those thousand searchlights and thousand flak guns filling the darkness with white puffs so thick they formed solid into clouds of cumulus, that I came out surprised on the other side anybody was alive. It was like I had expected my life to end right in a solid cloud of round balls of shrapnel bursts. Almost like I wasn't here now so I couldn't be alive even to doubt we'd see the French. So I went on in the waiting. And that's worse than ever being there.

WING COMMANDER RUSSELL

My body writhed in a nightmare about being torn apart by bullets and my flesh was torn with burning, bleeding holes. I lay twisting from side to side on the ground screaming. I woke sweating, my whole body covered with sweat.

It was dark outside. I could not remember what day it was. I got up. I must forget the nightmare. I told myself. I no longer could remain awake without falling asleep, no matter how hard I fought sleep. But I must fight sleep, the nightmare.

I tried to recall my past life to forget my dreams of fear and death and agony and terror. I walked back and forth, thinking of the past. I tried to remember everybody and everything that had happened to me and it all came back.

Now in my mind I saw the face of Jennifer's father during the company strike, the faces of the strikers at the gates and then suddenly the frightened faces of Mr. and Mrs. Fontaine. Were they faces I would never forget? Along with trying to be an English gentleman, practicing the accent and viewpoint and Jennifer's father saying British industry and British men are the best and believing the sound of his voice but not believing in the people unless he could exploit them and treat them like charity. And the face at the RAF enlistment desk with the poster behind him showing the RAF hero face. How madly I pursued the image of glory and success chasing happiness. And fighting for freedom against the Nazis. Why? I wanted to be a war hero and a business success after the war. And death did not exist then.

Then I stopped thinking and remembering because everything I remembered seemed phony about myself, and if it had been meaningful, yet what meaning could it have now? My life was finished. And chasing after Jennifer all those years. I knew I would not have done it if I had known I was going to die like this. Or would I? Was death only the end of a silly dream? To judge my life seemed absurd now. I had done many things but I was only a ridiculous ant among ants, chasing the dissolving sugar drops of eternity. And even as I tried to recall the things of life I had enjoyed I no longer could find joy in any of it.

The door opened and the guard came in accompanied by a German officer who spoke English.

'Would you like to write a last letter?' he asked.

'Fuck off,' Harry muttered.

'Don't you have wives or children?' the German asked.

'You heard him,' I said.

I wanted to write something to Jennifer but now it seemed absurd. The tenderness for her was still there beneath numb hardness. Yet even now as I felt it, it slid away, far out of my body that seemed to turn colder and colder. I thought of her lovely face and arms and throat, and I wondered if she were with me right now if I would care as I had once cared, for now as I thought of her in this instant I suddenly could feel nothing for her.

I looked at the wall and it seemed to be changing shape, darkening, and I looked at Harry and he no longer looked like the man I had met such a short time ago. He looked wizened. I felt sweat, cold and clammy, beginning to cover my body, coming up my legs and back. I shuddered, holding myself together in cold numbness.

SERGEANT CRAIG

Gifford sat high on the hearse and we went along slowly. His head was raised like he was trying to look over the tops of the trees on the rise up ahead. His eyes, though, were half-closed, his hair tousled back over his head like he hadn't combed it in four days which was about right. For the first time I thought his face looked sunken a little. Then I saw his lips part and his teeth showed. The crash of gunfire rippled across the air in a long dying echo. He wiped a piece of spit away from the corner of his mouth.

A man in a leather jacket and brown trousers approached out of the woods to the right of the road. He carried a sub-machine gun. Gifford raised his arm and waved. Then he beckoned the man forward.

'Craig,' he said. 'Tell him Boche inside.'

'I don't know French.'

'Tell him Boche!'

I started down the ditch. The man was watching me. He pointed the gun at my belly. I raised my hands above my head and walked slowly toward him. My arm pits felt wet.

'Boche,' I said, making the shape of the hearse with both hands. The skin on the man's face sagged from his eye sockets. His skin was pale. He nudged me with the gun muzzle.

'Boche,' I said. I pointed at the hearse which was almost even with us now. It was bumping along. Gifford waved at us to come over, waving one hand furiously. He said something to Reker and everybody began to move away from the hearse and slide down the side of ditch.

'Hurry,' I said.

I turned my back and began running toward the hearse. I felt and then heard the man running behind me.

The hearse stopped. Gifford sprang down, already running, gesturing furiously with both hands to follow him. He muttered something in French to the man behind me.

They ran around to the rear of the hearse. I slid down the side of the ditch. I thought I knew now what they were going to try to do.

Gifford began shouting in German. The Frenchman knelt in the road facing the rear of the hearse.

'Jesus,' Reker said. 'Jesus.'

Gifford snapped the ratchet back on the hearse door handle and sprang back flinging the door open.

The Germans came out running. I thought they were running on air the way they leaped running. Suspended in midair, still running, they were firing, but the Frenchman was below them. For a fraction of a second they seemed to hang against the sky as if they had been dropped from a great height.

I heard all the guns going fast *bopbop-bopbop,* slugs going into the dirt road. The horse was kicking in his harness and went plunging down the road, the hearse swinging back and forth.

One of the Germans was spread out on the road, landing face down, without dropping his gun. He shot wild and it ricocheted off a tree behind me.

The Frenchman must have been a lousy shot to miss them both coming out that way but he could roll fast and he rolled. He was down in the ditch.

The other German was across the road in the other ditch. He got off a burst at the Frenchman but all I saw was dirt bursting in the road.

Then I saw McWhinney running down the road toward us, and the hearse swinging up the road. McWhinney had a pistol. Then when he got close I saw it was a Luger.

He came running and then crouched and holding the Luger in both hands gave the

German lying in the road a burst. The German twisted as if he were hit, and then he swiveled around on his belly and shot at McWhinney as Gifford raised his head over the ditch and fired a pistol at the German.

McWhinney flopped, with both hands out in front. He raised his head and tried to lift the Luger again and his head sagged. By this time the German in the road was throwing a burst at Gifford while the Frenchman was putting a fresh clip in the Sten-gun.

I could see the other German across the road, just his helmet and a slit of his face and the machine pistol resting carefully on the top of the ditch. He was all settled down to give McWhinney a burst.

Then the Frenchman stood up, clear right out of the ditch, his face chalk-white, and plugged the German right where he lay in the road.

He started across the road and the German in the ditch shot him in the chest from fifteen feet. The Frenchman threw his gun in the air and sat down hard and went over forward.

McWhinney was trying to come up to his knees. He got his head up and he had the Luger in one hand. They must have left it on the coffin. Then the German came up, clear, walking straight down the road firing at McWhinney. I could see the slug marks bursting in the dirt, eating their way in a line toward McWhinney.

McWhinney's head came down and his hands covered his head. Gifford was working his way along the ditch and he was about even with them when the German got McWhinney.

Gifford stood up and shot twice past the German's side, standing there, the pistol jumping in his hand.

The German spun and the machine pistol lifted and Gifford dropped. I thought he was hit. He rolled down the side of the ditch. The German walked to the side of the road, and he was just getting the machine pistol level on Gifford, when McWhinney got his head up and the Luger in one hand that was lying in the road and shot the German three times in the back. Bloody good air gunner.

WING COMMANDER RUSSELL

It was strange losing the illusion of being eternal. Even at the most dire moments in the air I had never lost that illusion. Now here in this cell it was gone forever. Yet, in a strange way, I was relieved, for I no longer felt as if I were myself. I had the feeling of utter isolation and yet of being someone else now, of sitting outside my body, and yet being within it.

The female German doctor came in twice again and looked at us as if she were checking patients in a hospital. I half expected her to take my temperature. It was dark both times when she came in, turned on the light, studied us and left.

The young boy began to scream in his sleep, and we had to wake him he screamed so much. The trouble was when wakened though he would sit and cry and we could not stop the crying so we decided we could take his screaming more easily because it was only intermittent. The more I saw him sob the more determined I became to keep myself hardened against self-pity and crying. I made myself promise I would die without showing any tears to those bastard Germans.

So we sat in the dark and waited for dawn light and the boy fell asleep again and Harry and I talked about England and where we were born and went to school and we made the time pass until the dawn would arrive. At one point I thought I could hear a clock ticking somewhere and I asked Harry if he had a watch and he shook his head because I think he was suffering from the same delusion since the Germans had taken our wristwatches.

Then I heard the sound, baffling at

first, perhaps because we did not want to recognize it. The sound was muffled, and then it came back to me, the time we buried MacDaniels at Culthorpe, the muffled tread of marching, men marching across cobblestones, and the sound was beyond our window.

'Hear that?' Harry said.

'Changing guard,' I said.

'Oh? Like hell.'

'They don't shoot you in the night.'

'Oh, don't they?'

Then dawn came, purple light rimming the sky, then clear white light and day was here. The boy was still asleep. Somewhere shots crashed into the morning light.

'They're getting warmed up for us,' I said.

The female doctor came in and gave us the prisoner may have a hearty breakfast offer and we declined. The sound of shots came again and again.

A few minutes later two guards and a sergeant came in. He read off our names. The boy began to cry and fell on his knees. The sergeant told us to lift him up. We lifted him under his arms and his feet dragged. It reminded me of helping an airsick pupil out of the cockpit and across the tarmac. The boy's face was the same color as an airsick person.

The sergeant ordered us out. In the hall

an officer came up to me and told one of the guards to help carry the boy.

'Go on back to your cell,' he said to me in English. I turned away. They carried the sobbing boy down the hall. I went into the room. The door slammed. The lock clicked.

SERGEANT NORTON

Gifford came up to me grinning. He certainly looked like one. Caldwell was the only one who didn't look like a Kraut. Something too thin about his face. They finally got all the dead buried. Just carted them over to a big hole and threw them in, most of them stripped naked. They never had a chance when the ammo didn't get through to them, and we weren't going to have any chance in that hearse with the coffin all shot to hell and poor McWhinney lying in a hole of his own. He didn't live long, maybe five minutes in the road.

'You enlisted in the wrong army,' Caldwell said. He was smiling, and he was right about Gifford because he sure looked like a Kraut, right down to the sergeant's stripes.

'I hope he didn't have fleas,' Reker said, and the French standing around laughing and talking, about fifty of them, wearing bandoliers and new and old rifles and here and there a Thomson gun and a lot of Sten-guns.

'God,' Craig said. 'They shot them. Did you see that?'

'What the hell do you think the Krauts do with these frogs when they capture them?' Gifford said. He sounded browned off, tugging at the shoulder straps and trying to get the coal scuttle helmet straight on his head. There weren't any holes in the uniforms. They had stripped them and shot them after they surrendered.

They had caught the horse, too. He stood, snorting, in the middle of the field. And the coffin with the lid off lying on the ground beside the hearse and a couple frogs looking down at another frog stretched out in the coffin with his arms hanging over the sides like he was taking a bath in a big tub. The one in the coffin had a bottle of wine and was drinking and lifting his head back and laughing.

'What good are these uniforms going to be if we run into a bunch of strange frogs?' I said.

'Get it on,' Gifford said. 'If you want to stay with the frogs and sack up in the woods, don't let me stop you.'

'We ought to wait and get another coffin,' I said. 'And stick one of the

Krauts in it.' The sun was going down. The sky was the color of water, green, and getting darker. Still as water, too. Like I could feel some kind of threat waiting for us there in the sky.

'And let the Kraut bleed all over the coffin,' Gifford said. 'Come on, get in that suit.'

WING COMMANDER RUSSELL

I sat there alone and started crying. I had tried not to, but I couldn't stand it, hearing the shots outside every five minutes. I gritted my teeth but my teeth chattered and my whole body began to shake no matter how I fought to stay hard against the fear that was eating me up. I kept hoping they would come and shoot me immediately. Why don't they come? Why don't they come and get it over?

A few minutes later the door opened. Two guards marched me down the hall. We went into a room filled with school benches and a desk. Behind the desk sat an officer. There were papers on the desk, and he was smoking a pipe.

'Are you Wing Commander Russell?'

'Yes.'

'Where are the Fontaines?'

'I haven't the vaguest idea.'

371

The officer was tall and thin, quite old for an officer, with grey in his hair. He got up from behind his desk and came around and stood in front of me, our faces only a few inches apart. He stared into my eyes and smiled and blew smoke in my face. I could see he had never been near death if he thought smoke in my face was going to bother me. He went back behind his desk and sat down and looked up at me.

'You'll be shot if you don't tell us where they are.'

'You're losing the war, you know,' I said.

He laughed.

'You're losing your life in a few minutes if you don't talk.'

I did not speak. He picked up a piece of paper and put on a great serious act of reading but his eyes did not move. He was merely staring at the same word while he waited for me to speak. He was a bloody Nazi, if ever I had seen one, an officious old man, helping to kill and murder people for Hitler, for the good of the Third Reich, and Germany was filled with them, cruel bloody bureaucrats, calling themselves patriots, running slave camps, and killing women and children as hostages.

'Well?' he said, still not looking up,

still pretending to be concentrating on the paper in his hand.

'I don't know where they are,' I said. 'I imagine they have left town.'

'Where were they going?'

'I haven't the foggiest idea.'

'What about your companions?'

'I'm sure they're a long way from here.'

He took out a package of cigarettes and extended the package and smiled his thin smile as if he were amused in having offered me a cigarette. I declined.

'I'll give you ten minutes. If you don't talk in ten minutes, you will be shot.'

'I'm a prisoner of war,' I said.

'You shot an officer of the Third Reich while you were wearing civilian clothes. You are classified on our records as a saboteur.'

So they were going to sweat me some more. But what good could I do them. Fontaines surely had gone with the crew. They were hoping to break me down with more waiting, just more waiting to tighten the screws on my skin until I came to them screaming for mercy.

Or they were bluffing. I would have to sweat them out. My body felt drained of all energy, filled with a great sense of lassitude. I fought against lying down and falling into a stupefied sleep. I felt my eye lids trembling, seeking to close.

I rubbed my eyes and massaged my face and throat. I wondered why they didn't torture me. Perhaps they didn't torture officers. Yes, they were bluffing. I could tell them vaguely where Fontaines might have gone, and that might be enough, if they were not bluffing. But why die for the Fontaines? I had felt something for them when I had been thrown in here, but no matter how hard I tried to tell myself that I still felt something for those who had helped me and for my crew I could feel nothing for any of them. I told myself I must, I must feel something for them, but, no, it was all gone, all drained out of me. What did all of our lives amount to? I told myself I must believe now more than ever in the value of all our lives and yet I no longer could believe or feel this. Again I told myself I must and again a part of me said to hell with trying to feel this anymore when there was nothing left inside to feel it with. What real difference would it make if I died or the Fontaines. Who had done the most against the Germans and who could still do the most? Perhaps the Fontaines, but surely they were washed up in this town as far as being valuable to the underground. Oh, God, what really had any value now? I could make up a lie and perhaps escape being shot, and then I thought no I will fight doing that and I felt better thinking that way suddenly.

In a few minutes the guards took me back to the officer. I felt elated and I was smiling and I did not understand why. The officer had a monocle on his desk which he now inserted in his eye.

I said: 'You almost look good enough to be an English officer.'

One of the guards rammed me in the shoulder with a gun butt. I heard myself giggle.

'Well?' said the officer, removing the monocle. 'What have you decided?'

I felt my face sneer at him as if it were separate from my body which felt frozen and dead.

'I'll tell you,' I said. 'The Fontaines are hiding in the Fiocca cafe. Upstairs.'

I almost laughed because I knew there were only whores upstairs.

Almost at once the officer gave orders in German to the guards, then to me: 'If you're telling the truth ... if you're lying you'll be shot ... if you're telling the truth, you will live.'

The guards took me back to the room. I sat down, feeling calm, a child-like sense of amusement, as if I had tricked my nanny years ago. I imagined them rummaging through the whore's rooms, looking under the whores's beds. I began to laugh. I laughed a long time, and suddenly lay back and slept.

I must have slept several hours. It was evening when the guard came with food and the officer was with him. He smiled at me, pleasantly, almost courteously.

'Cigarette?' he asked. I stared at him stunned.

'Uh—' I heard my mouth say. 'Am I—'

'You may exercise after eating. Then you will be shipped to a prison camp, sometime this week.'

'But aren't you—?' I began, but already he was gone. I could not eat. I stared at the food. Half hour later the guards came and took me outside into what must have been once a school yard. About fifty prisoners were milling around. There were guards all around the yard. I felt as if I were in a dream. I couldn't believe I was here. I walked among the faces, almost without seeing them, not believing I was here and they were here, asking myself who I was. A man tapped me on the shoulder. At first I did not recognize him.

Then I saw it was the proprietor of the Fiocca cafe.

'Where are your friends?' he asked.

'They got away. What are you doing here?'

'I was going to ask you that. Everybody

in here is under death sentence.'

'They were going to shoot me,' I said. 'I don't know what happened. Maybe they decided to abide by the Geneva convention.'

'They raided the cafe last night,' he said.

'I thought they never bothered you because of the girls.'

'I don't understand it,' he said. 'I thought I had an understanding with them. The girls, you know.'

'Why then?'

'They were after the Fontaines. I had them upstairs.'

I stared at him stupefied.

'They stayed behind to bury money and valuables in their woods when your friends left. They wanted to hide with me a few days until things cooled off. They tried to escape down the back stairs. They shot both of them. And one of the girls who got in the way. The best girl we had.'

'The best girl you had!'

Oh, my God, I thought, and everything inside me blurred and I heard a voice inside me trying to laugh but nothing would come out and all I could hear was a crazy croaking noise coming out of something and then I realized it was me. I sounded as if I were being strangled.

Book Seven
THE GIRLS THEY LEFT BEHIND

46   EDA BRAUER

Among the fliers who were members of the squadron on which Sergeant Craig flew was a Flight Sergeant named Curtis. He had been shot down over Dortmund two months before Craig's crew went down. He had been so badly wounded that he had been repatriated to England through the Red Cross exchange of prisoners. He limped and walked only with a cane. He wore the DFC for having remained with his burning aircraft to the last second until his entire crew had bailed out and now on his first visit to the City of York (he had been reposted to his old squadron as an intelligence officer) since his return to England he was wearing a new uniform.

He was feeling depressed because he remembered the City of York as a place of laughter and gaiety in the pubs between missions. All that seemed long ago, years ago, to him now. He had come to enjoy himself with old friends, but all the old friends were gone, missing, killed or posted as instructors to Operational Training Units in the south of England. So now in the blackout he was walking from pub to pub looking for old faces, until he suddenly stopped, staring at a woman. She stood just inside a passage perhaps fifteen feet long that led into a pub. Half of the passage was in shadow, and the part near the interior was faintly lighted. The woman's hair was dyed jet black, eyebrows and eyelashes were heavy with mascara, and her cheeks bright with rouge and stark white powder. Her dress was new and obtainable only purchased on the blackmarket and she wore silk stockings. She was standing just inside, her face half in darkness and half in light, and she smiled and appeared to mutter something to the soldiers and sailors who passed. Curtis walked suddenly forward and stopped. The woman looked at him and averted her eyes and stared back into the pub.

'Eda?' Curtis said. 'Aren't you Eda? You used to go round with Craig?'

The woman appeared not to hear him. She stared straight back into the light of the pub, her face averted. 'I used to meet you with him in the Rose and Crown. I just got back from Germany. I heard about Craig. Sorry.'

'Yes,' she said. 'I heard you were dead, too. Curtis, isn't it?'

'You never know,' Curtis said. 'Craig might turn up.'

'Yes,' she said. Then she turned away. She drew back and slipped between him and the wall, turning to the darkness of the street, her lips curving in a smile again; it wasn't until fifteen minutes later that he saw her again. She was standing at the entrance of another pub two blocks up the street, just inside the door, saying something to each airman or soldier who passed. It wasn't until he was close that Curtis caught her voice.

'How about a little fun, honey?' she said. 'A little party? I'll show you a good time.'

He stepped forward.

'Eda ...' he said.

She looked up at him, this time with a smile that was cold and contemptuous. 'All right, you bastard, now you know,' she said, turning her smile to one of bright professionalism immediately. 'Do you want some fun, honey?' she asked in a low voice. 'Ten shillings. I have a nice place.'

Curtis stood there. She looked him full in the face, waiting, her stare quite dead and steadfast. 'Well, honey, make up your mind.'

My God, he thought, feeling ill. He

caught her elbow, and turned her swiftly from the doorway.

'Come on,' he said. 'Show me your place.'

MARY ALICE EVANS

She heard the sound of the band beyond the curtain, the din of squadron voices, and suddenly the grief was there again, the grief that would vanish for days and suddenly turn up like this again. She shuddered and shiverd and felt she was going to give way completely. God, how long since she had seen him? Now to have to come here to give a show at the field from which he had gone to his death. Oh, Rodger, Rodger, my dear dead darling. But she had to go on, five minutes, she had to go on, five minutes, go on, go on, sing, sing, sing. Sing what? What song was she supposed to sing? Dear God, she had been so sure the grief wouldn't come back like this, so suddenly. Was it being here at his squadron field? She did not recognize any of the faces that she had seen here before with Rodger. Must get ready. Must get ready. Must get ready. Here we go. Here we go. Sing. Sing. Sing.

She came out on to the small stage. It was the squadron briefing room. The lights struck her in the eyes and all she could see were the youthful mustached faces sitting in the front row and the sound of the band came, thudding, and the image of Rodger came between her thoughts of the song, and then the melody reached her and she began to sing *I'll Be With You in Apple Blossom Time,* and she knew how mechanical she sounded, but she had been doing this a long time, and she thought as she sang that perhaps they might not even know how wooden her smile was. Applause crashed over the stage in waves and the band blared for an encore and backed against the curtain, smiling, cursing herself for having accepted the request to sing here for the ENSA show.

She finished and the curtain closed in front of her and the applause rose in waves again for an encore.

'Mary, dear, please. What is it?' said her accompanist, a fairy named Fritz who was a composer for BBC. She leaned against the wall, crying.

'I'm all right. I'm all right,' she said. 'I won't sing any more. But I'm all right.'

She leaned with her head against the wall, trying not to think about Rodger but what else would there be in this place but thoughts of Rodger. She found herself thinking back to the evening, when her maid told her there was a flight lieutenant in the hall from Rodger's squadron and wanted to see her. She remembered that moment now because even then she knew why he was there, something had happened, but for a moment she had also refused to see him, thinking it was just another airman on the make and she had had enough of that since breaking up with Rodger. She did not want to hear anything about Rodger that day, nothing, nothing that would start up everything again since that meeting with his bloody awful father. But she went to the door anyway, and the Flight Lieutenant whoever he was with his tall blond looks was sober which was a change from most of them she met in London, and he was a considerate person. He told it simply: how Rodger had asked him to see her if he went for Burton and that was what it looked like. Then, after a pause, 'Miss Evans, there isn't any word on them. That was two days ago.' God in heaven, how many weeks ago had that moment been, she thought now. She had cried in a dozen plays, but she had never cried like that before or since, shuddering and catching her breath over and over again. And the existence in pain and anguish that had begun to diminish until she came here tonight. It was as though Rodger had ceased to exist and now here he existed again in the anguish and pain again.

She knew she would have to go back on sleeping pills tonight again.

Fritz said: 'Come on,' taking her elbow. 'Come on. Show's over. We'll have a drink with them and then back to town.'

'God's teeth,' she said. 'Do we have to?'

'Only one.'

'I'll wait in the car.'

'Have it your way.'

'Hurry, please.'

'Half a mo. You know they expect this. The after show drink in the mess. What'll I tell them?'

'I don't care,' she said and pushed the curtain aside and looked out at the empty briefing room. She flung her coat over her shoulders.

Outside it was dark. Buildings rose round and humped out of the moonless dark like stacks of hay, and she slipped twice on a duck walk and felt the mud splash her ankles.

She found the car. Somewhere a door opened, and the sound of music, a piano, tinkled brightly and was gone. She got into the car. She did not remember how long she lay with her head on the back of the seat, waiting, waiting, waiting, every minute a century long. She felt she had been asleep when she heard the door open.

'Fritz.'

She blinked her eyes and the ceiling light glared. A woman's face faintly familiar, or was she dreaming.

'Jennifer!'

'Hello, Mary.'

Jennifer Caldwell leaned down and embraced Mary. Holding each other briefly, Jennifer began to speak, then ceased and drew her head back, and then after a pause, 'I wanted you to know. Father's dead. He died a week ago. A stroke.' She shook her head. 'No, not a word about Rodger.'

JOYCE MOWBRY

She lay on the table in the doctor's office, looking up at the ceiling, and in that moment she knew—yes, she knew! It just came out of nowhere, and put away all the worry and anxiety she had had all these long weeks. It was that simple, like a bolt from the blue, as she described it to herself. But how could she be so sure? It might only be a coincidence, complete self-delusion, the desire so strong to believe what she needed to believe that the moment it came to her, she had believed it only because her need to believe made it believable. Oh, no! It was more than that! She knew it, knew it, down through her whole mind and body, and nothing, no one could ever make her believe now she was wrong. She had felt his presence, though Eddie Reker was miles away, she had felt his presence there in the room with her, his face and hands and voice, his eyes and hair and throat, not seeing him, yet feeling his aliveness—still alive, close to her, yet miles away, still alive.

She blinked, looking up into the doctor's face. He was a tall man and the stethoscope dangled like a crazy necklace around his skinny throat; pursing and unpursing his thin pink lips, his little eyes bland and tired behind tinted glasses.

She had never been in his office before. Her mother, of all people, the last person in the world one would believe would know about doctors such as this man, had brought her to this rather dingy address in London.

'A Canadian,' her mother said, not at all shocked by the first recognition of pregnancy as Joyce thought she would be, 'well, there's only one thing you can do. I shall arrange it. Lucky girl, he is missing, but Joyce, a Canadian! Really! I've always ... But to get involved with a Canadian.' Then, 'What could you have been thinking? You know how colonials are, here today and gone tomorrow.'

Her mother's reaction had shocked Joyce at first, for most of all Joyce had feared condemnation for being sent home from the service pregnant, but with Daddy overseas, Mother certainly had become more tolerant, or had less to worry about Daddy's wrath, but how on earth had Mother ever known about a London abortionist? Joyce was shocked.

She heard her voice speaking now, quite strange and remote, 'How long overdue, am I?'

He took off his stethoscope and set it on the table and removed his rubber gloves.

'I must talk to your mother first.'

Joyce didn't like either his eyes or his voice, something too, too benign and serpentine about him.

She sat up and smoothed her skirts and reached over for her pants and sitting on the edge of the table, drew them on.

'How long does the operation take?' she asked.

'Don't worry, my dear,' said the doctor. 'We shall have to wait a month.'

There was a soft tap at the door, and Mrs. Mowbry—looking lovely at forty-two, pink-cheeked, smiling—came in and asked the doctor for his opinion.

'Well,' said the doctor, straightening his tie. 'We're a little premature now. She's only two months and I couldn't do anything until the third month. Much too dangerous at this point. She needs a tonic, but, really, no worries about doing it in another thirty days.'

From outside, through the open window, came the rumble of London traffic, the far-faint music of a street band, horns and drums and saxophone. She saw the relief in her mother's eyes. And in that moment Joyce thought of Reker again, of all their tender moments together, letting her mind drink in that past that seemed so near, knowing he wasn't dead, knowing he was alive, knowing he had really been in the room with her for a moment, knowing he would never die, and she would see him again, and she would never lose him, and nothing, nothing in the world, must take this baby from them.

'We'll call in a month,' said Mrs. Mowbry. 'What about a tonic?'

Before the doctor could answer, Joyce laughed, looking at both of them, and they turned and stared at her, almost as if they expected to find her dead, their eyes shocked.

'Yes, a fine tonic,' said Joyce. 'I wonder if he would like milk stout.'

At once they saw she was mocking them. They could not speak.

'What about drinking?' said Joyce. 'Oh, just gin and orange. Will that harm me?'

'Joyce,' said her mother, her eyes fading like wax, pleading as if she felt her daughter had suddenly lost her mind. How silly mother looked!

'Oh, some alcoholic beverage would be beneficial,' said the doctor. His voice sounded husky.

Mrs. Mowbry stared at him and then back at her daughter as if she thought for a fraction of a second they were playing games with her.

And, down through the rumble of traffic, came the sound of a street band, thudding, somewhere over around Leicester Square.

The doctor nodded his head like an old monk and opened the door, and they were outside in the hall and going down the stairs before her mother turned and caught Joyce by the arms, gripping her hard, turning Joyce against the stair wall. Mrs. Mowbry's eyes widened with anger and fright.

'Oh, no!' Joyce said, her eyes blazing. 'He's going to live. I'm going to have him. Eddie's alive! I know he's alive!'

'You fool!' her mother hissed.

'Shut up!' said Joyce. 'If you say one word to me, tell me once more what I have to do, I'll write Daddy what you've been doing in the evenings. Working in a war plant? Don't make me laugh, Mother. I know now.'

She was only a girl but she looked older now in uniform, no longer just a teen-age face. She was tall. The uniform made her look taller and the way she wore her hair now made her look even taller than she looked if you had known her before she had gone into service. She wore her hair straight back now with a coiled bun of hair against the nape of her neck. She was sitting alone at a table in the pub. She did not look as if she were waiting for anybody. She looked like just another WAAF having a beer by herself, waiting for a WAAF to join her. The officer who came in through the door at the back of the room was tall and blond. He wore the navigator wing and the one ring of a pilot officer around the cuff of his tunic sleeve. A white handkerchief showed in the cuff of his tunic sleeve. Gold colored VR letters were clipped to the lapels of his tunic. He walked straight to her table and sat down.

A flight lieutenant who looked older than most of the fliers in the room and who was the only officer in the place wearing a DFC and bar stopped at the table and said hello to the pilot officer and the pilot officer said, 'Hello, George. Mary, this is

George Crawford. George, Mary Hunt.' They acknowledged the introductions and George went on across the room to a table jammed with air crew who were singing and shouting. The pilot officer said that George was on his third tour of missions and had been flying combat so long it was reputed he had flown on Mark 11 arrows at Crecy.

'What would you like?' asked the pilot officer whose name was Paul Spooner.

'Mild and bitter's fine,' she said.

'Sure you wouldn't like Gin and It?' said Paul.

'No, really.'

He handed her a pack of Gold Flakes and she took one and he lit her cigarette. 'Two mild and bitter,' he told the waitress and she left.

'Well,' he said. 'How do you like the service?'

'Fine,' she said, smiling through the cloud of smoke jetted from her nostrils, lifting her face back and away from the smoke.

'You're the prettiest girl on the squadron,' he said. 'Where are you from?'

'Actually, not too far from here,' she said. 'Where are you from?'

'Dorset,' he said. 'You probably never heard of the place. Little town. Maiden Newton.'

'Mine's about the same size,' she said. 'Did you ever hear of Goole?'

'Yes,' he said. 'About twenty miles west of here. We used to be stationed near there.' He smiled. 'Maiden Newton is a little larger.'

'How long have you lived in Maiden Newton?' she asked.

'All my life.'

'I've been there,' she said.

'Come off it,' he said. 'Nobody's ever been there.'

'I have,' she smiled. 'Actually, I know people who live near there. Long Burton.'

'That's twenty miles. Who?'

'The Buckfasters.'

'Do you really know them?'

'Why, yes.'

'Come off it,' he said.

'Really,' she said.

'You're pulling my leg.'

'Ian and Catherine.'

'Well, I was never quite in that crowd. I only know who they are. So you're from Goole.'

'Yes,' she said.

'Mary Hunt,' he said. 'You're the most attractive liar in Yorkshire.'

'Yes, sir,' she said.

'Look, Mary,' he said. 'Like I told you. I can get you a three day pass. We'll go to London.'

'But I've only been in service two weeks. No one—'

'The adjutant is a decent chap.'

'All the girls will start asking questions.'

'Compassionate leave. Simple.'

'No, then the adjutant will talk.'

'Freddy never talks. Soul of discretion.'

Just then a young man who was a captain in the hussar regiment came over to the table and stopped. He wore a tunic with a long skirt and big pockets and cherry-colored trousers and a cavalry regiment mustache.

'Mary,' he said, and she turned her head and looked up.

'Why, Reg!'

'Mary, what in blazes—?'

'About time I did,' she said and looked at her uniform and smiled.

'I heard about your brother. And your father. Sorry.'

'Won't you join us?'

'Can't. Just stopped for cigarettes. Troops are outside. We're on our way to Oswestry. Gunnery course.'

'You must come and see us.'

'There's only you.'

'Yes.'

'What about the Towers. Are you going to—?'

'Until the war's over anyway.'

'Well, cheer-oh.'

'Bye, Reg.'

And he was gone.

'Who's that?' asked the young pilot officer.

'Friend of my brother's.'

The pilot officer didn't say anything for a long moment and then just when it looked as if he were going to speak the waitress brought their drinks. He paid her and the waitress left them.

'Cheers,' he said, and lifted his glass and touched Mary's glass.

'Cheers,' she said and drank.

He drank and set his glass down and smiled.

'The Towers,' he said. 'Near Goole. Do you mean that big red castle?'

'Uh-huh.'

'Your people work on the estate?' he asked, watching her.

She reached across the table and touched his hand.

'Paul,' she said. 'I live there. He was talking about Father. He's dead. My brother's dead. In the desert. All very recent.'

'I'm sorry, Mary.'

'That's all right.'

'Who are you really?' he asked.

She squeezed his hand and smiled.

'Mary Hunt.'

'And you live in that—' he began. He

394

laughed. 'My God, maybe you could give me a job after the war. I used to be a game keeper.'

'Paul,' she said. 'Get me the pass. We don't have to go to London. We can go to my place.'

FRANCES MCWHINNEY

Sergeant Bert Haugen came out of the glass-roofed railroad station in the City of York and stood on the edge of the cobblestone street and took a look at his watch just as the sun started going down behind the spire of the York Minster. The intelligence people had kept him in London just long enough to make him miss the noon train, so that the girls he might have called in time to prevent at least one from going on the night shift at the engine factory, would have gone by now. He walked up the street to the Half-Moon and drank a couple of pints which made him feel better if not less weary. He ordered another pint and sat back sipping it slowly, trying to test his memory. He had left his little black book with all their names and telephone numbers back in camp, the day he had left as a volunteer for a raid on the French coast from which he had returned as one of fifty survivors out of a hundred. Ethel would be on the B shift. And Maureen. She had gone back to Ireland, he wasn't sure whether her sister had gone with her. It had only been a couple of weeks. It seemed like a century since he had been in York. And then he remembered Frances McWhinney.

Before he knew what he was doing he was outside on the street and standing in the telephone booth, telling himself he didn't want to get mixed up with her again, she was too serious. There would be pretty girls in the Half-Moon tonight, but there was a full moon and the air crew probably would be standing down on all the York based squadrons so the pubs would be full of airmen, shooting down all the pretty girls. No, he didn't want to have to fight for it or compete with the RAF for it tonight. And she was restful. She had a way about her. Peaceful.

He got the number from information and the operator put him through.

'Hello, Frances.'

'George?'

'No, this isn't George. This is Bert Haugen.'

The wire seemed to go dead and for a moment he thought she had hung up. And then, 'Bert? I thought you were posted away.' And then before he could say anything she added 'Are you in York?'

'Just down the street from the Half-Moon.'

'How are you?'

'Fine. Why don't you come down to the Half-Moon?'

'I can't now. Why didn't you write?' she asked.

'I've been away. I'll tell you all about it.'

'I can't now, but maybe, well, uh, there's Martha. She lives next door. She gets home about eight. I could come down for about an hour, if she'll sit for me.'

He didn't like that. It meant she'd have to go home soon as the pubs closed. Suddenly he had an idea.

'Look, I'll come over about seven.'

'Seven-thirty,' she said, and he knew why because it would be dark then and she wouldn't be embarrassed by the neighbours because they wouldn't be able to see a taxi stopping in the black-out then.

'Okay,' he said. 'Seven-thirty. I'll bring a couple quarts.'

He rang off and stood in the booth thinking. Well, even though it was a long taxi out to her house on the edge of the town it would be worth it, snug, too, and not fighting the bloody air force in every pub on the street.

He whistled while he shaved in his hotel room. He felt good, three more days of leave before going back to the bloody camp. You had to hand it to the Krauts, they had been waiting for them over there, and he was lucky to be one of the blokes who come out of it covered with horse shoes. It would be nice at her house, a cozy fire, the kid put to bed, and she wasn't a bad sort, really, a little too much on the serious side, but pretty and loving, yes, loving, poor kid, she was that. He whistled. A lad could do a lot worse than Frances. He wondered about her husband. Poor blighter was probably out in the desert. Everybody was out in the desert. He applauded himself for selecting her. When the fire burned low and the quarts were inside them, making them feel warm and cozy, and when he told her what he had been through, and it wouldn't be long and they'd be going back again soon, sure as bloody hell there was a second front coming, and God only knew who would live through that, if anybody did, so when he told her she would understand, he was sure.

She wasn't a whore, not a quick lay. She was all woman, and a lonely one, and she knew what it was to want and need a man. Her old man had probably been gone three years and when he came back they would start all over again, and infidelity didn't mean in war what it meant in peace. There wasn't much time and life was sweet. Tonight he wanted to hold a woman. More than he had ever wanted to hold a woman before. Not just to lay her but to hold one in his arms, one who wanted to feel the warmth he wanted to feel, the warmth he knew that put the thought of death away, because he had seen too much of it too closely last week, and he knew how short his time was.

He walked downstairs and drank a pint and walked up to the Station Hotel and looked for a taxi. The cabby was asleep and he woke him. It was dark now.

'Where to?' the hacker said, and Haugen gave him the address.

'Live out here?' asked the cabby.

'Not likely. Girl friend. Let's step on it.'

'All right, guv.'

Haugen settled back in the cab and lit a cigarette. He could see out the window. Everything was black in the street, but the moonlight was bright and the trees stood out clearly against the sky. Suddenly he saw a flare rise against the darkness and flick out like a dying match. Almost immediately the sound of sirens came wailing down across the air sad and mournful.

'Cor,' the driver said. 'You want a shelter?'

'Keep going,' said Haugen. 'They're probably headed for Hull. They haven't raided York in two years.'

They sped on through the darkness, down dingy streets. Flares rose against the sky, and from up ahead came the thunder of anti-aircraft fire.

'Let's go! Let's go!' Haugen shouted. Up ahead the sky filled with flashes of shrapnel explosions. Sirens screamed. People were running down the street. Searchlights sabred the darkness and flares burst among long white beams.

Suddenly the taxi swerved to the curb and stopped and the driver swiveled his neck.

'Cor!' said the cabby. 'Oi ain't goin' past 'ere.'

Haugen paid him and dashed up the street. He saw a pub and ducked inside. The bar was jammed with RAF and he wriggled through and managed to buy a pint.

He leaned against the bar, listening to the explosions and the reverberations of bombs, trying to estimate by the force of the reverberations how far away the bombs were falling. The bottles and glasses rattled on the shelves behind the bar. The flak ceased for a moment and in the silence he could hear the off-beat *vroom-vroom-vroom* of the German engines and the far-faint crackle of machine gun and cannon fire from a night fighter, making such a small noise as to seem harmless.

He finished two pints before the attack died away.

'Bloody sprogs,' the pilot next to Haugen said. 'They send their sprog crews to get blooded on Hull. Some bloody sprogs must have got off course tonight.'

The all-clear came mournful as the cry of hounds and Haugen walked out and up the street into the clanging and lights of rescue and fire fighting teams.

There was rubble in the street and fires were burning against the darkness. He picked out the street sign and turned down a narrow street, and then he saw the flames.

His heart jumped and his stomach twisted. The whole street looked like the street in the French town he had raided. There were no houses, no houses at all, only the roar of fire. He ran into the clotting of rescue and fire fighting teams. Where houses should have been there was only a blazing mass, and from the mass of fire came long and thunderous plumes out of whirling hot balls of fire.

There was no Frances McWhinney. There would never be a Frances McWhinney again.

Sergeant Haugen woke in the next

morning with a hangover, his mouth coppery, his brain dizzy and throbbing. The anonymous woman who lay beside him was snoring. He thought of Frances for a moment, but only for a moment, because the thought of her burning was suddenly more than he thought he could ever bear.

JENNIFER CALDWELL

Jennifer closed the door of her Nissen hut room. Just to be away from everybody for a few minutes. Grief was making her this way, a way she had never been before, not wanting to be around people, wanting to be by herself more and more every day, and the thought frightened her. At the end of the day, she usually sought the mess bar with other officers, but now—was it a month, three months? God, was she losing her memory, too? She could not recall how long she had been doing this, the moment she was off duty, going alone to her room and just sitting on the bed. Certainly the other officers noticed it and surely it would soon be brought to her attention, but they also ought to have the grace to understand why she felt this way. Even a stranger, if they knew the circumstances would understand, and would refrain from acting as if she were doing anything untoward each day, but she knew the other officers were changing their feelings toward her, too, because she was withdrawing from them, almost as if she had made them feel something was wrong with them, something hideous about them because they were alive, almost as if they didn't have a right to be alive. Yet it was a blessed moment to be alone just like this in one's own room.

She rose mechanically and went to the dressing table and picked up a package of cigarettes. They were Gold Flakes and she was the only officer who bought them regularly. For an instant she felt a little foolish for being so particular about her choice of cigarettes. She liked all kinds of cigarettes, even NAAFIS, if it came to that. Suddenly she began to cry. She had cried a lot in the past several weeks; in the first week for different reasons than now, and now she sought a reason for the difference in her tears at this moment, and then she realized it was because of a silly package of cigarettes. They were the kind that Gifford always smoked.

It was terrible to cry like this over something so trivial, a package of cigarettes. She put down the package of cigarettes and wiped her eyes on a towel. And she decided to let herself completely unwind, and as she thought about it, she stopped crying suddenly.

She looked at the phonograph. It was a portable with a hand crank, set on the edge of a dressing table. She tried to remember the tunes that Gifford liked and she could not think of anything special because he always seemed to like so many songs. She knew that her brother and Russell thought that Gifford lacked taste in everything, but taste didn't mean anything during a war. She liked his taste because she loved him. She knew he liked to dance to *Begin the Beguine* and she wondered why he liked a *Nightingale Sang in Berkeley Square*. It was from Charlot's Review which was before his time. She had seen the show with her father, and he had not approved of it, no, with her brother, and he had laughed, and then after the show had not approved of it. If Gifford hadn't come along, she thought, I would have married Russell, provided he lived through the war, and I would be the same person I was before the war, before meeting Gifford. Was it the war or Gifford who changed her viewpoint of life. God, she thought, I used to be stuffy ... But people could revert, and she supposed that when it was all over and she was out of the service and everybody else was out, and her true love was dead and gone, she would return to being the person she had been before the war, inwardly and outwardly, correct, proper, believing only in God, the King and business as usual, as the three most important things in the world, outside of a nice, comfortable husband who went into town every day on the train at the same time and came home every night at the same time and said the same thing every day for umpteen years.

Well, she was glad for one thing; she had stopped dreaming finally about seeing his machine going down in flames and all of them burning, falling in flames, falling and falling down through sheets of fire, eating up the machine. It was bad enough to cry suddenly during the day, but to have hysterics at night in a dream had become so unbearable she feared going to bed, and suddenly three days ago the dreams had ceased. She prayed they would not return. It was also hysterical to keep wondering about that other woman, Katherine Alcott, if she loved Gifford as much as she said she had. It doesn't even bother me, Jennifer thought, that she had an affair with him. It doesn't even bother me that he would because he's mine, but I can't stop wondering if her love for him was or still is more than mine. This frightened her. She remembered that day going to Diana's apartment and finding Katherine and her husband there, worrying about Diana, that she might mean something to Gifford, but finding her dead, no longer thinking of her, and yet knowing Katherine would never be free, and that Gifford's affair with her was only a fling in the hay, and despite all this, and knowing how much she loved Gifford, wondering if she could love him as deeply as Katherine had; or were Katherine's feelings merely the product of the woman who will forever hold a love unobtainable more dear than love obtained? Well, she would never know, and she was happy now for a moment as she remembered Gifford and tender moments with him.

Katherine's grief. Could it have been a performance merely to make Katherine feel alive when her own marriage was so dead and to make me feel jealous forever because neither of us would ever see him again? It didn't seem possible, but women were strange, jealous creatures, and would even claim allegiance to the dead over another woman. Hooey!

I ought to go to the mess and have a drink ...

And something else. Even the new wingco had hinted at it. A spot of leave, like aircrew took when they started getting flak happy, two or three weeks on the Devon coast, but did they really forget death down there? Could it be forgotten over nine daily holes of golf? Would eight hours of regular sleep daily for two weeks eradicate the cumulative erosion of daily anxiety? Would golf and bridge and new scenery take away the grief and shock? Maybe it would be the right thing to do. Strange, she could feel nothing for her father, and yet she had been fond of him, even loved him as a little girl growing up, but now there was no grief for him; it was almost as if the shock of Gifford's going had numbed her beyond any more grief. No, she could still cry; and, no, she was not going to take leave and go away by herself because she would be by herself no matter where she went and it wouldn't help at all. It would be unbearable.

Wasn't there somebody she could talk to? She wondered about Gifford's relatives and wished they were in England; she could talk to them, a sister, or his mother, just somebody to talk to, just anybody who knew him. She wondered what his family was like; he had never mentioned them. And in civilian life he had been a racing driver. Did he have any family? She must find out and write them. That's what she would do. Write them a long letter. It would be a way of talking about him to somebody.

But what if he didn't have any family? What if there wasn't anybody she could write to? ... God.

Go and see the adjutant and get Gifford's records and find out, that was the best thing. And try not to sit around the room like this alone every late afternoon, when off duty. Thinking this Jennifer began to feel differently; she felt relieved and better. Oh, God, everybody in the mess seemed so stupid and their conversations seemed so stupid, as if she had heard them all a thousand times, the same words crawling in and out of their mouths.

She lit a cigarette but could not taste it. She felt the corners of her eyes getting ready to cry again. Her mouth tasted rotten, and she could feel tears in the back of her throat though she had not started to cry. There was a knock at the door. It was the sergeant. She was a fat woman who doubled at being PT instructor for the squadron of WAAFs.

'New draft of girls just came in,' she said. Why at this time of day? How she hated having to go and give them a talk.

'How many?'

'Five, ma'am.'

'All right,' Jennifer said, still feeling tears quivering around the edges of her eyes. She touched her eyes, each lid, and the quivering stopped and she rose and put on her tunic and cap and followed the sergeant down the hall.

'I'll see them one at a time,' said Jennifer.

The first two were mousy little girls from

Sunderland, and one needed a bath, and the third was a tall girl from Scotland with an accent Jennifer could scarcely fathom. Jennifer was looking down at papers on her desk when she heard the door close behind the fourth new girl and she did not look up until after she heard the girl's heels click to attention. Then she looked up. At first she only partially recognized the woman's face. It was not the face of a girl. It was the face of a woman, but the hair was different, and there was no sign of recognition on the woman's face; the woman was looking straight ahead, straight over Jennifer's head, eyes perfectly front, and hands by her side, rigidly at attention. Jennifer wondered if the woman looked at her if she could see she had been crying, and suddenly she felt grateful, almost happy, and yet she wanted to cry again, to put her arms around this woman, to hold her, to have her embrace in return, to stand with her like that for a moment. Now she wouldn't have to find any one to weep with her for him, to talk to her about him, because that person was here, someone who would weep for her, too, and it was what she needed all along, someone to weep for her.

'Katherine,' she said. She almost smiled. 'What are you doing here?'

'Ma'am?'

'Katherine,' she said, rising. 'I'm Jennifer. Jennifer Caldwell. Don't you remember?' Jennifer started around the desk.

The woman stood there, until Jennifer put her arms around her, and they embraced without speaking.

Jennifer drew her head back.

'Whatever—?' she began. She sounded quietly astonished.

Katherine looked at her.

'I couldn't stand it. Just sitting around. I mean never intended coming here.'

'Cigarette?' said Jennifer and picked up the package of Gold Flakes and they both stared at it as if it were something alive as it lay in Jennifer's hand between them.

Book Eight
TOWARD THE SEA

47 FLIGHT LIEUTENANT JACK GIFFORD

There are times when one's luck just keeps running on and on and because it keeps running so well after a lot of bad luck you begin to get scared because the luck is running too well. And when it keeps running well you get more scared, thinking all the time, something has to go wrong, has to go wrong, it can't keep running this good. That's how it was for us. We were making about twenty miles a day, just walking right down the main road, nobody stopping us because we were all wearing German uniforms and I could speak the language, but even then I didn't have to because though we passed Kraut soldiers they simply nodded or we would give them the Nazi salute in return. We skirted all the towns and slept in the woods at night. It made me nervous. It couldn't go on this good. It couldn't be this easy. We had the weapons, if anything happened, and the Resistance had told us to keep off the back road or they couldn't promise we wouldn't get shot at, and they'd given us the place to go to in Marseilles. Sometimes I felt I could smell the sea, but I knew I was only trying to will the miles to go faster past us, I was more worried than ever before.

We just came over the top of the hill when it happened. A tank. I don't know what kind, but it was a tank. We didn't have a chance to hide. It was the first tank we had seen on the road, going either way, and it was coming fast. I shouted to just keep marching single file, and not move a muscle, and if it stopped I would do the talking. They all kept walking and if they didn't look as good as Kraut soldiers I thought they were a reasonable facsimile.

I should have taught them a Kraut marching song or something, but perhaps it was better the way it was, just the silent column and me in a Kraut sergeant uniform. I could hear Reker starting to spit which he always did when he was nervous and I told him to stop spitting.

The turret was pointing straight ahead so I figured they would pass us because it was also traveling damn fast. I watched it getting closer and closer. Then it began to slow down. I could hear Reker starting to spit again into the ditch. I loosened the grenade in my belt, and got ready, though I didn't stop walking. I figured if my German failed me, the officer in the tank would have his head out of the turret anyway, and I'd pop the grenade inside the tank before he could close the hatch. It was our only chance if my accent made him suspicious. The tank came abreast of us slowly, and then slowing again, stopped, and the turret hatch popped open and an officer stuck his head out the window. I halted the column and saluted. He wanted to know how far it was to Digne. Well, we'd passed around Digne the night before. So I told him fifteen kilometers. He popped his head down inside the turret and then just as we started to move off he stuck his head up again and from the corner of my eye I saw him give us a fast once over and then down went his head again, and the tank roared away as the hatch clanged shut. I hadn't thought my German sounded too bad but you couldn't tell. I couldn't see his face too well because he was wearing goggles and a metal tank helmet, so I couldn't see by his eyes how he felt about my German, but it was too easy, too easy, and it worried me. Reker was spitting again but I didn't say anything.

'How much further today?' said Norton. I didn't answer him. He knew we would walk as far as we could walk, until we were too tired to walk any further because it was safer in daylight in these suits. Somebody sure as hell would take a crack at us in the dark if they thought we were Krauts, and besides Krauts would start challenging us in the dark.

'Take ten,' I said suddenly. I wanted to talk to them. I had a feeling about that Kraut in the tank. I couldn't tell why, but I felt he was going to get down the road a piece and wonder about my accent. I had been tired and I think I sounded a little too much New Ulm, Minnesota Kraut rather than Bavarian; the way he had given us a once over the second time.

'He smelled us,' said Norton.

'You're crackers,' said Craig. 'He never twigged for a second.'

We sat in the ditch, lying back against the slope. It was sunny and warm, and the boots hurt my feet.

'What do you think?' I asked Caldwell.

'Just keep going,' he said. 'And keep our eyes open.'

'If he comes back,' I said, 'we've got to have a plan.'

'Run for it,' said Craig.

'Come off it,' said Norton. 'They'd cut us up in a minute.'

'It's a piece of cake,' said Reker, spitting. 'That Kraut took off like a blue-ass canary in a dust bin.'

'Craig,' I said. 'I want you off the road, about twenty-five feet inside the woods.'

You couldn't really call them woods, just bushes and trees, thin cover, but good enough to shoot through. And Craig had the machine pistol. It was a kind of sub-machine gun, faster and bigger than a Thomson.

'I can't keep up,' he said.

'We'll move slowly,' I said. 'You'll be able to keep up.'

His eyes watched me carefully.

'Can you work that gun fast?' I said. He nodded, not taking his eyes off my face.

'Now listen, everybody,' I said. 'If that tank comes back or if there are more coming, and it's radioed back to check us over, remember this. Craig will cover us from the woods. Keep your grenades loose. And if the tank stops, come in close, so close they can't nail you with the machine gun. Craig, if I raise my right hand and touch the back of my head, open up on the Kraut who's sticking up in the turret. You've got to nail him. The minute he's nailed I want the rest of you to start heaving grenades into the top of the turret. Okay?'

'Okay.'

'Don't miss.'

'I'm a sniper,' Craig said. 'I just got promoted. No flying pay.'

'You were overpaid in the air for what you did,' Norton said.

'Want to take my place?' Craig asked.

'You look like a Kraut sniper.'

'I've got news for you. Gifford's keeping you on the road because your head is so square they can't possibly mistake you for an Englishman.'

'Sure,' Norton said. 'Herr Norton.'

'Shut up,' I said. 'Don't any of you put your hands near those grenades when I'm talking to the Kraut. Norton, stand at the right hand corner of the tank. Reker, stand on my left. Caldwell, I want you behind me. Shoot over my head if Craig misses. Both you other guys! Hop up on the tank the second the Kraut drops inside and start popping grenades on him. Reker, you understand?'

'Yes, sir.'

'All right. Any questions? Okay? Fall in and start marching.'

It was a nice, sunny afternoon. We marched slowly. Not a sound. The country-side was beautiful, rolling trees and hills, and little farm houses set back in the fold of hills. Not a sign of war. It was difficult to believe we had ever heard or seen war. The sky was brilliant, the color of glass, domed a vivid-blue, cloudless and windless. Not even an aircraft in the sky. It didn't seem possible that anything could happen to us and the more I thought about the tank the more it seemed to me I was jumpy and as a result overly suspicious of anybody who looked faintly cross-eyed at me, and there was no reason why an officer might not take a second look at us, perhaps with the thought of reporting us because we were not the finest looking body of troops in Europe. Yet, if he wanted to report us he would have asked for our unit.

But if he did come back, and he did doubt us, we had only a fraction of a second's chance, because if he got that turret hatch down before he was dead, and even if he were wounded, we were finished. He had to go on the first shot because if he were wounded they would get the turret hatch down and the Kraut inside and pull away from us and mow us down with their machine gun. We would never make it to the woods and it wouldn't do any good to get to the ditch. It could come right down the ditch after us and grenades were not going to disturb the tracks on a tank that size. It looked like a medium sized tank. Maybe the best thing to do would be to hide in the woods now. No, that would create suspicion if they came back because there weren't any towns nearby and there were no troops in the field and if we just vanished into thin air they would surely look for us tomorrow and the next day and from then on in and we would never make it to Marseilles. If we blew the tank, it wouldn't necessarily look like we did it. It would be put down to the work of Resistance. I hoped. But right now I was willing to bet I had been overly-suspicious and it wasn't coming back.

SERGEANT ROBERT CRAIG

I watched Reker. He was spitting. Not nervous. Gifford thought it was because of his nerves. No. Reker gets mean when he spits. It was a good sign. I touched the trigger. It was thin. Gifford went on, looking first to the front and then to the back. Good man. I thought about the tank coming back. What would happen? Was I that good a shot? I doubted it. I better get him. I thought about hunting when I was a kid. The first time I understood wing shooting. What a surprise. Couldn't believe it. Pheasant coming straight at me. At least thirty-five yards high. Going fast. Somebody shouting: 'Aim behind and pull through fifteen feet.' I didn't believe it. How could you hit something shooting that far in front. Amazing, not even seeing the bird when I fired and everybody shouting and the bird sailing and sailing, sprawling suddenly across the sky, tumbling, wings and feet swinging every which way, fifty yards down the field. I wondered how tanks traveled. In pairs? I remembered seeing movies of them in columns, masses, going across the Russian plains. What was one doing alone? Maybe he was on the way to the garage to get something fixed. I thought about Marseilles. Gifford said there was a place there we would contact and they would get us aboard a submarine. How far was it? I thought about Marseilles. Would we make it? Had we come all this way for nothing.

Then I heard it and the column seemed to pause and as I heard the sound again, Gifford put his hand behind his back and beckoned everybody to keep walking, and then it came clearly. It's a tank, I thought, but it wasn't coming back. It was another tank, coming from the direction of the first tank. It would pass us going the opposite way, and it was too late to get off the road, too flat, it would see us now. The country was too open.

I could see their faces through the bushes. Caldwell looked like the typical British officer out for a Sunday afternoon walk in the park. They ought to spot him immediately. No foot slogger walked that erect with his chin held high and his head back. He looked like a Guards officer in Green Park. Norton and Reker ought to pull their heads back. They seemed to be leaning forward, trying to peer into the distance, trying to see the tank we could only hear now. Gifford's face was set. He looked like somebody going into a rugger scrum or a street fight. He ought to relax or maybe Kraut sergeants naturally looked that mean.

I looked at the trigger, and checked the safety catch. It was off. I tried sighting. I put the safety on. It was a light machine gun but I wasn't going to pick off anybody firing from the hip at this distance. I looked around for objects to practice throwing down on, slinging the butt against my shoulder fast. I did some dry firing on the column, first sighting on Gifford's head and shoulders. I stopped and stood still and pulled down on each man and held steady with the safety on. Head and shoulders. Five fast rounds. Have to nail him with one of the first three slugs. The gun would pull after that. Then I saw the tank. Big. Maybe bigger than the first one. The hatch was down. The turret was moving. That was bad. The turret on the first tank had not been moving. What was this one looking for? And besides it was not moving as fast as the first tank. Not nearly as fast because it was looking the country over.

The column moved along the road and the tank moved toward the column and I practiced sighting on everybody's head at least once, first walking and then standing still. It was a long shot with a gun that would jump after the first burst, and I certainly couldn't be sure of knocking him off with one shot. I would have to get him with a burst. But maybe I wouldn't have to get him at all. Maybe they would go right past, and keep going and never stop. Sure. Never stop. Stop kidding. If they were looking the country over, swinging a turret, they were going to stop and ask questions.

It was close now, and it was stopping, about fifteen feet in front of Gifford and the hatch opened, but not before Gifford got everybody up against the side of the tank, running. So they were all in close. I ran and ducked and ran and got even with the tank just as the hatch popped open and I sighted along the barrel just below the hatch cover.

A couple seconds passed and an officer's head popped out. He rose higher, head and chest out of the tank and sat on the rim of the open turret, and pushed up his goggles. He smiled. Gifford saluted.

I set the gun against the side of tree trunk and got it steady. I held my breath and held the sight on the officer's stomach. He waved a hand casually palm up and Gifford nodded. I could see the officer's lips moving and Reker and Norton sidled out from behind Gifford. They stood against the corners of the tank. Caldwell didn't move. He was directly behind Gifford.

Suddenly I saw the officer stop smiling and his lips moving rapidly. My eyes blinked and as they blinked it all happened all at once; Gifford's hand jerked toward the back of his head at the same instant I saw the officer jerking at the pistol in his waist holster. It took a split second to adjust the sight again to his stomach as he leaned back, jerking. The noise of the gun hammered in my ear. I let him have a long burst. I knew I had hit him. He fell backward out of the tank.

The tank suddenly shot forward. Reker and Norton already were on top. I saw them drop grenades into the open mouth of the turret and leap. There was a dull sound when the grenades exploded, and the tank went on rumbling down the road and then swerved and went down into a ditch and up the other side and came to a stop against a tree. The machine gun slanted down.

I ran back along the cover of trees. Everybody was in the ditch now across from the tank. I stayed in the trees and covered the tank.

A pair of arms stuck up out of the open turret and a man appeared, holding his hands above his head. He kept his hands that way. He jumped down on to the road and another head appeared above the tank and another German crawled out. His hands were in the right place, high.

'Craig!' Gifford shouted. 'Shoot them!'

Was he crazy? I didn't move. I looked at the two men. One was blond and one was dark. They did not look like members of the super race. They looked like a couple of miners, with broken noses and cuts across their faces. They were perhaps twenty-two or three years old. Blood ran down the side of the blond's face and I could see a dark stain in the shirt sleeve of the other.

He lowered one arm and pointed at the wound.

'Come on! Come on!' Gifford shouted.

No, this was murder, assassination. They couldn't defend themselves. They had surrendered. You didn't kill prisoners. I was no killer.

'Shoot them yourself,' I said. I did not move. Almost as I said it Gifford turned and looked at me over his shoulder, with his hand drawing out the pistol from his holster.

The blond one saw it and started to run and Reker fired and the blond rolled into the ditch against the tank. The dark-haired one stopped and started to go down on his knees but he never made it. Gifford shot him between the eyes and he never had a chance to kneel and ask for his life.

'Get those bodies in the woods,' Gifford shouted. 'I'll see if I can get this tank going.' He started down the ditch and stopped and called back: 'Caldwell, get the officer's uniform.'

FLIGHT SERGEANT EDWARD REKER

It was dark. We'd been on the road since sunset. It was really a jam with five of us inside the tank. It had taken me a while to figure out how to reverse the tank. The gears were easy, just like a car, but you had to turn the wheel when you reversed the gears. We had pulled into the woods and Gifford figured out how to run the machine. Simple. Just gears, so we were making about fifteen miles an hour down the highway. We figured to go as far as we could go and as fast at night. Gifford was dressed in the officer uniform. He sat up in the turret along with Caldwell who claimed he had figured how to operate the gun. Norton was acting as leader and Craig was sitting on the floor in front of Norton. It was a hell of a jam.

Up ahead the failing light that was almost darkness was pierced suddenly by a light beam. It wavered and wavered across the road. Then two lights glowed red on the road.

'Road block!' Gifford shouted. 'Caldwell, are you loaded?'

'Ready,' said Caldwell.

'Reker,' said Gifford. 'Start slowing and stop at the road block.'

We rumbled slowly forward, braking.

'Caldwell,' said Gifford. 'Stand by with the machine gun.'

'Right-oh.'

'I'll do the talking,' said Gifford. 'Caldwell, if I want machine gun fire, I'll tap your right or left leg, so just open up in that direction. Then we'll make a break for it. Off the road. Everybody bail out then and take off. I'll give the signal to bail out.'

'You mean you're going to try to run the road block, Gifford?' said Caldwell.

'Depends on the situation. We'll just play it as it comes.'

I could hear my breath. I was panting like bloody hell and my heart was pounding. The tank crept toward the light. The light splashed in a pool over the highway. My fingers grew tighter and tighter on the wheel. Suddenly a huge oblong of darkness loomed out behind the light and I was just about to yell when Gifford shouted.

'Tank! Stop!'

I stopped the tank.

The gun barrel of the tank looked twenty feet long in the light. A helmeted figure popped out of the tank and started walking toward our tank. Suddenly he ducked down in the ditch and I saw the tank gun traverse faintly and start to move downward. I started to open my mouth just as Gifford yelled: 'Fire! Goddamn it! Fire!'

There was a tremendous roar and I thought we were hit. The tank shuddered under the recoil and I smelled the cordite.

I slammed the gears into action and we shot through a swirl of flames. A figure disappeared under the tank.

'Off the road!' Gifford shouted.

I slammed the machine down into the ditch and up the side and into the woods. We crashed through the underbrush. It was dark and we went pounding along, expecting to hit a big tree any second. But we picked up speed. Suddenly we were out on a meadow, doing about twenty miles an hour. We went along like that for about five minutes, everything smooth, Gifford with his head out of the turret now, giving us a play-by-play account of the fire behind us.

'Must had only one tank,' he said. 'Nice shooting Caldwell.'

'Keep going south,' said Gifford. 'We'll bail out in the first woods we find as soon as it gets light.'

FLIGHT SERGEANT NORTON

It was foggy in the morning. The sky was still dark. The wind blew cold on my shoulders. As the darkness drifted I thought about eating breakfast. My stomach jumped. I thought about all the good breakfasts I had eaten, scrambled eggs, hot sausage, scalding hot tea with lots of milk, kippers and kidneys on toast, and I couldn't stop thinking about it, even when it started to rain. I must have been talking about it out loud to myself.

'Will you shut your mouth,' Craig said.

'You're not the only one who's hungry. Christ, they must have caught him by now.'

I had never felt hungrier in my life. My stomach kept turning over. I looked out through the trees and saw the light falling through the cold rain. We must be about three miles from where we ditched the tank. Gifford had left us.

'If I'm not back at noon, move out, one at a time,' he had said and gone out to check the area. Well, the rain was one consolation. They couldn't put dogs on us. The woods here were much thicker and the underbrush heavier than any we had seen in three days, and it was hilly.

'Don't you miss the squadron sausage?' I said to Reker. He looked real browned-off.

'I hope you get a lot of camping after the war,' Craig said.

'This is a nice spot for a camp,' I said. 'These are nice trees.'

'I hope you wind up in the woods after the war,' said Reker.

'I'm a city boy,' I said.

'With a bloody city mouth,' said Reker.

'I'm a city boy and outdoor man,' I said.

'Drop dead,' said Craig.

'Ss-s-s-s-h,' said Caldwell.

'Are you an outdoor man, sir?' I asked

Caldwell. I could see he had lost his sense of humor, too. But bloody hell who wasn't cold and hungry?

'Shut up,' Caldwell said.

'Turn yourself in at sick-call this morning,' Craig said.

'How do you spell Scarborough?' I said. 'The winner gets a free trip to the mouth of the Humber River on a house boat.'

'It's an order,' said Caldwell. 'Shut your mouth.'

'Listen,' I said. 'They got Gifford. Let's get out of here.'

'Wait till noon. That's what we're going to do,' said Caldwell.

'I have a bad memory,' I said.

'Norton,' Caldwell said.

'Stay here and get wrapped up,' I said. 'When the rain stops, they'll have a hundred Krauts in here looking for us, and they'll shoot us sure as hell.'

I got up and out from under the trees. I started walking. There were small bare patches in the woods. Trees had been sawed down and hauled away. The stumps were still there. They looked like fresh stumps. I walked about five minutes and started to feel alone. I felt my spine tingle as if a buzzer were warning me to go back. I felt disgusted weak and wanted to run. But I didn't feel strong enough to run. I wiped sweat from my eyes and leaned against a tree. The rain was cold. Something struck me a blow between the shoulders and I fell on my face. Somebody climbed on my back and sat there. I didn't give a damn. I lay with my face in the mud.

'You dumb bastard,' Gifford said. 'Where were you going?'

'I was looking for you.'

'Get up.'

I wanted to lie there, never get up, but I got up.

'Come on,' he said, pushing me. 'You dumb bastard. Running around with your stupid head cut off.'

'I was looking for you.'

'Now you found me.'

'Did you find anything to eat?' I asked.

'Better. A nunnery.'

'What?'

'Come on, dope,' Gifford said. 'They won't talk. Can't. Only one. The head one.'

'Silent vows,' I said.

'What?' he said. Who's a dope, I thought.

'They must have vows of silence,' I said.

'Come on. Pick up your feet.'

'Will they feed us?'

'Yes. Yes. And we can hide there.'

INTELLIGENCE REPORT

Documentary Records

EXCERPTS FROM CONVERSATIONS DEAL-
ING WITH EXPERIENCES OF MEMBERS
OF THE FRENCH RESISTANCE WHO
CAME IN CONTACT WITH MEMBERS
OF THE ROYAL AIR FORCE CREW OF
THE HALIFAX BOMBER W FOR WILLIAM.
CONVERSATIONS TOOK PLACE AFTER
THE WAR.
Speakers: British intelligence officer and
Madame Fetole, French Resistance worker
in Marseilles.

'I don't recall the exact time they
arrived. It was during the afternoon. No,
I was not notified. I heard about the
tank from our operator at Saint Santin.
They were brought to my apartment by
Rene Dusacq. They were all dressed in
Trappistine nun's habits. They were very
tired and dusty looking, having walked,
they said, twenty-five miles into Marseilles.
They were laughing about something and
Rene explained they had been stopped by
a German patrol and the big American
Gifford explained they were an order with
vows of silence. All of them were armed
under their habits. We were going to
send them out through Perpignan, but
our contacts were lost so we kept them

two weeks. We had in the city at that time twenty-five British fliers in various apartments. All were taken off in a British submarine on the night of the twenty-sixth. Yes, they obtained the nun's habits at the convent which sheltered them after they abandoned the tank. The nuns contacted Rene who met them in Marseilles. Their feet were in poor condition from wearing nun's shoes which were too small for them.

Book Nine
HOME AGAIN

48   JACK GIFFORD–
JENNIFER CALDWELL

The sun was shining on the trees on Cheyney Walk. Inside the wall surrounding the outdoor tables at the Chelsea Arms there were trees growing among the tables and the leaves were a beautiful pale sea-like green in the sunlight. The red bricks in the wall of the building were old but in the sunlight they were shining a dark red wine color. Jack Gifford and Jennifer Caldwell sat at a table in the center of the court yard. The sun was warm.

'What would you like?' Jennifer said.

'I'm up to here with beer since I got back,' Gifford said.

'Whiskey?'

'Miss,' Gifford said to the waitress who was about to serve the table beside them.

The girl finished serving and turned to them.

'Gin and orange and a whiskey,' Gifford said.

'Black Label?' the waitress smiled.

'Don't tell me we have a choice. We must be winning the war.'

The waitress smiled and left. Jennifer and Gifford looked at people while they waited for the waitress. The waitress brought the gin and orange in a cocktail glass and the whiskey in a short glass. Jennifer looked at the court yard. The tree in the middle was short, heavy with leaves.

Jack saw her looking at it; 'Is that a plane tree?' he said.

'Don't you have them in America?' she sipped her drink.

'I never saw one until I came to England.'

'You might have,' she said. 'Maybe you didn't know it.'

'No.'

Jennifer looked at the open newspaper on top of the table.

'There's a good show at the Shaftsbury,' she said. 'Have you seen Noel Coward?'

'He wears yellow polka dot pajamas.'

'This is a good show, actually.'

Gifford saw the waitress and waved.

'Two more.'

'Same?'

'Whiskey double. Jennifer?'

Jennifer smiled. 'Did you ever mix gin and whiskey?'

'Oh, come along.'

'Two whiskey?' asked the waitress.

'No. Double whiskey. Gin and orange.'

'I'd only get sick,' Jennifer said.

'Nobody gets sick. You just stay on doubles.'

'I'm not going to work at getting sick,' said Jennifer.

'Come on. We never had it so good.'

'Don't be foolish,' she said.

'Nothing is going to spoil my leave.'

She smiled.

'Cheers,' they touched glasses.

'Whizzo,' he said mockingly.

'Wizard. That's how we're supposed to feel, isn't it? Absolutely wizard?'

'If you say so.'

Gifford glanced at the plane tree.

'Bet you,' he said, 'we don't have trees like that in America. Never saw one in my life.'

'No bet.'

'Time for another,' he smiled.

Suddenly the tree paled faintly as the sun slid through a cloud and then after a long moment the tree began to bloom greenly.

The sun came out brightly.

'God, that whiskey is good,' Gifford said.

'Another?'

'Look,' Gifford said. 'He's dead. I've told you the whole thing.'

Jennifer looked into her glass.

'I asked intelligence,' he said.

Jennifer did not say anything. He looked at her hands.

'I want to marry you. Can't you get that through your head?'

'It wouldn't be fair without seeing him first.'

'You love me?'

'It's not that.'

'Listen, I'm going back on ops.'

Jennifer, holding the stem between thumb and forefinger, slowly twirled the glass.

Gifford leaned forward.

'You don't have to feel guilty about it. He's dead.'

'You don't understand,' she said. 'If I married you and he came back, face to face, how do you think I would feel?'

'He's dead. Listen to me!'

'No, not always thinking I cut him off when he didn't have a chance to see me.'

Gifford did not say anything.

'Oh, God, I don't know what to do, Jack.'

'Marry me. And don't worry.'

'If I do it, could we get out of here? America.'

'Now? That's impossible.'

'You know, Jack. I only really care about us. You know that.'

'Then let's get married.'

'Oh, God,' she said.

'Nothing's ever fair,' he said. 'You know that.'

Jennifer leaned back in her chair. She glanced up at the sky. It was one of those unbelievably radiant English days, the high sky vivid as glass, filled with whipped cream clouds. The high sky shimmered, bluish-white.

'We can wait until after the war,' she said. 'Then we'll know.'

'Don't try to predict anything.'

'Look at the sky. We could live here after the war.'

'No, we'll live in America.'

'No,' she said. 'I don't think we'll ever live anywhere.'

'Don't talk rot.'

'You are getting English.'

'All right. Baloney. Don't talk baloney.'

'Baloney,' she said.

'Listen, we're living now. How many nows do we get?'

'You told me not to predict.'

'Give me your hand,' he said. 'I don't know where you get such crazy ideas.'

'It's never going to work,' she said. 'I just know it.'

'Don't go clairvoyant on me.'

'I want another gin and orange,' she said.

'Sure. But be practical.'

'That's just what I'm being,' she said. 'Oh, let's forget it today and just enjoy ourselves, please.'

They ordered two more drinks and drank slowly and looked at each other across the table.

'You must realize,' he said, 'it was his choice. Nobody there could have ordered him to do it. I don't know—maybe you still love him.'

'After last night? Are you mad?'

'No, of course not. I want you all the time. I want you with me on the squadron.'

'I'm there now,' she said.

'But how do I know I'll be posted back there?'

'Oh, stop it,' she said. 'Let's enjoy the time we have.'

He lifted his glass and drank until the glass was empty.

'I want to marry you,' he said. 'This week. Now.'

'I won't even talk about it anymore. Go on. But I won't talk about it.'

He looked at his watch. 'Well, I can catch the five-forty,' he said.

'What?' she said.

'I'm going to catch the five-forty,' he said, winding his watch. He did not look at her.

'Oh, we're going to act that way.'

'Any way you want to call it,' he said. She smiled at him.

'All right. You better pick up your kit at the hotel.'

'I'll get it.' He put a shilling on the table. He got up and as she started to rise he touched her hand on top of the table.

'No,' he said. 'Stay here. When you make up your mind, write me. I love you, Jennifer.'

'You have a nice way of saying it. Goodbye, I love you.'

'When you make up your mind, let me know.' He stooped his head and kissed her cheek. She did not move. She watched him cross the court yard and vanish.

He caught a taxi back to the Green Park hotel and got his new kit bags and caught another taxi to St. Pancras

Station. He went into the station bar to wait for the train. He drank two pints of mild and bitter and read the evening paper, leaning on the bar. When he heard his train announced he walked out across the platform. A New Zealand pilot he had gotten tight with a couple times in London passed him.

'Hello, Jack,' he said.

'Lofty, how goes it?'

'I heard you were dead,' said the New Zealander.

'Not bloody likely,' Gifford heard the train whistle. He shook hands, turned and ran toward the line of coaches.

49 SERGEANT REKER– JOYCE MOWBRY

'No,' said Reker. 'I won't.'

'Please.'

'No.'

'Okay. Okay,' said Joyce.

'I'm sorry,' he said, and she didn't know he was thinking about the girl in France.

If you have never been in Reading, England, you are lucky. If you have been there, make the most of the train stop-over, don't walk around and look at the town. Joyce was thinking this as she had been thinking this for fifteen years without ever saying it in words to herself. Now she was getting it in words to herself. She looked at herself and thought of her mother, for what they were, for the first time. Oh, God, she thought.

'What's wrong with me?' she said.

'What?'

He didn't say anything for he saw suddenly she was more beautiful than ever before: svelte (he hated the word, but she was svelte). All smoothly plum-ripe, golden bright skin flushed smoothly with plum-wine color, the color beneath the flesh glowing beautifully. He wanted her right there suddenly at the bar table. It was the first time he had had any feelings toward anybody since he had returned. As he felt this he was at once happy and sad. Quickly happy and then sad because he could not hold the happiness for in that moment he felt it slipping away. He knew he had become strange to himself. No.

'I'm fine,' he said.

'Really. What is it?'

'I don't know,' he said.

'Oh, darling, darling,' she said. She looked straight into his eyes and something there, neither blank, nor cold, nor dead, told her that touching his hand now would mean nothing to him.

'Christ,' he said. 'Forget it.' His head was hung slightly with a rueful smile which served only to cover the lowering of his eyelids. Why can't I feel something toward her, he thought. She's carrying my child. Why can't I feel something? He didn't realize how much the child and death had frightened him. He had seen death before but never a child of his own to care for, dying.

'I love you so much,' he said.

'What's wrong with you then?'

'Oh, God, I'm sorry,' he said. 'Please understand.'

'What's happened to you?'

'I'll be all right.'

'I'm sorry,' she said.

'It's not your fault.'

'Don't say that. It may be. You know what I mean. You know, we understand each other.'

'Bullshit,' he said.

'What do you want me to say then?'

'Keep it up. It'll come out as if you told the truth anyway.'

'Yes.'

'Let's cut out, darling.'

He looked at her briefly as if he were sorry.

'You don't believe I still love you, do you?' he said.

'Rot,' she said. 'Bilge. Well,' she said. 'What am I supposed to do about it?'

'I don't know.'

'It's your child.'

'I know,' he said. He looked at her and touched her hand.

'Poor darling,' he said. His hands were cold.

'Oh, stop it,' she said. 'You're only acting. What's wrong with you? Ever since you came back. You're a different person.'

'Hell, I don't know.'

'That's for sure.'

'I do love you, Joyce.'

'Stop it.'

'I'm sorry,' he said, 'if I could explain everything to you, I would.'

'Don't bother. What's her name?'

'It isn't that,' he said, looking at her. 'It isn't that at all.'

'I'm sorry,' she said.

'If it was only just one thing I could put my finger on.'

'Have you talked to a doctor?'

'What the hell do they know? Half the time I feel sleepy and half the time I can't sleep.'

'You should tell somebody.'

'Sure,' he said. 'They'd think I was malingering. Trying to get off ops again.'

'I'm sorry,' she said. 'I try to understand, but when you kiss me it's as if you weren't really there. You don't feel anything, do you?'

'No,' he said. 'I guess not.'

'I'll have an abortion.'

'You mustn't do that.'

They looked at each other in silence for a little while.

'I don't care how you feel,' she said. 'You'll get over it. Please. I want our baby.'

'All right. All right.'

'I'll make you love me again.'

'Darling, you don't have to prove it.'

'Oh, God, what's happened to you?'

'Just a little numbness,' he said. 'It will probably go away.'

'It won't,' she said. 'That's what frightens me. I can tell when you kiss me.'

'That's what I mean. The trouble is I don't feel a damn thing about anything.'

'You don't have to with me.'

'Yes, I do.'

'When did it start?'

He did not answer again and she put her hand out and touched his hand again. The bobby was coming along the walk toward them. He had a big black Irish face. He looked at the other couples just like these two who were sitting on the benches in the park. There were sailors and airmen and soldiers, all with their girl friends, all young, sitting close. They all looked alike to the bobby. He strolled slowly through the park.

'Couldn't we get married before you go back to the squadron?' Joyce asked.

'What if I live?'

'Don't talk rot. Of course, you'll live.'

'But I told you. I don't love you anymore.'

Three soldiers went past whistling a marching tune.

'You'd never forgive me. It'd be like living with a dead man,' he said.

'I don't care. It's the child.'

'I know. All right, I'll marry you.'

'Do you have to say it like that?'

'How do you want me to say it?'

'You don't have to sound that way.'

'What way? How do I sound? How do you want me to sound?'

'Oh, darling, try to be sweet. Just try, please.'

'What time are we meeting Ann?'

'A few minutes. What's this Norton person like?'

'A loner. No girl friends as far as I know.'

'Is he like you?'

'I hope not. No. Don't worry. He'll be nice to her.'

'I hope so. It just about broke her heart. Not a word about him. Funny. He went missing the same night you did.'

'Parachute type you said?'

'Not actually. I don't really know. Something to do with radar.'

'It just about killed her. She's just coming out of it.'

'Don't worry about Norton.'

'Do you have to go back on ops?'

'I'll be okay.'

'Oh, God, nothing must happen to you, darling. I want you back. You'll feel differently when this mess is over.'

'Sure. There's Norton.'

They saw him coming along the walk. Norton was smiling. His voice was happy. He had had a couple of beers and he was quite in the mood for a party.

'Well, when's the big day?' he asked jokingly.

'You're going to be the best man,' said Reker, but his voice sounded strange, far away to him. He almost didn't recognize his own voice. He could feel himself slipping away into the nothing sensation that had been coming over him ever since he had returned to England. He tried to shake himself out of it.

He even felt he was not the same looking man he had been before he had been shot down. He looked at the girl coming along the walk toward them and when Joyce waved he knew the girl was Ann. She was pretty and blonde. They introduced her to Norton and the two couples got up and began to walk out of the park.

'Where would you like to eat?' Reker asked.

'There's a place off Leicester Square,' said Norton. 'A hole in the wall. Lot of show people eat there. It's a dump but they've got everything you can imagine, steak, fresh salmon.'

'Black market,' said Joyce.

'Let's go,' said Reker.

They came out of Green Park and started walking down Piccadilly. The street was full of traffic, and Norton started waving at taxis but they were all full and sped past.

'It's nice out,' said Ann. 'I don't mind walking.'

'If I never walk another step it'll be too soon,' said Reker.

But they went on walking, talking about themselves, asking questions about each other. Where do you live? How long were you in the services? Were you ever stationed at such and such a place?

'You boys certainly were lucky,' said Ann.

Norton laughed and appeared to scratch his chest. Then he tapped his chest and smiled.

'Luck,' he said. 'It got me out of bloody France.'

'What?' said Ann.

'This.' He unbuttoned his tunic and

drew out the little talisman he now wore around his neck which he had carried in his pocket across France.

At that instant Ann felt her breath stop, and her head swing suddenly in nothingness beginning to fill with faint, furious points of light. Silence all around her, as if all sound had stopped. Then she felt the silence slowly enveloping her like a substance. The soft rabbit's foot mounted in the butt of gold froze her gaze, and she began to say 'It's Peter's.' She heard herself through the stillness all around her saying it to Norton's ears. 'It's Peter's!' she screamed at him, standing in the sunlight, holding the rabbit's foot between his thumb and forefinger on the gold chain above his unbuttoned tunic. 'You killed him!' she screamed. 'It's Peter's!'

50 MARY ALICE EVANS

'Are you going to see him?'

'I suppose,' she said.

Oh, God, he hated her languid answer.

He didn't turn around because he didn't want her to see his face. He adjusted his tie. He felt his throat, checking to see if his shave were smooth. He looked at himself in the mirror, and yet saw her body on the bed across the room. You bitch, he thought.

'What do you mean, suppose?' he said.

She did not answer. She lay flat on her stomach, propping her chin in two hands and she looked out the window lifting her jaw away from her hands. She did not want to meet his gaze. She was frightened and she did not want him to see the fright she felt was in her eyes. She was naked and her body was long and beautiful.

But she knew she couldn't fool him. Yet she wished he were out of the apartment. His presence caused her to feel guilty, and she knew she ought not lie like this in front of him because she knew it would excite him and if she wanted him to go, she should cover herself. But she knew she was the cause of her own misery. Who would ever think Rodger's father would die? But what good was that? And she had supposed Rodger dead. Not a word on the crew so she had accepted it as death. She wondered if she were imagining an aversion Harold felt for her now as she stood looking down at her or was there real aversion in his eyes.

Yes, she could see the aversion in his eyes now, the stiffness of his jaw and neck. Harold was a good-looking man, ten years older than Mary Alice, but handsome in a Guard's uniform, and handsome at the wedding a week ago. Even at his age he had the pink scrubbed look of so many boyish Coldstream officers. He was such a good person; ten years of asking her to marry, so two weeks ago, she'd said yes. Oh, so tired when she agreed and all hope of ever seeing Rodger again gone, how many years can you last in the theater? Now the revulsion in his eyes, all because of the letter. How had Rodger ever found her? He had simply sent a letter to her apartment; and the only thing different about her apartment now was her married name was on the door: Major and Mrs. Harold Saunders.

'What do you mean, suppose?' Harold said again.

She did not say anything. She looked past him with languid indolence, remarking the nakedness of her back in the mirror across the room. When she spoke she was still looking at her image in the mirror.

'Well, just suppose, that's all,' she said.

It was a moment she had never dreamed would happen, and for him it was a moment he dreaded might happen, and now here it was, and there was nothing he could do. He must be at brigade headquarters in half an hour. He crossed the room and paused at the door.

'I'll call you when I'm free,' he said.

'Fine,' she said. As he closed the door she rolled over on her back and put her arms behind her head and stared at the ceiling. After a long moment she smiled slowly. She listened to him pause in the hall, and she listened to his footsteps go down the hall and the door close.

She rose and stretched and turned round and looked at herself in the mirror; tall, with full breasts and smoothly rounded hips, and hourglass figure. She ran her hands over the curve of her hips, and then began to brush her hair, smiling at herself in the mirror as if out of some secret reserve of contempt and amusement, the lips curving indolently. She got back into the bed and drew the covers up to her chin.

She drowsed until the ringing of the door brought her awake and tense. She rose softly and slipped on a white bathrobe. She listened to the bell ringing, almost peremptorily. She went along the hall as the ringing ceased. She opened the door quickly and looked out and the blood rushed to her face as Rodger Caldwell came in. He shut the door with a backward push of his hand and as it closed he embraced Mary Alice, kissing her throat and then her lips. Their mouths opened softly and their eyes closed and after a long, long kiss she drew back and kissed his throat and slid her tongue along this throat up to his ear. She put her arms in his, and drew him along the hall and into her bedroom. As she kissed him again she began to undress him and then she asked: 'How much leave do you have?'

'Seven days. Four left.'

She undressed and he undressed and naked they slid into bed.

'Darling, darling,' he murmured, feeling her body press against him as if out of some long pent-up sense of gratitude for his love.

'Oh, darling,' she whispered and stared into his eyes. He kissed her ears and throat and eyelids, and she writhed against him as with an exquisite pain.

'Easy, darling, easy,' he said. 'It's been a long time for me.'

'Me, too.'

'I want to love you first.'

'Darling, whatever you want.'

She lay in his arms a long while. Then she pressed him closer. He held her tighter, and then suddenly beneath her hands he went into her.

He said quickly: 'Easy now. Take it easy.' He kissed her closed eyes and lay still upon her.

Suddenly he said: 'While I was gone, did you—?'

'I had to.'

'Who?'

'I don't even remember his name.'

'You whore.'

'Don't tell me those French girls—'

'Don't believe everything you hear about French girls.'

She moved her hips up and down and he pressed her down.

'Easy, easy,' he whispered.

In the stillness there was no sound, only the soft silence of their mouths pressed together. He began to breathe faster and he dug his fingers into the flesh of her breasts and cried out:

'What about Harold?'

'He isn't you,' she murmured, kissing his chest. And she drew her lips down, murmuring. 'Not so fast, darling. Please, please.'

He went on faster and faster and then she cried out: 'Now.' And she drew herself away, drawing out the up-thrust stalk.

'Oh, God,' she said. 'It'll be perfect now.'

'All right. Easy.'

'Easy yourself,' she said tauntingly.

She held him with both hands pressed into the small of his back and he slid easily inside her and gripped her buttocks and lay quietly down on top of her. Soon their bodies moved slowly, then faster and smoother, their flesh blooming, nerve ends ravishing nerve ends, until at last each nerve in their bodies softened and became silent.

Silence going on, going on and on ...

They opened their eyes and looked at each other hearing the far-faint sounds of the city.

'Darling.'

'Oh, darling.'

'I know, but I have to be there in half an hour. Across town.'

'Once more.'

'We would have to do it too quickly.'

He drew back gently and turned on his side and she came over and kissed his throat and then lay back, hands clasped behind her head, and together they stared up at the ceiling.

'It's better than I ever knew it could be,' she said.

'Yes.'

'Who did you sleep with in France?'

'Nobody.'

'Tell me.'

'There's nothing to tell.'

'Come off it, darling.'

'Honest.'

'Do you really love me then?'

'You know it,' he said.

Then they did not speak for a long time. He turned toward her.

'Don't you have a matinee today?'

'I told you. We're off today.'

'How could you marry him?'

'Why not? He's pleasant enough.'

452

'Christ, you could have waited.'

'Forget it,' she said. 'He never did anything like that for me.'

Caldwell rose and began dressing. Soon he was a tall proper looking air force officer.

He looked at her naked body as he tied his necktie. Then he came and sat on the edge of the bed and bent over and kissed each breast. But in his eyes there was a sad look.

'What's the matter?' she said.

'You really mean it when you say you've never felt like that before with anybody? What about him? Do you do it like that with him?'

'Why should I lie to you?'

'You have before.'

'He asked about you today. Would I see you?'

The sad eyes stared down at her.

'Don't be stupid,' she said. She smiled and reached up and drew his head down on to her breasts.

'He won't be home this evening.'

'Are you sure?'

'He went away angry.'

Caldwell's face turned bitter.

'You're not going to tell him, are you?'

'No, but he'll be able to tell. I have to sleep with him.'

'You bitch.' He sprang up, his face

and eyes hot with anger and misery. 'All you want is somebody to make you come. It's all you want. If that's all, you can get that from anybody. You couldn't wait that long. You just had to have it regular.'

She sat up and drew him down beside her on the bed. 'Rodger, Rodger, darling, try to understand. I was so damn lonely and miserable after I heard about you. I didn't know where to turn, nor what to do. He's always been kind to me.'

'Do you do it that way with him?'

'No, no.'

She seized his shoulders and embraced him with protective love as if he were a lost child.

Tears ran down her face.

'Everybody I've ever loved has been either killed or lost,' she said. 'I couldn't believe you would ever come back. Nobody ever comes back.'

'What are we going to do?'

'Just as we do now. There's nothing else to do. I can't divorce him. He'll be in the invasion. I'm not going to send him out alone. I know what it's like to be alone. But we're not alone. We'll always be able to get together.'

He looked at her and began to cry, leaning against her naked shoulders. He held her naked body in both arms.

She said: 'Don't ever do that with anybody else.'

'How can I without you?'

'Do you have to go back on flying?'

'We're crewed up again. I suppose I could get screened, but I couldn't stand it. Ground pounding behind a desk, I'd go crackers.'

She smiled.

'What if it's you who makes me pregnant and the child looks like you? He would leave me then. He knows if we see each other what would happen and I haven't told him I wouldn't see you.'

'Can't you tell him?'

'How?'

'Just tell him. I'm back. You love me. That's all.'

'You don't understand. It would kill him. He'd try to get himself killed.'

'What are we going to do, then?'

She didn't answer. She put her head on his shoulder and he stroked her hair.

'This is the only way now. Maybe after the war,' she said after a long time.

'Then be good to him.'

She began to weep again, and he held her close.

'I have to keep seeing you and pretending with him. I'll write you care of your sister, and you write me the same way. It's all we can do.'

They sat silently on the edge of the bed, his arms around her shoulders, holding her with her head on his shoulder. Slowly the rapidity of their heart beats softened, became smoother and slower, and they sat silent in the embrace of tenderness and love. After a long while he lifted her face from his shoulder and kissed her tenderly, knowing they would always be one person.

'Oh, heavens,' she said. 'Look at the time.'

'Fine. They'll court martial me and throw me out of the service and then I can see you every day.'

'You must go.'

'Tomorrow?'

'Call me about nine in the morning.'

'Be good to him, darling.'

'Be careful, won't you darling, won't you, take care of yourself, be careful, won't you, darling ...'

51 SERGEANT ROBERT CRAIG– EDA BRAUER

It was a wonderful meal, the best he'd eaten since being home, real Yorkshire pudding, gravy, roast beef, dark ale. His stomach bulged. The room felt wonderfully warm and comfortable. A fire in the grate, and toes warming in front of coals that glowed like red jewels.

'Tell me all about it, Robert,' said his father.

'All about it,' Craig heard himself say, and thought, but what is there to tell? All a dream. What is there really to make real in a dream once it is over.

He tried to think of some way to tell them some amusing incident, but he could think of nothing they would understand. They would think he was making it up. Civilians. They all seemed strange. There was no point in talking to them. They wouldn't understand. France was as remote as Mars.

'I hear you had a bad air raid,' he said, trying to change to subject.

Yes, they had experienced war, too. His sister told him how long they had to sit in the air raid shelter. It wasn't a big raid, but a few houses knocked down.

He could hear her voice from far away, and he felt his mind wandering as she spoke. She looked older, though she was only fifteen. How much she has changed in a few months, he thought.

'Did you know Mrs. Marvin died?' his father asked.

'Really? When?'

'Week ago. She had a stroke.'

The coals in the grate pulsed and

glowed, red and blue. He rubbed the thumb of his right hand absently. A week ago, he thought. A week ago. I was at sea. I can hardly remember getting aboard the submarine. He felt his eyes closing.

'Where's Albert?' he asked. Albert was Mrs. Marvin's son.

'Albert's been dead a year,' said his father, surprised. 'You knew that. He was killed in the desert.'

A year ago ... Craig thought of all the faces in his flying school class. He could not recall their names now. How many were alive today? So many had been shot down in the last year. He had seen their names listed in the RAF casualty lists in Aviation Magazine.

'I forgot,' Craig said, opening his eyes quickly. 'Yes, I remember his being killed. Yes, I remember.'

His sister laughed softly. 'Bob,' she said with quiet astonishment. 'Did you really hear what Daddy said.'

'Of course, of course,' Craig said. 'In the desert, yes; missing, then reported killed, wasn't he?'

'He was only nineteen,' said his sister. She stared at him.

So he was nineteen, thought Craig. So what? So he's had it. So that's it. Pack it up, forget it. He's dead.

He listened to their voices going on and on about neighborhood gossip. He tried to sit up straight and pay attention, but his mind went on wandering.

He got up and went into the kitchen and poured himself a beer. He turned out the light and lifted the black out curtain and looked out at the night, the moon hanging high and white and naked, and suddenly he remembered other nights like his, and the sky above as if rising out of some vast dark shadow cast a scene across the sky: streaks of fire searing the darkness, a machine wrapped in flames plummeting—and the night sky criss-crossed with searchlight beams—the heavens dripping fire and torn with explosions—a night over Essen. For a second he could see the scene clearly against the sky and then it vanished, and the naked moon was there again, and the feeling of home all about him. Not yet again, he thought, not yet, and with a sense of relief covering fear, he turned away.

'Take it easy. Relax,' said his father. 'That's what a leave is for.'

'He is still tired,' said his mother.

'No,' Craig said. 'I'm all right. It's so nice and warm here that I haven't got used to it yet.'

'Well, stop fidgeting,' said his father.

459

'Would you like to go to bed?' his mother asked.

'Might take a little nap,' Craig said, and he went out and up the stairs to his room. It was the third time he had seen it in a year and it make him feel as if it belonged to somebody else. But it was good here to be alone. But he was followed, and his sister stood in the doorway looking at him.

'What's the matter?' she asked, watching him.

'Nothing,' he said. 'Nothing.' He thought of the cold Nissen hut room, the dim glimmer of the coke fire and lying in his flying kit to keep warm and all those nights on the road, starving and freezing.

He thought of this and could not understand why he was not happy here at home. He had been home only three days and already he felt fidgety and nervous, not knowing what to say to his family. They all seemed like strangers and all the rooms seemed so small and yet he had been away no more than a year.

'Any whiskey in the house?' he asked his sister.

'Why, Bob,' she protested. There was always a bottle in the house for colds, and now he felt embarrassed by the thought of asking his father for a drink. He would never understand. Two years ago he drank only a little beer. It would shock his father to ask him for whiskey.

'You never drank like that before,' she said. 'Mum would die if she heard you.'

'All right. All right,' he said, but he smiled to himself to think they would be so easily shocked.

He glanced at his wristwatch. He longed to get out of the house and find Eda. He had her new address. How strange the landlady had looked at him. What would her husband say if he took a chance and the husband was home and he simply knocked on the door and asked for somebody else. He realized that he ought to stay in with his family. They expected it, and they would be hurt if he went out, but he longed to be out of the house. Soon he would be back at the flying field, waiting, waiting, for briefing time again, wondering, what's the target tonight, the words going faster in his mind, listening to the sound of machines running up in the afternoon stillness.

He picked up his tunic and put it on.

'Where are you going?' his mother asked.

'Down to the Stag,' he said averting his eyes from her gaze. 'I won't be late, Mum. Walk will do me good. That dinner was too much for me. All that wizard cooking.'

'Be in early,' said his father. Craig smiled to himself. I'm still a boy in their eyes, all those hours and days of seeing things they'll never see nor feel, and I'm still a boy to them. Suddenly he felt a sharp stab of anguish in his heart, and he looked round the room at their faces. Ah, all the people in the world who loved him. All that has happened, he thought, is only a remote dream. Only here at home are we all real again, but in a flash the thought and feeling were gone. I am no longer the person I was a year ago and I never will be again, he thought. He opened the door and walked swiftly down the street. It began to rain.

He caught the bus at the corner and took the pieces of paper out of his inside tunic pocket and read her address again, eager to see her face again, as if she were some connection with the life of war he knew better than he would ever know the life of his own family again.

He looked out the bus window at the night reflected softly in the wet pavement. Moonlight flickered in the wind. The High Street lay underneath wet silvery evening mist. Other buses swam up through the darkness like huge mysterious beasts. The trees gleamed black and wet.

At the corner of Hampden Street he got

down from the bus. He thought of Eda. The world felt so warm and soft in the rain. An old feeling sprang up inside him, full, tremulous, wavering; the weeks and days and years of war were blotted out. A bright bridge of time seemed flung over the last months of his life and he was back again in a time with horizons of joy and fullness and youth.

He walked up the stairs to the door marked Thirty-Two. He knocked. As the door opened light flickered across a scarred face, and beneath it the tunic and golden crowns of a flight sergeant and a bottle of beer.

'Craig!' the scarred face shouted. 'I heard you'd gone for Burton.'

Craig stopped. 'Curtis!' he exclaimed. 'What're you doing here?'

'I live here,' said Curtis. He laughed. He turned his head and called over his shoulder. 'Oh, Eda! I want you to meet an old friend of mine.'

Craig stood still. His heart beating fast. Suddenly into the light he saw a face softly bloom. Eda! He felt his eyes shine.

'How do you do,' he said, taking her hand, feeling the fog drifting in behind him along the street, the cold, wet trees, the shining dark pavement, the sweet, inaudible music that had been alive in him, dying away into the cold dark sky.

Book Ten
NOW AND AT THE END

52   W FOR WILLIAM

When Jack Gifford came into the briefing room the younger fliers turned in their chairs and looked at him. He smiled at a few of the old hands and sat down with his crew. It was raining lightly upon the roof of the Nissen hut and water streamed down the windows. There was very little sound in the room other than the rustle of maps and scuffling of flying boots on the floor as the crews waited for the Wing Commander to enter.

The Wing Commander was young with a hook for his right hand which he had left over Dortmund. He was stocky and had once been a top rugger player before the war. As he rolled the curtain up from the big briefing map of Europe Gifford saw the red ribbon marking the flight plan out over England and the North Sea to the target. Gifford's heart froze for an instant in his chest. Essen! Every flier in the room gazed steadily at the ribbon on the map. There was no sound. Nobody moved.

The Wing Commander lifted the wooden pointer in his right hand.

'Most of you have been here before. This time we're going after the Krupp's works. We want a first class prang. That means each of you must bomb on the red marker. You have been briefed before how some of our recent attacks tend to fade away from the target after the first two waves. We will be in the third wave. Bomb on the red marker.

Gifford listened to a list of the defences, two thousand flak guns. It all sounded like the many targets he had heard about before but he knew Essen. Happy Valley! The bloodiest target in Germany.

He listened to the weather report, and then another short pep talk about bombing on the red marker, and then it was over. It all seemed meaningless, remote to him, but he knew everything clearly that he had been told.

He walked back to the Mess and stood at the bar with Caldwell and drank a couple of pints. He kidded Caldwell about British football and Caldwell played him darts for another pint and Caldwell won.

'What made you do it?' Caldwell asked.

'Hell, I'd go bats flapping around an O.T.U.,' said Gifford. 'I always say if you want to get killed fast get a job instructing at an operational training unit. If you survive that you'll survive combat. What made you?'

'Bored, I guess. I don't know.'

'Remember the last time we hit Essen?'

'Came back on a ropey engine, wasn't it?'

'Ropey?' Gifford laughed. 'It damn near fell out of the wing.'

'Jack,' Caldwell's voice was quiet as he set down his glass. 'If there's anything I can tell her ... anything before tonight.'

'No, she knows how I feel. We'll just have to work it out later.'

'Well, cheers.'

'Cheers.'

'See you, Rodger.'

It was still light when Gifford and his crew gathered at Flights. But the sun was dying and the sky was windless. They were all there, Reker, Craig, Norton, Caldwell, and two new gunners, both experienced, off on their second tour of ops. They stood outside Flights holding their kit, waiting for the trucks to take them out to the machines.

'Could use a little cloud,' said Caldwell.

Gifford snapped a half burned cigarette away.

'But not over the target,' said Gifford. 'Craig, if there's a cloud over the target and you can't see the markers and there are no sky markers we'll go round again.'

Norton nodded. He looked scared by the idea of going around again. By the third wave that flak will start to break up, Gifford thought. But he hoped he wouldn't have to go round again and make a second bomb run.

'Where'd you go on leave?' he asked Craig.

'Home.'

'Good time?'

'Not bad.'

'Reker,' he said. 'What's this I hear about you getting married.'

'Yes, sir.'

'Congratulations.'

'Thank you.'

Gifford wondered if there would be a lot of night fighters dropping chandelier flares lighting the approach to the target. He hoped the Pathfinder crews who dropped the dummy flares would be good and accurate and pull off some of the night fighters. Since he'd been back he'd heard losses were high due to new co-ordinated night fighter attacks made over the target in the light of gigantic chandelier flares.

'Let's go,' said Gifford as the truck pulled up. At the machine Gifford found a magneto drop in the starboard outer engine. God, he thought, we're not going to have to take off late again. He revved the engine over and over again and mag drops ceased. If only it had been right the first time. It scared him a little. He checked the crew. If only that engine doesn't go wonky, he thought. He ran up engines and taxied slowly out on to the perimeter track. He was the fifth machine in line waiting to take off. Why didn't they shoot the green flare? Were they going to abort the mission? Why don't they shoot it? He looked out at the other machines waiting, huge heavy beasts, thinking of each man in his place in the machine. He checked the engine temperatures and hydraulic and brake pressure.

Then the green flare burst against the darkness and the first heavily laden Halifax sped down the runway.

Then, it was his turn; he rammed the throttles open, feeling the noise of the engines beating into the aircraft; he snapped off the brakes, and though she moved slowly at first, she shot rapidly forward half way down the runway. He eased the wheel back. He felt the machine lift itself into the air.

He climbed steadily toward the Cromer light on the Norfolk coast and far to the west the sun was still setting. A ground haze was rising. They went on, climbing in the darkness, the western sky blood-red, slowly blending to purple and a soft golden light. Remote and lonely the machine flew out over England. Gifford found it hard to believe he was back on operations. He had the strange feeling of flying his first mission over again.

Below them came the coast, the sea foam breaking whitely, far, far down; a friendly light winking goodbye from the last dark headland of England.

The night was clear, too clear, and the moon was shining brightly. This was a bad thing, he thought, if only they could pick up some cloud cover just before and coming out from the target. But this moonlight was deadly. The night fighters could silhouette the machine against the moon. He watched the coast slide away and he eased himself back in his seat and stared out into the starry darkness.

'Seven minutes to the Dutch coast,' Caldwell said in a calm voice, and Gifford told the gunners to test their guns.

They passed over a convoy which fired off the colors of the day and almost immediately fired a warning salvo to stay clear.

'Reker,' Gifford said. 'Let's get that flare off before our British brothers shoot us down.'

Two reds and a green arched out across the darkness and the flashes from the water ceased.

The weather began to change and they flew in cloud, and came out still climbing.

Ahead, marking the Dutch coast, searchlights sabred the darkness and then far ahead, Gifford saw the target, a small glow against the dark. Flares began to fall singly and in pairs among the searchlight beams and Gifford saw the flares marking the turning point of the approach to the target. Dead ahead were cones of searchlights. Flash after flash of exploding shrapnel burst filled glowing sky.

Gifford called to Craig in the nose, 'O.K., boy. Let's go. Take us in.'

They flew on. Flak burst all around the machine. Sudden flashes of light on all sides. On and on toward the glowing fires far down in the darkness. Machine seemed almost to stand still, hang motionless. An aircraft passed, diving, the fuselage covered with flames. Gifford felt the machine lurch and dive and bound upward. A gigantic flash of light and faint sound of an explosion, muffled, beneath the machine. The aircraft heaved.

'O.K.,' Craig called. 'Bomb's gone.'

Caldwell's voice: 'Two eight zero magnetic.' The machine rocked violently. A huge chandelier flare, dripping green and yellow and white fire slowly descended, lighting the sky. Gifford studied a searchlight cone, watching it for fighters concealed.

Slowly they drew out of the immense bowl of light, reeling with searchlight beams and tracer fire. The moon high and clear hung above on the starboard side.

'Watch out for fighters now,' Gifford called. They flew on out of the range of the searchlights and then the tail gunner called out a fighter was attacking. The moonlight was shining on the Zuyder Zee, and the fighter was clearly visible against the water, at first a black dot, coming up on the tail, single-engined, climbing straight up. The tail gunner opened fire. The fighter whip-stalled, dived straight down. There was no sign of flame. The tail gunner watched the machine going down, down, down, and then suddenly a flash of fire across the darkness. A ball of flame into the water.

'Nine o'clock,' said the mid-upper gunner, and Gifford saw twin threads of tracer fire pass directly under the nose. Gifford kicked left rudder and dived and corkscrewed. Reker reported another machine signaling with a light on the port beam, and just then the tail gunner reported a machine coming up at six o'clock. Gifford could hear the machine gun fire and both gunners cursing. Tracer streamed over the cockpit and fell away.

'Buggered off,' said Reker. 'Watch the one with the light.'

'Dive port,' said the tail gunner.

The machine went down in a long shallow dive. Gunfire rattled. Norton cried he was hit. The method of attack was perfect; one fighter closing on the beam and as the bomber turned into the attack the other fighter coming up under the tail to get the clean shot without having to use any deflection. It was a well co-ordinated night fighter attack. The best Gifford had ever experienced. He was scared, his guts spasmed, his thighs stiffened.

'Six o'clock low,' screamed the tail gunner. The machine, twin-engined, with twin rudders, and extended stabilizers, shot past, directly beneath, so close Gifford banked hard as the machine burst out from under his nose.

'He never saw us,' called a gunner. Gifford couldn't tell which gunner was talking. 'Flat out of a cloud. Bloody well almost ran over us.'

'Watch the light! Port beam! Dive! Dive!' shouted the other new gunner. Gifford searched for cloud, saw only searchlights far away.

Then the air was silent. No searchlights, no flak, no fighters. They went on across the silvery darkness, reflected out of the Zuyder Zee, the moon high and white, shining down on aircraft and inland sea, machine and water and sky and stars and the men inside the machine for a moment one together.

'I got him! I got him!' the tail gunner said almost within the second the crew heard the rattle of his guns.

Norton moaned again. Gifford sent Caldwell back. Caldwell reported Norton was shot in the thigh.

Gifford looked back at the target, a monstrous layer of white sparkling glare, even as a cake frosting, perfectly shaped upon the aiming point.

A light winked. It was a star, greenish, Venus, and the tail gunner almost opened fire upon it, swinging the sight through the star to check its motion.

'Give me a rough course, Rodger,' Gifford said. He was holding the control wheel steady, about to begin evasive action when the instrument panel burst in front of him. He grabbed the wheel and hauled the machine around in what was almost a stall turn. He felt himself fainting, but he knew this was not true even though he felt relieved. Oh, God, he thought, oh, God, I'm tired. When I get home. When I get home. When I get home.

Then he saw the long blue searchlight from Amsterdam, the longest searchlight in Europe, so long and so blue, sweeping back and forth through the darkness which now held only this single beam of light.

We're free, he thought. We're free. We've made it.

Then they were past the Zuyder Zee and the moon was falling behind them, and then they were over the North Sea with the Northern Lights flashing like flak, and then the world became the inside of a dark round ball filled with stars, bottomless and topless; rivers of stars; darkness and stars above and below, and mackeral cloud drifted over the bottom darkness and Caldwell giving him the course.

And then instead of coming in over Dungeness they crossed the coast some place in the dark; he evidently had the wrong heading, and looking down Gifford saw the low mackerel cloud again, and knew he was out over the sea again. Then he called for a new course and Caldwell gave him a new heading and then they were in a round black ball filled with starlight top and bottom again, the stars filling the sea and the sky, and then they flew out of it, and Gifford looked toward the east and saw it, the sun, the morning sun, the beautiful morning sun, orange bright, hugely round, red hot, burning the fog and mist off the Cliffs of Dover. And then he knew he was home, home for ever. Just then the sun turned black, huge and round, and he felt the machine going straight at it and he hauled back on the wheel but the machine remained on course, level and steady, and the darkness was spreading out from the sun, coming out to meet the machine, moving across the sky, like a far-faint mist, thickening and darkening as it approached and then suddenly the darkness was there and the machine entered the sun's cold eye. And Gifford knew he was never going home again.

Book Eleven
WORLD WITHOUT END

53   WING COMMANDER RUSSELL– JENNIFER CALDWELL

The hotel room was warm. There was a fire in the grate. She lay with her head on his shoulder, staring at the firelight shadows on the ceiling. He kissed her and she said, 'I don't know why but it scares me. It really does.'

'All right,' he said softly.

'I can't help it,' she said. 'I just don't feel right.'

His insides felt dull and dead suddenly.

'What can I do?' he asked.

'I feel ashamed, that's all.'

'He'll never know, you know that.'

'What if he were here instead of you?'

'He isn't.'

'I never thought I could love anybody else, but those last few weeks with you here, everything has changed.'

'You've got to stop living an old dream,' Russell said and his voice was harsh.

She turned away from him and buried her face in the pillow and started to cry. After a while she ceased and apologized. Then she asked about his internment during the war, and he told her about missing the firing squad and being sent to a prison camp which American troops had liberated only a month ago, and she said, 'I keep seeing him dead.'

'He is. But we're not,' he said.

'It won't go away. He's dead and he sits there watching me.'

He kissed her cheek and she drew her head away.

'Don't,' she said. 'Please don't kiss me.'

'You're crazy. You mustn't believe what you're saying.'

'Do you want me to go?' she said.

'Do you want me to?'

'No. No,' she said. 'I want you here.'

He turned and lay on his back and

staring at the ceiling he fell asleep. When he woke he turned and touched her shoulders, pulling her toward him. She began to cry again.

'What is it?'

For a long moment she said nothing, then suddenly she spoke. 'Don't you understand? I let him go without loving him. I never gave him any love when I had so much of it for him.'

His back felt cold.

'Why?'

'Because I thought it wasn't fair unless I saw you first and told you how I felt.'

'Oh, my God.' He put his arms around her. 'You've got to pull yourself together. Wherever he is, Gifford would understand, and I would have.'

She went on crying, clinging to him.

'Darling,' she said. 'I do love you.'

'I know. I know. And I love you, too.'

'Could you leave me alone for a little while?'

'Surely.'

'Don't leave me, will you? I'm sorry. I just can't help feeling this way. Please understand.'

'Don't worry. Don't be upset.'

Dressing, he thought of nights in prison camp when you lay in your bunk and dreamed of having her like this beside you, warm and soft, all yours to love and hold all night.

'I know he doesn't know,' she said. 'But I just haven't been able to make love because I felt he was looking at us.'

'He is dead. It's the one thing you must realize.'

He looked down at her and kissed her forehead.

'I'll be back for breakfast.'

He went to the door.

'You won't leave me?' she called.

'Don't worry.'

'Please come back. I'll be all right.'

He shut the door softly and walked down the hotel hall. He went across the empty lobby of Flemmings and up Half-Moon Street and turned down Curzon Street. The air was cool and dark.

He cut through Sheperds Market and walked up Piccadilly to Hyde Park Corner, thinking of Gifford, 'Bad luck, chum, but remember one thing, you're dead and you're going to stay dead. And I'm alive. And she's alive. And we're going to stay alive together for a long time.'

Epilogue

'Workers in the Zoobruck Dike land reclamation project in Holland today reported that following draining of the western marsh, five aircraft from World War II which crashed in the marsh have been uncovered. Four of the machines are German and the fifth was identified as a Mark II Halifax bomber W for William.'

Excerpt from *The Times* of London, July 6, 1960.

This Large Print Book for the Partially sighted, who cannot read normal print, is published under the auspices of

THE ULVERSCROFT FOUNDATION